MERELY MORTAL

URBAN FANTASY ROMANCE

MERELY MORTAL
BOOK ONE

MICHELLE M. PILLOW

MICHELLEPILLOW.COM

ABOUT THE BOOK

All I want is a simple, normal life.

Unfortunately, normalcy is a luxury I can't afford as a lowly human born into a powerful supernatural family embroiled in magic. They've always been quick to remind me that I have an expiration date. Imagine everyone's surprise when it's me standing above their graves, not the other way around.

The fire that took their lives wasn't my fault, yet everyone is blaming me, especially the vampires. Now, I have a target on my back and a bounty on my head. Without the protection of my family, I'm caught up in a tangled web of supernatural dynasties and arcane power struggles.

So when a handsome stranger and his young daughter take pity on me and offer me a ride, I don't say no. It's a mistake. One I hope doesn't cost us all our lives.

Sometimes, being merely mortal really sucks.

Prepare for an exhilarating journey of magic, power struggles, and forbidden love like never before! Inspired by the author's short novella, Merely Mortal. (Inspired by, but completely different!) This book ends on a cliffhanger, but don't fret, look for book two: Mostly Shattered.

Mailing List

To stay informed about when a new book in the
series installments is released, sign up for updates:

Sign up for Michelle's Newsletter

michellepillow.com/author-updates

To my husband, John, you have been an amazing support throughout this creative process.

To my daughter, you are all things incredible and talented. You inspire me every day. I am so proud to be your mom.

To my family and friends, Thank you for always uplifting me.

To my readers, Your love and support mean more to me than you will ever know.

I love you all.

FROM THE AUTHOR

Lovely Readers,

As I celebrate my 20-year Authorversery, I know my writing journey is far from over. There is still so much I want to accomplish. But, mostly, I'm humbled and grateful for my readers who have shown me love and support over the years. I want to take a moment to express my deepest gratitude to each of you for giving my new series, Merely Mortal, a chance. This is the first time I have published a first-person POV book.

Your enthusiasm means the world to me, and I am thrilled to have you join me on this exciting journey into the realms of supernatural intrigue and urban fantasy romance. Writing Merely Mortal has been an incredible adventure. It's filled with twists, turns, and heartwarming/heartbreaking moments. I sincerely hope it brings you as much pleasure to read as it did for me to write.

Now, I must give you a little heads-up: Merely Mortal does end on a cliffhanger. Yes, I know cliffhangers can be a love-hate experience, but trust me, it's all part of the plan to make Tamara's journey as captivating and thrilling as possible. I promise the suspense and anticipation will be worth it. The next book in the series, Mostly Shattered, will delve even deeper into the mysteries of this new supernatural world.

I *promise* that will not make you wait years between installments!

Again, thank you for your unwavering support and for being an integral part of my author journey. I can't wait to share more of Tamara's adventures with you, and I hope you enjoy every moment of the ride.

When you're done, I'd love to hear your thoughts. Please consider leaving reviews and joining me on social media.

Happy Adventuring! Oh, and don't accept gifts from the necromancers. Trust me.

- Michelle M. Pillow

ONE

"It can die."

Guilt fills me as one of my oldest memories pops into my head. I'm not sure what triggers the thought. Maybe it's seeing everyone in black. Or perhaps it's that funerals can't help but remind me of mortality. Memories have been flooding my consciousness a lot over the last few weeks, crawling out from some deep vault I'd buried them under. I hate bad memories. I much prefer denial.

Oddly, this funeral feels more familial than the birthday party where the tragedy happened. People are dressed for mourning. Their solemn and respectful postures display attentiveness and empathy as they try to make me feel like I belong for once.

That word. *Belong*.

Being a part of something. Being accepted as a member of a community, organization, or place, according to the AI app on my phone. Yes, I made the chatbot talk to me in a fit of self-pity and loneliness. At least it doesn't judge.

Hell, I would have settled for my family's acceptance, let alone the red carpet to some secret paranormal cabal that controls the world.

"It can die."

It. Not she. Not Tamara. Not even that dreaded nickname I hate, Tammy. It.

At five years old, I hadn't even grasped the concept of what death meant, and yet those words, the way they were said, had stuck with me. In many ways, those words defined my childhood. All my life, I've been treated like some delicate butterfly that the supernatural world wanted to squish because that's what monsters do when they're bored. They hurt delicate things. I need to be careful. I need protection.

I need to not draw attention to myself.

So how is it I'm alive and standing outside a mausoleum at the funeral of three of the most formidable supernaturals I know—*knew*—my immediate family?

Well, not *all* my family. Conrad survived. But he is like me. Mortal. Normal. Human. If any members of the Devine family should have died in a fire, it was us. However, Conrad would probably prefer that I compare him to a moth drawn to the supernatural flame. No, that's not right either. Conrad would rather be the flame. My brother can have a nasty streak sometimes. He will burn shit to the ground if pushed to it. Metaphorically, of course.

I'm unsure why my cycling brain thinks getting this comparison right is important. It hardly matters. I guess I just don't want to face what's happening right in front of me.

Fuck. Fuck. Fuck. I want to be anywhere but here.

I can't look at the three caskets being carried by pallbearers, none of whom I recognize. They must be from the "distinguished" side of the family. Those distant relatives that Conrad and I were never introduced to.

Where the fuck is Conrad? He promised me he'd be by my side during this ordeal.

"What?" Uncle Mortimer leans closer, and I realize I had muttered the thought out loud.

"Nothing." I feel his judging eyes on me as I glance up from where I stare at the lush grass surrounding my high heels and then back down again. I'm balancing on my toes so my heels don't sink. Walking in these shoes across the grass has been difficult, and I keep waiting for the ground to swallow me under, not that I expect to be so lucky.

Have you seen those older men who always look like they're about to explode from the need to state their opinion? The wrinkled brows, the permanent lines of disapproval etching the creased valleys of their faces? That's Uncle Morty on a good day. Considering he tried to get me to pick out my gravestone for my birthday present—*"since at twenty-eight and mortal, you don't have much time left, Tamara"*—the confused look he's now giving me makes sense. I can see it in his eyes. He thinks it should be my body getting shoved into the stone wall. Everyone does. Even me.

The flutter of a damp handkerchief catches my eye. Someone waits in the wings to give it to me, should I need to snatch it from the beefy, sweaty paw of a hand. Not an actual paw, but I can imagine it would shift nicely into one in the right moonlight.

"It's up to you now, Tamara," Mortimer says, more to himself than to me. I can hear the frustration in his tone. "The bloodline must be preserved and protected above all else. You're too innocent to know it, but rival factions within our world will try to use you as a pawn because of who you are and the position you now control. Everyone is watching. Your mortality makes you vulnerable. There are those who would take advantage. But I don't want you to worry. I'll take care of everything. You might be the last of my brother's line, but we can fix that. You will be expected to carry on the legacy by marrying a person of great magic. I'll have to find the right spells, of course, but I'm sure we can have you pregnant with an heir within a year."

I furrow my brow and glance up at him, trying to hide my repulsion. Now is not the time for this conversation.

Actually, *never* is the time for this conversation.

"We must decide on a husband quickly. You don't have much time left," Mortimer continues. "Don't worry. I'll see to it."

"...since at twenty-eight and mortal, you don't have much time left, Tamara..."

Happy fucking birthday.

I don't bother to answer him, and I'm grateful when he stops talking. The last thing I want is to be a broodmare for some magical old dude my uncle picks for me. Still, I can't keep the images out of my head. My eyes flit around the crowd, landing on the gnarled wizard waiting in his long ceremonial cloak to seal the rest of our family inside their new home. I try not to gag.

Where is Conrad? He should be here with me. Though I am grateful he's dealing with security, so I don't have to. Detectives have been following us all morning. They're trying to figure out who did this, but they're worse than the reporters. I'm sure they recorded all five thousand guests entering and leaving the church. Fine, not five thousand. I seem to remember the church seating about half that, but it was standing room only, which would have made our mother happy. Only about fifty of those were allowed to come to the graveside.

I can tell everyone expects me to cry, not too embarrassingly hard, but a dignified amount. They keep staring at me. I feel their judgments, their concerns, their critiques. I want to tell them that my mind is numb, that I cried for two days straight after the accident. I remember someone reciting the stages of grief to me like a to-do list I needed to get through, but I couldn't seem to complete them in the correct order.

I make myself lift my head. The second coffin disappears into the mausoleum door. She is the only mother I've known, but there is a part of me that can't help thinking, *I guess I'm not the only one who can die, huh, Lady Astrid?*

The angsty cynicism only makes me feel guiltier, and I instantly wish I could take the thought back. My mind is jumping all over the place.

Someone pats my back and gives it a little rub.

The physical contact takes me by surprise. I want to lean into it, to cling to the rare moment of compassion. But I know the attention won't last.

Woodlawn Groves is the most prestigious cemetery in New York City, and the funeral is a veritable who's who of the supernatural world—not that most humans know that. I suppose it's always like this when the influential and wealthy die. Thankfully, security keeps the reporters away. The same can't be said for their overhead drones.

I adjust my wide-brim hat and resist the urge to look up as I hear another buzz pass. The funeral getup hides my face from it, but that doesn't stop the middle finger from extending from the clenched fist at my side. It's brief, but I hope the vultures catch it.

The sleek black dress, hat, and heels make me feel like a 1930s movie star, which in turn makes me feel like a fraud. I'm not glamorous. I'm not special.

Is it getting hotter? I need to get out of this graveyard.

Seriously, where the hell is Conrad? He promised to stay beside me.

My emotions are all over the place. Grief. Anger. Confusion.

Loneliness is the worst, but it's not new. I'd feel lonely in a crowded room or, in this case, outside a mausoleum.

My parents were assholes, for the most part. I had always explained away their elitist natures because they came from ancient magical lineages. It made them distinctive in the supernatural circles, and they knew it. They also had money, which made them respectable in human circles. Or if not respectable, untouchable.

Is it wrong to be thinking of this now? Outside their mausoleum?

What else am I supposed to be thinking about?

Where the fuck is Conrad?

Uncle Mortimer puts a hand on my shoulder and gives it an awkward pat as Mr. Beefy Fingers lifts the sweaty handkerchief for me to take. It's only now that I realize I've started crying again. A gentle breeze cools the warm tears on my cheeks.

Fuck.

Fine.

Poor, fragile little human.

This emotional breakdown is what they all expect to see anyway.

I snatch the slightly damp handkerchief and blot it under my eyes to catch the tears, trying not to think about the hand that held it.

"Conrad should be here," I manage, hoping one of those with magic will make it happen for me.

"He's just there," Mortimer answers.

I follow his nod to see Conrad crossing the great lawn, dodging tombstones as he cuts a direct path toward us. Relief floods me to know I'm not alone in this. His reddish-blond hair is slicked back, and his long coat jacket reminds me of the style favored by vampires. It's his latest thing. I think he secretly wants one of them to bite him and make him immortal. He's always so desperate to fit in with the paranormal. I forgive him for that.

It's difficult straddling two worlds and not fitting in either.

Conrad is adopted. I'm not. For most of my life, I thought I was born a freak mystery of nature—the human daughter of supernatural parents. But it turned out that even though my dad is my dad, my birth mom is the second half of an extramarital affair. Until a few months ago, I didn't know Astrid Devine wasn't my biological mother.

However, it did explain a lot, like why she would have looked at child me with that air of disgust while muttering, *"What do you want me to do with it, Davis? It can die."*

I'd been holding a puppy I had found at the time, but she'd looked at me while she said it, and somehow, I just knew she'd meant me. They'd been fighting in front of the servants, one of the rare times they let anyone see their displeasure.

I watch pallbearers carry the third coffin toward the mausoleum door and shiver as the gothic entryway swallows it like some great evil beast consuming a meal. How can it keep eating my family? Hasn't it taken enough? Someone will surely pull me out of this nightmare. Any second now...

Any second.

I can't turn away from the last coffin transporting my brother, their *real* son. Anthony doesn't deserve this ending. He'd always been kind to me. He might not be human, but he has his own secret demons.

Half-brother, I remind myself. And he *had* demons. Those secrets hardly matter to anyone now. They never mattered to me.

"Fire," I hear someone whisper. "Do they know how it started?"

"They are a family of magics," a woman says. "My guess is witch hunters. That lot likes burning things."

I'm too tired to pick apart who is talking, even though I recognize the voices, so I pretend I don't hear them.

"It's sloppy. They killed more than witches. Hunters are usually cleaner," comes yet another voice. "They'll be sorry once the vampires or trolls get ahold of them."

A woman chuckles softly and whispers, "I'd rather vampires over trolls."

"Not me. I'm not into torture like you," her friend answers.

The laughter is inappropriately loud, though I hear them muffling it with their hands. Mortimer pulls in a long, audible breath and lets it out slowly. The laughter instantly stops at the warning, and he doesn't even have to turn around to look at them.

"Excuse me." I step away from the gathering and move toward Conrad as he approaches. I won't listen to their speculation. I have been hearing it all week. No one knows who started the fire, thus the constant police presence.

I need distance. I need my bed.

I need them to stop looking at me, but I'm afraid of being alone.

Why can't this day be over?

Conrad sees my face and instantly lifts his arms to hug me. His chest bumps my hat, knocking it off my head. He is tall and slender, so it's more like hugging a dressed skeleton than a man. Still, human contact is comfort, and he's the only person I have left in the world who understands me.

My hand bumps a backpack hanging over one of his shoulders. I hadn't noticed it before. I release him and pull away.

"Are we going camping in Central Park after this?" I try to joke, but my voice comes out gritty and raw.

"I'll explain later. They're ready for us now," he says.

I turn and shade my eyes to watch the hunched-over wizard. His long hair and beard blow in the breeze as he leans heavily on his wooden staff. I wonder why no one points out to him how tacky it looks to have the worn yellow stars sewn into the navy material like patches around his shoulders. Still, I'm glad he's here. It sounds extreme, but we want a magical sealing. Otherwise, who knows what kind of mischief the necromancers would get into? The only thing worse than burying a family member is having them show up for dinner as a zombie.

Conrad swipes my hat from the ground and pulls at my arm as if he's in a hurry. I can't say I blame him. I want this to be over, too.

The drones buzz past again. He hands me the hat while we walk. As we near the mausoleum stairs, I try to get the hat to sit at the perfect angle. I trip on my heel, and Conrad slows his steps for me. He releases my arm and holds out his elbow for me to take. I thread my arm through his.

The gathering quiets, and all the attention is on us. I glance side-eyed at his chin and wait. It juts a little higher with an air of importance, and I know he imagines we're some grand family leading a procession. Conrad cares too much about what these people think. The familiar knowledge humors me in a dark and twisted way, but I hold back the small smile that wants to form. The impulse is short-lived as I feel the flickering shadows calling from inside the mausoleum. Someone had lit torches, and I suppose it's fitting there's no electricity as the dead don't need light switches. Still, after the accident, the fire seems a cruel taunt for the living.

My legs stop moving as I hesitate outside the mausoleum door. I do not want to be swallowed up by the great and evil beast that's been feasting on my family's coffins. I don't know if it's my imagination or a real scientific thing, but the air from inside feels heavy like gravity has different rules when it comes to the afterlife. It wants to suck us all into the dark void.

I think of what it means to have eternal rest. I wonder if my family dreams, even now, locked in a fiery eternal nightmare. Or is it nothingness? Everything ends and goes away? Or is it a version of heaven? Only lovely memories playing out for eternity?

Not knowing the answer causes me some distress. I hope it's lovely but fear it's not.

Conrad's muscles tense under my hand, and he pulls me with him. I want to resist, but I'm aware of the crowd behind us. They won't enter the vestibule, but they'll wait, watch, and calculate the correct amount of time we're to be stuck in the tomb.

Intricate gothic carvings adorn the stone walls, ornate and purposefully terrifying. The twisted figures are supposed to represent souls ascending toward stoic angels. At one time, the carvings were probably considered mystical things of beauty. In the modern age, the eerie scenes are creepy as fuck.

I was right about the air. It is heavier in the flickering darkness and smells smokey from the poor ventilation. I try not to think of what other smells the fire might be masking. The black stone walls absorb the light into inky depths.

The wizard doesn't join us as we're given privacy. I can't let go of Conrad's arm. Life and death blur within the quiet grave.

"What if they shut us in?" I whisper.

"Like burning the queen and all the possessions when a Viking king dies?" Conrad muses. His response does not put me at ease. He drops the backpack by the wall. "Lady Astrid would approve."

We stand, staring at the three open slots in the crypt wall, now filled with coffins.

"I wouldn't worry about it. Our parents were too

vain to want us with them," Conrad says. "They didn't bother to reserve rooms for us here in the luxury suite."

"Don't say that," I protest, though I can't say he's wrong. My eyes go to our grandfather's sealed resting place, and I instantly touch the necklace he gave me as a child. I wear the ruby amulet like a talisman to ward off danger, but really, it is just a piece of jewelry that gives me comfort. It reminds me that someone once loved me enough to create a magical story to make me feel safe.

"These three by fire. Grandfather by Covid." Conrad shakes his head. "I'm beginning to suspect supernaturals are not as all-powerful as they would have us believe. They want us to feel less than. Well, fuck their superiority. We're still here."

"Don't talk like that, Conrad," I scold him. "Any eavesdroppers won't get that you're joking."

"You're right, of course." He nods and sighs before turning his attention to the backpack. I'd forgotten about it. "Besides, we have more important things to discuss."

I don't like the tone of his voice as he says it.

"The police are coming for you." His blunt words are hushed.

I wait for the punchline that doesn't come.

He runs his hand through his hair in agitation.

"They say they have solid evidence that you started the fire. I convinced them to let us finish the funeral, but they're going to arrest you."

There has to be a punchline. This isn't funny.

"I'm not going to ask you why—"

"I-I didn't!" I protest. "I wouldn't."

"Shh." He glances at the door and lifts his hands. "We have a small window. I think you should run."

He must be joking. None of this makes sense. I was in the fire. Why would I start it?

My heart is beating fast, and I feel sick.

I try breathing deeper, but it doesn't help.

"I don't understand," I manage. "How can they think...?"

"I grabbed some things from the car." He motions at the backpack. "If you come back to the house, they'll arrest you. You'll be put into the system, and who knows how long before we can get you out."

"But...?" I can't think. This can't be real. I look at the coffins and then at the sealed door hiding my grandfather. I look at my hands. They're trembling. "I can't go to prison."

I'm hardly a roughened criminal. What little I know about prison I learned by watching movies. Things never work out well for the prisoners. If the other prisoners don't get them, the guards will. What if someone wants to make me their bitch? I don't want to be someone's bitch. I've had enough bad relationships to last a lifetime.

My heart beats faster, and I find it hard to breathe. The world around me begins to blur, and my ears are ringing. I want to escape, but there are only two ways out of this mausoleum, and it doesn't look like Anthony is going to slide over to make room for me.

Conrad takes my hands in his and holds them as if he senses my rising panic. He grips them tight, shaking them as he forces me to look at him.

"I can't do this," I say.

"Listen to me. You're going to run." His eyes are steady and sure, and I'm desperate for answers. "Someplace where they won't think to look. I'm going to finish up with this, and then I'm going to call the lawyers. I'll come for you tonight. Don't contact anyone."

"But..." I look at the bag and try to shake my head in denial. "What about you? Will they arrest you?"

"They know it's not me. I'm not a suspect." Conrad's grip tightens.

"Let go. You're hurting me." I flinch in pain as I try to pry my hands from him.

He waits a few seconds before loosening his grip. His tone is stern as he states, "Tamara. You don't have a choice. Do you understand? This isn't like the time you got caught shoplifting. They're not going to stick you in a room and wait for the lawyers to sweep it under the rug."

"Where do I go?" I whisper. He's right. If it's between hiding out and waiting for the lawyers or going to jail, there isn't much of a choice. The Devine family employs some of the slickest and sleaziest lawyers in the city. They'll get me out of this. They always get us out of our mistakes. I didn't do anything this time. Innocence has to count for something.

Right?

"Good girl." Conrad takes a steadying breath and nods in approval. He goes to grab the backpack and hands it to me. "I put an address in the front pocket. Be there at six o'clock. No sooner, no later. It's a small apartment building. Trust me, it's the last place they'll look for you. Get there and wait for me. I'll talk to the lawyers, and we'll figure out what to do. Extra cash, your wallet, and some other things are in the bag. Try not to use your credit cards. If the police do get to you first, say nothing."

"They'll know you warned me," I say. "Come with me."

I don't want to be alone.

"Let me worry about that. I can do more back at the house than I can by hiding with you." He glances toward the mausoleum door. I hear shuffling but don't turn to see who it is. "We're all that's left, Tamara. Just do what I say and let me handle this for you. *Ego sum avis stultus.*"

It's his way of saying it's us against the world.

I nod, relieved that someone else seems to have a plan because I can't think. Conrad is right. He's family. I can trust him. It's the one thing I'm sure about.

"It's just like when we were kids. Hide and seek. Easy." He helps to lift the bag over my shoulder. The weight of it presses into me, and the dizziness becomes worse. "You hide. I'll come to find you. Don't forget. Six o'clock on the dot."

"Shall we begin?" The old wizard hobbles into the vestibule to join us. He smells of cherry vanilla pipe smoke. My grandfather favored the same kind.

A tear rolls down my cheek as I look at my grandfather's tomb. I touch my necklace.

"Yes," Conrad answers for the both of us.

The wizard turns toward the three openings and lifts his hands. He mutters in some ancient language, but I ignore the muffled words as my heart hammers louder in my ears. Blue light illuminates the mausoleum wall as the metal doors appear to seal the coffins inside their crypts.

I try to whisper goodbye, but no sound comes out. It's not like they can hear me anyway.

Conrad's lips are pressed tight as if to control his expression. He sees me watching him and nods that I should leave.

I feel unsteady on my heels as I go toward the sunlight. I try to ignore that flashing blue behind me and what it means.

Time feels clumped together as if the past weeks are jumbled and squished into nonsensical order. Much like the ball in the pit of my stomach. *Death. Grief. Fear. Fire. Police. Alone. Run.*

I try to breathe as I meet fresh air, but the heaviness of the tomb stays with me. I grip the bag on my shoulder and hold it like a lifeline until my knuckles turn white.

"Is it done?" Uncle Mortimer asks.

I start to nod, but the gesture is weak. I glance around for the police but only see the eyes of the funeral guests on me. "Excuse me."

I hurry past him, torn between running and not drawing more attention to myself. I walk in the opposite direction from where the cars are waiting for us. My heels sink into the grassy earth, forcing me to pull them off. My naked feet offer no protection, but at least I'm steady. I carry the heels like weapons clenched in my fists, trying not to think of all the people buried beneath me as I pass by old tombstones.

The cemetery grounds are vast. I pick a marble building jutting from the manicured landscape in the distance and rush toward it. My skirt keeps my stride shortened. Strangely, the movement makes me feel better. My heart still pounds, but I'm away from the mausoleum and the watchful eyes, and there is relief in that.

The sound of water on concrete welcomes me to the building. I walk onto a stepping stone pathway and slow my pace as I move from grass to hardscape. Everything is clean and polished and sculpted, as if enough decoration can hide the truth of what happens here. The dead are clearly a lucrative commodity.

A large sundial catches my attention. Even though the sunlight is diffused, I can tell that it is not facing the right direction, and thus, the shadow cast from the gnomon onto the flat surface is not keeping the correct time. I only know this because one of our tutors made us build one as a project. In a way, that's a proper metaphor for the afterlife. In death, time loses meaning.

A woman reads a paperback on one of the benches in the shade near a fountain. Her leashed lapdog naps beneath her. It reminds me of the puppy I had for those brief moments when I was five. I turn my head away even though she doesn't look at me.

I find a somewhat secluded spot in the shade on a stone bench. It's chilly near the fountain, but I like the privacy and the sound of water against the stone. Nothing about my life right now makes sense. I should not be at this funeral. I should *be* this funeral.

The grief tries to rise but is confronted by the terror of my life in freefall. I feel as if my heart might explode.

The dog peeks around the corner at me. If not for the leash, it might actually come over.

"It can die. It can die."

I hear the words in my head like a mantra in the cold clip of Astrid's annoyed voice. The dog needs to stay away from me and whatever curse I carry. The seamed edges of the backpack press into my chest as I hug it. I feel the lumps of what's inside. I should be thinking about the police, but I can't get that memory out of my head.

"It can die. It can die."

A monarch butterfly catches my attention, and I turn my head to watch it land on the gnomon. Is it trying to warn me that my time is up?

"Does your mom live in a vase now, too?"

CHAPTER TWO

A vase?

It takes me a second to realize the small voice doesn't belong to my memories. A young girl stares at me as if she'd been standing in front of me for a long while. Her black slacks and white button-down shirt —the latter of which is a size too big—make her look like a waiter-in-training. The worn, stuffed puppy she clings to and her hollow eyes make her look like a reflection of my insides.

"My dad says my mom lives in heaven now, but we can visit her here," the girl says. "They put her in a vase."

I don't have much experience with children other than once having been one. This one might be five or six. She keeps focused on me like I have some kind of answer for her.

"I don't like talkin' sometimes, either, when my heart feels broke," she says as she sits beside me and mimics my pose by hugging her dog against her. "Did you bring snacks?"

"Oh, um..." I glance at the backpack clutched in my arms. "Are you hungry?"

She shakes her head in denial.

"Are you," I glance around, "lost?"

She again shakes her head.

The idea of ghosts in a graveyard is nothing new, neither are mental breakdowns, and I find myself poking her arm.

"Why'd you do that?" She watches my finger withdraw.

"To see if you are really here." My psyche is stretched too thin to think of a good lie.

"Oh." She accepts the answer. "I don't like it here."

"Me either," I say.

"Your necklace is shiny. Can I—"

"Diana!" The panicked shout breaks into the tranquility of the hiding place.

The girl doesn't stand, so I don't either. I feel a strange kinship with her, sensing she might be as shattered as me.

"Diana!" A man appears from around a corner. His athletic arms swing wide in his frantic state, and he looks desperate. He wears the subdued uniform required of such a place—a suit jacket and black slacks. He must have pulled at his dark blue tie because it hangs cockeyed around his neck like he wants to escape this place as badly as I do.

I'm too mind-numb to call out, so I merely watch his panic like a play. A small voice whispers that this makes me an asshole. I don't listen. Thankfully, the girl next to me doesn't have the same problem.

"Dad," Diana says, her voice calm. "I'm here."

His striking light brown eyes find us at the exact moment she says the words.

The man rushes toward us, relief warring with his heightened state. He barely seems to register me as he lifts the girl into a bear hug. "Don't run off like that. You know better. I said you could look at the fountain if you stayed where I can see you."

The panic is still in him, rippling through his jerky movements. He holds Diana against him, and she submits to his affection, resting her head easily on his shoulder as he sways back and forth. The scene still looks like it comes from a movie, so I watch. My father never held me like that, and I can't recall a time he ever came looking for me.

The man's longer brown hair is slicked back in an attempt to subjugate the waves, but a few gelled pieces have broken free. Handsome men are plenty in the world, and he can count himself amongst their numbers. I like that he looks *normal*—not rich, not prepped for an internet following, not ready for reporters. There is a vitality to him that radiates. He knows a hard day's work, and I can easily see him at a local pub drinking a beer and watching a football game instead of some fancy uptown bar. He has strong hands, too, blue-collar hands, so he's not afraid of hard work. But those hands are gentle with his daughter, so he's not afraid of love either. I always feel I can tell a lot about a man by his hands.

After some time, Diana kicks her feet to indicate she's ready to be put down. He obliges with a deep breath. I watch, wondering where the scene will take them next. I expect them to leave, to walk out of my life, so when he looks at me expectantly with his sexy brown eyes, I'm momentarily stunned. I watch for changes within their depths that would hint at him being something more than human. They don't change, except for how they catch the light.

"This is my friend," Diana introduces me. "She has a sad heart, too."

"Thank you," he says softly.

The words confuse me.

"For looking after her," he explains.

I nod, though I hardly deserve the recognition.

"I'm Paul." He holds out a hand for me to take. "Cannon."

"Oh, um." I slide the backpack off my lap and stand. I place my chilled hand in his warm one. A tiny shiver rolls up my arm at the contact. "I'm..."

It takes me a moment to finish the thought.

"I'm, ah, Tamara. Tamara Devine," I say. Only seconds later does it occur to me that maybe I shouldn't have used my real name. I apparently suck at being on the run from the law.

This can't be my life. I have no clue what I'm doing. All I know is that I don't want him to let go of me, so I hold his hand a little too long as if silently begging him not to leave me alone.

"You're shaking," he observes as he places a second warm hand around mine. The electricity of his touch works itself into me. They say funerals are like strange aphrodisiacs, but until this moment, I never believed it to be true. "You're freezing."

He releases my hand, and I let it hang awkwardly between us. My reactions seem to be ticking seconds past what is polite.

"Here." Like a gentleman, he shrugs out of his suit jacket, but there is nothing refined about the muscles now visible through his dress shirt. He whisks the jacket over my shoulders as if it's the most natural thing in the world.

The transferred warmth from his body feels like a hug, and I pull the jacket closed around my torso. I never realized how intimate such an act could feel. The jacket smells of him—light cologne or scented soap. I can't be sure which, but I find myself breathing deeper.

I know I should speak, but I don't want to leave this moment. Paul's eyes are kind, and they smile at me.

I should be standing with Conrad at the mausoleum.

No. I should be home listening to my mother bitch about something that annoyed her over family dinner while Anthony texts on his phone under the table, and my father gets up with a half-baked excuse to leave early.

"Are you...?" He hesitates on the question as if contemplating whether it would be rude to finish.

"I'm sorry about your wife," I say. My gaze goes to his hands, but I don't see a ring. That doesn't mean anything. People who work with their hands often take their rings off.

It occurs to me that he doesn't appear heartbroken. His eyes are sad, yes, but not inconsolable. Instead, he looks at his daughter as if all his energies are focused in her direction. I wonder at the reaction.

"Thank you." The words are abrupt, as is his nod.

"Who did you put in a vase?" Diana asks.

"It's called an urn," Paul corrects before saying to me, "I'm sorry. She's curious by nature. It's okay if you don't want to talk about it."

I look in the direction of the mausoleum, but I can't see past the fountain. As strange as it sounds, I miss the companionship of the funeral. I don't want to be alone.

"We can leave you be." Paul tries to usher his daughter away. "Thanks again for keeping an eye on her."

"I lost my ride." I don't know why I say it, except he seems like the type not to leave a damsel in distress. "They left without me."

"Oh? Can we give you a lift somewhere?" he offers, proving me right.

"I don't want to intrude." It's a lie. I do want to intrude. I want to go with them. It feels desperate and dumb, but I can't help it. Diana is staring at me with her lost eyes, and Paul is talking to me as if I'm normal like them. It's a relief not to be faced with magical beings and their constant judgmental examinations.

"No intrusion. Do you need to get to a wake?" He gives a slight nod, indicating that I should follow.

31

I think of the house with its servants and trays of food waiting. And booze. So much booze. All anyone will be talking about is the fire and, evidently, how I started it.

Then, there is the police waiting to take me into custody.

I feel tears burning their way into my eyes, threatening to spill over. "No."

"Dad," Diana says with an exasperated sigh. "She's already awake."

He looks as if he's about to explain but then doesn't.

"Where should we drop you?" he asks.

I don't even know.

I go to the backpack and unzip the front pocket. Digging around, I find a wad of cash that Conrad had shoved next to a piece of torn yellow paper with an address. I hand the paper to Paul. "I have to be here at six."

Again, not the best at running and hiding. Maybe I shouldn't have told him. The buzz of a distant drone catches my attention, and I automatically reach for my hat, only now realizing I must have dropped it somewhere.

He looks at the paper and then glances up at me. "This is in the Bronx."

It's news to me, but I nod. "Is it too far?"

I hope he says no. I don't like riding the subway.

"Are you from here?" He again looks at the paper.

I nod. "Manhattan."

"Just making sure you're familiar with the boroughs. Not all parts of the city are safe for tourists. If this is where I think it is, crime rates have increased in this area."

His concern is sweet.

"I'll be fine." I know Conrad would not have sent me into danger.

Paul studies me momentarily, looks at my backpack, and then at his daughter. "Six?"

I nod.

He comes to stand right in front of me, and I can't help but look up at him. He's the perfect height for me, and it wouldn't take much for me to lift on my toes to meet...

I can't think like this.

Paul reaches into his suit jacket pocket and pulls out his phone. "We have time, and I need to feed this little munchkin. What do you say we stop for a bite somewhere first?"

I nod again, relieved that my big escape has come together so nicely. Conrad will talk to the lawyers and get me out of trouble. In the meantime, I'll kill time with Paul. And tonight, Conrad will pick me up in the Bronx and tell me the plan.

All will be well. It has to be. I'm not a criminal. I didn't do what they are claiming I did.

I try very hard to convince myself all that is true.

A fatalistic part of my personality worries that it sounds too easy. I shiver, feeling like I'm being watched. Now is not the time to get cocky. I listen for the drones but don't hear them past the fountain.

"Are you usually this quiet?" he asks with a small smile. Is he flirting? He doesn't step back, and there is a moment when our eyes meet.

The question takes me by surprise. My thoughts have been churning like a chorus of crazy, jumping from topic to topic.

"Dad, come on," Diana pulls at his arm, taking him away from me.

If he is flirting, the sound of his kid breaks any spell. Paul clears his throat and glances at his phone. "We're parked this way."

I find my heels lying on the ground and pull them on. Paul lifts the backpack to carry it for me. I see him pressing his hand against the fabric as if subtly trying to figure out what's inside.

It occurs to me that he's a stranger, and I should be careful. But the warning bells aren't going off in my head when I look at him. I feel like I'm a pretty good judge of character when it comes to bad people. Maybe it's from a lifetime of knowing about vampires, dark magic, and moon howlers. There's an air of superiority that supernaturals get around humans. Paul doesn't have that. Plus, if he were supernatural, he'd have recognized my last name.

I don't pay attention to where we're heading as we enter a building. We pass through a long stone corridor. Diana walks with her head down, placing her feet carefully on the tiles to avoid the cracks. Her stuffed puppy dangles from one hand. Her actions are subdued.

The soft echo of our footsteps disturbs the quiet. Small doors line the wall where cremains are stored. Benches are placed where visitors can sit, but they're all empty. I remind myself that Paul and Diana were here for a funeral, like me, and I start to feel as if I've taken advantage of their kindness.

I watch them both, wondering where their loved one is, but they don't stop moving.

Not loved one. Wife. He buried a wife.

I try to use that thought to suppress any attraction I feel for him. Although, if there is ever a time to make stupid mistakes with a stranger, it's after a funeral. There is a big part of me that is up for spending the afternoon parked somewhere secluded in the back seat of his car. But having a child chaperone puts a damper on that idea.

What is wrong with me? I don't mess with single dads, let alone freshly grieving ones. He's not crying, but then neither am I. It's strange that I'm studying him as the others had studied me at the mausoleum. I tell myself to stop analyzing him.

Grief is a complicated thing, and he has it times two because he has to help his daughter through hers. I don't need to add my needy ass to that mix just because I'm lonely and want to be held by his callused hands and muscular arms.

No one speaks, and I feel like holding my breath until we exit the hallway of resting death. Will I end up in a place like this? Shoved in a stone box in front of empty benches that no one visits? Conrad wasn't wrong when he said we didn't have reservations in the Devine mausoleum.

Paul catches the glass security door as Diana pushes through and holds it open for me. The sounds of the city are more pronounced here, away from the white noise of the fountain.

Paul glances down at my shoes. "I can get the car and come pick you up."

"I'm fine," I say, not wanting to wait alone. In fact, I want to keep moving away from the cemetery.

Diana drops back to walk beside me. "Can I try your shoes?"

"No," Paul answers for me.

Paul pulls his keys out of his pants pocket and lifts them. As he unlocks the doors, the security alarm beeps on an older crossover SUV parallel parked next to the curb. He opens the back door for Diana to climb inside before putting my bag on the floor behind the driver's seat.

"Seatbelt," he says to her before shutting the door.

He turns to me now that we have some privacy. We're surrounded by the sound of engines as cars rumble past.

"She's barely spoken to anyone since her mother died." Paul's handsome eyes meet mine, and he keeps his voice low. "She has nightmares she won't talk about. She's also started carrying around Mr. Plop. She's barely played with it this last year, and now he goes everywhere with her."

I can see that he wants me to understand, so I nod, but the truth holds that I know little about kids.

"I wouldn't normally bring a stranger into our lives. Not now. Never with her. But she's talking to you for some reason."

I can also see he doesn't trust me as much as I assumed.

Paul takes a deep breath. "She's delicate."

I don't know why he's telling me all this.

"She's everything." He glances at the keys in his hand.

"We buried my mother today, too," I tell him. He starts to speak, and I cut him off. "And my father. And my brother."

The words tumble out like I'm ripping off a bandage.

Diana knocks on the window.

There is a helplessness in his eyes, as if he's suddenly added me to his list of concerns. He starts to reach for me, words hanging on his firm lips.

Diana knocks louder. Her little face smooshes against the glass as she stares at us.

"We're both broken," I say. "Maybe she senses it, and that's why she talks to me."

That sounds smarter than I think I am.

Or profoundly stupid.

Traffic again catches my attention, and I see a police cruiser with flashing lights. It's a stark reminder that I need to hide.

"Listen to me. You're going to run." Conrad's words stir in my thoughts and spur me into action.

I walk around the front of the SUV before Paul can change his mind. Opening the passenger side door, I get in.

Seconds later, he joins us in the vehicle. As he starts the engine, he quietly says, "I'm sorry about your family."

"I'm sorry about your wife," I answer.

"She wasn't..." He stops himself and looks at Diana in the rearview mirror. "Let me hear the click."

Diana unbuckles and then buckles her seatbelt. "Tamara, you have to make it click."

I reach for my seatbelt.

"My mom wasn't wearing her seatbelt. That's how she died," Diana says. The words are so matter of fact.

I fumble at the admission but manage to buckle up.

"Is that how your family died?" Diana asks, revealing she'd been able to hear us from inside the vehicle.

I don't want to talk about it.

The police cruiser appears next to my window, and I turn my back on it to look at Diana. My heart is pounding fast, but I try to hide the fear. "No. They were all in a fire."

THREE

Two weeks earlier...

Smoke billows, filling the hallway. It hits me like a sledgehammer to the chest, knocking me to the floor. With each breath, scorching heat sears the walls of my lungs. Yet, somehow, I'm able to crawl on my stomach like a snake through the carpeted hallway away from the inferno that is the banquet room. Screams of panic disorientate me, and I want nothing more than to curl into a ball and make it all go away. But something inside me won't let me give up.

I crawl faster, digging my toes against the floor to propel me onward. I think I'm going in the right direction, but I don't know for sure. The combination of pot and liquor in my system doesn't help.

I never wanted this stupid party, and I sure as hell don't want to die here.

My muscles strain, and my entire body heaves for oxygen. The harder I try to breathe, the worse the pain becomes until it feels like I'm being stabbed in the back and chest. I can't see into the smoke, and I begin to cough violently. I cover my mouth with my arm and roll to lie against a wall.

A large vampire bat flies past me, a blur of flapping fire in the smoke. His screech of pain is enough to make my ears bleed. With a hard thud, the creature crashes into a wall. The screeching stops. I hear a second thud when it drops onto the floor.

Fire burns where the bat landed.

I push up and feel material against my cheek. It's one of the old banners hanging in the hallway. I jerk it off the wall. The rod along the top strikes my back, causing me to flinch as it knocks my head against the floor.

I crawl toward the bat, dragging the banner to smother the flames. The vampire has transformed back into his human shape and isn't moving. As I push down, his body turns to ash. I'm too late.

Ash and smoke surround me. My cough worsens, and I collapse against the floor, hacking and gasping. The air is gone. I'm going to die in here.

My life doesn't flash before my eyes. Instead, I'm

locked in fear and regret. I don't want to die. I'm not ready. I'm only twenty-eight.

My body is weak. My eyes burn and tear. My legs flail. I try to pull myself somewhere, anywhere, but it's like my limbs have stopped working.

Curling into a ball, my hand strays to my necklace. My grandfather said it would always protect me. I know it was just a story, but I'm desperate for it to be true. I clutch it like a personal talisman and wait for that white, peaceful light everyone talks about seeing when they die.

The light doesn't come, and I remain in dark pain.

It feels like an eternity before I see the faint beam of a flashlight zip past. I try to call out but only manage a croak. Everything is a blur as I'm jerked off the floor. Time feels stunted. One moment, I feel arms holding me. The next, I'm on my back on the sidewalk, an oxygen mask on my face, with ambulance lights flashing around me. People are poking me with things and asking me questions that I can't comprehend.

Conrad is standing behind the EMTs, watching. His mouth is pulled tight, and a strange light is in his eyes. I try to yank off the mask to get a better look at my surroundings. Where there was pain moments before is now only a dull ache.

An orange glow shines from the windows of the old stone building. Smoke pours from broken panes, staining the night sky. Embers flutter in the darkness like fleeting butterflies, swarming and dying as they drift into eternal ash. How can something so awful, like a fire, produce something so beautiful? It doesn't seem right.

Streetlights illuminate the tragedy, and emergency vehicle lights flash all around. A spotlight passes over the gargoyles, staring down from a small clock tower. It might be a trick of the light, but it appears as if the creatures move their heads. I can't be sure. Something sizable lands next to the gnarled figures, only to fly away.

The oxygen seems to be working, as my lungs feel better. Or possibly it's just being out of the smoke that helps.

Shouting voices come over the static of radios, creating chaotic music accompanied by the pounding of feet and the clang of emergency equipment.

"Easy now," a woman says. Her hands move over me methodically. "I'm Stacy. We're friendlies. We're taking you to the private clinic."

The private clinic is an exclusive wing of a hospital that treats supernaturals. They rarely need it. Mainly, it caters to vampires and other ghoulish creatures shopping for blood and discarded body parts.

I try to pull the mask to tell her I'm not special.

Stacy's eyes flash with a tint of red that could easily be mistaken for the flash of emergency lights. Her partner leans close, shielding her with his body as she lifts my hand.

Before I realize what's happening, Stacy bites below my thumb. I flinch at the puncture of fangs in my palm. I try to jerk away, but her grip is firm.

Recoiling, she tosses my hand aside and says to the partner. "Ugh, she's only a human. Drunk. High. Who knows what else? We'll lock her in quarantine until we figure out who she is, but I'm sure she's unimportant."

"She's probably someone's dinner." Stacy's partner laughs as he tightens the straps over my chest.

"She does taste like someone was preparing for a fun blood feast," Stacy agrees.

"You know how the rich do," her partner answers.

Stacy's interest in my well-being fades quickly as she stops paying attention to me. I search for Conrad, but he's not standing behind them. The EMTs' movements become rougher as they raise the gurney.

They push me close to the ambulance but don't put me inside.

I have just enough wiggle room to lean forward and pull off the oxygen mask, even as the straps pin down my torso and upper arms. I frantically search for my family, not that I'm worried. They're supernatural and would have made it out all right. But I want them with me. I don't want to go to the hospital alone.

"We found another one." The digitalized voice comes over one of the emergency workers' radios.

"Another what?" I try to ask, but they're not listening to me. I no longer matter.

"Make that two dead in a closet," the voice corrects.

My blood turns to ice. My brother and his friend Louis were hiding out in a closet. It's where we had smoked the joint to escape the birthday party.

It can't be Anthony. It can't. It just can't.

I'd left them to go to the restroom. I try remembering what happened after that, but it's a blur. I'm still high and drunk and must have blacked out. One moment, I was leaving, and the next, I was on the floor surrounded by smoke.

What happened? Why?

"Conrad?" I croak, trying to yell as I struggle against the straps holding me down. "Conrad!"

I search for Conrad and my parents. I need them to tell me it's not Anthony and Louis.

"This is a fucking mess," a firefighter mutters as he stomps through the chaos staring up at the flames before he says into a walkie-talkie, "Watch your asses, boys!"

"Someone barricaded the doors on the north end," a voice answers.

I find Conrad standing with his arms crossed over his chest, staring at the building. My parents aren't with him.

"Conrad!" I yell, using all my strength to push through the pain in my throat.

He turns in my direction briefly before looking back up.

"Shut her up," Stacy says.

"On it." Her partner comes at me with a syringe.

I kick to keep the man away, but he laughs at my restrained movements. He jabs me in the thigh, and I feel the drugs flooding my system. The medicine overtakes my will even as I fight to stay awake.

FOUR

No one speaks as Paul navigates traffic. It's as if they're waiting for me to expand on my statement, but I don't want to discuss the fire. Just saying the words aloud causes a flood of memories I'd rather not think about. In my nightmares, I can still feel the straps of the gurney holding me down, leaving me completely helpless.

Time from that night slips and fades from one moment to the next. I remember the smoke. I remember being pulled out. I remember coming to on the sidewalk, then again on a gurney. I remember meeting Stacy. Well, *meeting* if I am to stretch the word's meaning. I press my fingernails into my hand, mimicking the feel of her fangs before rubbing the spot to try to erase them. She cared when she thought I was important, stopped caring when she found out

I was mortal, and then cared again later at the hospital when she learned my last name. Her partner's face was more of a shadowed blur. Not that any of that mattered in the end.

I remember feeling as if someone sat on my chest, making it hard to breathe. I remember Conrad and the strange look on his face as he watched me on the gurney. I'm sure he was traumatized, but we never talked about that moment. Neither of us seems to want to relive it.

My heart beats fast, and I feel like I want to throw up.

The police cruiser is ahead of us. I find its rearview mirror, hoping the driver doesn't look back and somehow see me. I want to beg Paul to turn, but he's unconcerned by its presence, and I can't think of a good reason to ask him to do so.

My hands shake, and I can't make them stop. My fingernails are again digging into my flesh, and I have to force myself to release their hold. The red mark indentations cause me to hide the damage beneath my legs.

I want to fill the silence, but I'm unsure what to say, so I again check the police cruiser for signs of suspicion. I tell myself it's just paranoia because I don't want to go to prison.

Or would it be jail? Jail, then prison.

No, the family lawyers won't let it get that far. I need to lie low as they work this out like they always do.

Yes, I know I'm privileged, and it embarrasses me.

My thoughts churn, jumping around in my head. I don't know what I'm doing.

It's an eternity before the cop car turns. I instantly breathe easier.

My attention goes to Paul's hands on the steering wheel, and I watch him drive. The subtle movements of his fingers instantly give me naughtier ideas—a hope that they could make me feel anything but the depression I've been carrying around inside of me. I shouldn't be having these thoughts. I have to be careful who I trust right now. My baser instincts tell my cautious brain to shove it where the sun don't shine.

The colloquialism feels appropriate because it's not the only thing I want shoved where the sun don't—

"I think I saw the fire you're talking about on the news. It was downtown, right?" Paul says, politely showing interest in me. The words are like the verbal equivalent of slamming on the brakes and letting the tire screech to a sudden stop. It rips my thoughts out of the gutter. Thankfully, he can't read my mind and all its chaotic ramblings. "If you want to talk about it..."

He lets the invitation dangle and waits to see if I'll pick it up.

My knee-jerk reaction is not to answer. Reporters have been circling for the story, and I don't want my family's pain used for entertainment.

But I look back at Diana, her saddened eyes staring at me, and I know that isn't what they're doing. They navigate their own pain. We're strangers with kindred afflictions on the same path.

"Yes. It was the fire downtown," I answer, my tone hoarse and somewhat off-guard. I clear my throat before rebounding with what I hope sounds calm. "We were all there for my birthday, mostly, kind of. Everything went wrong."

These are not the words I want to use to describe what happened. In my preferred version, *fuck* and *hell* would pop into the sentences more.

I glance back at Diana and then at Paul's strong hands. For some reason, those hands fascinate me. They are sturdy and safe, and I feel anything but.

"Kind of?" Paul prompts, and I hear his curiosity as he tries to understand.

"It was my birthday, but it wasn't about me. It was more for associates of my parents, so there were all these people there I didn't really know." I can't believe I'm admitting it out loud. Normally, I sugar-coat my family drama to outsiders.

"How old are you?" Diana asks.

"Twenty-eight." I look back at her, surprised and relieved that is what she wants to know. "How old are you?"

"Five and a half." She holds up her stuffed dog and adds, "Plop is five and a half, too. He was born the same day as me at a zoo."

"You were born at a zoo?" I ask, unable to help myself.

Diana giggles. It's a short, tiny sound, but I see Paul let loose a breath like a weight is temporarily lifted. He looks at me and nods in what I can only assume is appreciation.

"With the monkeys," she says.

"I'm boring. I was born in a hospital," I tell her. I mean, I assume that's true. I didn't know my mother wasn't my real mother until a few months ago. For all I know, I could have been born in a back alley.

The break in the sorrow lifts a little of the weight off me, too, if only for a few seconds. I turn to Paul. "And how old is your dad?"

I try to make it sound like a playful question and not to analyze my asking too closely, but I want to know.

"Three hundred," Diana answers.

It takes me a moment to realize that she is joking. In my world, three hundred is a believable answer. I remind myself that they're human.

"You look good for your age," I say with a small smile.

Shit. Am I flirting again?

I need to stop flirting. The man just buried his wife and mother to his kid. That makes me a creepy asshole deluxe.

As we stop at a red light, Paul adjusts his rearview mirror to look at his daughter.

"Knock a zero off the end. I'm thirty," Paul corrects with fake sternness.

"Yeah, *old*," Diana shoots back. "The store didn't even have enough candles for your cake."

Paul readjusts the mirror so he can drive.

"He was born with..." Diana stops and screws up her face as she thinks really hard. "In the sewer. He's a boy. Boys stink."

I can't say I agree with that assessment. I still have his coat around my shoulders, and there is nothing wrong with his smell.

Paul turns into the parking lot of a small diner. "Does this work? You're probably used to fancier. I can—"

"It's perfect," I say. No one will think of looking

for me here. Even if the funeral guests don't go to the wake, they would never come here.

I pull down the visor and flip open the mirror as he finds parking. I'm horrified at the puffy-eyed mess staring back at me. My mascara has rubbed off a little—*waterproof my ass*—and a light smear crosses my temple. I lick my finger and rub my face to clean the smudge the best I can. That morning, I tried to tame my brunette, naturally curly hair, but several strands had come loose. I smooth them back the best I can before giving up.

I close the visor as Paul gets out of the car. He opens the door for his daughter.

I follow them inside. The diner looks like it was birthed in the 1950s and then led a hard life, though someone had cared enough to clean it. Utensils clank a little too loudly to accompany the murmur of conversations. The smell of burgers permeates around us like a bad perfume.

I think I love this place.

A busy waitress waves her hand toward the only empty booth. I pause to squirt hand sanitizer on my hands out of post-pandemic habit. Paul grabs menus from the hostess stand, and we follow the waitress's directions. People glance up as I pass, but their attention doesn't last long. They're more concerned with their own lives.

I look down. The moment feels surreal. It's my feet moving over the cracked tiles, but this is not supposed to be my life. This is not where I'm supposed to be, but I don't want to leave.

Maybe I don't have to go back. Maybe I can slide from my life into Paul and Diana's like I'm sliding into the booth.

The fantasy is fleeting. Stupid, honestly.

I can't have this, not beyond this stolen moment. Eventually, they'll realize who I am and that I don't belong.

It's the story of my life. My last boyfriend only wanted to get close to my family's power and money. I have no idea why I put up with his supernatural misogyny for so long. Then there were my parents. They hadn't wanted me. Sure, my father loved me in his neglectful way, but I was like another living doll in his collection of children. And Lady Astrid pretended I was her mortal embarrassment. Although, it seems she had considered my mortality less embarrassing than the affair. I wonder if she didn't know about my affliction when she let everyone think I was hers.

"Tamara?" Paul's voice disrupts my unraveling into self-pity. He's offering me a menu. Diana is sitting next to him.

"Oh, thanks," I say.

"Bathroom." Diana tries to slide out of the booth.

Paul points at the restroom sign. "There and back."

She leaves Plop behind as he lets her out of the booth.

He cranes his neck to watch her until she disappears behind the door.

"How did you get left behind at your family's funeral? Won't someone go back looking for you?" he asks. "I think someone would notice you're gone."

"No. I had to get out of there." It's not a complete lie. I don't say *why* I had to leave.

"I get that." He nods. "Funerals suck."

Indeed, they do. Everything about them.

"Good on you for putting your self-care first." He looks at the menu, and I do the same.

I only pretend to read it. My mind can't focus on the words, so I stare at the once-glossy pictures. Even the salads look unhealthy under the greasy lamination.

The waitress appears, and I set the menu down. I ignore her perfunctory greeting before saying, "Coffee."

"Same," Paul says, "and an orange juice. Thanks, Bonnie."

I glance at the woman's name tag before she hurries away.

This moment is so normal, so *human*. It suddenly makes me uncomfortable, like I'm missing something important about my environment. These people can't all be benign. I find myself scanning the other patrons. The guy in the corner could be half-troll. He has the features for it. Then again, trolls aren't known for their love of milkshakes, and he has two. The woman with blue hair and facial piercings looks like she has a scar on her neck. She could be feeding herself to vampires. The lady with the white cotton ball hairdo, pearl earrings, and pink button-down sweater stuffing sugar packets into her purse could be a serial killer. Hey, it's always the ones you least expect, right?

The panic rises in my chest as I work myself up.

I look out the window, searching for police cars.

"Do you have someone?" Paul asks.

His question turns my attention back to him. "No. I'm not seeing anyone."

A small smile cracks the corner of his mouth, and he glances up from the menu. "I meant family. Someone you can talk to about today."

"Conrad. My brother. Well, adopted brother." I try to hide my embarrassment at automatically thinking he was flirting again. "And my mother."

He lowers the menu to the table and furrows his brow. "I thought you said..."

"Birth mom. I haven't met her. I've been looking, but..." I shrug. "It is what it is. My father had an affair. After I was born, he and his wife raised me. I only discovered Astrid wasn't my biological mother a couple of months ago. It's all very soap opera."

"And Conrad?"

"He was in the foster system. I think they got him because he was like..." I force myself to stop before I say he's like me, not supernatural. "I don't know. So, yeah, it's just me and Conrad now. What about you guys?"

"Nancy was an only child, and her parents have both passed," he says.

"That's Diana's mom?"

He nods.

"And your family?"

"My parents live in Kansas City. My mom hasn't been feeling well, and they couldn't make the trip. She's a nurse. I hated her working during the pandemic, but it's a calling, you know. She had to quarantine away from my dad. We worry that it's affected her health long term, but she says she's fine. My dad is in construction, which apparently is hereditary because so am I. Only he works on giant skyscrapers, and I have no desire to hang out forty floors in the air. He's also a fireman. Most of my extended family lives in the Midwest. I've been thinking about taking Diana there for a visit. Might be good for her to get out of the city."

Paul rubs the bridge of his nose and sighs. There's a vulnerability in him that he tries to keep hidden, but it resonates with me.

"I wish they handed out a manual to parenting at the hospital for your exact child so I could know how to fix things. Chapter one, she'll get diaper rash. Chapter two, she'll try to eat sand when playing chef and scare the crap out of you, so you end up in the ER. In chapter three, the neighbor kid will break a window and try to say she did it."

"Chapter four, her mom dies, and she has nightmares?" I ask.

He nods. "The school counselor says to talk about her feelings. The internet says I should be talking about my feelings and telling her details about the death, so she doesn't wonder for the rest of her life. Honestly, I don't think either of those would be helpful to her. Memory boxes. Rituals. Routines. I followed all the guides, and she stopped talking."

This topic is way beyond my scope of expertise. I can barely figure out my own problems. I can't give him advice about his.

I say nothing, hoping he will continue to talk. I find myself drawn to the soothing timbre of his voice.

"But then you appeared, and she—" His eyes

dart to the side, and he stops talking. He stands to let his daughter into the booth. "Did you wash your hands?"

Diana holds them up to show him before sliding into the seat.

I turn my attention back to the window as they discuss the menu. I could never be a parent, constantly putting myself on hold to take care of someone else. As attractive as I find Paul, his focus is entirely on his daughter—as it should be. Still, a selfish part of me wants to finish our conversation before the interruption.

Bonnie arrives with our drinks. I take the coffee and start plying it with sugar and creamer as they order. When it's my turn, I give a slight shake of my head.

"I don't want anything either," Diana says, even though she'd ordered a grilled cheese.

"You should try to eat." Paul glances at his daughter and then back at me, his eyes widening.

I want to tell him it's not my responsibility and that I have my own worries, but she's just a child. Guilt instantly floods me, and like everything else in my life, I find myself trying to please those around me.

I point at a picture of a hamburger on the menu and say, "That."

Bonnie tries to leave a millisecond into me saying the word.

"I want that too," Diana states.

"All right, then." The waitress hurries away before anyone else can change their mind.

Paul stares at me and gives a small nod of thanks.

Aside from a few niceties, we fall back into silence, and I don't know what to say to fill it. Everything I want to talk about would be considered flirting, and I can't do that with him here, today, in front of Diana.

My thoughts bounce from my problems to theirs, to random memories from my childhood. I worry about the cops, Conrad, and what the future means for us without family protection from the supernatural. I think of Uncle Mortimer assuming the role of patriarch and wanting to auction me off into an arranged marriage. Sometimes, the universe feels too full, and I can't process everything. Maybe that's what grief is, feeling everything pressing in all at once.

The food appears, and I find myself eating, not because I'm hungry, but because it's there. The burger looks nothing like its picture, and it occurs to me that not many things in life look as advertised.

"Your burger all right?" Paul asks.

I realize I've been staring at it. I glance up to see Diana is holding her burger the same way.

"Yeah, it's good." I take a bite. Diana does the same.

When I put it down to grab a fry, Diana copies that too. Paul doesn't appear to notice. Or maybe he does, but he's too weary from the day's events and chooses to ignore it. I grab my drink to see if I'm paranoid. I'm not. Diana takes a drink.

So that's weird.

I put my hands in my lap and sit back. Diana does that as well.

"Finish your hamburger," Paul tells her.

She stares at me and doesn't move.

I don't want her to get into trouble, so I start eating again and try to ignore it. This is only one meal.

"So," I hesitate before asking, "you said you are a contractor like your dad?"

It's small talk, but it's better than silence.

"Somewhat. Not on the skyscrapers. I prefer houses, apartment remodels, whatever needs doing."

I look at his hands. That makes sense.

"How about you?" he asks.

"I'm a searcher," I say.

Diana holds a fry and mimics my hand gestures.

"What does that mean?" He watches me as if

he's really listening for the answer. His eyes are kind and inviting.

And safe. He makes me feel safe, and he shouldn't.

Damn. I wish he'd do something to make me less attracted to him. I glance around the diner. The blue-haired vampire bait is on her phone. Her eyes meet mine, and she stares at me while her lips are still moving. Is she talking about me or staring because I looked at her first?

"Searcher?" Paul prompts me to get back into the conversation. He glances over his shoulder to see what I'm looking at.

"Let's see." I turn my attention to Bonnie, who hasn't returned to the table since dropping off the food. "I've been a waitress. A barista. A florist. A shipping clerk for my father's business. He fired me because I messed up a shipment for one of his important friends."

I don't know why I admit that last part. Maybe it's because they don't know any of the players. I'm still unsure what was in the cargo container, but it had to have been questionable, even by supernatural standards.

"Your dad fired you?" Paul shakes his head as if he can't imagine it.

That further proves my assumptions about him

are correct. He's one of the good guys, and I'm a visitor in his normal world.

"It's fine." I shrug it off, reminding myself not to speak ill of the dead. None of that matters now, anyway.

"So you haven't found your passion yet," he concludes.

"That's a kind way of putting it." I glance at my little copycat and take a giant bite, finishing the burger by shoving it into my mouth. She tries to do the same and ends up squishing it on her face.

"Diana," Paul says in exasperation, reaching across the table to grab napkins from the dispenser to wipe the mess. He gives up and slides out of the booth. "Come on. Let's clean you up."

I watch them leave me alone in the booth. This is not how I thought today would go.

Vampire Bait side-eyes me as she leaves the diner. She holds her phone in such a way that she could be taking my picture. The attention makes me uneasy, but I can't look away. She flips me off before disappearing down the front sidewalk out of my view.

Bonnie passes by and drops off the check without saying a word. I realize I don't have any money on me. The backpack is in the car. The reminder makes me think of the police and the legal mess I'm in.

"It's almost over," I tell myself.

Even now, Conrad is probably talking to the lawyers. I think ahead to when I'll be back home, soaking in a bathtub, trying to forget this long day. Usually, that would include a bottle of vodka, but I haven't drunk liquor since the night of the fire.

Strangely, the thought of leaving Paul and Diana makes me sad. I don't know them, but I'm drawn to their kindness. They represent a life I've never lived.

It'd be selfish to introduce them into my dangerous world. After today, we'll part ways, and that will be it. Paul would become a pleasant fantasy filled with what-ifs that could never be. Perhaps, someday, in random passing, I'll hear of how a woman named Diana graduated from college, and the thought will make me smile as I remember back to this normal moment.

That is all this can be. I can't make it into more.

CHAPTER
FIVE

"Are you sure you want to be dropped off here?" Paul leans forward on the steering wheel and stares out the window while the SUV crawls through the sketchy neighborhood. The scarcity of other cars on the road feels ominous. The electric door locks click several times as if he's nervously tapping the button out of protectiveness. "This isn't the best part of the city to walk around in, especially after the sun goes down. I don't even like driving through here. Let me take you somewhere else, *anywhere* else. I can drive you into Manhattan. It's not a problem."

"I'll be fine," I say.

Though, I see what he means. The graffitied avenue of sadness that makes up this street is littered with people and their broken dreams. I can't imagine they all wanted to be strung out and dirty when they were children fantasizing about their lives. Or perhaps I'm just being judgmental as we watch them from the safety of Paul's car like we're on a safari through urban decay. Not everyone is sad. A man laughs hysterically as he talks to himself, pacing back and forth on the sidewalk. With each step, he swats frantically at imaginary tormentors.

At least, I hope they're imaginary. Sometimes, those crazy people you see on the street aren't so crazy.

"You okay back there, Di?" Paul asks.

"What's wrong with that man?" she counters.

"He's, uh, sick," Paul says.

Some of the graffiti catches my eye. The symbols are familiar, though I can't translate them, indicating vampire hunting territories or something just as sinister. Why would Conrad send me here? He knows I don't share his fascination with the undead.

I remind myself that this is the last place anyone would look for me. The knot of dread in my stomach is just my fear overreacting. Sunset isn't for another hour or so, and once inside, I should be safe from any night threats. Conrad knows what he is doing. I can trust him.

I finish tying the laces on my running sneakers before shoving the heels into the backpack on the floor between my feet. Conrad had grabbed my workout clothes. They were probably the only thing he'd found in the car. The shoes don't go with the funeral dress I still wear, but thankfully, the socks are clean.

I check the address and mumble to myself, "Apartment 204."

"Seriously, Tamara, I—" Paul touches my arm briefly as if to stop me physically before instantly letting go.

"I won't be here long," I cut him off. "It's fine. I promise. You've helped enough just giving me the ride."

His look says he doesn't believe me. "I can wait."

His fingers drum the steering wheel, and I can imagine the battle going on with his conscience.

"Diana shouldn't be here," I insist. "You should take her home."

"Why can't I come with you?" Diana protests.

I turn to look at her and shake my head in denial. "You just can't. Sorry."

"I think this is it, up ahead," Paul says.

At least the small apartment building doesn't look like a crack den. The steps leading to the front door are well-maintained and free of litter. I can't say the same for some of its neighbors down the street, where decrepit houses are in paint-chipped disarray, with broken windows and trash hugging the edges of their concrete lawns. Paul slows the car but doesn't stop completely as he watches a couple stumble past. Their unsteady steps give evidence of their intoxicated state.

"You're not here to..." He again hesitates as if choosing his words carefully. I assume it's for his daughter's sake.

"Score?" I give a small laugh. "No. Not my vacation of choice."

"We are going on vacation to Kansas City," Diana offers. "You can come with us. Grandma can make any cookie in the world."

"Diana," Paul scolds, his voice tense. "You can't just invite people on vacation. Besides, the decision isn't final. I said we'd see."

"Why not?" the girl shoots back.

"Because—"

"You said we could do what I wanted after the funeral," Diana persists. "I want Tamara to go to Kansas City with us."

"I meant to a park or out to eat." Paul appears frustrated.

"That's not what you said. You said *anything*."

"Thank you for the ride," I interrupt their back and forth, sliding my fingers onto the door handle.

"Let me get closer to the front door." Paul swings the car around and pulls up along the sidewalk. He takes his phone from the center console. "Here. Call your phone so you have my number. I can come back and pick you up if things don't work out."

"So can a taxi," I answer.

"No car service is coming down here," he denies, insistently bouncing his phone, "especially after dark."

Logic tells me giving my number to him is a mistake. The goal should be to cut off future contact for their sake more than mine. Still, I find myself taking his offer and calling my phone. I notice he has several missed text messages, but I resist the urge to tap the notification to look at them. Hearing a ring in the backpack, I end the call and give his phone back to him. Our fingers touch briefly, but the feel of the contact lingers on my hand.

Why am I obsessed with his hands?

"Thank you again for the ride." It seems stupid since I've already said that, and it's not at all what I want to tell him. What I want to say isn't fit for the chaperone in the back seat. I remind myself this is not the end of a date. "Diana, pleasure to meet you."

"Will you come to my softball game?" Diana asks, wiggling against her seatbelt.

I feel bad for the kid. Her tone is almost desperate, and I know what she's been through today. I can't bring myself to tell her no.

"We'll see," is all I can think to say.

"That means no," she counters with a pout.

I take off Paul's jacket and leave it as I get out of the car. Slinging the backpack over my shoulder, I cradle my hand against it and lean back in to look at him. "Are you sure I can't pay you back for dinner or gas?"

He frowns and waves dismissively, indicating that the idea is absurd. "I should be thanking you. This ended up being a much-needed distraction from today."

It's been the same for me too. I didn't think anything could distract me from a triple funeral.

I find myself not wanting to leave them and the safe life they represent. I have to keep reminding myself that I'm a visitor in their normal world. And, in order for it to remain safe and normal, they should get out of this neighborhood.

"Bye, Paul, Diana." I make myself shut the door before saying more as an excuse to linger.

I resist the urge to look back as I scan my surroundings and make a beeline for the entrance. The list of names on the old intercom system is unreadable. Still, I buzz 204 to let me in. I'm not sure the system is working. Nothing seems to happen, and no one answers.

I glance toward the street. Paul and Diana watch

me from the parked car. It's sweet that he's making sure I get safely inside.

I try the glass security door. It sticks a little, but it opens. It's not exactly like breaking into Fort Knox. I look back one last time and give a wave.

A layer of grime covers the lobby floor. Someone had tried to mop but only sloshed the dirt around the tiny space. A waft of urine mixes with what I can only describe as dying flowers. The wall of dented mailboxes has seen better days. Florescent lights flicker. The sound of them is abnormally loud.

I don't see an elevator, so I head up the stairs. The smell becomes mustier, like old plaster and mold.

I touch the amulet on my necklace to ensure it is hidden under my shirt. Now that I'm here, I have to question Conrad's logic.

Why would he send me to this place?

Maybe he gave me the wrong address.

Is this one of the Devine family holdings? How did he even know about it?

I think of the vampire symbols outside. Conrad has been very into vampire culture lately, at least superficially. Did one of his friends tell him about it?

At the end of my mental storm, I decide it doesn't matter. I'm here. Conrad is talking to the lawyers. This will all be over soon.

A small security camera is pointed at the top of the stairs. Someone had anchored it to the ceiling. I duck my head, wondering who would be watching in a place like this.

Apartment 204 is easy to find. My hand shakes with nerves as I knock. I wonder who will answer and pray it's not vampires. They made me nervous before. Now, without my parents acting as an invisible shield, I feel much less protected.

I panic and start to turn away. If I run, I might be able to catch Paul. But it's too late to change my mind. The slide of a lock clicks. I back up and press against the other side of the hallway. Chipped paint crunches along my back as I make contact. I hug the backpack against my chest like body armor.

The woman who answers the door looks frail, but her jerky movements appear angry. The smoke from her cigarette dances and curls as she holds it in her mouth. Graying brown hair is pulled back to the nape of her neck, but I can see personal appearance is not a priority. Her arms are made up of loose skin and sores. I see them briefly before she finishes pulling on a sweater jacket to hide them.

"Did you bring my money?" She pulls the cigarette from her lips, walking away as she leaves the door open for me to follow. It occurs to me that she's not scared of letting a stranger inside. I find that odd.

Her bare feet shuffle on the wooden floors and worn rugs. A dusty poster of a rodeo cowboy is thumb-tacked to the entryway. I wonder if the woman is a fan of the sport or simply likes the display of abs.

"You're expecting me?" I follow cautiously and shut the door behind me without locking it. I want to make sure I have a way out. I glance into a small, empty kitchen. I get a whiff of rotten food from the dirty plates littering the counter and the overflowing trash can. I move closer to my hostess.

"Welcome to my shithole." She grabs a pack of cigarettes and a lighter from a shelf before falling back onto an old couch. The cushions are intact but worn and sagging with the imprint of her body. The stark light comes from a lamp minus its shade on a scuffed end table. A half-empty whiskey bottle waits next to a plastic cup and soda can. Balled-up fast food wrappers lay scattered at her feet.

This place could do with fresh air. I glance at the windows behind her but see the thick bars welded over them and the nails poking out of the frame to keep it shut.

She takes a long draw off the cigarette and crosses her arms as she stares at me. Smoke unceremoniously furls from her mouth as she speaks. "You happen to have more smokes in that bag of yours? Food?"

I give a slight shake of my head. "I didn't know I was supposed to bring them."

I swear she looks at me like I'm an idiot. Though, I really don't know her well enough to judge for sure. It's possible that annoyed irritation is just her natural resting state.

"I'm Tamara," I say. "Thank you for letting me hang out here."

The woman cackles as the lit cigarette dangles from her lips. I get a glimpse of yellowed teeth. The cigarette bounces as she mutters. "I'm not letting you do shit."

She reaches for the cigarette pack and pulls out a new one. I glance up to see a security camera anchored to the living room's ceiling.

"May I ask who's watching us right now?" I point toward the camera.

"Oh." She fingers the new cigarette and uses it to point in the same direction. "My son put those in for me. He's a good boy. Takes care of his mama."

She laughs as if it's the funniest thing ever said before choking back a long drink.

"Your son?" I prompt, still standing. I start to feel a little lightheaded.

I tried to be polite, but this place is gross.

"You got the cash?" She nods at the bag.

"Who's your son?" I repeat. I adjust the backpack on my shoulder. Is this why Conrad sent cash with me? To give it to this woman?

She flicks the old cigarette's ash into the soda can she's using as an ashtray before tamping it out. "Look. The deal is cash to crash. This isn't a fucking bed and breakfast, and we're not going to chat and be friends. Now, do you have my cash or not?"

This woman is a real piece of work.

A series of loud thuds reverberate behind me, and I turn to see Diana flying into the apartment. I startle in surprise, but before I can move, she collides into me.

"I want to come with you," she says, wrapping her arms around my legs.

"Whoa, whoa," my bitchy hostess protests. "No one said anything about kids. This ain't no fucking daycare."

I pry the girl off me so I can look at her. "Diana, what are you—?"

"Ugh, it stinks in here!" Diana holds her nose and gags.

She's right. It smells like old Easter eggs, and it's getting worse.

"Di!" Paul's yell comes from far away.

"I don't need this. Get the fuck out of my house."

The woman stands, shooing with her arms to get us to move. She throws back the liquor in her cup before putting the cigarette in her mouth.

I'm lightheaded, and I'm starting to feel a little nauseous.

Oh fuck.

Gas.

"Diana!" Paul yells, closer than before.

The woman lifts the lighter.

"No!" I sweep my arm across Diana's chest, half lifting and half dragging the girl as I run toward the door.

I hear the spark wheel turn.

The loud whoosh of an explosion ignites behind us. The force of it pushes us through the door. Diana screams. I feel the heat on my back and wrap my arms around her. My yell joins hers as I close my eyes tight.

I don't expect us to make it.

I gasp for breath, stunned that I can breathe. I open my eyes to find a soft blue glow emanating from my skin like a protective shield. I'm not magical, so I have no clue where it's coming from. The flames crackle and roar all around us. The apartment is engulfed, and the fire has spilled into the hallway. Smoke clouds the air.

Adrenaline pumps through me. I grip Diana tight

and run toward the stairs. It's hard to hold on to her and the backpack at the same time, but it's strapped over my shoulder, and I can't drop it.

"Diana!" Paul is there, screaming toward the flames. We crash into him, all three tumbling a few steps down before he manages to stop our fall.

"Go, go, go!" I yell, guiding Diana's back to make her hurry. Paul pulls his daughter into his arms.

The fire rages, and all I can think of is survival. I cover my mouth with my sleeve as I run down the stairwell.

We hit the bottom of the stairs. Paul grabs my arm while still holding his daughter. He pulls me behind him toward the front door. I let him guide my steps as I look back.

People gather on the sidewalk outside to watch the flames against the night sky. Shouting comes from those trying to escape the blaze, adding to the chaos. They jump from the second-story windows.

"Yo, dude, what happened?" A guy yells, puffing out his chest as he tries to stop us.

Paul sidesteps him and keeps going. His car is parked halfway up the block on the wrong side of the street. It's up on the curb, and the engine is running.

He sets Diana down and grabs her face. "Are you hurt?"

She cries and gasps for breath. Her words are incoherent whines between sobs.

Paul feels her arms and legs, searching for injury, as he says in relief, "You're okay. It's okay."

He opens the car door and lifts her inside.

Paul turns to me and holds my face, searching my eyes. "Are you hurt?"

He starts to repeat the panicky process of checking for injuries. His hands start running down my arms. I'm relieved he came back, even if it was for his daughter.

"Hey! That's them. What'd you do?" a man yells. Some of the crowd has turned toward us.

I stop Paul's hands. "We should get out of here."

He nudges me to go around the front of the car as he gets into the driver's side.

Something strikes the car window. As it resonates through the vehicle, Diana whimpers in fear. She quickly curls into a ball on the floor behind her dad's seat, seeking refuge from the threat.

I reach for the door handle. Paul stomps on the gas pedal, and we accelerate down the street before I close the car door, leaving tire tracks behind us.

CHAPTER
SIX

"What the fuc—?" Paul catches himself. He shoots a precautionary look in the rearview toward Diana, but I doubt he can see her on the floor. His hands white-knuckle the steering wheel as his body writhes with adrenalin. He glances warily at me as if going through a mental checklist while trying to understand it all. "Are you hurt?"

I shake my head as I realize how fast the car travels down the inner-city street. I brace myself on the dashboard. Paul notices, but it doesn't deter him. I feel shaky and numb. My stomach churns and knots at the same time. I don't know if I'm going to pass out or throw up.

A strange, acrid taste lingers in my mouth, the flavor of smoke and ash.

Fire.

My mind can hardly process the word. I should be dead or at least in a hospital burn unit.

I rub my arm, wondering at the blue light I saw, but then realize it was probably reflected from the gas fire. Natural gas in stoves burns blue. That has to be it. The simplest solution is usually the answer.

Still, there is a nagging thought in the back of my brain warning me that this might be magic. Not that I'm magical. I've been alive long enough to know that's not happening.

"Natural gas burns blue," I whisper, cementing the answer in my mind before my thoughts carry me down a magical conspiracy rabbit hole. I mean, honestly? If the supernatural wanted to kill me, there were much easier ways for them to go about it than a gas leak. Plus, I saw her light a cigarette.

"Di, hon, it's all right, baby," Paul tries to soothe the whimpering girl behind us.

I need to think of someone beyond myself. Diana is just a kid, and she's terrified. Paul is confused and trying to be brave. They're in this situation because of me.

I push out of the passenger seat and crawl into the back, which causes Paul to ease off the gas pedal. As I peer out of the back window, I'm unable to see the flames. It doesn't matter. They're still blazing vividly in my mind. I can almost feel the scorching heat on my skin, not to mention the cloying smell that haunts every breath.

I reach for Diana, pulling her off the floor and into my arms. As I hold her close, a wave of uncertainty washes over me. My actions aren't altruistic. I need a hug as much as she does.

The girl clings to me, shaking. I don't know what to say to make any of this better. I don't even know what to think.

Fire.

That word keeps churning in my thoughts.

What are the odds that I'm in two fires so close together? Two random events? Intentional?

A new fear creeps in. Authorities think I started the first one. What if they think I'm to blame for this one, too? There were cameras. People saw me there.

But why would I want to hurt that woman? Why would I want to hurt anyone?

No, the cameras would prove I'm innocent. I didn't do anything.

None of this makes sense. I want to close my eyes and wake up from this nightmare.

Paul slows the car and pulls aside. Firetrucks zip past, sirens blaring.

"We should go to a hospital," Paul says.

"We're not hurt," I tell him. "We'll end up sitting

in the waiting room for four hours around sick people."

Post Covid, I find myself wanting to avoid such places at all costs. I think a lot of New Yorkers feel the same way. We all remember what it was like during the pandemic. I touch my necklace and can't help but think of my grandfather.

"We need to call someone," he insists.

"They know." I turn in my seat to look behind us. The fire trucks' lights flicker long after the vehicles disappear from sight.

"We should go to the police. Tell them everything we know," he says.

"No." The panicked word comes out more harshly than I intend. "I mean. We didn't do anything. We don't know anything."

I can't talk to the police right now. What if they detain me?

"But..." He struggles with my logic.

I can't blame him, even if he doesn't know my selfish reasons for making the argument. The right thing would be to go to the police and tell them we're witnesses.

I'm not going to do the right thing. Not now.

Besides, I'm not sure it matters. I don't know anything. The arson investigators will figure out it was a gas leak without my help.

I admire the goodness in him, even as it works against me. Leaning forward, I gently stroke his arm. The contact strikes me as more intimate than it should be. "It'll be fine. I'll have the family lawyers reach out on our behalf. Right now, you have to think about Diana. You don't want to expose her to a police station. We'll be stuck there all night, and she's already freaked out."

I know it's manipulative, even as I say it.

"She's terrified, Paul," I insist. My hand stays on the solid muscle of his bicep even as I tell myself to let go.

The manipulation works. He reluctantly nods. I expect to feel relief, but I don't. Instead, I feel self-centered and mean.

Unwillingly, I force myself to loosen my grip on him and let go, even though every part of me longs for the contact. There is no denying I feel a sexual pull toward him. I have been attracted to him since I saw him wildly searching for his daughter after the funeral.

I want to feel safe in his arms. I want him to hold me. And I hate that I can't act on my desires.

There are several rules I live by when it comes to dating. Don't date the undead, no matter how sexily mesmerizing the vampire's power can be. Don't date my parents' friends or their heirs. I won't make that mistake again. And don't date single dads. There are some complications I know it's best to avoid. They're the type of commitment I can't handle. What do I know about being a mom figure? I never plan on having kids.

Planned. Not plan.

"It's up to you now, Tamara... You will be expected to carry on the legacy by marrying a person of great magic. I'll have to find the right spells, of course, but I'm sure we can have you pregnant with an heir within a year."

The words play like a bad song stuck in my head. If Uncle Mortimer has his way, I'll immediately begin replenishing the family stables with the next generation. Try as I might, I can't keep images of cult-like rituals out of my head. Ole Morty said he'd work magic to ensure I conceive a supernatural baby. Nothing kills sexual desire like the idea of ancient dudes watching as I...

I physically gag and have to cover my mouth.

Goodbye, sex drive.

"...since at twenty-eight and mortal, you don't have much time left, Tamara..."

The SUV swerves a little in the road before righting itself, jerking me back to our current problems.

This mess is my fault. I might not have started

the fire, but I should never have accepted a ride from Paul. I knew if they stayed around me, my chaotic life would spill over onto them. I didn't expect it to happen so soon.

Diana's grip remains tight. I meet Paul's gaze in the rearview mirror. "Why didn't you leave?"

"I did." His brow is furrowed, and his lips are tight. "She jumped out of the car and ran after you. Thankfully, I wasn't going fast."

It's sweet, I guess.

I know there is something I should say to Diana, but I have no clue what it is. She's five. What do I know about five-year-olds? I don't even know why this one likes me so much.

I guess it all comes back to being broken. She senses it in me, like I sense it in her.

I want to protect her. I'm not sure from what. Maybe from me.

No one else will give me the answers I need right now, so I have to force myself to think logically about our situation.

What if this fire wasn't an accident? What if both fires were intentional? I again think of the cameras. Someone was watching. They would have seen me come up the stairs and into the apartment. I hardly think my bitchy hostess was a target—unless she owed a drug dealer money or gave one of her tricks an STD.

Okay. That's mean. It's wrong to call her bitchy now that she's probably dead.

It's like I can't stop being a horrible person. Thank goodness no one here can read my thoughts.

I saw vampiric symbols in the neighborhood. Is someone after me because of my family? The Devines weren't exactly benevolent and loved— more like feared and powerful. I want to call Conrad about it, but I can't talk freely in front of them. I tell myself he's at home. He's safer there than anywhere else.

Diana doesn't look like she will let go of me anytime soon. She almost died. I can't blame her.

A sinking feeling overwhelms me. What if they saw Diana on the security feed? What if they know I'm with them? What if they were watching outside? And saw his car? And his license plate? And what if that puts this family in danger?

Who the hell is *they*?

Is there even a *they*?

What is the answer here?

"We have a guest bed," Paul says. I know where he's going with this. He's too nice. Kindness is an attractive quality in a man, and my dirty mind is all too willing to suggest ideas about what to do with that guest bed. I can't take him up on the offer.

They can't go home. Not until I know what the threat is.

The sun is setting. I can't see it behind the tall buildings, but I can tell by how the light falls. Night is a dangerous time to be an unprotected human. My heart still pounds from our brush with death.

I look up, trying to see the sky. A dark shadow flies past. Most people would assume it was a large bird and ignore it. But I know what's out there and what it's capable of. I don't think I've been this scared in a long time. Probably not since I was a kid when I watched Anthony practicing defensive magic and realized I didn't have any.

"Kansas," I blurt out.

"What?" He adjusts the mirror as if that will help him see me better.

"You said you wanted to go to Kansas." I try to loosen Diana's grip on my waist. I see her stuffed dog on the floor and grab it. I hand the toy to her. She pulls it into the hug but doesn't let go.

"I said I was considering it, but now I don't know..." He sounds doubtful.

Experience tells me that if I were to explain that their lives might be in danger by some unknown supernatural force—*oh, yeah, and by the way supernatural things exist*—they're not likely to believe me.

"Don't you want to get out of the city? What's

stopping us? It doesn't have to be Kansas if you don't want to go there. Let's just drive. Anywhere. Road trip." I try not to sound as desperate as I feel. No one will think to look for me in Kansas. And, by the time we get there, Conrad and the lawyers should have some answers for me. I can hop on a plane and come back to the city.

Paul slows the car as we enter traffic.

"I want to get out of the city." Diana's muffled voice is barely audible.

Paul rubs his brow. His gaze meets mine. He looks worried and desperate. I know he's trying to figure out the best course of action. He already confessed he is unsure what to do for Diana in her grief.

I wish I had answers for him, but I'm not a mom. I am, however, terrified for all of us.

"Please," I mouth.

I see his eyes dip as he thinks about his choices. The weight of this day is on all of us. It's a palpable force pressing down and making the air thick. Funerals then nearly dying in a fire. How can we not think about mortality?

How can we not want to run?

The car stops moving, and his head drops forward. "We don't have anything packed."

"We'll buy supplies on the road," I insist.

He runs his hand through his hair, and I see the fingers gripping together as if to pull it from his scalp. A horn honks behind us, prompting him to resume driving.

As if coming to a decision, he says, "We can stop at home and pack. It'll be better to leave in the morning anyway."

"It's still early." I touch his arm and feel his muscles stiffen beneath my fingers. "Please, Paul, just keep driving. I can't breathe here."

Diana lifts her head. "Yeah, Paul. I can't breathe. Keep driving."

"This is crazy," he mutters to himself. "What am I doing?"

"Dad," Diana insists. "Keep driving."

This copying is getting out of hand but damned if it doesn't work.

"Okay." He tosses his hands as if giving up. "Fine. Road trip."

I sit back but don't feel relief from getting my way. I can tell myself I did it to protect them, but I know the truth. I manipulated a man's concern for his daughter because I'm scared.

Fuck, I'm a selfish asshole.

With the decision made, Paul seems to relax into his role as driver. I've noticed that about most men. They want a defined purpose, a logical blueprint to fix whatever situation they're in. Or maybe he craves the mindlessness of his task, to drive into the distance without having to think.

The truth is, I can assume all I want about him. I can try to read his expressions, but I don't know him, no matter what kind of kinship I feel at this moment. I remind myself that I am a visitor to their world—an interloper dragging trouble behind me.

Interloper. That's a good word.

I lean my head back and close my eyes. Fear won't let me sleep, but I feel the exhaustion from the day in my bones. I can hardly concentrate on one thing, so I let my mind drift.

I'm glad not to be alone.

Traffic is a good thing. There is safety in numbers, and with so many people around, an attack is less likely.

Why would someone want to hurt me? I'm not special.

My mother would hate that I'm wearing these shoes with this dress.

My father would hate that I'm entangled in legal drama.

Poor Anthony. He seemed to have everything— the golden boy of the Devine family—but he'd lived a life of secrets and lies.

Conrad will be worried about me. No, he has my

phone number. He'll call when he has something. He probably doesn't know about the apartment fire yet.

"You should be in a seatbelt." Paul's voice causes me to open my eyes.

I realize Diana's grip has loosened. Her eyes are closed. For a second, I think she's copying me, but they stay closed.

I'm not sure what to do. "She's sleeping."

"That's probably for the best." He turns a corner.

I don't pay attention to where he's going, just as long as we keep moving.

"Thank you for being here for her." His eyes try to meet mine, but I purposefully avoid them. "I don't know what I would have done if I lost her."

His gratitude makes my guilt worse. I hear the pain in his voice. It wasn't there before. I wonder if he'd been trying to stay strong in front of his daughter.

"It's nothing," I dismiss. "We're all just trying to make it through this fucked up day."

"I keep a blanket in the back."

I slide Diana off my lap onto the seat and turn around to find the blanket. It's next to a first aid kit, bottles of water, and a toolbox. The man is prepared.

A tiny shiver of apprehension works over me, and I look out the back window. The tinting on the car behind us is too dark to see into. I don't know if I'm being paranoid or if it's some kind of self-preservation sixth sense kicking in.

"Find it?" Paul asks.

"Yeah, yeah, got it." I take the blanket and try to ignore my nervousness. A couple of worn paperbacks fall from within the folds. I leave them.

I recline one of the seats and do my best to maneuver the girl without waking her. She frets a little but doesn't open her eyes. I buckle her in and cover her with the blanket. When she's secured, I crawl back into the front seat.

Paul glances at me a few times before reaching over to pat my shoulder briefly. "You got a little…"

I look at my dress to find the material singed. It's odd, but my skin is unharmed. "I'm fine."

"You're lucky." Paul glances back at Diana before saying, "You want to tell me what happened back there?"

"Diana showed up. I smelled gas. The woman I was with lit a cigarette and," I shrug, helpless to explain it better, "boom."

"Did she do it on purpose?"

"I don't think she noticed the smell. She…" How can I say it diplomatically? "She seemed like she'd lived a rough life."

"Who was she?"

"I never got a name."

"Then why were you visiting her?"

I contemplate how to answer that honestly. I don't want to lie. "It's a family matter."

I can see that he wants me to explain more, but I can't. If I say *supernatural*, he'll kick me out of the car before I can even get the word out. Two seconds into meeting him, anyone can see that Diana is his world, and he'll protect her at all costs.

I admire that about him.

It also means I must be cautious if I want to stay with them until I can assure myself they're safe.

I look into the side mirror and see the car with tinted windows driving beside us. I can't shake the feeling that something isn't right.

I tell myself I'm paranoid and that I'm making up threats in my head because I don't want to be alone. I hope that's true.

"I'm sorry she followed me," I say.

"It's not your fault she jumped out of the car." He sighs, and I see him struggling with his thoughts. "She's...I guess you'd say she's attached to you. It could be because you lost your mom, too, and she recognizes something kindred in you. I know I'm asking a lot. You don't know us, and you don't owe us anything, but—"

"Hey." I touch his arm. I can't seem to help myself. I feel his warmth beneath my fingers, and I don't want to let go. "Maybe... I don't know. This might sound all new-age-y or whatever, but possibly we were meant to find each other today. Maybe, right now, we're all broken, and we're just three people trying to get through this moment the best way we can. And I don't know about you, but I can't be in this city right now. So, let's just drive. And be safe. And be gone. And be..."

I don't even know if I'm making sense.

"Be anywhere but here," he finishes for me with a nod as if I've made the most logical proposal in the world. "Any other time, I would say this is insane. But I get it. I feel the need to reset and regroup, too. If I'm honest with myself, I don't want to go home yet."

I imagine that's what someone innocent of any wrongdoing would say in this situation.

My touch has lingered too long, and I force my hand to drop to my lap. Even now, I can feel my fingers tingle where they made contact with him. It's a physical awareness so profound and startling that I know I'm in trouble. It radiates deep into my stomach. I'm becoming more attracted to Paul by the second.

There are thousands of reasons why that is a bad idea. And I can't think of a single good one.

CHAPTER
SEVEN

"Tamara."

I resist the call of my name, wanting to stay inside the darkness of sleep.

"Hey, Tamara, wake up."

Someone taps my shoulder. I startle and blink rapidly until I finally realize it's Paul. He's no longer driving. One second ago, I was staring at the taillights of the car ahead of us, and then... I don't remember going to sleep.

"Where are we?" I suppress a yawn and stretch.

"Shh." Paul motions to the back seat. If his eyes are any indication, he's clearly exhausted.

Diana is still sleeping. We're in the parking lot of a gas station next to an open field. We've made it out of the city.

He keeps his voice soft. "Near Pittsburgh.

There's a hotel across the street. I figured we'd stop for the night and make a plan in the morning."

The plan is to drive. I don't want to stop, but I don't say as much out loud. It's unreasonable to expect them to spend the night in the car.

"I'm going to get snacks. Any requests?"

I shake my head in denial.

"I'll be right back." He starts to get out of the car and then stops. "I think someone was texting your phone."

He leaves me alone in the car with his daughter. I check on Diana in the back seat. Her neck bends to the side at a dramatic angle that makes my muscles ache just looking at it, and her limbs sprawl in what must be an uncomfortable position. It seems odd that Paul would trust me to watch her, even if it's only for a brief time in the car. If he knew how little experience I have with kids, he might change his mind.

I dig my phone out of the backpack and get out of the car to stretch my legs. It's nighttime. Streetlights illuminate the area, but I can still see stars. I hear cars from the nearby interstate zipping past.

I search for signs of trouble. A tattooed man in leather fuels his motorcycle next to a schoolmarm type in a sedan. The biker seems harmless enough, but the woman looks like she wants to eat him for dinner...and not in a fun way. It's always the benign-looking ones we need to watch out for. Danger loves hiding under the façade of innocence.

Face recognition unlocks my phone. My parents put all of our devices on what they called a supernatural protection plan to keep them from being hacked or tracked, prompted by all those naughty celebrity cell phone photos being leaked online. Apparently, they were less worried about finding me via my GPS than me doing something to cause them public embarrassment.

For the record, no, I do not make sex videos with my phone.

I see Paul through the gas station window. Though, I could be tempted to...

Just saying.

Paul watches us intently. I guess he doesn't trust me as much as I thought. I lift my hand toward him in acknowledgment. A blurred version of my reflection mimics me in the glass. It's warped and faded, making me feel like I'm slowly disintegrating into the surrounding landscape. My scorched funeral dress and sneakers have a sad Miss Havisham decaying vibe to them. Only, instead of a wedding day that never happened, I'm eternally dressed for my funeral that didn't come—locked in a place where time no longer makes sense.

It should have been me who died in that fire. Not my family.

As diverting as it may be to compare myself to an iconic madwoman in a Dickens novel, this gas station is no manor house in Great Expectations.

Checking the phone, I see I have several missed messages from Conrad.

"What the hell happened? There are fire trucks."

"Where are you?"

"Answer me."

"Tam?"

"Tamara?"

"We need to talk."

"Tell me you're alive."

"Call."

I dial Conrad. Paul is still making his way through an aisle, pausing to look at the SUV every few steps.

"Tamara?" Conrad's hushed voice answers.

"I'm okay," I tell him.

"Hold on." The garbled sound of movement comes through the phone. When he finally returns to the call, he says, "Are you still there?"

"I'm here." I lean against the SUV's hood and watch an old van pull up beside the motorcycle at the fuel pumps. Smoke drifts from the cracked windows.

I stare at it. My heart begins to beat faster, and I feel sick to my stomach.

"Tamara, are you listening? Where is *there*?" Conrad demands.

The insistence in his voice brings me back to the conversation. I take a shaky breath. "I'm not sure."

He sighs loudly, and I know he doesn't like my answer.

"I went to pick you up. Police and firefighters were everywhere." Conrad sounds confused, and I can't blame him. "They're saying a woman who looks like you was seen fleeing the scene with some guy and a kid. What the hell is going on? What did you do?"

"I didn't do anything." Anxiety unravels inside me, spreading throughout my entire being and taking hold of me in its vice-like grip. "I'm innocent. You must believe me, Conrad. I didn't start any fires. I didn't hurt anyone. It was an accident. I smelled gas, and then that woman lit a cigarette and—"

"I know," he cuts me off. "I believe you. You're not a murderer."

My body contorts, the frustration evident in my clenched fist.

"Of course, I know you didn't do it." His tone softens. "You're my sister. I never thought you did. I'm just worried."

I exhale and then draw a deep breath. Hearing him say it is a relief. It gives me a sense of comfort. He is the only member of my family left. Well, not counting the mysterious birth mother I have yet to find. I hardly think she counts.

A man gets out of the van and slams the door. I jump at the loud sound. He stops to talk to the biker, and the woman in the sedan snarls. Her mouth quickly snaps open and shut. My instincts were right. She's not human, and she's hunting.

"Did everyone make it out okay?" I bite my lip to keep it from quivering and try not to draw attention to myself.

"No. They're still searching the debris. Six so far." Trust Conrad not to sugarcoat things.

"Who was that woman in the apartment?" I ask. Paul is standing in line at the register, watching me. I lift my hand to indicate we're all right. "Why did you send me there? I could have just gone anywhere and waited for you to call—"

"Tam, listen," he cuts me off. "I can't talk long. I'm here with the lawyers. They're waiting for me in the other room. It's worse than we thought. The police claim they have solid evidence that you had something to do with the birthday fire. We're trying to determine what that evidence is, but it will take time to grease the right palms. The detective on the case is a real hardass."

I shake my head, even though he can't see me. I want to scream, but I'm really scared. Like *really* scared. "They can't have any because it's not true."

"You know the truth doesn't matter, only perception—optics, sis," Conrad says, sounding like a jerk. "The lawyers are on it. Just don't get arrested in the meantime. You cannot go into custody."

"I know. I don't want to be in the system." I hear a car engine, and I glance to see the schoolmarm driving away.

"I don't care about the system. Fuck the system," Conrad says. I wish he had come on this trip with me. I draw comfort from the surety in his familiar voice. "Human legal problems are human problems. We have bigger ones. Word's gotten out in the supernatural world that you're to blame. They're pissed. A paramedic told the vampires you were covered in death ash when they found you."

I flex my hand, remembering Stacy's bite.

"They know you were with Costin when he died," Conrad continues. "His ash was found next to a metal rod they use to hang tapestries. They drawing their own conclusions."

My hands tremble as I glance anxiously around

the parking lot. I envision eyes watching from the shifting shadows.

"Tell me honestly," Conrad's voice lowers as if he's scared of being overheard. "Did you stake Costin? I know how aggressive he could be around you ever since we were kids. But if you killed him, that's... Dammit, Tamara, that's some serious shit we have to deal with. You need to tell me if you started the fire to hide a murder."

Tears burn my eyes as I search every corner of the surrounding darkness. Vampires move quickly. I could be dead before I even realized they were coming. My body is frozen in place, but I want to run at the same time. "He was on fire. Everything was. I tried to put him out with the tapestry, but I was too late. He..."

"Tam, if you go into the system, you'll be a sitting duck holding a giant neon target for the hunter to shoot at. I don't have to tell you that vampires have very powerful connections. You won't come out alive."

I draw my arms close to my body, feeling helpless. That fear of death is still inside me. "I didn't kill him. Costin just poofed when I tried to put out the flames."

"You need to stay hidden," Conrad persists. "Tell me where you are now."

"A gas station."

"In the Bronx?"

"No. I left the city. I'm safe. I'm with friends." I see Paul paying the cashier. It's not really a lie. He's a new friend, and he makes me feel safe—well, safer than being alone. "We're heading west."

"West?" I can hear his unease.

"Kansas City." I have no reason not to tell him, but I instantly wish I hadn't.

"Kansas?" He gives a short laugh of disbelief. "To what? Visit Dorothy and Toto's farm? Are you insane?"

The Wizard of Oz movie is probably the only thing he remembers about Kansas.

"No one will think to look for me there," I say.

The smoker bumps fists with the biker and returns to his van without fueling.

"Who with? That man and kid you were seen fleeing with? Who are they?"

"Nobody you know."

All my fears are coming true. We made the right choice leaving the city. If Conrad already knows I'm with Paul and Diana, it won't take long for other people to figure it out. It's one thing to be on the run from the police, but another matter entirely to be hunted by vampires and the supernatural. They don't give a shit about laws and due process. However, they do enjoy a good torture session and revenge.

"I have to go talk to these guys. I'm sure they're fine sitting on their asses drinking all our high-end bourbon, but Mabon and Beck are charging us a thousand dollars an hour. Don't do anything stupid. I'll figure out somewhere safe for you to hide while we figure this out. Keep your phone on." Conrad hangs up on me.

I slowly lower the phone.

"Oh, what a precious baby girl!" someone exclaims.

I gasp sharply in surprise and spin around at the closeness of the sound. The schoolmarm stands on the opposite side of the car, peeping into the window at Diana. She must have circled back since I didn't hear her creep up. So much for being vigilant. I'm off my game. I should never have let Conrad's words distract me from my surroundings.

I glance down to see the girl is still asleep before charging around to back the woman away.

She tries to smile at me as she reaches toward the door handle. "Do you think I could hold her? She looks just like my granddaughter."

I slide between her and the car, slapping her

hand back. It's an instinct, a feeling I can't explain. Technically, I've been trained to defend myself in a fight, but real-world brawls differ significantly from a paid instructor on a floor mat. His number one lesson for a human against the supernatural was to run. "Not happening."

"Excuse me?" She blinks, trying to look innocent, but I know it's an act.

I've been around enough to recognize the hunger in her eyes. When I look closely, tiny worms appear to be swimming in her irises. I'm sure her kind has some fancy name, but I simply know them as soul eaters. They feed on people's energies, driving them into madness if they're unlucky enough to survive the attack.

"We're not on the menu." I'm taller and make a point of looking down at her. It's easy to be brave in front of a brightly lit convenience store with plenty of witnesses and security cameras, which I glance at for her sake.

Her mouth opens wide, and her jaw clicks as she bites at the air. She sniffs hard as if trying to determine who I am.

"Hey, how's it going?" Paul appears next to the car carrying two plastic bags. They swing in his rush to get to us. His tone is pleasant, but I see his concern.

The soul eater closes her mouth and resumes her smile. The expression is tight and shows no pleasure.

Paul comes close to me. "We ready?"

"Yeah." I nod. To the schoolmarm, I say, "Sorry we can't help you."

I know she's pissed by the way her body jerks, but she steps back and leaves us alone.

"Takes all types," Paul says.

I arch a brow and turn my face toward him even as my eyes stay on the soul eater. She shuffles toward her car parked in the shadows at the edge of the station.

"Always sad when drugs take hold of a person." He leans against the car next to me. "What did she want?"

I think about how to tell the truth without actually telling the truth. "Dinner, but I didn't like the way she was trying to look into the car."

Paul reaches into one of the bags and goes after the woman. "Wait, hold up."

I start to stop him but hesitate. I don't want to make a big scene.

The woman turns, and I watch Paul try to hand her a sandwich. She snarls at him and waves a hand in dismissal. The movements jerk violently, and I hope she doesn't pounce. Clearly, she's losing control and, with it, her ability to hide what she is.

Paul jogs back to the car with the sandwich. "Good call sending her away. She's definitely high on something. Pity."

"We should go," I prompt, hurrying to get into the car.

Paul lifts himself into the driver's seat and hands me the bags. "I grabbed some snacks, toothbrushes, and some very fashionable t-shirts. I figure the hotel will provide soap."

I hold the bags but don't look in them. I'm more interested in watching the soul eater stumble in the parking lot. I wish there was something I could do to stop it, but I've long had to accept that there is evil in the world. Much of that evil can't be killed, at least not in any way I am capable of. All we can do is try to protect ourselves.

"She'll probably go sleep it off in her car." Paul suppresses a yawn, and we leave the parking lot.

I glance back at Diana. Her stuffed puppy has fallen on the seat next to her. She'll never know how much danger she was in tonight.

It's a short drive down a frontage road to a hotel. I watch the soul eater disappear from view, still hunting the parking lot. The stranger she acts, the more likely it is she'll scare potential meals away. The thought gives my guilt little comfort.

I think of the look in her eyes and know she

didn't recognize me. Even if she had, it would not have mattered. Conrad and I are no longer protected as members of the Devine family. Not anymore. Not when everything scary about that name is currently rotting in a mausoleum.

EIGHT

Devine Country Estate, Twenty-Two Years Ago...

I rush through the halls of the country house, eager to see what birthday surprises await me. The puffy princess dress my mother is making me wear is stupid and sparkly, but I don't care.

My father promised me a cake as tall as I am, with fairies skating in the icing. And, since I behaved all year and did everything I was supposed to, he promised I could get a puppy for my sixth birthday—one I could keep. I've thought of many potential names but will not decide until I know my new best friend's personality.

This is going to be the best day ever.

I'm going to take such good care of my puppy. And he'll love me as much as I love him. And we'll be best friends forever. We'll do everything together. Everything!

My entire body shakes with excitement, and I can't sit still. Grandfather would say I have unicorn ants in my pants. The thought of tiny unicorns makes me giggle. He's the funniest person in the world.

People have been coming all day to prepare for the festivities. I've watched from the top of the staircase and have seen the crates and flowers entering the house. I've never had a party this fancy before, at least not that I can remember from looking at my baby pictures.

My feet start running. I can't stop them. I have to see.

I hop down the stairs and burst through the large wooden doors carved with supernatural creatures. Sparkly lights hang from the ballroom's ceiling, and vases filled with flowers are on top of tablecloths. Usually, I don't like cut flowers because they wilt so fast, but today, they're perfect. Workers arrange the place settings according to how my mother likes them. I run through the maze of round tables toward my father.

"Where is he? Where is he?" The words just burst out.

"Stop." Lady Astrid appears before me. The chill in my mother's voice instantly causes me to freeze.

She's always irritated with me, so I try to stay out of her way. She snaps her fingers. "Davis. Give her the thing. We need to get dressed. Our guests will be arriving in a couple of hours."

My father has his hand on a skinny boy's shoulder and steers him toward us. I look around the floor, hoping to see my puppy.

"Tamara, stand up straight," my mother orders.

I obey, pretending a steel rod is attached to my back so she doesn't magically put the brace back on me to straighten my posture.

My mother smells heavily of flower perfume, and the scent will linger in a room long after she's gone. She also looks like a movie star. My father isn't as glamorous, but he's fun when he's around. He wears well-pressed suits and smells like the special drink he keeps in the fancy crystal in his office.

"Tamara, this is Conrad," my father says. "He's your brother."

I look at the boy and can't help but roll my eyes as I giggle. "No, he's not. Anthony is my brother."

"Conrad is your new brother." My mother studies the boy. "This is Tamara. As we discussed, it is a big brother's job to look after his little sister."

"Yes, Astrid," the boy says.

My mother arches a brow.

"Yes, Lady Astrid," the boy corrects.

"Are you at least a werewolf?" I scrunch up my face as I look Conrad over. That would kind of be like having a puppy.

Conrad frowns at me.

"Where's my puppy?" I can't stand waiting a moment longer.

My mother waves her hand. "You're not getting a dog. I will not have it pissing all over the carpet."

"A brother will live longer," my father says. "And he's mortal, like you. You'll have someone to play with while Anthony is away at his special school. Won't it be fun to have a brother to attend human school with you?"

I want to go to school with other kids, not have someone go to the tutor with me.

"But you promised," I remind my father. I already have a brother. I don't want another. "You said if I behaved, I could have a puppy and a cake with fairies."

"Ew!" Anthony appears behind me, bumping his shoulder into my back as he walks past to join us. "You want to eat fairies?"

"No," I protest. "They'll skate in the frosting and make the cake float."

"Anthony!" our mother scolds, her words coming over mine. "I told you to get dressed for your party. Tonight is very important."

"I came down to tell Tamara happy birthday." Anthony is brave. At seven, he's a year older than me and is never scared of our mother. It's probably because he has magic and can throw fireballs.

I wish I could throw fireballs. Anthony tried to give me one once, but it burned my hand. We got in trouble.

Anthony leans over and whispers in my ear, "Fairy eater!"

I scrunch my face up at him in defiance.

"Conrad." Anthony reaches out his hand. "I'm Anthony."

"Hey." Conrad tilts his head back and juts out his jaw. He doesn't shake hands.

Anthony takes the rejection in stride.

"Anthony, get dressed in your robes before the wizards get here," our mother says. "Tamara, show Conrad the house and tell him the rules. Then take him to the yellow guest suite in the protected wing. That will be his bedroom. I expect you both to be out of sight when our guests arrive, or there will be consequences."

"But..." I look around, confused. I try not to cry. "Where is my puppy? Where is the cake?"

This is supposed to be my party. Not Anthony's.

"It will not be safe for humans to wander around

tonight," my mother says before prompting in her firm voice, "And why is that?"

I sigh. I hate lessons. "Because someone might eat us."

"Or?" she insists.

"Maim us," I mumble. "And magic won't be able to put us back together because humans are fragile."

"Tam-tam," my father says. "Tonight is very important for your brother. The wizard council is coming to coronate him into his first magical order. We'll have cake tomorrow."

"She doesn't need more sweets," my mother tells him.

"Leave her be, Astrid," my father scolds.

I feel like they're about to start bickering, so I grab Conrad's arm. "Come on. I'll show you the house. Don't touch *anything*. It might kill you."

"Astrid's mean," he says when we're out of the ballroom. I take him across the foyer to the library. "She doesn't want me here."

"Sh." I press my fingers to my lips to tell him to be quiet before pointing toward a maid. I lead him into the library and shut the door so it's safe to talk. "They are all tattletales."

Conrad has a sad face. I feel bad for him.

"She is the most beautiful lady in the world. Everyone thinks so." I point at my parents' portraits on the library wall. "Anthony says she has to be like that. It's not easy running an empire."

"What does that mean?"

I shrug. I have no clue.

"Do I get to name you?" I try not to be sad, but I really wanted that puppy.

"No. I have a name," Conrad answers. "It's Conrad Muller."

"I hate my birthday," I say, sniffing back tears. "And I hate their stupid Anthony party. They promised me a puppy, not a brother."

"I've never had a birthday party," Conrad says.

"Never?" I try to see if he's joking.

He shakes his head. "Never."

"Not even a cake?" I insist.

"Nope."

I can't decide if he's telling the truth. "Do you have a birthday?"

"Of course, I have a birthday. Everyone has a birthday." He stares at me, looking me up and down. "How old are you?"

"Six."

"I'm eight," he says. "That means I'm older and in charge."

"No." I purse my lips in defiance.

"You heard them. It's my job to be the boss of you."

I don't want another boss of me.

"Did they adopt you too?" he asks.

I shake my head. "No."

"Then how come you're human?"

I shrug again. "I don't know. How come you're human?"

"My parents are human." He finds an old fireball stain on the wall and stares at it.

"A wizard drunk too much adult punch," I explain. "That's why the paint won't cover it."

"Can you do magic?"

"Anthony said he'd teach me spells and potions when I'm older. He has to learn them first." I stop under Anthony's portrait. It hangs close to my parents' and shows him standing in a fancy suit. "He bought me fireworks. Those are kind of like magic."

"Where's your picture?" Conrad asks.

"I don't have one yet," I answer. "Lady Astrid says I have to grow into myself first."

"Why do you call your mom Lady Astrid?"

I laugh at the silly question. "That's her name."

"It's weird." Conrad starts to reach toward my mother's picture frame.

"Don't!" I grab his hand. "It's poison."

He frowns. "That doesn't make sense."

"It'll make you sick. It'll make your insides

explode," I say. "Lady Astrid says it's to keep from printing fingers on it."

"Fingerprints?"

"Yeah, those." I nod.

"That's stupid." Conrad doesn't try to touch the picture again.

"We can sit in these chairs when we're reading." I point at the reading nook before showing him which shelf has books safe for humans to read. "You can look at the books on this shelf."

"Why not all of them?" He starts to reach for a book on a higher shelf. The magical shield zaps his fingers, and he jumps back, shaking his hand and saying bad words.

"Cause it's illegal for humans." I find it weird that he doesn't know these things. If he's living in this house, he should know. "They're written funny anyway. Anthony showed them to me. The words are jumbled. You need magic eyes to see them."

His stomach growls.

"Are you hungry?" I ask.

He nods. "They didn't feed me before my flight."

"You fly?" I look at him in excitement. "Like a fairy? On a dragon? Oh, did you use wings?"

He furrows his brow. "On an airplane."

"Oh." That's much less interesting. "Where did you fly from?"

"Missouri," he says. "That's where your parents found me."

"What's a Missouri?" The library is boring, so I decide to take him to the kitchen.

Conrad doesn't smile. His face looks like he's about to yell, but his voice remains calm. "A state."

I pause at the door and plug my nose. My voice sounds funny as I say, "This next room smells. It's called the smoking room. A guy died in there a really, *really* long time ago, like forty years ago. Anthony said his ghost is in there farting. If he touches you, you'll smell like that forever."

I run through the stinky room.

Conrad doesn't hurry, and he bravely looks around. "I don't believe in ghosts."

"How do you not know about ghosts?" I pull his arm to get him out of the room faster and slam the door shut behind us. I walk him through the maze of hallways toward the kitchen. "Didn't your father tell you about them?"

He shakes his head. "My dad is dead."

I'm confused. "Is it because he told you the supernatural are real, and they had to kill him? Humans aren't supposed to know. It's illegal."

"You know."

"I'm special. I'm not allowed to talk about it unless my parents say it's all right."

He puts his arms over his chest. "Maybe I'm special too. I've seen goblins before."

I stop walking and pet his arm. "I think you are, even if you're not a puppy."

He lifts his shoulder and steps back, so I stop petting him.

"I'm sorry your dad is dead."

He shrugs. "Doesn't matter. I never met him."

"Why didn't your mother keep you in the Missouri?"

"My mom didn't want me." He starts walking again but misses our turn.

"This way," I say. "Did she give you to me for my birthday?"

"She left me at a gas station when I was a baby."

"Lady Astrid locked me in a closet once when her magic friends came to visit," I say. "To keep me safe."

"But she came back to get you," he counters. "Mine didn't."

"She got busy. A maid let me out," I explain. "Maybe your mother got busy and forgot to come back."

"Your parents bought me from foster care. My mother isn't coming back."

I don't know what to say because I don't understand. Instead, I start running. "Race you!"

"Hey!" Conrad chases after me. "No fair, you cheated!"

I almost topple a maid.

She doesn't fall over, but she screams nonsense after me. "...running around...halls...like a little street urchin..."

I don't care.

I glance back to see Conrad passing the angry woman. He hits the bottom of her tray, sending her drinks flying. "Don't yell at her."

The woman's screams become funny gibberish.

I stop running. Conrad smiles for the first time as he catches up to me. He turns to jog backward a few steps to watch the maid picking up the mess.

"She's going to tell on you," I warn. "You'll be in trouble."

"So what? She shouldn't have yelled at you." Conrad might be the bravest kid I've ever met—not counting Anthony.

He's no puppy, but this new brother might be all right. At least I won't be alone on my birthday.

"I'll show you the food we can eat." I lead him into the kitchen. "And then I'll show you where we can hide on the protected balcony to watch the supernaturals arrive. Trust me, you don't want to miss it."

"Why?"

I giggle in anticipation. "They wear the funniest outfits."

CHAPTER
NINE

"You look like your mind is far away, Tamara. What are you thinking of?" Paul's voice interrupts my reminiscence.

He sits next to me on the hotel couch. A partial wall hides where Diana sleeps from view. Light from the bathroom casts just enough for us to see each other while leaving the two queen-sized beds in darkness. This place is nothing like the hotels I'm used to, but that's only because I usually travel with my family. But since Paul and I went halfsies on the room, it is one I can currently afford.

Everyone thinks I'm rich, but I'm not. My parents were rich. They gave me a living allowance as long as I had a job. Now, everything is tied up with the lawyers. My parents never expected to die, so it's been a mess. More than a few of those lawyers have pulled me aside to comment that I was the last "actual" Devine by blood, like that somehow made a difference, like that meant I could cut Conrad out if I wanted. I hope they didn't say as much to him as I would never consider it.

Honestly, I have been too eager to let Conrad deal with the legal mess while I hid myself away in bed.

I stare, mesmerized by the plastic-wrapped snack cake in my hands, and finally mumble, "Fairies and puppies."

"Okay," he says with a small, confused laugh. His cell phone dings, and he reaches over to silence it without looking at who texted him.

It's late, but I don't feel like lying down. Memories keep haunting me. I worry they'll spill over into my dreams. At least awake, I can control where they go.

It seems weird that I'm sharing a room with them, but I don't want to be alone. I'm afraid of what I'll do if I am. Everything about this situation is unusual.

Paul's hair is wet from showering. Mine has started drying, but I feel the damp weight against my back. I wear my exercise clothes from my backpack. Shorts and a tank are more comfortable than a dress. Paul had changed into one of the shirts he bought at the gas station. A cartoon turtle appears to dance on his chest while holding a gas can next to a spilled drink.

Paul sits close, closer than he needs to since there is plenty of room on the couch. Our bodies don't touch, but I feel the heat coming from him. I wonder if it's on purpose or if he's just tired. I want to tell him I'm scared. No, terrified. I want to warn him that there is danger outside. I want to explain vampires and soul eaters and magic. I want to say I'm sorry for Diana being brought into my world. But, most of all, I want him to believe me when I tell him the truth.

I can't force any of the words to come. If I say it, he'll leave me, and I'll be alone.

"How are you?" I've been thinking about myself all day. He obviously has a lot going on.

"I'm glad today is over." He leans forward and puts his head in his hands briefly before leaning back on the couch. "And I'm thankful to be out of the city. Leaving was a good idea."

We keep our voices low so as not to wake Diana.

I set the snack cake down, uneaten. I hear my mother's voice in my head telling me I've had enough sweets. I draw my knee onto the couch to sit sideways and study him. "Can I ask what happened to your wife?"

He hesitates, and I see him considering his answer.

"Diana doesn't know this," he whispers, turning to face me as he mimics my position.

I lean closer and nod that I understand.

"Nancy and I were getting a divorce. We've been separated for over a year. I've been saving money to move out and meet her—we'll call it an alimony demand." He takes a deep breath. "I shouldn't talk like... There's no point in speaking ill of her now. She's Diana's mom. I don't need to be an asshole about it."

I can see there is more to the story. I gently touch his knee in support.

Despite his words, he keeps talking. "Even before we separated, she was faithfully challenged."

"She cheated?" I clarify.

"Yes," he says. "I didn't see it for years. It started with the waiter at our wedding dinner, then her boss at work, then some clients at work, and God knows who else. I found out when she tried to seduce my best friend. Hector told me about it."

"And you believe him?"

"It was harder for him to tell me than it would have been not to. He had no reason to lie. Besides, Nancy eventually confessed to all of it."

"I'm sorry that happened to you. It's not the

same, but my last boyfriend, Jasper, cheated on me. He was only with me because of my family." I give a dismissive shrug. "All that to say, I understand a little of what you might be going through."

"Yeah, it sucks." His hand slides over mine on his knee.

"So what happened to her?"

"She was on a date. He drove off the road. They crashed into a construction dumpster. Her neck was broken, and she died instantly. He passed at the hospital hours later." He presses his lips together, and I can tell he's suppressing some emotion. I'm not sure if it's grief or humor. "She was..."

Paul makes a weak noise and gestures toward his lap.

My eyes widen as I stare at him. "She was giving him...?"

He nods. "I'm such an asshole. The entire funeral, all I could think was she died like she lived with some other guy's thing in her mouth. Then I felt guilty for even thinking it."

I cover my mouth and force myself not to laugh at the dark humor.

"Well, I mean..." I give a small shrug. "Was that in the news? I don't remember hearing about it."

"They hinted at it but left her name out, thank goodness." He sighs. "Diana doesn't need that memory of her mother, and I don't need some kid at her school being the one to tell her about it. Only a few people know the full details. Most of them are emergency responders."

"I feel honored that you trust me," I say.

"I don't know why I do. I just feel like I can."

His admission makes me feel guilty. I think of all I'm hiding from him. I take my hand out from under his and pretend to stretch.

"I had thought I'd gotten lucky that a bigger story was taking over the news cycle." He looks at his hand still resting on his knee where I'd left it. "I'm sorry that news story ended up being the fire that took your family."

"My mother liked living as the center of attention. She'd be upset if the news stations weren't obsessed with her death," I admit.

His hand reaches for mine, drawing me back to him. Our eyes meet. There is vulnerability in his gaze. A feeling of calm comes over me, giving me a reprieve from the usual frantic dialog cycling in my head.

"I'm glad I met you," he whispers. "And not just because Diana has taken a liking to you. Today was unbearable until you came along."

I feel drawn to him. I see his pain, and it reflects my own. I don't believe in love at first sight without a potion or a spell, but I do believe in need. Need is an angry, dark monster that reaches up from the void and tries to suck in everything around it. It's desperation and sadness and loneliness. It's my oldest friend.

"I hate today," I whisper back. "Funerals. Fires. I can't deal with it all, Paul. I need it to be over."

"It's after midnight." His voice is soft like he's whispering a secret. "It is over. We got through yesterday."

I feel safe when I'm looking at him. He seems so steady and sure.

"I'm sorry Diana was in the fire. I don't know why things keep going up in flames around me. I feel like I'm bad luck. Maybe you should just leave me here and go on to Kansas without me." It's not what I want, but it's the right thing.

"I can see why you might feel that way, but it's not as unheard of as you think. I read once that fires are the most common emergency in New York City. The fire department responds to over three hundred thousand emergencies a year. In the Bronx, there is an average of about twelve hundred structural fires a year. Most fires are caused by cooking and heating accidents. You said you smelled gas in the kitchen."

I furrow my brow. "You read once? That's a lot of information about fires. Do you have one of those photographic memories or something?"

He gives me a half-smile. "I looked it up on my phone when you were sleeping. And before you worry, we were stuck in traffic. I didn't search my phone and drive at the same time."

I lean closer, mesmerized by his mouth. Knowing he was separated from his wife for a year changes things. "Were you worried I was dangerous?"

There I go. Flirting again.

"Oh, I know you're dangerous." His tone becomes husky. He's flirting back. "But I don't get a fire starter vibe off you."

I've had a really crappy couple of weeks, and I'm helpless to resist the way his gaze dips to my mouth and back up again. The invitation is unmistakable.

"What vibe do you get?" Yes, I'm fishing for compliments.

"I think you're sad and a little lost, but who wouldn't be after what you've been through?"

It's honest, but it's not exactly what every girl hopes to hear from a boy she likes.

The disappointment must show on my face because he adds, "You're also beautiful, and sweet, and kind, and—"

I close my eyes and broach the distance between us. I press my mouth to his. I don't think of consequences. In fact, I don't think of anything beyond his touch. The contact sends a tingling sensation over my body, and I moan softly. After a moment, I realize his mouth is not moving against mine.

Mortified, I pull back to see him staring at me.

I'm not sure what to do or say. Do I apologize? Do I run and hide in the bathroom?

I can't make words come out.

"I'm sorry." He lifts his hands as if to push me away without touching me. "I didn't mean to take advantage of you."

"Wait." I tilt my head in confusion. "What?"

I kissed him.

"You're vulnerable, and I..."

"Wait, what?" I shake my head. "I think I'm taking advantage of you. I'm the one who convinced you to give me a ride. You've been nothing but a gentleman by helping out my damsel in distress sorry ass."

Now, he looks confused. "I told you my sad story, and you feel sorry for me now. You're also grateful for the ride. I'm seducing you and taking advantage of your fragile emotional state. I promise I'm not *that* guy. I like you. I don't want to ruin any potential by jumping you the first chance I get."

This has to be the strangest conversation I've ever had with a man. I maneuver on the couch and lean my head back to stare at the popcorn ceiling. I've been ignoring my exhaustion, but now I feel it filling every inch of me.

"Are we arguing?" I ask because I'm completely unsure at this point.

"I don't think so." I feel him move next to me. When I glance over, he's reclining to mimic my position. I can't see his expression clearly in the shadows. "Possibly?"

"Can we not? I think I'm too tired to have this conversation." I'd rather be kissing him, but we've headed into bizarre, almost awkward territory. I close my eyes.

"I know I'm too tired to have this conversation," he mumbles.

"What else did you find out while I was sleeping?" I like the sound of his voice and want to hear more.

"I called Hector to let him know we decided to go out of town. He's going to cover a few construction jobs for me. I answered job email queries." He lets loose a long yawn. "As much as I want to pretend I don't have any responsibilities, bills don't pay themselves."

I listen to the rhythmic sound of his breathing in the quiet hotel room. I have no idea how long we sit, but we must have fallen asleep because my neck is hurting. When I look down, Diana is curled on the couch next to us, using my leg as a pillow. I try to untangle myself from the situation but don't want to wake her.

I nudge Paul to wake him up. He inhales sharply and looks down at his daughter. Without saying anything, he stands, swoops her off the couch, and walks her to one of the beds.

I stretch as I cross to the hotel window to peek at the parking lot. It's still dark outside, but the street lights illuminate the cars below. I can't shake the feeling that there is someone out there, in the night, hunting and waiting. There are a million reasons to fear the dark, and my tired brain is all too eager to tell me about them.

Not seeing an immediate threat, I shuffle to the unclaimed bed. Paul is sleeping next to his daughter with his back turned to us. Diana is snuggled under the covers across from me.

I pull the covers up around my head and close my eyes. What is it about blankets that make us feel safe against the horrors of the world? We burrow like little soft bunnies. But predators aren't scared of bunnies, and they do not respect the sanctity of the blanket.

Fuck, I want my thoughts to stop churning. I want to sleep for an eternity and not think of anything ever again.

CHAPTER
TEN

The hotel's complimentary breakfast was a sad affair. Pre-packaged plain yogurt and granola sat on a coffee-stained counter. In the background, a pristine but empty breakfast buffet promised more. I don't care. Stress has taken my appetite.

Unfortunately, a grumpy Diana does care. She has been talking about waffles nonstop since we left the hotel. I tune her out.

Well, I *try* to tune her out.

While I slept, my dreams were haunted by fiery nightmares. Every time I woke up, I found myself peeking out the window at the parking lot and night sky. I can't shake the feeling that something is hunting us.

Now, I stare out of the car window at passing

vehicles. My fear builds, but I don't want it leaking onto my traveling companions.

Diana wears an oversized gas station turtle t-shirt like a dress over her funeral slacks. It matches her dad's style for the day. I'm still in the workout shorts and tank top, and I'm using Paul's jacket like a blanket over my legs to block the air conditioning from my skin. Diana tried to get me to put on a dancing turtle, too. To her vocal disappointment, I couldn't do it. Matching outfits would scream to the world, hey, look at us! We're a family, a matching set. We belong together.

It might be a stupid stance, but I couldn't take the lying to myself.

I've offered to drive, but Paul declined. He seems the type that likes to have a task in front of him. Or maybe he likes control. Or perhaps he's just worried I'm not on his car insurance. Or that I don't know how to drive. I'm not sure which, if any, is true.

I wish my brain would shut off. I'm over-analyzing everything.

I wish Diana would stop whining about waffles.

I wish Paul would have kissed me back so I wouldn't feel awkward around him now.

Fuck, I'm in a bad mood.

Diana kicks the back of my seat. "I'm bored."

"Put your headphones on and play a game," Paul says.

I hear Diana moving around as she pulls something from behind my seat.

My phone dings and Paul glances over at the sound. He's been quiet, and I wonder if he's uncomfortable around me. I worry that in the cold light of day, he regrets agreeing to this trip.

I automatically flip the switch on the side of my phone to mute the notification sounds as I check my messages.

A text from Conrad asks, *"Safe?"*

I send him a thumbs-up, and he sends back a link to a news article.

My heart sinks and forms a rock in my stomach. The headline reads, *"Police Search for Suspects in Bronx Arson,"* and pictures of the apartment fire accompany the article.

"Everything okay?" Paul asks.

"Uh, yeah, all good," I lie. "Just my brother checking in. He worries about me."

My hand shakes as I hold the phone. It's not a long article, but my vision keeps blurring, and I have a difficult time reading the words. I need to start over a few times to comprehend what it's telling me.

The article says a gas line had been tampered with, and a timer device had been discovered.

Authorities concluded it was arson rather quickly. Three people were found dead. Sources saw an unnamed man and a woman fleeing the scene with a child. The couple is wanted for questioning.

Legally speaking, it's a mess. I know I'm innocent. I trust the lawyers can eventually get me out of trouble with the cops. Unfortunately, I can't say the same for the vampires. First, they blamed me for Costin and the fire at my party. Now, all three of us are wanted for questioning regarding the apartment fire in vampire territory.

Fucking hell, it looks like I'm trying to start a war with the vampires. It doesn't make sense—none of it. I've spent most of my life trying to stay off the supernaturals' radar.

Vampires aren't exactly known for due process and innocent until proven guilty. When it comes to humans, they have more of an eat-first-worry-about-it-never type of justice system. Their long lifespans and natural lack of compassion for their meals lend themselves to a type of apathetic boredom. Hunting and torturing me will give them a diversion to live for, if even for a short while.

I pretend to look at my phone while side-eyeing Paul. He's a handsome man. The more I look at him, the more attractive I find him. In what can only be considered twisted self-deprecation, I find the fact that he didn't return my kiss makes me want him more. I watch his thigh muscles flex beneath the slacks as he speeds past a long line of semi-trucks in the right lane. I want to touch his leg and run my hand upward.

Is this how Nancy felt, sitting in the car next to her lover moments before giving in to the sexual temptation? Was there something in her life she wanted to escape? I can't imagine anyone wanting to escape Paul. Did she know some secret about him that I'm not seeing? Or was she just broken and selfish?

I suppose we humans are all broken. We're all just fumbling our way forward, navigating our short lives.

Not only is Paul sexy, but he's also considerate and kind. It would be easier knowing what I've dragged him into if he weren't so thoughtful.

I try to think of ways of telling him what's happening. All of them end with the vision of me being left on the side of the road like a crazy person. It's hard enough telling people about the supernatural without proof to show them—not that I will ever admit out loud that I've tried. It's like the number one rule: Don't.

No, that's not what would happen. He's too much of a gentleman to dump me on the side of the road. He'd leave me somewhere safe—like locked in a hospital psych ward.

His phone dings, not for the first time, and he ignores it. It's rare to see someone not addicted to their electronic devices.

"Do you need me to drive so you can answer those?" I offer.

"They'll wait," he says, reaching over to silence his phone without checking. "If it's an emergency, they'll call."

The highway lines come at us, repetitive and hypnotic. Riding next to Paul makes me want a different life, a normal life. I wonder what it would be like to be ignorant about magic, to never have that fear embedded deep into my soul.

"Are you sure you're all right? You've got a death grip on your phone." Paul gives me a half smile.

I force my hand to relax and pinch the bridge of my nose. "Headache."

"Crawl in the back. There are water bottles and a first aid kit," he says.

"I'm hungry," Diana demands.

"You should have eaten breakfast," Paul answers.

"I. Want. Waffles," she protests with light kicks to the back of my seat to punctuate her words.

My headache gets worse, and before I can stop

myself, I grumble, "Enough with the freaking waffles."

Paul stiffens.

I instantly feel like an asshole. "I'm sorry. I didn't mean..."

"It's fine," he says.

"No, it's not." I rub my temple. "I'm sorry. She's just a kid."

And she's dealing with a lot. The kid lost her mother. Her world has been shaken.

Shit, I'm such the asshole in this situation.

Anxiety fills my stomach and tightens my chest. I press my hand between my breasts to try to force it back down. I want to cry. I want to scream. I want to jump out of the window and splat against the pavement. Usually, I wouldn't go for suicidal ideation but fuck if life isn't screwed up right now.

"We all need to get out of the car to stretch our legs. We'll stop for an early lunch and a supply run." Paul leans forward in his seat and stares at the road.

The man definitely is a problem solver. He's a fixer, a helper. Lady in the cemetery needs a ride? He gives her one. Woman in the parking lot is hungry? He tries to give the druggie a sandwich. Older gentleman needs help lifting suitcases into his car outside the hotel? He runs across the parking lot to help.

I want Paul to fix me so I don't have to fix myself.

I stare at him, trying to figure him out. No one can be this nice, this decent. Even Conrad, who loves me, isn't this patient with me. Sometimes, I wonder if Conrad would even like me if our bond hadn't been forged on the fires of childhood trauma and neglect.

"Why did you say yes to this?" I ask.

"To what?" He glances over at me.

"To this trip. To me coming with you."

"Haven't we talked about this already?" He leans back in his seat. It's the first sign of real annoyance I've seen. It's slight, but it's there. "It's good to get away from the city and for Diana to see her grandparents. She needs a sense of family to remind her that she has a support system."

The phone vibrates in my hand. Conrad is trying to call. I don't answer and instead text him, *"Give me a minute."*

Paul takes an exit off the highway that leads to gas stations, fast food restaurants, and discount stores. We don't speak as we turn into a small strip mall. He stops at a place that boasts all-day breakfast.

I take my phone with the intent of calling Conrad. "I'll meet you both inside."

I wait for them to reach the front door before calling my brother. He doesn't take long to answer.

"Where are you?" Conrad asks by way of a greeting.

"Ohio, I think." I wait for him to speak, but he goes quiet. "I didn't do it, Conrad. I didn't start either fire. I don't know what happened. I went to her apartment, and before I could even sit down, everything was in flames. I barely made it out of there alive."

"I believe you." He sighs loudly.

"What the hell is happening? Are we cursed?"

"Don't be dramatic." His tone grates my nerves. "The police aren't on to you about the second fire, but it won't take them long to piece together that you were there. They're looking for a couple with a child for questioning. The lawyers are monitoring it."

"But I didn't do it," I insist. He says he believes me but isn't acting like it.

"Forget the police," Conrad dismisses. "Vampires know you were at the second fire. They're looking for you, and their resources are greater than any police department. They were here at the house last night questioning me. They put out the word to the supernatural network. Everything scary out there is looking for you. I need you to let me know where you are at all times."

Conrad doesn't sugarcoat his words to make me feel better.

"Who was that woman, Conrad?" I ask. He didn't answer me the last time we talked. "Why did you send me into vampire territory?"

"What isn't vampire territory in this city?" he counters.

"The woman?" I insist when he tries to avoid answering. He'd changed the subject yesterday, but I won't let him do it again.

"She was..." He sighs again. "Darlene Muller was my birth mother."

"Your...?" Stunned, I stare at the front door of the restaurant, watching a couple walk inside. I barely register them. "Why didn't you say anything?"

"I reconnected with her about a year ago," he admits. "You saw her. Why would I want to tell people I was related to that? It's embarrassing. Darlene was a drugged-out mess. I offered to put her into rehab, but she didn't want it. You can't force common sense on people."

"Conrad, I'm so sorry."

"Why are you sorry?" He's grouchy and under a lot of pressure, so I forgive his tone.

"That she died," I explain. "I'm sorry you lost her."

He snorts. "I'm not. I wish I never met her."

"But she's your birth mom." I know, deep, *deep* down inside him, he must have some feelings about it. The emotions might be complicated, but they have to be there.

I think about the birth mother I never met. Even if she turned out to be that drugged-out wreck I met in the apartment, I wouldn't wish her dead.

"Conrad—"

"Tamara, stop," he cuts me off. "She was a whore who got pregnant by some random dude while turning tricks on the street. The only good thing she ever did for me was abandon me at that gas station. Do you know what she said when I asked her about it? She said she forgot where she left me. Some guy showed up with five bucks and a teenth of meth. She climbed into his truck and never looked back."

My chest is tight, and I frown at the phone. "If she was so horrible, why did you send me there?"

"I had all of three minutes to come up with a plan. Forgive me if I had a lot on my mind dealing with cops outside our family's funeral." He doesn't sound apologetic. He sounds annoyed that I'm questioning him about it. I remind myself that Conrad is my brother, and he loves me, even if he doesn't say it. "You should have been safe there. We needed a place where no one would think to look for you. I thought that was it."

"I know you care more than you're letting on. There were security cameras in her home."

"She said she was being harassed."

I look around the parking lot and see a woman staring at me from inside a car. I turn my back on her.

"You have to tell the vampires," I whisper, though I don't think anyone is close enough to hear me. "And the police. Show them proof that it wasn't me."

"Tamara, the cameras were dummies. There is nothing to show. They just made her feel better."

My heart sinks into my stomach. "What? Why would you—"

"Would you want footage of the mother who abandoned you as a baby having sex with strangers for drug and liquor money? I can only imagine the illegal activities she was involved in. Having proof didn't seem like a great idea."

I think of the mother I've never known. He has a point. I wouldn't want to see that. I wouldn't want visual evidence that's what her life is.

"But she was being threatened," I insist, wishing I could send him back in time to make the cameras work.

"She also said she was the Queen of the Nile, the Princess of Wales, Mrs. Rodeo Royalty 2014, and Cleopatra reincarnated. The woman was batshit crazy. I sent over a few groceries, paid her rent so she wasn't thrown out starving on the street, and did my best to avoid situations where she tried to blackmail me for money. It's about all I could do."

He's right. I should let this topic go. I think of the rude woman and her dirty apartment. I can see why Conrad might be embarrassed by her. "Even if she had a mental illness, I can't believe you didn't tell me you found her. I'm your sister. We share these things, right? I told you the second I found out that Astrid wasn't my bio mom."

"Listen," he changes his tone, and I know he's done discussing it. "While I have you on the phone, there is something else I need to tell you. I was going to wait until after the funeral, but..."

He's breathing heavily, and I can tell he doesn't want to have this conversation with me.

"What?" I prompt him.

"There isn't really a great time to tell you this. I heard from Wick a couple of days before the funeral. He's located your birth mother. Her name is Lorelai Weber, and she lives in California. He gave us a phone number."

If he wanted to distract me from questioning his decisions, this was the perfect way to do it. Wick is the private investigator we hired to track my birth mother down.

"Are you sure it's her?" I ask.

"Would I tell you if I wasn't?"

"Did you see her? What does she look like? Did Wick talk to her?"

"Slow down," Conrad says. "No. I have no clue what she looks like. Wick says she has no social media presence and lives a secluded life. I couldn't find much information online either. He didn't contact her. I told him not to."

I find it hard to breathe and begin pacing in the parking lot. I see the woman in the car window still watching. I hear the sounds of traffic all around me. My vision blurs, and I hide from the woman behind Paul's SUV, leaning against the back to steady myself.

Lorelai Weber.

My birth mother's name is Lorelai Weber.

She's alive and in California.

Lorelai Weber.

"Tamara?" Conrad asks. "Are you still there?"

"This is a lot to take in," I say.

How am I supposed to feel? Part of me is numb and doesn't know what to think about it, and another part is terrified to have an answer. It's different knowing she's out there in the abstract compared to actually having a way of confronting her. All the imagined conversations I've had with her try to surface. I don't like confrontation. I like things to be friendly and smooth. Now, I feel like I have to ask the hard questions, starting with why.

"I can't..." I don't know what to say. There are too many thoughts in my head. Vampires. Police. Fires. Mothers. Paul and Diana. "I can't think."

"I'll text you her number, but I don't recommend calling her. You need to be focused on the present. Not the past. She left you, Tamara. She's not your family. She's just an incubator. Trust me. I learned that the hard way. My mother lived what Wick would call a secluded life, too, with no social media profile. There is nothing there for you. Let the idea of her go."

I hear his wisdom and what can only be genuine concern in his voice. Sure, it doesn't sound like concern, but I need to believe. I trust his advice. Still, a deep fear causes my hands to shake in anticipation. I don't say it to him, but I want to feel like I belong to something, to someone.

I push away from the car and turn toward the restaurant. Diana's face is pressed to a window with her hands next to her cheeks. She stares at me with anxious eyes while Paul reads the menu.

Still embarrassed by my outburst in the car, my eyes dip down to avoid contact with the girl. Unfortunately, they focus on a symbol drawn in the dust on the back of the SUV. It's a vampiric tag matching the graffiti we saw outside the apartment. Someone marked us.

"Tam?" Conrad asks. "Are you still there?"

I spin around, scanning the parking lot for signs of the supernatural. It's daytime, so vampires and other nocturnal creatures won't be active. That doesn't mean their human minions aren't around. I don't know what I'm looking for. Everyone is a threat.

"I have to go," I say.

"Wait. I should have a safe house lined up for you by the time you reach Kansas City," he says. "I'll send you the details when I have them."

"Okay. I'll get in touch when I'm closer." I hang up on my brother. He's my only real ally left in the world, but I need to focus on my surroundings.

I don't feel safe. Something is tracking us.

The woman who'd been watching me from the passenger seat of a car is currently being driven off by a man. Nobody seems to be paying attention, but I can't be sure. There are so many parked cars and people walking around the shopping center.

I rub my hand over the symbol to erase it.

I catch my panicked reflection in the window. I feel exposed and fold my arms like I'm pulling an imaginary coat around me as I rush toward the restaurant. I push my way inside and slide into the booth next to Diana. Paul is on his phone answering texts.

"Do you want pancakes?" Diana asks. "They have sparkles on them."

Her resilience is inspiring, and I smile, relieved she's not mad at me.

"Everything okay?" Paul puts down his phone and slides a coffee in front of me. He notices my trembling hands, and I clasp them together in my lap to hide them.

"Yeah. And with you?" I nod at his phone.

"Check-ins. Work questions." He shrugs. "It never ends."

A melancholy guitar plays on the radio, and the accompanying voice evokes feelings I'd rather not have. I grab the mug and gulp hot coffee in an attempt to look normal. It burns my tongue, and I cough in surprise at my stupidity.

Emotions run rampant through my body, aching and burning their way to my core. A warm tear slips from the corner of my eye. My hands grip the cup like a clamp, and I can't force them to relax even as the hot coffee uncomfortably heats my fingers.

"Hey." Paul reaches for me, holding my wrist as if to steady me. "Whatever it is, it'll be okay."

But it won't. He doesn't know.

There is so much kindness in him. I feel as if I've

known him my entire life, but from a distance—like a girl staring out from her glass cage at the bigger world, longing to be a part of it. I've always wanted to be here, with someone like him, but I'm keenly aware that I don't belong.

"I'm sorry you met me," I whisper.

He frowns and leans closer.

"Three sparkle cakes," Diana announces loudly. "Extra sparkling."

The sound causes me to jerk, and I see a waitress approaching. She has distinctive blue eyes encased in black eyeliner and dark shadow. Is she a shapeshifter? Will she report me to the vampire council? There is no way to tell. Shifters look like everyone else in their human forms.

"You got it, sweetie." The waitress glances at me as she stands next to the table. I can see she's curious, but she doesn't comment.

I swipe at my face, dashing the tear into oblivion before reaching to toy with my necklace.

"Anything else?" the waitress asks.

"That's all," Paul says, handing our menus to the woman.

Diana reaches for me, and before I can think of reacting, she's got her arms wrapped around my shoulders. Her head presses to my neck. The heat from her breath hits my skin as she says, "It's okay if you want to cry. I miss my mom too."

I touch the edge of the amulet against my lips. Every stranger seems to be staring at me. I feel danger all around. I don't know if it's my imagination or if it's really there.

Actually, I feel a little sick to my stomach. Judging from the tabletop advertisement, sparkle pancakes are nothing more than candied starch patties smothered in whipped cream and sugar cookie sprinkles. Lady Astrid would never have allowed such a breakfast.

I try to steady myself. "I have to go to the restroom. I'll be back."

I push free and rush toward the back of the restaurant. When I enter, a kid is at the sink washing one hand. The other is in a brightly colored pink cast covered with stickers and signatures. I lock myself inside a stall.

I hug my arms around my waist and stand, trying to muffle the sounds of grief and fear erupting inside of me. I watch the girl through the open slit created by the door, staring more at the pink cast than at her.

My hand strays to the amulet as if the simple contact can make me feel safe. It doesn't. I can't help but think we're all going to die, and it's going to be my fault.

CHAPTER
ELEVEN

Devine Country Estate, Sixteen Years Ago...

Conrad and I stand on the upper balcony looking down at the fancy town cars and carriages pulled by horses with glowing red eyes. I let my toes dangle over the edge as I lean on the railing. We've been exiled. Again. They say it's for our safety, but I can't help but feel jealous that Anthony is allowed to attend. Even if it's dangerous, it must be more exciting than listening to the muffled sounds of a party echoing across the house. If my life had a soundtrack, it would be stifled music from another room.

I'll be the first to admit that I have a slightly reckless and rebellious streak inside of me. The reality of my mortal life has been drummed into me like a terminal disease, and that knowledge has created a strange duality. I've been told repeatedly to be cautious, but I'm also keenly aware that life is short, and I want excitement. My tutor says that makes me rash.

"Remember the first night you came here?" I glance at my brother. That was the first time we snuck out here together to watch the supernaturals arrive. Since then, it has become our thing—two humans tucked away and forgotten. Laughter and shouts come from the floor below, and I see a trail of blue light bouncing across the lawn from the tree line.

"I remember you wanted to eat fairy cake," Conrad says.

I laugh. "I remember being so disappointed you weren't a puppy."

Conrad hands me a pouch. "Happy twelfth birthday."

"What is it?" I ask. My birthday has technically passed, but I take the gift anyway.

"Flying dust," he says.

"I'd still prefer a puppy," I tease.

Conrad points to the drive. "I think I saw a hellhound tied to the carriage down there. Why don't you try taking it for a walk? See if you still want a puppy afterward."

I follow his finger but don't see the hellhound.

More flashes of light zip across the lawn, and a group of boys emerge from the shadows. They're zapping each other in the backsides and laughing.

"There's enough dust for both of us."

His words turn my attention back to my gift. "I've never heard of flying dust."

"Anthony's friends sold it to me," he says. "We're going to try it tonight."

I press my fingers against the material to feel the dirt-like substance inside. I can't help the excitement I feel at the idea, and the fear. Magic easily works against us mortals but rarely for us.

Conrad and I have become obsessed with finding ways to harness power. Well, mostly it's Conrad, but he's my brother, and I support him. He's always reading about enchanted objects and old potions. I try to accept that I'm not extraordinary, even if I want to be. But Conrad's life has been difficult. He grew up in foster care and not in the best of situations. I've seen the old scars on his body. I heard one of the staff say they looked like cigarette burns. Conrad told me that goblins attacked him while he lived in a group home, but no one believed him, and he was labeled as a troublemaker. The truth is my brother has a mean streak he usually manages to hide. I only know it's there because we spend so much time together.

To me, it's simple. He's my brother and I love him. He doesn't have to be perfect, and I make allowances for those imperfections. Conrad never says it, but I know he wants more than anything to belong.

He stares at the boys as they play their magic games. His hands grip the rail so hard that the blood stops flowing through his fingers, turning them white. He breathes deeply. I can tell he's emotional, but I know he won't cry or yell. He doesn't like to show his anger.

"Hey." I touch his arm gently. "At least we have the best seats in the house."

The joke usually makes him smile, but it doesn't this time.

"They think they're so superior," he mutters.

Conrad may not be my brother like Anthony is my brother, but I'm closer to him because of the things we share. I love Anthony, of course, but Conrad understands what it's like to be unremarkable in the Devine family.

"You're a better present than any puppy," I tell him, trying to make him feel better.

"People shouldn't be presents," he answers. "Remember what Mr. Dorkens said about people being property?"

Mr. Dickens, aka Mr. Dorkens behind his back,

is our current tutor. He's been focusing on European and American history—and incidentally is obsessed with making us read Charles Dickens novels, but that's beside the point. He tells us the old stories so we don't feel bad about our situation. He constantly reminds us that we're lucky and shouldn't complain. Our family is rich and well respected. They chose Conrad, and I was born lucky. It could always be worse.

I get his point. I don't think Conrad does.

"How does this work?" I lift the present and try to sound upbeat.

Conrad's attention goes to the pouch. Excitement replaces the anger in his eyes. "It's easy. We sprinkle it on our heads. Shout *ego sum avis stultus.* And then we jump."

He nods toward the ground.

Jump?

I look over the edge, and my legs begin to tremble. I don't want to jump. I shake my head. This is a horrible idea. "I don't know."

"It's magic," he insists, taking the fairy dust from me. "You said you wanted wings to fly like a fairy."

I can't remember saying that, but I say a lot of things.

He lifts the bag and pours dirt on my head. I wince and instantly cover my eyes with my hands.

When I again look, he's emptying the rest of the bag on his head.

Conrad climbs onto the rail and sits to face the long driveway. He holds out his hand for me to do the same. I'm shaking. I can't help it.

"You have nothing to be scared of," he says. "It's magic."

He's right. I've seen plenty of flying creatures, especially out here at the country estate where mortals can't watch them. It's why supernaturals like coming here so much.

I manage to climb onto the rail and sit down. I take several deep breaths, and my heart pounds hard. I can hear it thumping in my ears.

"Lift your arms to the side. Shout the spell and jump." Conrad lifts his arms to the side and waits as I am slow to do the same. "*Ego sum avis stultus!*"

"*Ego sum avis stultus,*" I repeat. I can't make myself leap.

"Jump!" Conrad pushes my back from behind. I scream and flail. I hear the boys from the yard laughing as I fall.

There is no flying, only the rock driveway coming at me fast. My body twists in the air as I try to avoid the inevitable.

"Tamara!" Conrad shouts in panic.

My body strikes the ground, and pain explodes

throughout me. I can't catch my breath to scream, but I try anyway.

"Oh, shit, run!" I hear a boy shout.

A demon horse angrily paws the ground like it wants to trample me. Thankfully, it's tethered too far away.

Conrad doesn't land next to me. Looking up, I don't see him on the railing above.

"Hello there, little castoff." A shadow falls over me as a vampire leans to block the view of the railing. Costin's long black hair and mode of dress make it appear like he crawled from the pages of a dark vampire romance novel. I don't see how women think these pasty monsters are beautiful. They're glamorized in movies and books, but really, they're just well-connected serial killers.

I'm not too innocent to know his eyes swirl with bloodlust. His pale skin is ethereal, almost translucent in the dim light. His fangs seem to grow sharper the longer I stare at them. On a fair night, I couldn't outrun this creature. Broken and breathless, I don't stand a chance in hell. And that is precisely where this vampire wants to take me.

His movements are so fast that I only see a blur before he's kneeling beside me. Cold fingers caress the nape of my neck. His fingernails scrape my skin before he pulls them away. Blood stains his pale flesh, and he licks it off his fingers, just like my brothers and I eat stolen cake batter. He closes his eyes and makes a strange noise of pleasure.

"So fresh and innocent," he whispers.

I know I'm going to die tonight. My body quakes. Tears roll down my face. Pain radiates from my fall. All I can manage is to mouth a winded, "Please."

"Constantine, step away from her."

I've never been so relieved to hear my grandfather's voice. Costin's nostrils flare, and his eyes narrow. He doesn't like the command.

"She's protected," my grandfather George insists.

The vampire hisses through his teeth. His body thrashes violently before it becomes a blur and disappears as if he was never there.

My grandfather is instantly at my side. He is dressed in an immaculate, old-fashioned suit, complete with a custom-made vest. The attire looks as if it just came from the tailor despite its vintage style. I don't know why he came to search for me, but I'm deeply grateful that he chose to leave the party to come to my rescue.

His hands travel over my legs. "What hurts?"

I cradle my arm and flinch.

"Your arm looks broken." He feels along my neck before touching my scalp. "Your head is bleeding. How did this happen?"

My eyes move toward the railing. Conrad still isn't there. He's left me to fend for myself.

My grandfather turns to look upward and frowns.

"Why, little dove?" His concern is impossible to resist. It draws an answer out of me.

"They said we could fly." I choke back a sob, finally able to draw a deeper breath.

"Who?" He looks around the drive. The demon horse paws in agitation.

I shake my head. I don't want to say. Tattling on supernaturals doesn't tend to go well for mortals.

He sighs. "We need to get you to the hospital. I'm going to petrify you so you can't feel it."

The idea terrifies me, but I can't protest as his magic surges over me, bringing with it a wave of darkness.

When the sensation ends, I feel as if no time has passed, but I'm in a hospital bed with a white cast on my arm. My parents are at the end of the bed.

My mother looks annoyed as she stands with her arms crossed, staring at me.

My father appears distracted by his phone. He glances up and smiles. "Hey, there, Tam-tam."

"Conrad?" I manage.

"Locked in his room for fighting," my mother says. "That's where you should have been. This wouldn't have happened if you two hadn't been running wild outside."

"Leave her be," my father says, though he sounds more bored than authoritative.

"Fighting who?" I ask.

They ignore me.

My grandfather appears in the doorway. "Why don't you two head back to your guests? I'll wait for the doctors to discharge her. I'll make sure she makes it home."

My mother closes her eyes briefly and sighs. Knowing her, she's relieved someone is there to deal with the problem. "Thank you, George." She taps my father's arm. "Come on, Davis. We need to check Gregory's pockets before he leaves. Last time, he tried to smuggle out half our library."

She's exaggerating. The dwarf tried to steal two books—an ancient, priceless grimoire and an 1800s fairy tale featuring a colony of dwarfs. I can only assume the second was for his vanity. I'll never understand why they keep inviting him back to their parties. I suppose when you are friends with blood-suckers and demons, a kleptomaniac dwarf is tame in comparison.

"Right," my father mutters, barely glancing up as he types on his phone. As he reaches the door, he pauses and looks at me. "Do what your grandfather says, Tam-tam."

I nod, but he's already leaving and doesn't notice.

"I figured I'd save you from their caretaking," Grandfather says with a smile. "I love my son, but those two don't have a nurturing bone in their body."

"Thank you." I know I'm supposed to love my parents—*and I do*—but sometimes they make me feel worse. "Is Conrad okay?"

"He tried beating up a couple of Anthony's friends. They hit him with magic." He sits on the edge of my bed. "I take it they're the ones who gave you the fake flying powder?"

I nod. There's no point in protecting them if he already knows. As the Devine patriarch, my grandfather has powerful magic. He could draw the truth out of me with a snap of his fingers if he wanted to.

"Does your arm hurt?"

I look at my cast and nod.

"Once we return to the house, I'll whip up a potion to help you heal. But in the meantime..." He pulls a slender jewelry box out of his pocket and hands it to me. "I had planned on giving you this for your next birthday."

"What is it?" I ask.

175

"Open it." He smiles and watches my face.

I open the box to find a fancy red jewel hanging on a chain. There is no way my mother would let me have something so beautiful. Family jewels are kept in a safe and only brought out on special occasions. I never have a special occasion.

I know not to smudge it with my fingers, so I study the jewel without touching it. "Thank you. It's pretty."

"It's an amulet. Some people call them talismans or good luck charms. It's to keep you safe." He reaches for the necklace and lifts it out of the box. "Once you put it on, it's yours. It won't work for anyone else. You can't share it. Ever."

I don't understand why he's being dramatic, but I nod.

"You're not like the rest of the family, Tamara," he says. "You have our blood, but the magic didn't take root for some reason. But our blood, our lives, who our family is, all of that puts you in danger. Wear this. Always. And know that every time you look at it, you are loved."

His words scare me. He holds the necklace insistently. I lean my head forward so he can place it over my head. The weight falls against my chest, and I pull my hair free.

I don't feel any indication that magic radiates

from the jewelry. I've been told enchanted objects are rare. My arm doesn't magically heal, my head aches, and my neck is stiff. I know about lucky rabbits' feet, four-leaf clovers, and horseshoes nailed to doorways. This is no different. Objects only carry the faith people put into them. Nothing else.

My grandfather loves me and wants me to feel safe. He once joked about trapping me in a magically protected tower like a human fairytale princess. Being ordered to the protected wing of the estate all the time isn't much different.

"You still have to be careful," he insists. The warning confirms my guess. If this was truly enchanted, I wouldn't have to be careful. I want to tell him I'm too old for these children's stories and fairytales, but he seems pleased with himself, so I don't interrupt. "I need you to promise you'll stop dabbling in magic without talking to me first. Conrad is too impetuous. He doesn't think before he charges into these situations. You are humans, and you must accept the way of things."

"I know. I'm a delicate butterfly in a world of fiery dragons," I answer dutifully, repeating what he's told me since I was little.

"That's right. And there is nothing wrong with that." He makes a show of glancing toward the closed hospital room door.

He gives me a sneaky grin as he tosses his hands into the air. A swarm of butterflies magically appears, fluttering all around us. I know it's a simple glamour, but they look real, and I watch their delicate beauty in awe. One lands on my cast and instantly disappears, bursting like a bubble. The others pop as the tiny spell ends.

"The world needs butterflies, Tamara, as much as it needs dragons. Probably more. We all have our place." He kisses the tip of his finger and then presses against my forehead. "Conrad is not going to be able to find what he's looking for, and I don't want him hurting you to further his pointless quest."

I nod. It feels like a promise, but I'm unsure what I'm agreeing to. Still, it makes him happy, so I see no harm in giving him what he wants.

"Good girl." He pats my head.

I love his smile. It's always so kind. He's the only supernatural in my life that doesn't make me feel less than. He's the only one who doesn't give Anthony more attention because he's special.

I can see he wants to talk, and I want to be entertained. I touch the amulet. "Where did you get it?"

"This is a piece of a larger necklace crafted for an ancient Pagan goddess," he answers. "The legend goes she was so beautiful and rare that other goddesses hated her, and gods kept trying to force her to date them. So trolls made a necklace to protect her."

I know it's a lie. No one would let me have something so rare. Still, I let him think I believe it. "I'll be careful with it. I promise."

"Just be more careful with yourself." He touches both of my cheeks, and I feel the tickle of magic in his fingers. "You ready to get out of here, butterfly?"

"Yes, please."

"I'll light a fire under the doctor to hurry up the discharge papers." He turns as he reaches the door and winks. "Don't worry. Not literally."

I watch him leave as I touch the amulet, tracing my finger over the edge. My attention moves to the cast on my arm. The amulet doesn't take away the pain. Flying was a complete bust. And now I'm stuck with a broken wing.

"Ego sum avis stultus," I whisper, wishing I'd had the magic to make the spell work. Nothing happens, and I'm not surprised. I'm merely a helpless mortal, after all.

TWELVE

This is it. The end of everything.

Red and blue flashing lights glance off the side-view mirror. The siren sounds far away, even though I know it's close. I want to throw up, and I think my heart might explode out of my chest like a bad horror movie. I feel trapped, and it's hard to breathe.

"Daddy, what is it?" Diana demands from the back seat.

State troopers are pulling over Paul.

"Nothing, just stay in your seatbelt," Paul answers in frustration. To himself, he says, "What the hell is this? I wasn't speeding."

The admission does not make me feel better. If he'd been speeding, at least there would have been a reason for him to get pulled over.

"Don't stop." I reach for his arm as he starts slowing the vehicle. "Just keep driving."

Paul frowns and glances at me. My grip tightens. He shakes his arm to knock off my hand. It's a rare crack in his usual calm. "It's just a ticket."

But it's not just a ticket. I frantically search for the words that will convince him to step on the gas and make a run for it. My mind draws a blank. I regret not explaining the danger sooner.

Shit.

Shit. Shit.

"You didn't do anything." I wish for him to understand.

He pulls the car over. "I assume you're not serious. You should know I'm not in a joking mood right now."

Short of grabbing the steering wheel and slamming my foot on the gas pedal, there's nothing I can do.

Please, please, *please* be a ticket.

Paul puts the car into park and turns off the engine. The interstate is next to a field and a line of trees. The bumpy ground will be hard to run on, but I could try to make it.

Without the troopers seeing me?

I can't leave Paul and Diana behind.

What do I do?

Fuck. Fuck.

Fuck!

I focus on my breathing. I'm afraid to move as if doing so will somehow ripple the universe and worsen my fate. I need to look normal and beyond suspicion.

Okay. Normal.

This is so far from freaking normal.

We'd stopped at a discount store and picked up supplies. I wish we had taken the time to change into the new clothes. Paul had insisted it wouldn't matter since we'd be stuck in the car all day, but it feels like it matters now.

I tug on the hem of my shorts to cover more of my legs. It doesn't help.

The cruiser's reflection pulls into the side mirror's frame. Each disorienting flash of light momentarily overpowers my senses and feels like a sharp, stinging slap across the face. I recoil even as I try not to. As a steady stream of traffic flows past, I yearn for a sudden, dramatic event—screeching tires, a sudden swerve, anything to divert attention away from our current predicament.

The sound of a car door slams. It's wrong to wish for an accident, yet here I am, praying for someone else's misfortune so we can escape the approaching officer.

"Tamara?" Paul's hand is outstretched, and he's leaning toward me. He grips his wallet against the steering wheel. "Registration? In the glove box? I want to get this over with."

He says it like he's been speaking, but I didn't hear a word. It takes me a moment to react. I open the glove box and pull out the white envelope inside.

Paul takes it from me. "Thanks."

I finally dare to look behind us. Diana is craning her neck to stare out the back window. I follow her lead and watch the trooper.

The woman stands with her hand resting on her holstered gun as she carefully approaches the front of her cruiser. The stance is unnecessarily aggressive. Her head is tilted as she stares at the back of the SUV. I think of the symbol I erased.

"What's she doing?" Diana asks.

"Quiet, honey," Paul answers.

A second cruiser pulls behind the first.

Crap. She called for backup. Cops don't normally need backup for a simple speeding ticket, do they?

The second trooper joins the first. The woman says something to him and gestures at the car.

This isn't good.

Act normal.

I need to act normal.

I shift my weight and stare forward, unease running through me like an electrical current. My leg bounces nervously, creating a rapid staccato against the seat. Each beat of my heart feels as if the organ is slamming into the walls of my chest. I struggle to regulate my breathing, desperate to conceal the rising panic, but the sound is deafening.

Paul's hand presses against my knee to stop the repetitive movement. "Hey, what's going on? Are you—?"

A knock on his window interrupts him. His hand leaves my leg, and I make myself sit still. I look at his feet. I could reach the gas pedal if I swung my leg over the center console.

Paul rolls down the window. "Afternoon, officer. What seems to be the problem?"

He sounds so calm.

"License and registration." The female trooper leans to look inside the car. Her poker-faced, judgmental affect doesn't change. She eyes Diana and then us like we've got the kid on a brick of heroin.

Paul hands the items to her.

I catch movement in the side mirror. The male

officer walks around to my side of the car, snooping in the back windows.

"Is something wrong, Trooper Jennings?" Paul asks when the woman studies his license longer than seems necessary. I glance over but can't read her name badge.

"Where are you heading?" Jennings asks.

"We're going to Kansas City to visit my parents." Paul taps his fingers on the side of his leg. He's irritated, but his voice doesn't show it.

"This your wife?" She nods at me.

"No, this is—" Paul begins.

"A family friend," I insert.

"License, family friend," Jennings demands.

I reach for my backpack. The male trooper suddenly appears by my window, startling me. I jolt in surprise. His mirrored sunglasses are lifted, and I don't like the suspicious way he's staring at me.

"What's your name?" Jennings leans into the window and looks at Diana.

"Plop," Diana says. She sounds defiant.

"Diana," Paul answers for her. "My daughter."

I'm careful opening the bag and taking out my wallet. I keep my head down and move slowly. When I was younger, one of Anthony's school friends sold me a magically enchanted fake ID. I've had it since my misspent teenage years sneaking into clubs. The enchantment part is that the license ages with me, never expires, and whoever looks at it believes it to be real.

I reach past Paul to hand the card to the trooper. She takes it with a flick of her wrist. I still don't like the way both officers are looking at me. I tell myself that's just how cops look at people, but what if they know who I am?

It's daytime, so they're not vampiric, but they could be enthralled by a vampire.

The trooper at my window moves. I get a brief glimpse of a creepy smile as he stands, taking his face out of view. I stare at his back in the mirror as he walks toward the rear of the car. It's taking every-thing inside of me to maintain my composure.

"Looks like everything is in order. Here you are, Mr. Cannon." Trooper Jennings hands him his license and registration papers before reaching across toward me. "Ms. Bennet."

Paul gives me a questioning glance, and I pray he doesn't say anything.

"Drive safe now," Jennings says, tapping the open window.

"Wait, why did you pull us over?" Paul asks.

I want to tell him to shut up and let them leave. It doesn't matter as long as they go away.

"Your car fits a description." Jennings doesn't give any further explanation.

A loud, shaky breath escapes me before I can stop it.

Paul rolls up his window and watches the rearview mirror. Diana is turned around in the seat, staring out the back window.

I can't look as I listen to their car doors slam.

Paul holds out his hand and looks at where I clutch the fake ID. "Can I see that?"

"I can explain," I say, gripping it tighter. It's a lie. I can't. At least, not in any way that will make him stop looking at me the way he is now.

He keeps his hand out. I have no choice but to give it to him.

"Mary Bennet?" he reads.

"I..." What can I say?

Paul flips the ID over a few times, studying it. "I thought you said your name is Tamara."

Diana is looking at me now, her expression more confused than anything.

I reach into my backpack and pull out my real driver's license to hand to him. "It is Tamara."

He looks at them side by side before handing them both back.

"Jenny Rhoades told everyone her name is Moonbeam," Diana says. "Randy told her that's a stupid name, and so she dumped a bucket of dirt on his head. And Randy has an imaginary friend who he says is a ghost, and he told Jenny that he is going to have Mr. Scary haunt her and she better watch out. And Jenny cried. And then Mrs. Larsen said they couldn't have a recess for three days, and they had to sit and think about what they've done. Also—"

"Put your seatbelt back on," Paul tells her as he starts the car. I feel the agitation radiating off him.

"You can be Mary if you want, Tamara." Diana pats my shoulder. "We won't put you in time out."

I'm not sure how I feel about a kid coming to my defense. Paul doesn't appear pleased by it. I hate that I never know how to explain things to him. I want him to understand so badly, but the truth does not make me look good. He'll think I'm crazy. I need proof, but any supernatural proof that finds us would be a bad thing.

Paul waits for the troopers to leave first before pulling into traffic. He won't look at me, and I can't help staring at him.

"Paul..."

"We'll talk at the hotel," he states.

I can hear the frustration in his voice. I can't blame him.

The sky darkens with the threat of a storm. I

hadn't noticed it coming before, but I have been preoccupied.

My life is a fucking mess. My hand strays to the door handle as the vehicle picks up speed. Not for the first time, I think about opening the door and jumping out onto the passing interstate. One quick splat and it could all be over. And then nothingness. Silence. Blessed silence. No more churning thoughts. At least, that's my hope. But who knows what the afterlife holds?

I can't do that to Paul and Diana. I can't scar them like that. It's sad, but that's the thought stopping me. I've done enough to them.

Guilt fills me as I think of Conrad. He should have been my first concern. I'm the only family he has left, and he's doing so much to help me.

Then I think of the phone number from the investigator. My birth mother. I haven't tried calling her. She must have known where I was my entire life. Why hasn't she tried to see me?

My father was a formidable man to know. Was she afraid of something? Did she not want me?

Actually, no, I can't deal with those thoughts right now.

The atmosphere inside the car has become unbearable, as if the reality of our impulsive decision to drive cross-country as strangers is crashing down on us. Diana is a kid. She can't be blamed. But Paul and I are adults. We should have known this was irrational.

Paul grips the steering wheel, his hands twisting lightly as if strangling the car. For all his rightful irritation, he isn't threatening me. I'm not scared of him. I'm scared of what he's thinking about me. I'm scared of him leaving.

None of this is logical. I barely know him and can't be this desperate for attention. In the scheme of everything, this is only a tiny moment in our lives.

Everything inside of me is trembling, and I rock in my seat.

I want to scream.

I want to bang my head against the window.

I want to shake something.

I wish I knew the perfect thing to say.

"Please don't dump me on the side of the road." The words are out of my mouth before I can regulate them. "I'll tell you whatever you want to know."

Paul's hands instantly stop wringing the wheel. He takes a deep breath. "No one is dumping anyone anywhere."

"I'm bored," Diana announces from the back seat. "I don't want to drive anymore."

"Yeah, I think we all need a break from the car." Paul looks at the road with renewed determination.

I want to ask him what he means by that. I don't.

Diana starts talking, but I can't concentrate on the words. Honestly, they're a long drone of noisy sentences, and my brain can't process them. It's like she's trying to diffuse the situation the only way she knows how, by filling the silence with distractions.

The car slows, and I glance up to see we're taking an exit. A raindrop hits the windshield, and I can't help but think it's a warning shot from the universe.

CHAPTER
THIRTEEN

"They say grief makes you do foolish things." Paul doesn't meet my gaze as he peers at the motel parking lot. "Maybe that's all this trip is. An illogical thing we're doing because we don't know what else to do with ourselves."

This is not what I thought Paul would say once we were alone. And I didn't expect him to appear so calm.

"With death, nothing makes sense, does it?" he asks, but he's not looking for an answer. I stay quiet as he continues. "It just happens when it wants. And we're left trying to figure it all out. I keep trying to think of a reason to tell Diana about why her mother died. I want to be honest, but I don't want her to know those things about Nancy. I don't want her to hate the half of herself that came from that woman, but I'm struggling. I love the daughter we created and will never regret any of it because of that. But Nancy? Part of me is glad she's—"

"Dad, this stupid shit is not working!" Diana yells through the open door from inside the motel room.

"Hold on." Paul takes a deep breath.

From the surprised look on his face, I realize he won't finish the thought. The words that tumbled past his guard will not be released again. It was a momentary slip, a second of weakness that almost caused him to speak his deepest shame. I don't even know if he meant what he was about to confess. People say all kinds of things when they're lost and frustrated.

Paul leaves me alone on the sidewalk. To Diana, he scolds, "Watch the potty mouth."

"You said it before," Diana counters, trying to sound tougher than she is. The cursing would be funny if this situation didn't suck so badly. Poor kid. I'm sure she's feeding off our tension. She's trying to be brave under unusual circumstances. Parts of her remind me of me at her age. I had the same desire to keep everything even-keeled when the family seas were rocky. But her innocence, that's different. I wonder if I was ever really innocent. I grew up knowing monsters are real. Diana probably has a vague fear of the unknown fueled by imagination.

I don't want that to change for her, but the monsters are coming.

I can't help but note that the roadside motel looks like something out of a horror movie. It's partially isolated like a complex of abandoned office buildings had tried to swallow it whole only to choke the weather-bleached motel out as unpalatable. On the other side are dense trees covered in vines. The interstate is close. I can hear the cars, but I can't see them.

I peeked inside the lobby window while Paul checked us in and noticed taxidermy guarding the front office. I'm pretty sure this is the exact setup that the psychotic killer from that old movie had—the one with the mom in the basement and the knife shower.

What the heck is that movie called? It's driving me crazy. The guy dressed up like his dead mother. Larry? Tate?

Argh.

The sound of the television comes through the open door behind me, and I hear Paul telling Diana to calm down. Her response is lost as the impending storm makes itself known.

Lightning cracks across the sky. The threat of bad weather isn't helping the death-trap atmosphere. The temperature is dropping at a noticeable rate, but

I still want to stand outside on the sidewalk. The roof juts out over the walkway to provide shelter from the drizzle. Our room is at the end of a long L shape, far from the creepy lobby.

"I ordered pizza." Paul reappears next to me.

"Norman Bates!" I say at the same time. I'm momentarily happy to have the mind puzzle solved.

Paul looks at me and then around at the motel, confused.

Diana is on the bed playing. I hear the steady squeaks of her jumping on the mattress.

I wave my hands in dismissal. "Never mind. What were you saying?"

"I ordered pizza," he says. "It's the only place that delivers."

"Cool." I'm uncomfortable and don't know what to say. I rub my naked arms and think of the new lightweight jacket in the bags.

Paul's hands rest on his hips as he studies our surroundings. He tries to hide it under a show of quiet strength, but I see a vulnerability in him that mirrors my own. "I guess this does kind of look like the Bates Motel."

"Right?" I nod in agreement, starting to laugh.

His face tightens. "The storm looks like it's going to be a strong one."

My smile drops. He's not laughing with me. In

fact, he appears to be thinking that this is another problem he needs to solve.

"It's fine, Paul. I was only joking. We're already here, and taking off in this weather isn't a good idea. This place is as suitable as any. It's got character." It sounds like I'm trying too hard.

Paul releases a long sigh. "Yeah, I guess."

An invisible barrier has risen between us, casting doubt. It's deeply uncomfortable, and I know it's my fault. I want so desperately to mend the rift, but I can't. They say honesty is the best policy, but I don't think *they* ever had to explain a vampiric threat.

"My name really is Tamara," I blurt. The words have been bubbling inside me for some time. "I didn't lie to you. I didn't tell you some things, but I didn't lie."

Paul glances over his shoulder into the room and listens to Diana for a moment before turning his attention back to me. "What things?"

A rush of random facts fills my head as if my brain is trying to get me to retreat from the truth that needs to be told.

"The police are looking at me as a suspect for starting the fire that killed my family. I didn't, I swear, but I was there that night." I can't look him in the eye. Not yet. I need to get all of it out.

"I would assume they look at family and friends first," he answers. "That sounds pretty standard."

Why is he always so composed and understanding? That makes no sense to me.

"Then when the second fire..." I don't know how to explain it.

"You thought that made you look guiltier," he finishes.

"It does. I went there to hide because I didn't want the police to take me in for questioning after the funeral. I couldn't deal with them, not with everything." I run my hands through my hair in frustration. "These last weeks have been one giant blurry nightmare. I keep waiting to wake up."

He listens patiently, and I feel his attention focused on me.

"The woman who died in the apartment fire was the birth mother of my adopted brother, Conrad. He recently reconnected with her. He thought I'd be safe there until the lawyers could talk to the police and clear my name. I'd never met Darlene before you dropped me off. I can't explain why someone... I don't know what is happening to my family."

Too many thoughts are trying to come out at once in my desperate attempt to convince him I'm innocent. Paul's not accusing me, but it feels like I still need to defend myself. When we were kids, Conrad used to tell me that I act like I'm being judged even when I'm not. Often, this led me to confess when no one was even asking questions.

I make the worse criminal.

"I know you didn't set the second fire. You didn't have time," Paul says. "We should go to the police, and I'll tell them that. You'll see you're worried for nothing. We'll tell them what we know like we should have done right after it happened. I'll explain that we'd just come from the funerals and were not thinking clearly. It's going to be fine."

Paul takes a deep breath, like a giant weight is being lifted at the decision. He gives a small nod of self-approval.

It's a bad decision. I need to make him see that.

"You didn't go inside. They'll say you can't know for a fact what I did or didn't do," I protest. "I'm connected to both events."

Paul touches my shoulder, startling me. He keeps his hand there until I settle, and then he lets go. I instantly miss the contact.

"It sounds like Conrad is more connected to them than you are," he says. "Maybe you should consider—"

"Don't." I stiffen and shake my head in warning.

"I'm not saying he did it. I'm saying that it was his birth mother at the second—"

"Stop," I interrupt, refusing to listen to him badmouth my brother. "You don't know him. Conrad would never put me in danger. He didn't do this."

Paul looks like he has more thoughts on the subject but wisely keeps his mouth shut.

"Besides, they're not looking at him. He's not a suspect. I am." I know it sounds like I'm trying to divert blame back to myself while also protesting my innocence. But I trust Conrad. People don't understand what our lives have been like. If I don't have Conrad, nothing I have left makes sense. I need to know that at least that connection is solid.

Conrad would never hurt me.

I think of the time I broke my arm.

Conrad would never purposefully hurt me.

But what if he did something unintentionally? Like believing dirt could make us fly? What if this mess is inadvertently Conrad's fault?

I hate myself for allowing the suspicion to surface. Fear will only lead me down the wrong path. I must have faith in what I know to be true. Conrad is my anchor, and I can rely on him. It's the only way to preserve my sanity.

"You don't have all the facts." I sound defensive, and this is not the convincing reasoning I want to convey.

Why do none of my conversations with Paul go how I need them to?

This is so frustrating.

"You were only inside for about a minute," he says as he crosses his arms over his chest. "You saved my daughter's life. That's what I know for a fact. I couldn't have survived if anything happened to Diana."

It suddenly makes sense why he's putting up with me. He thinks he owes me, a stranger. Giving me a ride after a funeral was a kindness. Everything after is a debt he believes he needs to repay. I'm not sure how to feel about that. It's understandable as far as reasons go, but it's not the one the woman in me hopes for.

"I can't force you to do anything," he continues, "but I strongly feel we should contact the NYPD and have a conversation. I think you'll feel better when this is all cleared up. I know I will."

He unfolds his arms and starts to reach for me, but he stops himself and shoves his hands into his front pockets.

"There's more." Everything in me screams to shut my mouth. Apparently, everything in me is a coward. But no. I must get through this. "There is another reason we can't go back. It's not just that it's the police. It's that it's the vampire-controlled police."

I tense and wait for his response. He says nothing. We stand quietly for so long that I start to doubt he heard me. My hands shake, and I clasp them together to make them stop.

"Paul?" I ask, finally daring a nervous glance at his face.

He's staring at me as if weighing his thoughts. I wish I could hear what he's thinking.

"Come here." He reaches out his arms.

I wince and automatically take a step back.

"Come here," he says again, his voice soft. He bends his fingers as if to gently will me toward him.

I hesitate before moving into his embrace. He hugs me tenderly. His hand strokes my back like a feral animal needing to be tamed. As good as his touch feels, it's weird.

He believes me? I can't believe he actually—

"It's going to be all right," he soothes. "We're going to get you help. I promise. There is no shame in taking care of your mental health. You're not alone."

He doesn't believe me.

He thinks I'm insane.

Can't say I'm surprised, but...

Dammit.

"You're dealing with immense grief. It makes

sense that it would come out in unusual ways. There is no right or wrong way of dealing with things. We just deal. You're not alone, Tamara. I'll make sure we find you the help you need."

He keeps talking, his tone soft and soothing. I'm not sure what to do.

I push away from him. "I'm not crazy."

"Hey, I never used the word crazy," he says in that same composed, firm voice. I find it irritating and slightly condescending.

"I know what's real." I take a deep breath. He already thinks I should be committed. I might as well say it all. "The supernatural exists. Those things humans are scared of? The bumps in the night? They're real. Very real. And we should be scared of them. Terrified. *Petrified.* I've known about them my entire life. There are creatures that crawl out of the belly of the Earth every hundred or so years so that they can wear a human skin suit and stretch their legs before their next big nap. Werewolves are controlled by the moon. Giant monsters live in the ocean. Dragons fly the Norwegian skies in protected territory, of course, so that's why you don't see them. And vampires are just as monstrous as you think they might be. It's not all Hollywood happy endings. This is real. I'm not crazy, and I didn't start those fires."

He glances around the parking lot. The rain

seems to come a little heavier. "Do you see them now?"

I look at the cars. No one's around. I scoff. "Of course not. I'm not hallucinating."

The important conversations in my life never go how I want them to. I wish I could come off as charming and sophisticated, but I can never get the words out right. And with Paul, it's worse because I really care what he thinks of me. After this outburst, I'm sure all he feels is pity.

Great. Just what every woman wants. A sexy man to pity her.

Fuck my life.

The explosive outburst should have made me feel better like I was getting a weight off my chest. It doesn't. I feel like a freak.

"I guess that explains the jars of minced garlic I found in your shopping bags," he says, more to himself than to me. "Let me guess. It's a blood thinner, and vampires are naturally repulsed by it."

"Think of it more like a severe allergy or poison." I see no point in hiding facts now. "Can I have the keys? I want to get my bags out of the car."

At this point, if he sneaks off in the middle of the night and abandons me here at the Bates Motel, I won't blame him.

"Your clothes and backpack are inside the room."

He gestures over his shoulder. The squeak of the bed playground has settled down.

I wonder if Diana overheard us. I feel like I can't get anything right. The last thing I wanted was to traumatize a child with my rantings.

A scream of frustration builds inside me, and I fight to keep it bottled.

"I need all the bags before it gets dark," I manage through a tight throat.

"Sure." He pulls his keys from his pocket and points the fob at the small SUV. "Just... Don't say any of this to Diana."

"Yeah, of course." I nod. I'm not an idiot.

I hear the beep indicating the door is unlocked before he puts the keys back in his pocket.

I run through the rain to the back of the SUV and reach to lift open the door. My hand hesitates as I see the vampire symbol redrawn in the dust on the vehicle like some magical tracking signal. Moisture streaks the design, but it's there. I instantly rub my palm against the door, erasing it into a muddy smudge print.

I check the parking lot, trying to peer into the empty cars. I don't see anyone. Still, I feel watched. I'm not sure if it's paranoia or a sixth sense.

The car locks click and then beep a couple of times. I startle at the sound, but I hear feet coming at me before I can react. I turn to see Paul reaching for the door handle.

"Having trouble?" he asks, his voice louder as the rainfall continues to thicken.

The door lifts upwards, creating a metal umbrella above us as the storm's primitive drumbeat intensifies.

My heart is beating fast. I look at my dirty, shaking palm as if it's proof to validate my fear. That trooper had spent time examining the back of the car. Did he mark us? Or was it someone here in the parking lot?

I rub my hands in the rain to clean them as if that can erase the threat. I hate unanswered questions. Not knowing is the worst.

I don't want to die here tonight.

Paul reaches into the back. The moisture molds the t-shirt to his body, and I can't help but notice. "Run inside. I got these."

Instead, I kneel on the wet ground and look under the chassis. A muddy puddle wets my knees and hands, and tiny bits of gravel push uncomfortably into my skin. Water creeps into my shoes.

I have no clue what I'm looking for, but in the movies, a tracker always has a little blinking light, right? I don't see anything. I have to tell myself this isn't a movie. It's real life. There are tiny trackers on the market now. I reach to feel along the bumper. My fingers glide against clumps of mud to knock them off.

"Tamara," Paul says sternly as if struggling to bury his frustrations. "Get up."

He pulls at my elbow to keep me from crawling under the wet car. I don't know what I'm doing anyway, acting like I'm some sort of trained spy.

"No, wait. I just..." It's the only protest I have. I'm reacting in pure panic.

Paul urges me to my feet. His grip is firm but doesn't hurt.

We stand under the door umbrella. The rain is coming in thick now and creates loud splatters against the concrete all around us. The dark clouds make it feel later than it is. But sunset is close, and that means danger won't be far behind.

Paul is staring at me, gripping the bags in one hand and my arm in the other. He's breathing heavily. His fingers work against me, kneading. Something about his eyes makes him appear lost.

"I don't know what I'm doing," I say. My skin is wet. My soaked clothes cling to me uncomfortably, and threads of my hair stick to my face. Everything about me is a hot mess. I feel as if the world is ending, and I can't do anything to stop its painful finale.

He drops the bags into the back of the car and reaches for my face. "Neither do I."

Paul pushes his mouth to mine. I'm not expecting it, and so I stiffen in initial surprise. Oh, but his body is warm and strong, and I'm drawn to lean into him. His heat infuses the wet on our clothes.

At my movement, his kiss deepens. His tongue slides past my lips. His hand leaves my arm, snaking around my back to pull me fully against his length. The world fades away into this moment. Raindrops cocoon us, blocking out all other noises but for a rumble of thunder.

I feel safe in his embrace. Pleasure and desire swirl inside of me. I breathe him in and deepen the kiss as my hands move over the indentation of muscles on his arms. It's been so long since I've been connected to another person. I want the mindless pleasure only sex can offer. I need to be touched.

It's easy not to think beyond the intimate press of his hips to mine. When you're this physically close to someone, all other pretenses fall away, and you can't hide your attraction. It's animalistic. I circle my hips in primal invitation at the lift of his obvious arousal. I want to tear off his clothes and let the rain hit our naked bodies.

The attraction that has been building between us explodes. I need to feel anything that isn't death and fear. I don't care if people can see us. He can take me right here in the back of this SUV if he wants. I won't stop him. In fact, I want him to.

I claw at the dancing turtle holding a gas can, wanting to rid him of the shirt. My leg lifts along the outside of his thigh. The hunger is intense and causes a physical ache inside of me.

A thought tries to warn me that I'm being shameless and desperate. I ignore it. I don't care. I am desperate to end the loneliness and pain.

He moans and tries to pull his mouth back. I can't let him break the spell of his kiss. I grip his head to keep him there. This can't end.

He can't leave me.

Paul keeps kissing me, but he won't lift his arms so I can strip him of his shirt. That's fine. I don't need his shirt off. I reach for his waist and begin tugging at the fly of his jeans. His hands slide over mine to stop me.

With my hands trapped, he ends the kiss. He's breathing heavily, and his eyes are wild. I know he wants more.

I try to lean toward him, but he pulls his mouth out of reach with a long, staggered breath.

"Tamara, we..." He sighs and shakes his head.

"Please," I whisper, well aware of how pathetic begging sounds. "Don't think."

Please just kiss me.

"Diana," he states.

The word is like a block of ice crashing on top of my head. I blink, stunned, and we both lean to look toward the open motel room door. Diana stands at the entrance and waves.

"I don't think she saw," he says.

I say nothing. There's nothing to say.

Diana starts to step into the rain as if to come to us. Paul grabs the plastic bags from the back and sweeps them behind my back to gently guide me toward the motel room.

I don't want to leave our little alcove. I want to rewind to the moments before.

The sense of danger washes back over me to combine with my sexual frustration and disappointment.

"Stay there!" Paul yells to Diana, pushing me more insistently toward the motel.

I tuck my head and run through the rain. Paul slams the car door shut, and I hear his feet splash as he follows me back to the room.

Diana sticks her cupped hands into the rain, catching the droplets. The expression of joy on her face at her small swimming pool is enviable. She's so innocent. And there is so much danger in the world that she can't even comprehend.

When I rush toward her, Diana flicks her hands in my direction and laughs. The small amount of water doesn't matter when my clothes are already soaked. As if the temptation is too much to resist, she jumps out into the storm before following me into the room.

I stand near the doorway, dripping. Paul stops under the overhang and shakes off the moisture the best he can.

A weather-beaten hatchback pulls up next to him. On the side panel, the logo of a beaver holding a pizza box announces our dinner. I find the logo odd. What do beavers have to do with pizza?

The kid driving doesn't get out of the car. His passenger window rolls down, and two pizza boxes are thrust into the rain toward Paul. I guess it's lucky the kid didn't just chuck them at the open door like frisbees.

Paul grabs the food, and when he turns to bring the boxes inside, the hatchback's tires spin in a puddle, creating a reverse waterfall from the street onto the sidewalk. The dirty water barely misses the back of Paul's legs.

I see Paul's lips move to form a silent curse as he carries the boxes into the room and sets them down on the nightstand.

"That was rude. You shouldn't tip him," Diana says, her tone matter of fact.

"The tip is already on the bill when we order," Paul answers in his usual steadiness. "Fast food drivers are underpaid as it is. Plus, he drove our food here in a storm. I think we can be grateful for that."

"Mom wouldn't have tipped him," Diana mumbles.

I hate to admit it, but my first reaction to having my food shoved at me into the rain wouldn't have been to tip very much, either. Paul is a better person than me by far.

Paul disappears into the bathroom and returns with a couple of towels. He tosses one at me before dabbing at himself. The unspent desire lingers, and there is nothing I can do to help it. I watch him for a moment but force myself not to stare for too long.

My mind is a jumbled mess of confusion and guilt.

I go into the bathroom and shut the door to compose myself. The room smells of mildew and disappointment. I never realized disappointment had a fragrance until now. The combination of chipped paint and peeling wallpaper announced its sad, neglected state. It feels fitting to my situation somehow.

The walls are too close, creating a cramped,

suffocating space. A dim light flickers and buzzes, making my shadow dance behind me as I stare into the old mirror. The edges are clouded, vignetting my face in the tarnished glass. A faint crack in the corner reveals where someone had tried to tighten its metal clamp too tightly against the wall.

A drowned rat of a woman stares at me in accusation. I barely recognize myself. Lady Astrid would have had a fit to see me like this. What's the saying? She'd be rolling over in her grave?

The fact that I don't know what I'm doing has become an inner mantra.

I see myself as my mother would have seen me at this moment, with all the imperfections and mortality. Astrid was a great beauty—so elegant, so perfect. She was a fierce figure of a woman from a powerful Scandinavian witch heritage. I can't remember a time when her hair or makeup was out of place.

I'm only twenty-eight, but it's only a matter of years before wrinkles overtake my face and weight spreads my hips. Twenty years might feel long to me, but to the rest of the supernatural world, it's a blip on a timeline. I'll be dead and forgotten soon. At best, I can hope to be a footnote to a story—probably not even my story, but someone else's. The fairytale of a mortal girl who survived the death of her supernatural family only to be killed by vampires. What would the moral of my story be? You can't outrun fate? Mortals are stupid, fragile creatures? Life is unfair? Vampires do what vampires do?

Boo-fucking-hoo.

This self-pity isn't helping. And it sure as hell won't keep the three of us alive.

My eyes go to the amulet. The jewelry has become as much a part of me as my own arm.

"I'm a delicate butterfly in a world of fiery dragons," I whisper as if my grandfather can hear me somewhere out there in the universe. If he were here, he'd warn me to be careful.

I may be fragile, but this butterfly isn't going down without a fight. I just need to be smarter than the bloodsuckers.

I angrily pull out of my wet clothes and get some pleasure from the loud splat they make on the yellowed linoleum floor. The building fight feels better than defeatism.

I turn on the shower, and the rusty showerhead releases a stream of hot water. It doesn't take long for a misty fog to overtake the bathroom.

"Welcome to the Bates Motel," I mutter under my breath as I step into the tub and pull the curtain closed. The plastic barrier is new and seems out of place.

Chipped blue tiles line the shower wall. As water

splashes between my lips, I notice it has a metallic taste. That can't be healthy. I instantly shut my mouth and turn my back toward the stream. Despite the disrepair, the hot water hits my skin like a welcome embrace. The white noise of the shower is calming, drowning out all other sounds when I lean my head back into it.

The cheaply scented motel soap boasts of being a relaxing lavender vanilla blend, but its overpowering scent is more like a discount store floor cleaner. It isn't exactly what I'm used to, and it leaves my skin feeling tight and a little itchy, but it doesn't matter. I make quick work of washing off the traces of mud.

I want to do more, but I don't let my hands linger in any one place. Any self-pleasure would be a poor comparison to the real feel of Paul kissing me at the back of his car. Plus, it's just weird knowing they're eating pizza on the other side of the thin bathroom door.

I don't understand Paul. He didn't believe me when I told him about vampires, but still he kissed me. Maybe the man is attracted to crazy? It sounds like his late wife had been a piece of work.

Vampires.

The thought lingers in my mind like a bad omen. It prompts me to get out of the shower and dry off. I clutch the towel to my chest and poke my head out of the door while using the barrier to hide my half-naked body. "Can someone hand me my clothes?"

"Tamara, do you want pepperoni or gross adult pizza?" Diana yells.

"She'll be out in a second." Paul shushes her. He appears holding a plastic bag with the clothes I bought. He reaches through the crack in the door. "Here."

As I take the bag, his hand lingers through the opening longer than it needs to. His eyes hold mine, full of questions like he's worried about me. I don't know what to say, so I merely nod and shut the door.

FOURTEEN

I eat a slice of loaded vegetable pizza because it's expected. Diana is back to mimicking my movements and taking bites in time with mine, only she has pepperoni. She even chews and swallows with me. For some reason, she reminds me of a chatty baby duckling that imprinted on me. It is equal parts adorable and sad. I feel as if I've crawled out of my family's grief bubble into theirs.

I'm thankful for the warm clothes we picked up at that discount store. The t-shirt, yoga pants, and matching jacket provide more protection and comfort than my exercise shorts. Diana also wanted yoga pants and a jacket; only hers came in baby blue to my navy, and they have butterflies embroidered on them. I find the coincidence of the butterflies strange as if the universe is reminding me of how vulnerable Diana is to the dangers of the world.

Paul appears from his shower in cargo pants. I assume he bought them because he thought he could use them for work when he gets back to the city, but they hardly seem like comfortable pajamas. I can't help but wonder if he's planning a quick getaway.

He still wears that dancing cartoon turtle. No, correction: he wears a dry, clean turtle shirt. I'm guessing it's the one he bought for me at the gas station. Apparently, they were one size fits all.

Diana took a shower after me, insisting she also needed to clean up before we ate. Now, the pizza is barely warm. I thought it might be polite to wait for Paul to join us, but Diana had no such qualms.

We picnic on the bed. There's no couch or table, just a nightstand and a random chair. The mattress is lumpy, and the sheets scratch as if their thread count is two. The front desk gave us a portable cot as a second bed with some blankets and an extra pillow.

The curtains barely do their job as flashes of light come through the frayed floral material. Olive green and harvest gold date the décor. In a strange paradox, someone had taken care to clean the place. There isn't any dust, and the worn carpet has the marks of a vacuum. Still, the wallpaper peels at the seams and emanates with the scent of decay and age. The cracked vinyl chair has a cigarette burn along the edge.

Paul stares at the worst places in the room as if guilt is eating him for his rash decision to bring us here. It was the only motel at the exit he took. A few times, he starts to apologize and then stops himself. He looks exhausted—not just from the long drive but completely mentally drained.

Diana doesn't seem affected by our surroundings as she focuses more on copying me. I envy her innocence and sense of adventure. Still, an air of sadness peeks through. I wonder if she's trying to be strong for her dad. I also wonder how it would've felt to lose Astrid at her age. For all my mother's flaws, I still loved the woman.

I find it odd that people talk in the past tense when someone dies. We say I *loved*, not love. Death didn't change my feelings. Finding out Astrid wasn't related to me by blood didn't make her any less the woman who raised me—it explained a lot, but it didn't change how I feel. My emotions when it comes to my parents are just as complicated as ever.

Ugh, I want to stop thinking about this.

Night creeps over the motel like a looming threat. It darkens the stormy window through the crack in the thin curtains. With each passing second, a sick feeling settles deeper into my body.

When I glance in his direction, Paul tries to smile at me, but I feel alone. The protection of my last name no longer holds. An empire ruled by two humans will not subdue supernatural creatures. Conrad and I will never be able to hold on to all that power. I'm not sure I even want it, but I can't abandon my brother.

I touch the amulet. The hard edges are as familiar to my fingers as my own skin, but the stone no longer holds the illusion of comfort. It can no more protect me than my flesh and bone.

I fear the end is coming for us. The thought terrifies me. I don't want to die. Not here in this motel that time forgot.

Still, I try to hold on to hope. Hope that they don't know we're here. Hope that the vampires won't come. Hope that we'll all see the morning.

I cross to the window and lean to peer outside through the opening in the curtains. I hear the duckling behind me. A small hand fits into mine. Lightning flashes, illuminating the parking lot. Anthony would have joked that the gods were partying hard tonight.

"Don't be scared of the storm," Diana says. "It can't hurt us."

I should be reassuring her, not the other way around.

"Di, why don't you see what's on TV?" Paul suggests. "Find us something to watch."

I stare at the parking lot for signs of trouble. I feel a chill coming off the glass. Goosebumps rise over my flesh as if to warn me. On the other side of the motel, I detect the tiny glow of fire from a lighter brightening under the overhang before disappearing. It's not often I notice cigarettes. Most people seem to prefer vape pens. Or maybe it's the flame reminding me of the danger that makes it so noticeable now.

I recall the sound of Darlene's spark wheel seconds before the apartment explosion.

Paul and Diana move around behind me as they flip through channels on the television. I pull the curtain in an attempt to keep myself hidden as I peek out to get a better look. A flash of lightning reveals the shadow of a man smoking, and the sound of thunder follows seconds later. I don't think the smoker is a vampire, but I watch him anyway. He could be enthralled to one. He could be watching the room. Or he could be a motel guest with a nasty habit.

I feel hypervigilant. That's the word, right? I heard it on one of those catch-the-serial-killer shows.

My heart beats too fast. I hear a thump through the walls. I wonder who's next to us. The motel is old. I bet a vampire could crash through the thin walls. Or a werewolf. What if they send a shifter?

I try to keep my paranoia in check, but the real fear is in what I can't see and what I don't know.

"Tamara, watch a movie with us." Diana's voice is more of a demand than a request.

I lean over, trying to see if the moon is full. The storm hides it from me.

"Hey." Paul's voice is gentle. He's right behind me, and I startle.

His hand slides over mine on the curtain. He's warm to my cold. I realize I'm shaking.

"I know this room is not what you're used to," he says. "But it's warm. It's dry. There's a bed."

Great. He thinks I'm a spoiled brat.

"The room is a room," I answer, refraining from adding that he couldn't have found a better stage for a bloodbath. "It's fine."

"Then you're scared of the storm?" He pulls my hand off the curtain and continues to hold it.

"I told you what I'm afraid of," I whisper.

Another thump sounds from the room next to us. We both turn in unison toward the noise. His grasp tightens enough that I notice but not enough to hurt me. He's trying to look relaxed, but he's on edge. His lips press together.

I don't recognize the movie Diana is watching,

226

but it's full of silly noises. They're out of place in the current situation, but she giggles, not caring. She rests on her stomach, lightly kicking her feet against the bed.

"There's nothing we can do tonight," Paul whispers, as if he is nearing the end of some internal debate.

Every instinct inside of me prickles. I'm terrified of what's coming. I want to stop time. If only I had the magic to make that happen.

I turn back to the window. The smoker is gone.

The storm rages on. I stare into the night, waiting for a flash to illuminate our surroundings. Lightning strobes over the landscape, and I see a blur move across the parking lot. It's fleeting and impossible to tell what caused it or if it was even real. I rub my eyes and keep staring into the shadows.

"Tamara, come take your mind off things." Paul urges me to join them on the bed where they watch TV. I close the curtains to block people from looking in, but I'm not sure the thin material will do the job.

The pizza boxes are closed at the end of the bed. Diana stays on her stomach, watching and laughing. Paul lounges against the headboard and motions for me to sit beside him. I crawl into the domestic scene reluctantly.

I stare forward, but I don't see the show. Instead,

I see the various ways we could all die. I imagine how the police might find our bodies—strewn over furniture, right here where we lay, chopped up in the tub. Or perhaps they'd only find Paul's car in the parking lot, and we become an unsolved mystery.

What if our ghosts get trapped here for eternity? Then Paul, Diana, and I end up haunting this sad room in this rundown motel, seeing things that no person should see.

I can't get the thoughts out of my head.

"Hey, hey, easy," Paul soothes. He runs his hand down my arm to where I'm gripping the edge of the pillow with a tight fist. He tries to pry my fingers open while whispering, "Breathe. I promise everything is going to be all right."

There's a big part of me that wants desperately to believe him. I see the certainty in his eyes. I feel the gentleness in his touch. He is so confident of his place in this world.

I mimic his breathing, slow and steady, trying to calm myself. The knot in my chest grows tighter. I want to shake him, yell that he should be panicked, and that monsters are out there in the night hunting us.

Another flash causes my attention to move toward the window. I gasp to see the outline of a colossal figure on the other side of the thin glass. My pulse races.

"Paul." I grip his hand in warning. "The window."

Another bolt of lightning strikes and the shadow is gone.

"I don't see anything," he says.

I watch the curtain, unsure if it's just my imagination and fear.

Paul reaches his arm around my shoulders and pulls me against him. I lean into the solid warmth of his embrace. "You're shaking. Try to relax. I promise everything is going to be all right. I know you're probably not used to places like this, but it's just an old building. There's nothing to fear."

A loud bang sounds on the wall as if to debate him. Diana instantly pushes up from her spot to sit on the bed. Her rounded eyes turn to look at us. The sound of loud laughter follows.

"Noisy neighbors," Paul tells her.

Diana nods but remains seated as she turns back to the television. Her posture is stiffer than before.

"We should try to rest. The night will go faster if we're sleeping," Paul suggests.

I don't think I could sleep if I wanted to.

"You two can have the bed. I'll take the cot," Paul says.

I don't want him to leave my side. "No, I—"

Another loud thud comes through the wall.

Paul frowns and reaches over his head. He pounds his fist against the wall to tell the other room to keep it down.

The warning sparks inappropriately loud laughter on the other side. His frown deepens.

"Oh, you better watch out, Billy!" a woman's muffled voice teases.

"Bring it, asshole!" a man screams.

"Dad?" Diana asks, worried.

"Just ignore them," Paul answers. "Remember that guy at the neighborhood potluck?"

"Mr. Thompson, who drank too much beer and began yelling at a stop sign?" Diana giggles.

"Yeah, sometimes adults who drink too much act stupid," Paul says. "We need to stay away from them."

Another thud sounded.

"Drunk people are stupid," Diana states with a nod. She slides off the bed and lifts her arm as if to pound on the wall.

Paul leans over to catch her fist. "We should leave them alone."

"But you did it," Diana pouts.

"I shouldn't have," he says.

I slide off the bed and cross toward the window

to check outside. It's a compulsion I can't control. My hand shakes as I pull back to peek through the curtains.

"Tamara?" Diana asks. "Is something out there?"

I glance back to find her concerned eyes staring at me for reassurance. I smile, trying to appear brave for her. I know the expression is wavering. I tilt my head and manage a soft, unconvincing, "No."

A scream pierces the night, and I spin around to look outside. It sounds like it comes from the far side of the motel. I focus on where the smoker had been standing. Lights flicker inside his room as if someone is swinging a lamp back and forth.

Suddenly, Paul is beside me. "What was that?"

I point toward the smoker's room. It goes dark.

"Dad?" Diana asks, her little voice quivering.

"It's all right, honey," Paul soothes, but his tone is not believable. He touches my elbow. "We'll be safe in here."

I refrain from pointing out that his ability for denial is unrivaled. Merely stating something out loud does not will it into existence.

Well, unless you have magic and are casting a spell.

Paul takes a deep breath and starts toward the door. "I should check—"

"No!" I deny him exit, pushing in front of him. "Don't go out there."

"Someone might need help," he insists.

Did he not get the memo? We're New Yorkers. We stay out of everyone else's business.

"Call the front desk. It's their job to handle guests." I don't want him to leave us alone, and I sure as hell don't want him hanging himself out as bait. Let creepy taxidermy man deal with it.

"It'll only take a minute," he answers. "I'll just walk down there and see what I see."

I don't move as I mouth the word, "Diana."

It's the only thing that will keep him here.

It works. He nods. "I'll call the desk."

The room doesn't have a landline. Instead, a piece of paper laminated to an end table has the front desk's number on it. Paul reaches for his cell phone and calls.

I watch the other end of the motel intently, scared I'll miss something important if I blink. A prominent figure emerges from the smoker's room. It's too big to be the smoker and too fast and twitchy to be a human. If I had to guess by the terrifying build, he's male in form. The creature goes to the next room as if searching for his victim. Even though his inhuman strength could easily smash through the door, he knocks before violently pushing his way inside when the door cracks open.

Oh, fuck.

Oh, fuck, fuck, fuck.

Vampire.

They've come.

Heavy metal music starts playing next door. The steady thump of the dense beat makes it difficult to hear what's happening outside. A raw, aggressive voice projects over the music as the singer hungers for blood and boasts of living for an eternity. Fuck me if the tune is not appropriate for a vampire attack. The universe certainly has a morbid sense of humor.

"Dad, I don't like it here," Diana whines.

I can't say I disagree with her.

"They're not picking up," Paul says in frustration, glaring at his phone as if that can change the outcome of the unanswered call.

Run or hide? Run or hide? The thought ping-pongs in my head.

A man cries out. I see him trying to run out the opened door before being forced back inside the room. His arms and legs trail behind him as he is lifted into the air. He doesn't stand a chance. The lights go out.

"We have to run." My tone makes it clear it's not a suggestion.

Paul hesitates as if trying to process the right thing to do.

"Now, Paul!" I order.

"Yeah, yeah." He nods. "Uh, Diana, grab your bags."

I want to yell, *fuck the bags!*

My focus is on the second room's door. I see the curtains from other guests swish open, but no one leaves their rooms to help. I can't judge them for it. I'm not exactly ready to charge into battle against the undead.

The rain isn't letting up. I scan the parking lot for other movement. It looks like the vampire is hunting alone. Figures. They wouldn't send an army after a simple mortal.

The metal soundtrack isn't helping as the singer screams at us to feed him with our blood.

Movement catches my eye. Never mind. I was wrong. The vampire is not alone. There is a second figure crouching on the roof. The first vampire moves across the motel extraordinarily fast.

Just perfect. Two vampires are hunting us.

"Keys, keys..." Paul is mumbling to himself. I hear them moving behind me.

"Dad. Here."

"Ready?" Paul appears next to me, holding my

shoes for me to take. His arms are loaded with our bags, and he's wearing my backpack.

Instead of taking the shoes, I reach into a bag for a plastic jar of minced garlic. I untwist the lid and pull off the safety seal.

"Really?" he questions in frustration.

I ignore his tone. I reach my arm out to stop them from leaving as I watch the roof. "Wait. Not yet. Wait..."

My heart is pounding, and I can't catch my breath.

Paul leans to see what I'm looking at. "I don't..."

The vampire comes out of the second room and goes for the third. The second one jumps down to the sidewalk to join him.

"What are they doing?" he asks, his words barely above a breath.

I'm not going to answer that. The look dawning on his face says he already suspects.

"Stay close, sweetheart," I whisper to Diana. I hug the jar to my chest with my arm. "We're going to go straight to the car."

The vampires break through the third door. A bloodcurdling shriek soon follows.

"Unlock the car, Paul," I tell him.

He lifts the hand with his keys while adjusting

the bags hanging from his arms. I see lights flash on his SUV.

"Go. Now!" I dart for the door and fumble with the lock to open it. My shaking hands lack my usual coordination.

I grab Diana's hand and glance down the sidewalk before dashing toward the car. My arm doesn't come with me as Diana stops on the sidewalk under the awning. I grunt in frustration as I turn and sweep her under my arm to make her run with me. Debris in the parking lot stings the bottom of my feet as I splash through puddles, but I don't care. We weave through the cars.

Diana yelps and trips, causing us to stumble. Paul crashes against my back. One of the bags swings into my elbow, and I drop the jar. I manage to stay on my feet somehow, but I'm bent over and off balance.

A growling noise pierces the night. Diana wriggles against me as I try to right myself.

"Dad?" she cries out in fear.

A blur of movement precedes a loud splash as boots land close by in the water. Shaking, I turn to see the hulking shadow now in front of us. The rain encases all of us but doesn't seem to bother him as it pelts his leather coat. Lightning chooses that moment to flash, giving us a clearer picture of the threat. The vampire stands tall and imposing, his burly frame even scarier up close.

Wet hair hangs in strings. He holds his hands at his sides, the long fingernails shaped like pointed claws. He makes a show of sniffing the air. His skin is rosy as if he's fed, but the low growl rumbling from his throat and the piercing determination in his eyes say he's not yet full. Hunger and anticipation fill his monstrous expression. I've seen that look of malice before when I'd snuck out to watch my parents' party guests.

The creature looks at me. His words come in a slight hiss as he says, "Someone wants to see you, blood sack."

Diana's breathing catches as she starts to cry.

"Get to the car." Paul tries to push us behind him. The bags drop off his arms. Then louder, he states, "Listen, buddy, we don't want any trouble."

The vampire doesn't move. He's enjoying watching us squirm. A slow smile cracks his face, and he exposes the tips of sharp fangs. The sound of breaking wood cracks the night as his friend crashes into the next motel room.

"Paul, get Diana to safety. Don't look back." I slowly reach for the jar as I keep my eyes on the vampire. Some of the minced garlic has spilled into a puddle. "They're not here for you."

"Dammit, Tama—" Paul tries to protest, but the creature surges forward with a gurgling snarl.

Paul lifts his fists to fight. Diana screams. He takes a swing, making contact with the vampire's jaw with a loud *thwack*. Despite the strength behind the blow, the punch barely moves the creature's head.

I grab the jar and inelegantly chuck the contents toward the vampire before Paul can swing a second time. A strange bluish light flashes around us. The wet plastic slips out of my hand, and the jar strikes the vampire in the chin. The creature howls in pain and recoils, swiping at his face.

"Run!" Paul yells as the vampire is distracted. He picks Diana up and pushes me toward the car.

I crash into the passenger door as Paul darts around to the other side. Diana is sobbing, her raspy breath unable to catch as she gasps for air. I turn to look behind us, leaning against the metal frame as my fingers blindly search for the handle. Light shines behind me as Paul opens the car door.

I feel the vehicle rock with the force of his movements.

"Tamara," Paul yells in a panic.

The rain is relentless as it obscures the thrashing, howling monster. He charges angrily toward us.

My hands find the handle, and I fall more than step into the car. The engine roars to life. I kick my feet to push into the seat. The car starts to move before I have the door closed. Paul backs up. He hits the brakes, and my door slams shut at the abrupt stop. Paul puts the SUV into drive.

My attention is on our attacker when a loud crash reverberates from the roof. Diana screams behind me.

"Stay down, baby!" Paul yells.

The second vampire slides down the front of the windshield, grinning as if this is all a game. The sharp fangs are unmistakable, and his eyes glow with a supernatural light. His body turns on the glass as he hooks his fingers onto the top edge of the hood. Rain has diluted the bloodstains on his white shirt into a soft pink, but the splatter is unmistakable.

Paul slams on the gas before hitting the brakes hard a second later. The creature slides off just as our first attacker reaches my door. Paul hits the gas again. Our tires should have thumped over the vampire's body, but the road is smooth.

Diana continues to whimper. I turn to watch behind us. One of the vampires gives chase, but the car is faster. He fades into the distance.

"Hold on," Paul warns.

Diana is on the floor behind his chair, her body folded over into a ball. My backpack is on the seat.

The tires squeal as the car takes a series of turns.

The movement tosses me back and forth. We slide in the rain, but Paul quickly regains control of the vehicle. The backpack slides toward Diana's head. I lean between the front seats to grab hold of it, shoving it onto the floor behind me.

Diana's stuttering crying is only outdone by the harshness of my breath. My heart is pounding so hard that I think I might be having a heart attack.

"Diana, it's okay, baby. We're all right. It's all over now." Paul grips the wheel as we speed onto the interstate. "We're okay."

We're all drenched, and the cold is becoming noticeably uncomfortable. I step on the toes of my socks to pull them off my feet.

Paul reaches into his pocket to pull out his phone. His hand trembles as he taps his thumb against the screen.

"What are you doing?" I ask, leaning my head against the window to search the sky for signs that they're flying after us.

"We left them. There are so many," he mumbles, holding the phone to his ear. "Oh, thank god you're there. You need to call the police. Two tweakers are breaking into rooms and attacking your guests. They're... They're like fucked up on something. PCP or something. Yeah, yeah, okay. I—"

Paul pulls his phone away to look at the screen.

"They hung up," he says. "But they said the police are coming. So, we're good. We don't have to..."

Paul nods his head, the gesture agitated. He grips the wheel with one hand as he flexes the fingers on the other. His knuckles are red from where he punched the vampire.

Our speed is a little fast, and I touch his arm. "Slow down. We don't want to crash."

He obeys. I watch the speedometer drop.

"Dad?" Diana's voice is tiny.

I crawl into the backseat. "Come up here with me, sweetheart."

She's trembling as she moves onto my lap. "Where's Plop? I want Plop."

"Shit," Paul swears under his breath.

"Are you hurt?" I ask her.

Diana shakes her head.

"Is she hurt?" Paul glances back before moving to watch the road.

"No," I answer, even as I see a scratch on her arm. "She's a brave girl."

"Where's Plop?" she asks louder.

I look around but only see my backpack.

"I'm sorry, honey, I think Plop..." Paul makes a sound of frustration.

"I think he went on an adventure," I finish. "I'm sure he's happy wherever he is."

Diana cries harder. "You mean he's in heaven like my mommy? I'll never see him again."

I have no clue what the correct answer is, so I go for distraction.

"How about we get you into a dry shirt?" I reach for the bag even as she clings to me. "Do you want to wear my clothes?"

Diana tries to nod, but the movement is small.

"Tamara?" She sounds so traumatized and shaken.

"Yeah, sweetheart. I'm here." I give her a slight squeeze.

"Drunk people are stupid."

CHAPTER
FIFTEEN

There is something comforting about the lines in the middle of the interstate coming at me as I drive. They're hypnotic and constant, mesmerizing me to keep me on track. Paul finally relinquished the wheel. It took some convincing, but in the end, I think it was his daughter needing him that did it.

I feel him breaking inside. It's not anything I can define. It's in the tightness of his movements, as if every gesture needs to be in control. His kind expressions have turned to worry. He doesn't act as if he blames me, but it's my fault. I did this to them with my selfish need to be saved and my desire not to be alone.

Diana is curled up next to him in the back seat. For the longest time, I'd glance in the mirror and see his eyes staring back, but now they're both sleeping beneath one of his emergency blankets. If I had to guess, I'd say he fought to stay awake, but the days of driving and the letdown after an adrenaline rush were too much for his body. I'm too amped to rest while it's still dark outside.

It seems cruel at this point of our journey to tell them vampires can transform and fly or that bats, by nature, can blend into the night. Paul is still coming to grips with the fact they're real. He kept trying to convince himself that they were on some kind of new designer drug or part of a satanic cult. But he had difficulty explaining why punching that vampire felt like hitting meat hanging in a refrigerator unit.

My clothes have dried, for the most part. There is a dampness along the inside of my thighs that reaches around to my lower back. It's uncomfortable, but I don't want to stop the car. Since I gave Diana the t-shirt in my backpack, the only other option was my wrinkled funeral dress. Putting something like that on feels like bad luck, like tempting fate. I don't want to bury anyone else I care about.

And I do care about Paul and Diana. They've become very important to me.

As I drive, the constant hum of the tires on the pavement fills me with dread. I keep as close to the other cars as possible, hoping to find safety in numbers. The image of the motel flashes in my mind, reminding me that no matter how close I am to others, it won't guarantee our protection against a vampire attack. But I know that being isolated is far worse, as it makes us an easy target for their blood-thirsty hunger.

I try not to think of the guests in the other rooms. The guilt is undeniable. I remember hearing a debate once at trivia night in a bar. They were talking about old action movies and how a hundred innocent bystanders would die in the hero's effort to save one woman. But because they were unnamed extras, the audience didn't care.

Well, this isn't an action movie. It's real life. And I care. I just can't do anything about it.

Those people died because of me. Sure, I don't have proof that they're dead, but vampires aren't exactly known for letting their snacks live.

How did my life come to this?

I don't recognize myself.

I find myself toying with the amulet, rolling it against my fingers. My grandfather would've known what to do. Out of everyone, he had the most patience for me. Conrad cares in his own unique way —*I know that*—but he's jaded. And right now, he's busy dealing with the estate and getting me out of legal trouble.

I'm alone.

Utterly human. Utterly alone.

At least Diana and Paul have each other. And Paul has his parents in Kansas.

Family.

I think of the number Conrad sent me for my birth mother. Even if I didn't suspect what fate probably has in store for me, I'm not sure I'd be ready to call her. This is a woman who gave up her baby to be raised by her lover and his wife.

My feelings toward Lady Astrid are torn. She raised me and is the only mother I've ever known. But did she love me? With her, it's hard to tell. That's the one question I never allowed myself to dwell on. Love wasn't a priority in the Devine household.

I like to think that if I had a kid, I'd walk through fire to get to her.

What if Lorelai didn't want a baby?

What if she resented me for ruining her affair, and it was easy for her to give me up?

What if my parents pressured her? Or cast a magic spell to make her forget?

What if she didn't care?

What if she did care?

Why didn't my grandfather tell me about her? Surely, as the Devine patriarch, he knew. If he did, he'd have a good reason. Maybe she was dangerous? Or a druggy like Conrad's birth mother?

To hell with my churning mind! Why does my brain always have to roll every thought around in fifty thousand directions before it can stop?

I grip the wheel, blinking against the highway hypnosis and wishing for a shot of espresso to make me more alert. The first peek of dawn coloring the horizon releases a tight hold on my chest. Vampires will be slinking back into their nests. We're safe—*well, safe-ish*—for another day. That doesn't give me much time to come up with my next move.

Lorelai Weber lives in California.

We'll be in Kansas City soon. Paul will be stopping to see his parents. No matter how much I want to stay with him, I shouldn't. I should keep running and lure the vampires away. I'm the one they want.

"Someone wants to see you, blood sack."

That's what the vampire said as he looked at me. The creature had barely glanced at Paul and Diana as if they were inconsequential.

So California? I need to go somewhere.

I'll have to call her first. Even if I don't go to meet her, even if I don't survive to see her next week, I'd regret not at least hearing her voice and hearing what she has to say.

I can't help but think of Conrad's mother, drugged out on the couch, wanting money for her next fix.

Whatever the truth reveals, at least I'll know.

I force my hands to loosen their death grip as I take a deep breath. It's decided. I'll call. I'll leave.

The best thing for Paul and Diana is never to see me again. I'll be that fading memory of the woman they met after a funeral.

"How long was I out?" Paul's voice is low and sleepy. He moves behind me.

I feel a wave of guilt at hearing his voice right as I decide to cut ties. Clearing my throat, I guess, "Four hours?"

I look in the mirror and see him readjusting a sleeping Diana on the seat.

"I feel like I'm coming out of a coma." He leans up between the seats and rubs the bridge of his nose.

"It's good. You needed rest." I blink and concentrate on staying in my lane.

"It's been," he chuckles to himself but doesn't appear amused as he shakes his head and finishes, "a rough couple of weeks."

"The important thing is it's almost over," I tell him. Well, it's not almost over for me, but this moment isn't about me. "You'll be with family soon."

He nods, but I see reservation in his expression. I can't blame him if he doesn't want me around the rest of his family after last night.

"My brother is making arrangements for me in

Kansas City," I say to let him off the hook before he has to turn me away.

"Oh, but you can stay—"

"There are family things I need to deal with." I try to think of a good excuse. "Legal estate stuff, you know. And you said your mother has been ill. She doesn't need the drama that seems to be following me around. Besides, I think I will be heading on to California."

Seeing an exit that looks promising, I signal to turn off the interstate.

"Oh?"

"Yeah, our private detective found the contact information for my birth mother, so... yeah. Could be the best thing. She's my biological mother. I should meet her." I slow the car. My lower back aches and my exhaustion headache worsens. I need to stretch my legs and splash some cold water on my face before I pass out. "I mean, thank you for getting me this far, but I think, you know..."

"This conversation... It's like we're dancing around trying to be overly cordial." Paul lifts a hand as if to touch me but lets it hover. "I think we should be frank."

I nod. "I feel awful about what I've brought into your life."

"I don't blame you for anything that's happened."

He drops his hand. "I should never have stopped for the night in a questionable neighborhood. I let my frustration get the better of me when we were pulled over."

Okay. He wants blunt. I'm tired enough to give it to him. I pull into a parking lot and stop the car. Unbuckling my seat belt, I turn to look at him.

"Paul, my life is a mess. There are rules to being a member of the Devine family. When my parents were alive, I was protected. They were so powerful that no one would dare to fuck with me. I don't mean rich, though they were. I mean powerful. Magical. Like ancient magic. Now that they're gone, Conrad and I don't have that protection anymore. And that's why vampires think it's okay to come after me now."

"You're magical?" He rubs the bridge of his nose and glances behind him at Diana. "Let's talk outside."

As he silently exits the car, I let loose a deep sigh. I follow him out into the nearly empty gas station parking lot. It's not lost on me that my wet crotch probably makes it look like I peed myself.

Could I be any less attractive?

Early morning traffic fills my ears as we stand by the roadside. The nearest people are at the gas pumps, ignoring us as they go about their day. Crisp air sends a shiver down my spine, but I inhale it deeply, relishing the fresh scent of dawn.

"I'm not magical. I'm human. My father came from a Welsh witch line." I feel the words rush out of me like a bumbling, rambling mess of a confession. "My mother, or the woman I thought was my mother, Lady Astrid, is from an even older Norse line, descended from the gods of old. Anthony inherited all that. I have a human mother, and I didn't inherit magical powers. Conrad was adopted, so he's all human. And since we're mortal, we're not scary and—"

"Whoa," Paul puts his hands on my shoulders. Strong fingers massage my tense muscles. His eyes bore into mine, steady and sure. "Calm down. Take a breath."

"I'm so sorry I put you both in danger." Tears well up in my eyes. I'm exhausted, and frustrated, and scared. I shrug and toss my hands to the side. "And I know you don't believe me about magic. I wish I could prove it to you, but I'm…"

"Shh." He pulls me against his chest and wraps his arms around me. Holding me close, he whispers, "I believe you."

A tiny sob escapes me at the admission, and I pull back to see if he's placating me. He looks serious.

Paul doesn't let me go. His gaze focuses on my

necklace. "I'm not saying it's not a lot to take in, but I believe you. I thought my eyes were playing tricks on me the night of the fire. But then, last night, I saw the same thing. Something, some force, protected you and Diana from danger. And I don't think it was throwing a jar of minced garlic, or at least that wasn't all of it."

I touch the necklace. Its protection was only a story to make me feel better. Wasn't it?

"I notice you play with that when you're nervous," he says.

I don't release the amulet and ignore the observation. "I don't think anyone has ever just trusted me."

"You protected my daughter, Tamara," he answers as if that one thing erases all the craziness. "Twice. Of course, I trust you."

"Then trust me when I say we need to part ways. The fires, the vampire attack, the resulting legal troubles, they're connected to me and my family. If I'm not with you, you'll both be safer. Always be cautious of strangers, and if anyone ever asks, just tell them I paid you to give me a ride to Kansas City." No part of me wants to leave him, but I know it's for the best.

A soft knock sounds on the window. Diana's face is pressed to the glass next to her splayed fingers.

"You're exhausted." Paul sighs and glances around. "Nothing must be decided this second. Why don't you try to sleep in the car? I'll take Diana to get us all some fresh clothes, then breakfast. Okay?"

I nod. Paul reaches for the driver's side door as I make a point of walking around the vehicle to check for markings. I don't know when anyone would have had the opportunity, but I look anyway. The car is clean after the rainstorm.

"Diana, hop in the front. Tamara needs to lie down," Paul says as I open the back door to get in.

I crawl into the bed that Diana left behind. I can sense the warmth from her body still lingering on the covers. I bunch up a corner of the blanket to use as a makeshift pillow and turn to face the seat back so that my fellow passengers won't see the tears streaming down my face. I pull the blanket over my head to block out the light as I try to suppress my emotions.

I'm tapped out. I don't want to feel anything.

CHAPTER
SIXTEEN

I wish I could say rest is a cure-all. It's not. I still feel like someone threw me out of a fifty-story window. Every muscle aches. My head pounds. And none of that compares to the tight knot in my chest choking every breath. I don't want to be me.

I don't think I've ever wanted to be me.

How could Nancy have thrown away her family by cheating on Paul? He's perfect. Diana's a sweet kid. I would give anything to have had a chance at that life.

Why does everything have to be so complicated?

I wonder what my life would have been had Lorelai Weber kept me instead. What if I was raised in California instead of Manhattan? What if I never knew I was a Devine? Tamara Weber. The name sounds odd, but I wonder who that would have been.

Human daughter to a human single mother. Even if she was a flawed parent. Even if we had no money. Even if she hated me.

My hands shake, and I can't seem to make them dial the phone.

I pace the gas station restroom, ignoring the movements copied by my reflection. I did my best to clean up in the sink with hand soap and paper towels. Paul did a decent job of buying me a change of clothes. The gray drawstring pants and dark blue T-shirt are loose but comfortable. I'm too warm for the athletic fleece jacket, so I've tied the sleeves around my waist. He even got me a pair of sneakers to replace the ones we left in the motel parking lot, which beat the high heels from the funeral.

Is it strange that the man figured out my shoe size?

I'll go with it being sweet that he paid attention.

In my best game show contestant voice, I tell my reflection, "I'll take things my brain should not give a shit about right now for two hundred."

A quick knock sounds on the door, and I jump in fright as it interrupts my thoughts.

"One second," I call.

Another quick knock relays the person's urgency.

I open the door to a woman wiggling desperately. She rushes through the door, knocking me aside and muttering a half-apology as the wood slams in my face. She's not the only person waiting in line for the restroom. I try not to meet the annoyed stares of strangers as I walk past them to leave. Figures that there are more people in this world who are mad at me.

A person can only take too much before they either break down or scream like a lunatic in a psychotic episode. I wonder what will happen to me. I honestly can feel it going both ways.

The only thought keeping me on my feet and quiet is that being in a locked ward at a hospital is about as bad as being in jail. I'd be ripe for a vampire attack.

I know feeling sorry for myself is a pathetic look, but I'm beginning to wish I was never born. No birth, no fiery birthday party. No birth, no birth mother to call for a rejection. No birth, no—

I see Paul, and he smiles at me with his kind, non-judging eyes. It brings me out of my head, and I instantly feel better. Diana is skipping around the concrete yellow bollards along the edge of the parking lot like she's invented a game.

It's such a simple moment—me walking toward them, Diana lost in her little girl world, Paul smiling at me. Everyone takes these things for granted, but I wish I could live in this moment for an eternity. Just me, Paul, and Diana in a gas station parking lot in a town whose name I can't remember.

Out of all the failed spells Conrad and I tried in our youth, I wish the stopping time spell had actually worked. I could use a little of that magic right now.

"Feeling better?" he asks as I come near.

I nod.

"Did you call her?"

I shake my head. "There was a line outside the restroom, and I..."

I chickened the fuck out.

"Go ahead. We're fine here," he says, gesturing along the bollards, where I can find some privacy. "Take all the time you need."

I nod again, wishing he had given me an excuse to avoid calling.

"Dad," Diana demands, breathing heavily. "How fast was that?"

"Three minutes and sixteen seconds," he answers, not actually looking at any kind of time-keeping device. "I think you can beat that. Go again."

She takes a deep breath in determination and gets into her ready position.

"On your mark. Get set. Go!" Paul yells.

Diana takes off, skipping along her path.

"Go," Paul mouths to me with an encouraging smile.

I pace away from him. My hands are shaking, and I find it hard to catch my breath. When I look back, it's to find Paul glancing between me and Diana. I give him a small nod as I press the phone number in Conrad's text to dial.

"Hello," I practice whisper. "My name is Tamara Devine."

The phone rings, and I pray she doesn't answer.

"Hello. You might not remember me, but I'm your daughter, Tamara Devine."

The phone keeps ringing.

"May I please speak with Lorelai? Hi, Lorelai. Would you be interested in saving money on your car insurance?"

I'm an idiot.

"Don't answer. Don't answer. Don't—"

"Hello, June?" The voice sounds expectant.

I open my mouth, but no sound comes out.

"Hello?" This time, she seems more annoyed, as if she's checked the number and realized I'm not a friend. "Whatever you're selling, I'm not interested. This number is on a do-not-call list."

"Um, wait, I..." I clear my throat. "I'm not selling anything. Is this Lorelai Weber?"

"Who is this?" she asks instead of answering. I can't blame her for the tone. The only unknown numbers that seem to call people anymore are scammers.

"My name is Tamara," I manage. I wish I were more confident. "You might not remember me, but—"

The sound of a muffled crash cuts me off, and I wait nervously. I glance at the phone screen to see if she hung up.

"Tamara?" she asks after a long pause.

"Yes, ma'am." Who the hell says ma'am in this situation? I roll my eyes at myself. "My name is Tamara Devine. You, um, knew my father?"

Well, this conversation is going about as smoothly as a ship into an iceberg.

"Tamara?" she repeats.

"Yes. My father was Davis."

"Tamara," she states. "I heard about what happened to your father. I'm very sorry for your loss. Did he tell you to call me?"

"My mother, I mean, Lady Astrid, told me about you a few months before they died. I had hired a detective to find your number, but he just now got it back to me."

"Astrid," she whispers, and I hear a deep breath. "Yes, I heard about her passing as well. And your brother. I'm very sorry for your losses."

She heard? So she was keeping tabs on the family? Or did she just happen across the news?

"I was, um, thinking of coming to California for a trip," I say.

"Okay."

"And I thought we could meet for like a coffee or something?"

I lean my head down and cup my hand around the phone to better listen to what's happening on her end. I can't be sure, but I hear what sounds like a throat clearing.

I don't know what to think. "If that's not cool, we don't have to—"

"No, no," she interrupts. "Coffee would be good. When do you think you might be here?"

"Few days?"

"Oh? That's soon. Oh, okay, sure, yeah."

I can't think of what else to say, but I find myself not wanting to hang up, even if it is awkward.

"Do you know about...?" I stop myself from saying supernaturals.

"About your family?" she finishes. "Yes. I know what they are—*were*."

That's at least somewhat of a relief.

"I heard about your grandfather's passing. He was a decent man. Covid was a rough one, to be sure."

"Yeah, he was." A small pain tightens my chest.

My grandfather knew about her and never told me. "I miss him. I mean, I miss all of them, of course."

"Have they figured out what happened? How the fire started?" Lorelai instantly backtracks. "Never mind. That's none of my... We don't have to talk about... This isn't the time for a conversation about such things."

Why is she mentioning the fire? Is that a normal thing for her to ask on our first call? Or should it worry me?

"They're still investigating," I say, keeping it vague.

I remind myself that I don't know this woman and I shouldn't let my guard down because I'm desperate for a little familial connection. She's just a stranger on the phone. There could be a reason my grandfather never told me about her. Or my father. Astrid only said something because she could be a vindictive bitch.

I glance back at Paul sitting against one of the concrete bollards. He sees me and gives a tiny wave of his fingers.

"My ride is waiting in the car for me," I lie. "I should go."

"Oh, okay. I guess call me when you're in town? Or before. Or whenever. Or text. Anytime. This is my cell phone."

"This is my cell phone, too," I say.

"Got it."

"Okay."

"Okay."

"Bye."

"Bye, oh, and Tamara. Happy birthday."

"Thanks." I pull the phone away to hang up and take a deep, shaking breath.

I grip my phone and turn back to Paul. His expression has become one of concern. To Diana, he says, "Two minutes. Six seconds. Last one."

Diana groans but gets into her starting position.

"Ready. Set. Go!" Paul sends her skipping around the bollards.

I walk toward them.

"How'd it go?" he asks.

"Um, yeah, fine, I guess."

"Was she nice?" He lightly touches my arm and rubs it up and down.

I shrug. "She was fine. Nervous, maybe. Surprised. She said she was sorry about my family, and we're going to meet up for coffee when I get to California."

"So you've decided? You're going?" He looks disappointed, even as he tries to hide it.

I nod and look at Diana. "I think it's best. My brother sent the address where you can drop me off."

Paul's brow furrows.

"What?"

His frown deepens. "I'm just thinking of the last address your brother sent you to. Why don't you let me give you some cash for a hotel? A proper hotel this time."

"You don't—"

"You can pay me back when you return to the city," he cuts me off. "I'm not worried about it. I know you're good for it."

He's trying to make a joke. I do my best to smile, but I know the look must appear strained. I don't have the heart to tell him that when we say goodbye today, it's forever. I can't keep bringing my madness to their doorstep.

"I think we should get you something to eat first. You'll feel better with some food." He says it like he's trying to reason out an advanced calculus problem instead of something that's a fairly simple equation. One plus one equals two. Monsters plus danger equals my leaving.

"Dad?" Diana demands, breathless. I'm grateful for her interruption.

"One minute," he announces. "Well done! Go get in the car."

"What about my prize?" she asks.

"You get to pick where we stop for lunch," he answers.

She runs for the car, and we follow behind at a slower pace. Paul unlocks it with the key fob.

"Let's do our best to keep her from picking sparkle pancakes again," he jokes.

"You're only a kid once." I watch Diana through the window. She opens her mouth wide against the glass and blows to puff up her cheeks. "I say if she wants sparkly pancakes, then let her have them. Life has given us very few things we can smile about recently."

"Yeah, I suppose you're right." Paul gives in easily. "One more day of sugar won't hurt us."

I walk around the back of the car, automatically searching for symbols. There are none.

I look at my phone and pull up my texts. Typing to Conrad, I write, *"I'm going to California alone. Ditching my ride for the safe house. They don't know anything. Our angry friends hit the motel we were at, so they're eager to be rid of me. Need cash and ticket."*

"By the way." Paul stands by the driver's side door, waiting for me. "I searched the news. Nothing about the motel came up."

I nod that I hear him.

"Ready?" He pulls open the car door.

I answer by getting into the passenger seat.

"I miss Plop," Diana says as we shut the car doors.

"I know, honey. I'm sorry." Paul starts the engine. "Have you decided what you want to eat?"

"Not yet," she answers.

My phone dings and I glance down. Conrad texted, "*On it.*"

I see Lorelai's number in his earlier message.

Conrad is my brother. He's the closest family I have. He's suffered the same traumas.

Lorelai is my blood, closest to me in genetics, biologically a part of me. She's also a complete stranger.

Paul and Diana have only been in my life for a short time. They're not blood. They did not grow up in my household. I'm ashamed to admit it, but if forced, I'd say they're the family I would choose. They represent all those things I have wished for in my life. Normality. Humanity. Love without conditions or boundaries.

Just wishing it makes me feel guilty.

Guilty about Conrad because there is a part of me that would leave him behind, even if it's only in a fantasy.

Guilty that I'm not excited to meet my birth

mother, and I would skip going to see her if I could stay in Kansas City safely.

Guilty that I would consider bringing more danger to Paul and Diana for my own selfish need not to be alone.

The car dings a warning, and I reach to put on my seatbelt to make it stop.

Guilt does me no good. My desire to be someone else does no one any good.

There is only one thing that gives me hope. If I can figure out who started the fires and why, then I may be able to get my life back. Then, maybe I can be a part of Paul and Diana's futures...even if only from a distance.

"Tamara, what was your favorite food in the entire whole wide world when you were my age?" Diana asks.

My mind instantly goes back, and I answer, "Cake. My mother never let me have any, and so that made me want it more."

"Why didn't your mother let you have cake? Were you allergic?" She leans to better see my face. "Bobby's allergic to peanuts. If he eats them, he'll swell up like a balloon, and all his air gets trapped inside until he pops."

Diana puffs her cheeks as hard as she can to demonstrate.

"He won't pop," Paul corrects as he pulls into traffic. "It's called anaphylactic shock, and it's not funny. It's very serious. If it happens, you must run and get an adult right away."

"Right." Diana nods seriously but keeps focused on me. "He swells up until he shocks."

"My mother preferred I eat vegetables." It's the most diplomatic way I can think to say she didn't want a fat accessory in family photos.

"What kind is your favorite?"

"Vegetable? Broccoli, I guess."

Diana giggles. "No, cake!"

I think of the birthday I got a brother instead of a puppy. "When I was your age, all I wanted was a birthday cake as tall as I was, with fairies skating in the icing. I also wanted it to float and sparkle. I didn't care what flavor, but I think strawberry with vanilla icing. Or vanilla with strawberry icing."

"Maybe you should have told your mother you wanted carrot cake," Diana reasons. "Those are vegetables."

"Yeah, maybe." I try not to laugh in the face of her innocence. Even after last night, she still manages to see the world with childlike rationale. "What is your favorite cake?"

"I don't know." She presses her lips together. "I think I like strawberry with vanilla icing the best."

I wonder if my baby duckling is just saying that because of me, but I don't challenge the answer. Whatever memories these two take away from our time together, I want them to be good. Not monster-filled, funeral-fueled thoughts they avoid completely.

For all of Diana's mother's faults, she must have done something right. I think of my childhood days spent hiding from monsters in the protected wing of the country house, watching them come and go from the balcony. I think of logging treadmill hours as a teenager under the supervision of a nutritionist. Kids should be eating cake and skipping around concrete yellow bollards. Instead, I was running from history lessons to self-defense practice.

"All right, chipmunk, keep an eye out. We're coming up on some restaurants," Paul says. "If you see anything you like for lunch, shout it out."

Diana's attention is instantly diverted out her window.

I can't stop thinking about family and childhood and birthdays.

Someone in my life started that fire. It was my birthday. Sure, the party wasn't really for me, but it was still *mine*. If I'm the detectives' best suspect at this point, that means they have no clue what occurred that night. Although there were many people present, I'm certain that someone would have stood out. I just need to force myself to think back to the horrible night, moment by moment. The key to solving this mystery must be among the party guests.

SEVENTEEN

Two weeks earlier...

It might be my birthday, but this party isn't for me.

The banquet hall's décor feels more like a debutant ball than a birthday party. A DJ plays classics—and by classics, I don't mean classic rock. This shit predates rock and roll by like a millennium. Venetian waltz, anyone?

Twinkly fairy lights shine overhead, showcased in pink gauze like they've been ripped out of a six-year-old's dream palace. Crystal goblets and rose-tinted plates surround large flower arrangements. The scent of roses can't hide the underlying char of spent magic that seems to cling to some of the guests like a bad cologne.

I'm only twenty-eight, but everyone around me

acts like I'm sitting in death's waiting room anticipating my appointment. Most women my age are still enjoying the spoils of spring break and drunken mistakes. And their parties look nothing like mine. Very few of them are thinking about mortality.

Not that this crowd understands what it means to be human or the milestones that come with age.

More than one has asked me what it means to be human, what it's like to walk around with that kind of short expiration date tattooed across my soul. I never know what to say. They act like I'll have some profound truth. The only truth I know is we're all bumbling around. Humanity is nothing but a collection of small moments and big dreams.

I guess I could tell them humanity is a series of stupid, little mistakes we never learn from. Like that first drunken bender...the fourth, the fifteenth...

And this next one since tonight is shaping up to be a doozy.

I snatch a champagne glass off a passing tray and sit by myself at an empty dinner table. I'm hidden beside a wall behind a large floral centerpiece. It seems I've spent my entire life watching the supernatural crowds. There's a gift table loaded down with presents, but I won't open them. My mother's staff will take care of all of that.

So, what is my profound truth? What moments define me?

I toss back the full contents of the glass and instantly start looking for another. Seeing Annabeth, I return to my hidden seat. The succubus slept with my ex, Jasper, while we were still together. He was the stupidest waste of three years.

Gee, thanks for that, mother. Who else did Lady Astrid invite? The kids who used to torment me and pick on me? How about the six other women Jasper had affairs with? Oh, or Jasper himself. Wouldn't it be fun if we gathered all my ex-boyfriends into one party?

I think about the secret teenage boyfriend whose name I was too embarrassed to whisper out loud, not even to my closest friends. In reality, the only thing wrong with him was that he was mortal from a middle-class family. My mother would have hated those facts. My next boyfriend was imaginary. He was a magazine-insert poster I hung on my wall of a teenage heartthrob that prompted endless familial teasing. I fantasized that he'd magically step off the paper to whisk me away. I tore him down after a week as if I didn't even deserve a fantasy.

The memories make me sad because they remind me of how lonely I've always felt, how isolated.

I scan the crowd, trying to speculate who the

oldest guest is. You can't always tell by looking at them. Seeing a wizard who could probably recall the 1100s with ease, I know no one would treat him like he is on borrowed time.

I've spent my entire life worried about what all these supernatural creatures think of me. Quite frankly, it's exhausting. Most of the paranormal community treats humans like we're helpless children. Or food.

Vampire bats enter the banquet hall. They fly into a formation of ancient symbols before shifting to land on the dance floor in their human forms. The synchronized dance moves look well-rehearsed.

Showoffs.

As a Devine, I'm protected, but that doesn't mean an occasional drunken guest hadn't tried to snack on me over the years.

A reedy laugh catches my attention, and I cringe. I sink into my chair to hide behind the flower centerpiece.

Chester Freemont.

Why did Lady Astrid invite that tool?

Chester is the man who thankfully got away after a series of botched dates set up by my parents. They pushed him on me like he held the last life vest on the *Titanic*. I'm smart enough to know I don't want to marry a supernatural, even if he *is* a Freemont, and especially one who openly admires the stable of mistresses his father keeps. I'd rather be alone.

I watch Chester pass. He doesn't see me, and I let my captured breath go.

Where the hell are those waiters carrying liquor trays? I do not want to be sober right now.

A brood of vampires saunter by like they're starring in a Dracula reunion tour.

"Well, if it isn't our little Tiddy Mun." Leviathan appears and blocks my view of the vampires. He's in a dark, floor-length cloak with openings for two black sleeves.

I cringe at the nickname. It might mean bog creature to the over five hundred crowd, but to the rest of society, the term is one that humans would use to denote a rather unblessed chest size.

He grins as if proud of his teasing. Him and the sixty other people who came before him with that same tired joke.

Tiddy Mun is a child-sized bog spirit from England that appears in the mist and is followed by the sound of running water. When I was little-little, before Conrad came to live with us, I couldn't keep up with Anthony and his friends. So I cried. A lot. Anthony started summoning mist when I tried to go with them on their little adventures, so his friends teased me and gave me the name. Kids being asshole kids was one thing. But it stuck with the older crowd.

"For you." Leviathan hands me a small brown box. "Happy birthday, Tamara."

When an elder from the Sacred Delegation gives you a present, the recipient should know better than to refuse. I make a show of peeking inside the box at the ring. The stone setting is made to look like an eyeball. "It's beautiful."

"You should wear it," he instructs, wagging his eyebrows. "It's enchanted with an old family recipe."

A loud crash sounds across the banquet hall, followed by laughter as some of the guests mock a member of the waitstaff. I feel sorry for the person. This is a rough crowd to serve. The later it gets, the rougher they get.

Leviathan frowns at the commotion. "I take it your brothers are here."

"I haven't seen them," I lie.

"Hum."

I force a smile. "It's good to see you again, Elder Leviathan. Give my best to your wife."

Levi's wife passed years ago, but he summons her nightly to his bed.

And that is why necromancers are more than a little creepy. It's also why there is no way in hell I'm putting that ring on my finger. Under no circumstances do I want a necromancer's gift.

"Until we meet again, Tiddy Mun." Like the others, he leaves me to mingle with the more influential members of my family. I'll say it again. This party isn't about me. It is an excuse to get an informal audience with the Devine matriarch—my mother.

I set the jewelry box on the table and flick it away with my fingertips. I might be human, but I'm no fool.

"What did that dirty old man want?" Conrad sets two scotch glasses on the table and slips into the seat beside mine. I breathe a sigh of relief to see him.

"To give Tiddy Mun her birthday present." I gesture toward the ring.

Conrad frowns at the nickname even as he reaches for the jewelry box. He looks inside. "Creepy ass bastard."

"I'm sure he means well." I feel a little guilty. Leviathan is a longstanding family friend. "He said it was an old family recipe or something. It's probably an heirloom."

"I've read about this design. It's the original peeping tom," Conrad says.

I curl my lip and shrug, not understanding.

"Peeping tom?" Conrad repeats, tapping the lid of the box with a chuckle. "The perv wants to spy on you. It's like a magical live cam peep show. Nothing sicker than a motivated necromancer."

"Ugh!" I recoil from the box.

"Incoming," Conrad says under his breath before taking a drink.

"There you are, Tamara." Uncle Mortimer materializes out of thin air, causing me to jolt in surprise.

"Uncle Mortimer." Conrad lifts his glass and takes another drink.

Mortimer ignores him. He briefly studies me before saying, "You look...well."

"Thank you." I start to stand, but he holds up his hand to stop me.

"Our gift for you. Since there is a time urgency, what with your circumstances, I thought I should make sure you saw it." Mortimer hands me a catalog and a pen.

"Oh?" I arch a brow.

"Since at twenty-eight and mortal, you don't have much time left, Tamara," he explains. I really wish he wouldn't have. "Circle your choice, and we'll have it constructed. I put stars by my favorites."

I smile politely as I glance down at a catalog of tombstone designs and high-end mausoleums. I feel the expression freezing on my face. Conrad snickers behind his glass and turns away to hide his laugh.

"The collection on page sixty-three holds up.

We've had friends buried under those for nearly a hundred years, and they maintain well." Mortimer reaches out as if to touch me, hesitates, and then pats me lightly on the head. "Happy birthday, dear heart."

Somehow, I manage to keep smiling. "So kind of you."

Mortimer sighs and nods sadly before teleporting himself to the other side of the room.

"Stop laughing." I kick Conrad's leg. "It's not funny."

"If nothing else, our family is entertainingly full of assholes," Conrad answers, snatching the catalog. He starts flipping through it. "Let's pick the most expensive one."

"Let's not."

Stopping on a page, he lifts it to show a pink-tile-inlaid mausoleum option next to a hand-drawn star. "Ooh, pink! Your favorite. I bet we can get Lady Astrid to put up twinkle lights."

"I hate you a little right now," I mutter.

"No, you don't," Conrad dismisses. "You love me."

"Like I love a common cold I can't get rid of."

"Be nice. You need me." His attention turns toward a leprechaun, and he tosses back the rest of his drink and stands. "Drink that. You'll need all your vitamins and nutrients to get through tonight."

I take a big gulp of the liquor. It burns its way down my throat, but I'm used to it. I've been drinking a lot longer than I'll admit to.

"Meet me in the back hallway by the restrooms," he says. "I'm going to see if I can score some gold nuggets for us and luck into party favors that are a little stronger."

"That is the sweetest thing I've heard all day." I lift my scotch to carry with me as I attempt to slip through the crowd.

It's hard going. No one steps aside to let me pass. I bump into a cold arm. Even clothed, he feels like an ice cube. My eyes lift to Costin's and quickly dart away. His long, black hair is pulled up at the sides. He exudes an intense magnetism when I'm near him that I don't get off the other bloodsuckers. I've heard vampires can mesmerize. I don't want to give him a chance.

"Hello, little castoff." His tone is low and seductive, meant to draw humans in. I'm not falling for it. His hand lifts, and I see long fingernails reaching from pale fingers.

"Thanks for coming," I murmur, stepping back so he doesn't touch me. "Enjoy the party."

I arc around two goblins. Someone taps my shoulder, and I feel a tiny wave of energy tingling its way up my arm. The small infusion of magic makes me lightheaded. I take a few steps before turning. The crowd blurs.

"There she is!" Anthony hooks my arm and swings me around. The family's golden boy is all smiles. "Come on, birthday girl."

I blink heavily. "Where?"

"To the real party," he says.

He weaves me through the crowd, guiding me past the supernaturals. Unlike me, they part in respect for him to pass. A few of them state their birthday wishes, and I do my best to smile as Anthony answers them for me. He's a master at the small talk and quick getaways. When he cuts off a conversation, the other person never feels like he's shortchanging them.

We round the corner away from the crowd into the long hallway leading to the restrooms. I sigh in relief. The murmur of conversation follows us, but we're alone in the hall.

Anthony drops my arm and begins dancing backward. His movements don't keep time with the classical music. Grinning, he reaches into his pocket and pulls out a joint. He waves it between us. "The best spell humans ever cast is right here in this little piece of forgetting."

I feel a little off balance, and my path weaves as I follow him. He stops by a janitor's closet, looks both ways and then lifts the joint to his lips like a finger. "*Shhhh.*"

Anthony does a series of knocks like he's entering a secret clubhouse. The door cracks open, and a hand darts out to pull Anthony inside. I follow, hearing laughter.

Anthony reaches for my arm and jerks me inside the closet. I've met Anthony's secret a few times. Louis is a pleasant enough guy. I doubt he's ever met a party he didn't like. The couple had met on a beach in Miami, and Louis dresses like he's still there with rolled suit sleeves and pastel colors.

"Happy birthday, Tam-tam," Louis says, kissing both my cheeks. "Welcome to Club Janitor."

Anthony tucks the joint behind my ear with a laugh and hands me a lighter before giving his boyfriend attention.

Our parents have many rules, none of which are designed around our happiness. I've never seen Anthony happier than he is in these stolen moments. For that reason alone, I'll always keep his secret. You'd think supernaturals would be more tolerant. They don't care what happens behind closed doors, but Anthony is expected to marry a powerful woman and carry on the bloodline.

The liquor has hit me hard. I should have eaten something before, but that doesn't stop me. If anything, being drunk only helps fuel my questionable decisions. I don't want to be at this party. I don't want to be me. I don't want to feel my death hovering overhead like a cartoon anvil.

The thump of dance music sounds from Louis' phone as he places it on a wooden shelf. The man moves like we're at a nightclub.

As I light the joint, time becomes a blur. I can see the music in the trails of light. My body moves, dancing as if I'm under a spell. I hear my brother laughing. Bits and pieces come through my fog—playful banter, chords of music, being shushed for singing too loud.

The only thing missing is Conrad. I forgot about Conrad.

I feel dizzy, and I hold my head. "I need to use the restroom."

I fumble for the door knob.

"Take your time," Anthony says playfully, smiling at Louis. They begin kissing, and I know this party is suddenly too crowded for the three of us.

I slip out of the closet. It's only pure luck that no one sees me.

Leaning my arm against the wall to stay upright, I slide to the ladies' room. The light seems brighter in the restroom, and I flinch, shading my vision. Stumbling to a stall, I feel the churn of liquor making a reappearance.

I lose time and wake up on the restroom floor inside a stall. The air feels thick inside my lungs, and I try to cough the sensation away. I don't even want to think about the taste in my mouth. I try to push up from the cold tiles, but it's as if my muscles are jelly.

Crawling on my hands and knees out of a restroom stall after having puked and passed out is not my finest moment. No one can see me like this. I need to get back to the closet to hide. Anthony will help me get home safely.

The air smells wrong. White smoke curls under the doorframe. I blink, wondering if it's real or if I'm hallucinating from the joint.

What the hell was that thing laced with?

I grab the handle and pull myself to my feet. The door swings inward under my stumbling weight. Smoke billows, filling the hallway. It hits me like a wall, knocking me to the floor. With each breath, scorching heat sears the walls of my lungs. Yet, somehow, I'm able to crawl on my stomach like a snake through the carpeted hallway away from the inferno that is the banquet room. Screams of panic disorientate me, and I want nothing more than to curl into a ball and make it all go away. But something inside me won't let me give up.

My head spins. I think about finding the janitor's closet, but that would be stupid. No one needs me to save them. What I need is to find a way out. Anthony will be fine. He's magical. He'll make sure Louis is safe, too.

I dig my toes against the floor to thrust my body forward. This has to be the right direction. Right?

Everything aches, and each breath tastes like burned vomit. My chest tightens, and I start coughing as my lungs desperately search for oxygen.

I never wanted this stupid party, and I sure as hell don't want to die here.

EIGHTEEN

"Who are these people?" I ask Conrad, pacing outside the diner as we talk on the phone.

I'm confident that Diana picked it because of the giant statue of a chicken in a tux holding a hamburger on a tray. Other than the statue, it looks like every other roadside diner in the Midwest. I can pretty much guess the menu without even looking at it. I suppose most people find comfort in the familiar.

"Marge and Larry Turnblad." Conrad's voice draws my attention away from the window where I look for Paul and Diana. I don't see them.

"And who are Marge and Larry?"

"Does it matter?" he counters, sounding annoyed. "Don't you trust me?"

I forgive his tone. I should be there helping him with the lawyer and estate instead of bringing more problems to his doorstep. He lost our parents, too. I remind myself to be patient.

"Don't ask stupid questions." I force my voice to remain calm. I know how stubborn he can be when he gets into one of his dark moods.

"*You* don't ask stupid questions."

I take a deep breath and bite my tongue. Silence comes from the phone, and I wait. I again look for Paul but don't see him. I walk along the sidewalk out front to get a better view of the diner's interior.

"They were one of the better foster families I stayed with," he finally answers. "So they're used to having strangers in their house. I wired some cash for you to one of those send-cash-to-anyone-anywhere places, so it can't be traced. Larry will have it ready for you. And there will be a ticket to California waiting for you at the Kansas City airport check-in kiosk. I used Mary's name. You still have that ID, right?"

"Yeah, good old Mary Bennet," I answer. "Never leave home without her."

"Good," he says. "And you're sure about this? About California?"

Fuck, no. Of course, I'm not sure. It's the only plan I can think of. "Yes."

"Fine." He's frustrated, but at least he's trying to hide it. "Just, Tam..."

"What?"

"Don't expect too much. I mean, the woman abandoned you. She didn't want you. Don't forget who your only family is. You and me, sis."

"I know, Conrad. You and me." My heart sinks a little. I finally find Paul sitting at the counter, watching me.

"No one else knows what it's like to be us," Conrad insists. "How can they understand?"

"I know."

"I don't want you getting your hopes up. You tend to romanticize things in your head. You're fragile right now, and it's my job to take care of you. You remember the day I joined the family, right? Our parents said you're my responsibility. I'm in charge."

I frown and turn away from Paul so he can't see my expression.

I don't think that's a fair assessment of past events. Conrad is not the boss of me, even if he likes to act like it sometimes. I find it slightly manipulative that he is using the what-the-dead-parents-wanted argument now.

"I'll bet you even convinced yourself you have a crush on that guy you're traveling with," he says.

I don't like the slight mocking in his tone.

"You know he isn't—"

"Was," I correct. "I *was* traveling with them. And

no. I don't have a crush on some...*guy*. It's your fault I even needed a ride. You sent me off after the funeral with no warning. It's not like I had enough money to hire a cab to get me out of the city."

"I saved you from being arrested. And I warned you about the vampires," he says. "You're welcome."

"I'm lucky I came across someone willing to let me in their car," I amend, trying to stop the tension I feel brewing between us.

"Right? What an imbecile. Who does that? It's like he's never seen a true crime drama." Conrad starts laughing at me. "God, could you imagine? You playing suburban stepmom to some brat? I just got an image of you wearing sweatpants and dropping kids at soccer in a minivan."

I shift my gaze downward to the drawstring pants that Paul bought me, feeling defensive. My heart beats a little faster, and I realize I'm boiling for a fight. I manage to say, "Yeah, crazy, right?"

"Oh, hey, don't be touchy," he scolds, still laughing. "It's not our fault we are the way we are. We didn't have good parental role models. Besides, kids are the reason people like us hire nannies and tutors. We have more important responsibilities. The Devine empire isn't going to run itself."

He can keep the empire.

No. I take that back. I would never abandon him.

"I should go find a ride," I say. "I have a little cash left. It shouldn't be a problem getting there."

"Shouldn't be too hard. Midwesterners are rubes. I remember that much from living there."

"I'll text you when I'm close. Talk later." I hang up on him, unable to take any more of his superior attitude.

It's not exactly Conrad's fault. How can he comprehend the glimpse of normality Paul has given me? He has never experienced it himself. Yes, we ultimately grew up in the same household, but Conrad had to endure certain traumas during his early life that he might not have fully come to terms with yet. Meeting his druggie mother has made it apparent there are things I don't know about what happened to him before he came to be my brother.

All he ever wanted was to be special, powerful, magical.

All he got was frustration and a deep need to be accepted and looked at as superior.

Ego sum avis stultus.

I can't think of the distant past now. I need to figure out today's problems. I've been over the party, again and again, trying to remember every detail, and there is nothing out of the ordinary. The supernaturals were being elitists, like usual. I didn't like the way Costin looked at me like I was an amuse-bouche, but he died. I last saw Conrad trying to score some good luck from a leprechaun. Anthony, Louis, and I got stoned in a closet. My parents were being their normal social selves.

A digital bell dings as I go inside. I want to be next to Paul. I want every second of our time together.

It feels different somehow. Maybe because our time is almost over. Maybe because I lied to Conrad about him when I implied Paul was nothing to me. That lie feels wrong. Necessary, but wrong.

I give a quick survey of the diner. A few customers glance in my direction, but none seem that interested in me.

"Is everything okay?" Paul stands as I near and reaches for me.

I take his hand, needing to feel connected to him. I know it's not real supernatural magic, but I feel as if my energy is flowing into him and his into me. It would be the most natural thing in the world for me to continue into his arms—chest to chest, mouth to mouth, his breath coming into me.

I don't.

Of course, I don't.

But, fuck, I want to.

My gaze flits down to his mouth.

"Tamara?" He arches a brow.

"Tamara," Diana pipes in behind him, "I got you a big surprise!"

I know she's just a kid, and I like her—*I do*—but I want one tiny moment alone with Paul.

Okay, not tiny. I want a big minute. A big steamy minute with no interruptions so we can finish what was started by the back of his SUV.

"What is it?" I force a smile and pleasantness to my tone as I lean over to see Diana kicking her legs from the circular stool. It's bolted to the floor and rocks back and forth without spinning all the way around.

She scoots in her seat and gestures to something hidden under a napkin on the counter. "Open it!"

Paul simply shrugs and nods before tilting his head that I should do as Diana says. I sit beside Diana and pull the napkin to find a strawberry cake donut covered in sprinkles.

"Happy birthday!" she cries, throwing up her hands.

"Shh, honey, not so loud," Paul says.

"Look, it's your favorite, and it has little fairies on it." She points at the sprinkles.

"So it does." I feel myself getting a little choked up at the gesture.

"And..." She reaches for the plate and lifts it off

the counter and wobbles it in the air while making a spooky ghost noise. "*Ooo-ooooh-oh.*"

"It floats," I whisper, wiping at my eye before a tear escapes.

"Okay, that's enough." Paul taps Diana's shoulder.

Diana puts the plate down, grinning.

"It's..." I don't know what to say. It's probably the sweetest thing anyone has ever done for me. "Thank you."

Diana giggles. "You can eat it."

I pinch it between two fingers and take a big bite. With my mouth full, I say, "Mmm, this is the most delicious thing I've ever tasted."

Diana laughs louder. "You're eating fairies!"

"They tickle," I answer before taking another giant bite.

It's best I don't think too closely about how this idea would offend real fairies. Also, that'd be gross.

I tear the donut and offer an unbitten piece to Diana. "Want to try?"

She eats it and giggles. "We should have fairy cakes every day. Can we, Dad?"

I meet Paul's eyes over her head. His soft smile says he's grateful and a little sad. I know the feeling. Our time is almost over. I don't think he's told Diana that I'm leaving them yet.

"It's not a good idea to eat cake every day. I think we should save it for special occasions," he tells her.

"My teacher, Mrs. Larsen, says every day is special," Diana counters.

"Kid makes a good point." I shove the rest of the donut in my mouth.

"Yeah, Dad, I make a good point," Diana repeats.

A waitress appears. "Did your mom like her surprise?"

Diana's expression falls.

"Oh, I'm not..." I hold up my hands and shake my head to correct the mistake.

The waitress quickly sweeps her assumption aside. Something about her face reminds me of a goblin forced to socialize—not how she looks, but how she's trying really hard to appear pleasant with a plastered smile. The expression doesn't meet her resentful gaze. "What can I get you to drink?"

Vodka.

"Water," I answer.

"Water," my duckling mimics, her tone not as excited as before.

"Coffee," Paul says. "Thank you, Ivy."

"Done, done, and done," Ivy answers abruptly as she leaves.

Diana's mood has dampened, and I don't know what to say to bring it back up.

"Why don't we look at the menus?" Paul slides a kid's menu in front of her and reaches down the counter to grab a cup filled with crayons. "You can have whatever you want."

Diana nods as she rubs her cheek.

"Hey," Paul whispers as he leans closer to his daughter. "That lady didn't mean to make you sad. She didn't know. But whatever you're feeling right now is okay. I'm here anytime you want to talk about your mom."

Diana doesn't move. "I want Plop."

I want to say something, but I have no clue what that should be.

"I know, baby," Paul whispers.

I feel like an idiot. I've been thinking of how resilient and innocent Diana is, but she's more than that. She's hiding her pain.

I remember when I was her age. I would do anything to please my parents. It was important for me to make them happy, even if it meant concealing my own anguish and discomfort. Lady Astrid did not have the capacity to deal with disobedience. She'd rather lock us away and not deal with us. But if I was good, if I swallowed my feelings and pleased her, if I logged my exercise hours and listened to the nutritionists and excelled with my homework, then I gave her something to brag about, and she was more likely to let me out of my cage.

Well, cage might be harsh. It was a protected wing of a giant estate.

Then there was Conrad. He did the opposite. He acted out. He was willfully disobedient at first. Even when there was no reason to be defiant, he was anyway. He terrorized the staff with pranks, broke the rules, and touched forbidden books and objects. Then, as the years passed, he became sneakier.

Diana reminds me of me.

What would I have wanted someone to tell me?

"Your dad is right," I say, unsure if this is helping. "It's okay to feel sad. I feel sad about my mom."

Diana gives a small shrug.

Ivy comes back with the drinks. "We ready to order, or do you need a minute?"

"Hum." I pull Diana's menu toward me. "I can't decide between a happy face pancake or chicken tenders and fries. Oh, and mac and cheese. Got to have mac and cheese. What do you think I should get? Mac and cheese pancakes?"

Diana gives a small laugh. "Chicken."

"Awesome. I'll have chicken tenders, fries, and mac and cheese," I tell the waitress.

"You have to be under twelve to order off the kid's menu." She doesn't write it down.

"I want mac and cheese pancakes," Diana giggles.

Ivy sighs and puts her hands on her hips. "We don't have that."

I'm already annoyed with this woman for dampening Diana's mood. I put my hand flat over the menu and give the woman a firm stare. "Then get me the adult version of mine and bring her the pancakes *and* mac and cheese."

She huffs a little and rolls her eyes a bit as she starts writing the order down. All I can think is, *you have one fucking job, lady*. We've had a bad couple of weeks and don't need her taking her shit out on us.

"Uh, yeah, same, the chicken," Paul orders.

I grab a blue crayon and start coloring the picture of a tuxedo-wearing chicken on Diana's menu. It prompts her to do the same. Paul gives me a small nod of gratitude.

A sudden prickle of warning runs up my spine and spreads throughout my body. This feeling has become all too familiar to me lately, and I hate this knot taking up permanent residence in my chest. It's like my mind is on constant high alert, always searching for potential threats even in situations where there aren't any. Despite my attempts to rationalize the feeling away, the unease persists, leaving me on edge.

I glance around at the other tables. Two kids are bickering as their tired mother stares out the window. A young couple appears more interested in their phones than each other. An older man watches his hands as if the mysteries of the universe are hidden inside his coffee cup.

I envy their normal.

The dread doesn't go away. My gaze lifts to a security camera in the corner. It's pointed toward the register.

"Everything all right?" Paul asks. He glances meaningfully at my neck as if to say he notices I'm nervous.

I realize I'm playing with my necklace. I drop the stone and force a smile. "I think we just invented mac and cheese happy face pancakes. What could be wrong?"

CHAPTER
NINETEEN

Here is something I now know for a fact: Syrupy happy-face pancakes, fruit, and whipped cream topped with greasy diner macaroni and cheese is a disgusting idea that should never have existed. For putting this monstrosity out into the world, I feel I must apologize to any future person who tries it.

Then again, there seem to be no new ideas out in the world. I'm sure someone thought about this before me.

Regardless, the disgusting combination made Diana laugh, even if she ended up sharing my chicken tenders and fries. As a bonus, the mess she made of the creation annoyed the waitress, Ivy. Normally, I would respect the waitstaff and not want to make someone else's job harder, but the grumpy woman unceremoniously dropped our plates on the counter and then never checked on us again. Unless you count glaring at us from across the restaurant.

"Leave it. You never know what's going on inside a person. She might be dealing with something horrific we know nothing about," was all Paul said when I offered to throw a fit and flag her down for his coffee refill.

That one comment keeps circling in my head as we drive toward the address on my phone. That is why Paul makes a great parent and why I would not. Conrad is right about that much. Whereas Paul taught empathy and patience in the situation, I would have taught Diana to throw a fit and make a scene.

Or if I were Lady Astrid, the nanny would have watched with disinterest, and I would have been jet-setting the world demanding that the nanny be fired when I saw a roadside diner was on the children's itinerary.

And if I were Lorelai? Well, I would have abandoned my baby to be raised by someone else.

Every logical thought inside me says it's best I sever ties with my road trip companions. And safest.

But that's not what I want. I selfishly want to keep driving on this road forever. I want to feel normal. I want to be tired of the car. I want having a flat tire or defending Diana against grumpy waitresses to be the biggest concern of the day.

I want to be someone else. Anyone else.

I just want to belong.

My father once told me that for mortals, wishes were like riding unicorns. Sure, it might sound fun, but those deadly beasts are meaner than hell and will stab you in the end.

Needless to say, we did not have unicorn sleigh rides that winter.

"Should we...?" I glance back to where Diana is listening to her headphones.

"What?" Paul prompts.

"Should we tell her about where we're going?" I keep my voice soft. "Does she know you're dropping me off?"

"I've been thinking about that," he says. "Yes, of course, we need to tell her. I just didn't want to disappoint her until I had to. She's been better with you around."

Cars pass us, and I notice he's going a little under the speed limit as if he doesn't want to reach the destination. I don't mention it.

"I can't stay," I assert.

"I know." He takes my hand in his. "That doesn't mean I can't wish otherwise."

"Dad, bathroom," Diana says loudly due to the headphones. I hear her feet kicking lightly against the seat behind me.

"Should be a rest stop coming up soon." Paul releases my hand long enough to give Diana a thumbs-up signal before clasping it once more.

I stare at his touch, trying to memorize the sensation. Not for the first time, I feel as if our energies are transferring into each other, like blood, like life. If I let it, the ache the contact causes would create a deep chasm of desperate need inside of me. Instead, I feel the denial hollowing me out, making me face the lonely mortality of my future.

I can't release his hand.

Everything inside me wants to cling to him.

As we near a rest stop, the car slows, and he needs his hand to steer. I'm forced to let go. I feel the pressure against my skin even when he's gone.

The end of us is approaching.

The rest area isn't very busy, but it's daytime, and the manicured grounds are easy to see across. A woman walks her dog over the grass. Empty picnic tables wait for guests. A couple of big rigs are parked in a separate section.

As we all get out of the car, Diana rushes ahead, her hurried footsteps echoing on the sidewalk. Paul strides after her until he reaches the women's restroom door. There, he pauses momentarily, his hand hovering over the handle before he steps back and turns to look at me. Without a word, I nod and follow Diana to ensure it's safe.

Everything about the public space is hard concrete and tile. It smells musty with subtle hints of bleach. I scan the area for potential threats, walking the room length and glancing past the open stall doors. The sound of a broken, running toilet trickles in the background. Except for Diana, the bathroom is empty. Satisfied that she's safe, I exit the restroom and find Paul waiting patiently outside.

"I'll tell her when we get back into the car," he says.

"I wanted to say thank you." I reach for his hand.

I feel the deep need churning inside of me. Yes, it's sexual—*oh my god, yes, the sexual desire practically sizzles off my skin*—but it's more than that. I feel that great big hole inside me needing to be filled with moments, with caring and connection, with belonging, with love.

Love.

I want so desperately to be loved and to love him in return. I want to be worthy of it. I want to pull Nancy out of her vase and shake her. What the hell was she thinking, throwing this family away?

But I was not born for such ordinary things. I

have a life that demands more from me, especially now with the death of my magical family. I think back to what Uncle Mortimer said at the funeral, of how I'll be expected to carry on the bloodline by marrying a person of magic. The thought revolts me now even more than it did then. I won't dwell on it. That's a problem for another day.

"You helped me when I was down, and I will never forget that," I say. "Know that I am forever grateful to you and your daughter. I wish you both nothing but the best."

"You're talking like we'll never see each other again." He frowns, and my emotions mirror his disappointment.

"Our lives are..." I struggle to find the words. Why do the right words always elude me? "We come from different..."

"You mean you come from wealth and power." He starts to pull away, but I don't let him.

"I come from a family of powerful individuals with supernatural responsibilities. You saw how dangerous those things were at the motel. I need to keep that away from the both of you. Once this misunderstanding is cleared up, I'll have to return to that world. I can't leave the entire mess for Conrad to deal with. He would never abandon me, and I can't do that to him. We're all we have." My grip on him tightens. "Please tell me you understand."

He looks reluctant, but he nods. "I understand family and responsibility. I do. I get it."

I knew he would. He's a good man with a good heart. It's one of the reasons I'm so desperately attracted to him.

I try not to look at his mouth. If I focus on it too long, I'll try to steal another kiss.

"Your trouble should stop once I'm gone." I pray that I am right. "But, as a precaution, if you run into any legal issues about any of this, I'm going to send you the private number to the family lawyers. Don't worry about the cost. They're more than compensated. Tell them it's on my account."

He glances at the restroom door, and he gives me a stiff nod. Somehow, I don't think he'll ever call the lawyers for help. He'd want to take care of his own responsibilities. His hand lifts to my cheek. I close my eyes and lean into his touch before reaching to put my hand over his.

"Good. Please use them if you need them." I squeeze his hands harder and stare intensely at him. "Now, this is the most important thing I will ever tell you. I have given this a lot of thought and think I have the best solution. If, at any time, something supernatural tries to mess with you or Diana, I need you to tell them George Devine said you and your daughter are Devine protectus. It's Latin for protected."

"George?" He appears skeptical. I can't blame him.

"George was my grandfather. We lost him to Covid. He was a very respected and powerful man."

"Covid?" Paul repeats as if surprised.

"I know what you're thinking. How powerful can he be if...?" I let out a small, helpless sound, not wanting to revisit the painful memory. It is still difficult to talk about. "The irony was not lost on anyone. He lived for over two hundred years and then was taken out by a complication due to a virus. Even so-called immortals are not immune to the natural world. That's all magic is, really—a manipulation of nature. Covid had everyone on edge. The vampires were wary of their blood supplies. Fairies, wizards, shifters, everyone panicked right alongside us humans. Trolls and goblins were probably the least affected, but they enjoy hiding away in their caves, so the stay-at-home mandates are a way of life. Immortal only means they won't die of old age. It doesn't mean they can't die of something else."

His eyes have widened, and he stares back at me. Softly, he whispers as if memorizing a list, "Trolls, goblins, shifters, fairies, vamp—"

"Hey." I give his hands a small shake. "Listen, don't focus on that. If anything happens, just say, George Devine said you are Devine protectus. They'll think twice about messing with you, even after his death. If not out of respect, out of fear that they'll enact some kind of curse. Trust me, it sounds awful, but humans aren't worth the bother. Not many mortals have that kind of status, so don't go telling it to everyone. If too many people say it, it'll stop working. Protectus takes a lot of magic to enact, and supernaturals are incredibly superstitious. If they ask how, tell them you helped the Devine family with a private matter. Never, under any circumstance, tell them it's not true. Tell them you can't speak of it."

When I return to New York, I'll write their names in the family ledger in case someone checks it later. No one else needs to know that it's not true, and I won't even tell Conrad. However, I like to think that if my grandfather was still around, he would have given Paul and Diana protection for helping me.

He nods. "George Devine said we are Devine protectus."

"Teach it to Diana, too."

"Why didn't we just say that at the motel?"

"That wouldn't have stopped them. They're

hunting me. Once I'm out of the picture, you'll be safer. They have no reason to go after you, especially under protection. Tell them I forced you to help me." Okay, so that's kind of true. It's such an archaic practice that I honestly didn't think about it until after the motel attack. Plus, it doesn't often occur to me to lie about magic when I don't have any.

He keeps staring at me, and I see so many emotions churning through his expression. "Tamara, I wish things were different for us. That we had met under better circumstances and not at funerals."

"I know. Me too." This time, I let go of his hand and reach to touch his face. "But today has to be our goodbye."

I know he wants to kiss me, but we deny ourselves. Any hope for a relationship falls under the wrong place, wrong time category.

"Diana is taking a long time," he says.

I nod in understanding. "I'll go check on her."

I walk into the restroom and take a deep breath. I hear a soft sniffle.

"Diana?" I call, heading toward the sound. "Is everything okay?"

She's around the corner, leaning against the painted cinderblock wall, her face stricken.

"Sweetheart, what is it?" My first instinct is to check the room for danger. I stride past the stall doors, looking inside to make sure they're still empty, before rushing back to her. "Did something happen?"

"You're...going to...leave me," she manages through choked breaths.

I try to touch her, but she jerks away. She's shaking, and I don't know what to do.

"Diana, I—"

She rushes out of the restroom. I hear Paul trying to stop her and then the sound of feet running as he chases her.

"I'm sorry," I whisper weakly after her.

I catch my reflection in the mirror through a streak of dried cleaning product. I don't recognize myself. My clothing is not the neat uniform demanded of my position as a Devine. My hair needs styling products, and my eyes look hollow beneath the mask of dark circles. What is happening to me?

The only familiar thing is the amulet winking back at me in the light. The symbol is fitting—pretty and rich and from an ancient line but containing no actual power. It's me in stone form. Well, me when I don't look like I do now.

My body feels as if I've been steamrolled. Pressure weighs my shoulders, and a grip inside my chest won't ease up.

I've felt the presence of my expiration date since I was old enough to understand death. Never did I think it would come at the age of twenty-eight. Surely, I should get another sixty years.

I think of Anthony, only a few years older than me. He thought he'd live forever like they all do. I try to remember him that last night, but his dancing smiles are a blurred memory of pot and alcohol and only come in flashes.

"*Happy Aging Day, Tam-tam*," his distorted voice teases with a distant laugh. "*Don't worry, I'll find a way to make you immortal. Louis, too, right baby?*"

I can't look at myself. My gaze drops to focus on a puddle of pink hand soap beneath a dispenser on an otherwise clean sink.

Grief unexpectedly bubbles up inside me, bringing along its sister emotion, regret. The sorrow crashes over me like a tidal wave, choking my breath.

I should have told him I loved him and accepted him for who he was.

I should have been the one who died in the fire.

Anthony was prepared to mourn me eventually. I never thought I'd have to mourn him.

I know my brain is avoiding thinking about leaving Paul and Diana. Regret invites guilt to the party.

I'm mentally cycling. I know it.

Two teenagers enter the restroom, chatting

happily and laughing. The sound startles my attention away from the soap. They wear matching yellow shirts with a school logo on the front and athletic shorts. One has house slippers that drag with each step.

I don't want to face that look on Diana's face, but I also don't want to listen to teenagers gossiping about which not-so-sexy old dude golf player from the country club they'd have sex with if they had to pick one to survive their imaginary apocalypse.

They stop and look at me as I stand aimlessly in the middle of the public restroom. Instantly, they start giggling, glance at each other, and not-so-quietly whisper in unison, "Drugs!"

Great, now the golf-whore teenagers are taking potshots at me.

Fuck my life.

I want to tell them that in an apocalypse, they'd be rounded up into a pen and used like breeding cattle by vampires and other variously unpleasant undead. The comeback is a little wordy, so I keep my mouth shut. Also, they're not wrong. I look like shit.

Fuck, fuck, fuck my life.

I leave the teenagers in the restroom without saying anything. Their laughter follows me like a mean girl taunt straight out of high school. I catch part of their jokes as they continue to mock my appearance.

Even though I'm seething with irritation, I force myself to suppress my feelings and try to stop the interaction from occupying my thoughts. Now is not the time to start slap fights with teenagers. I remind myself that those girls hold no significant importance in my life, and I shouldn't allow them to affect me.

What had Lady Astrid taught us? *"Holding on to negative feelings toward insignificant people can only bring you down, and you should focus on the things that truly matter."*

Sound advice, I guess. Although truth be told, our mother considered practically everyone insignificant compared to her. She might not have held on to the negative feelings, but she sure as hell would act on them. Evidently, the thing that truly mattered was always having the upper hand.

Yeah, I don't think Lady Astrid's life teachings can help me out right now.

I see Paul standing near the car, holding Diana. Her head is buried in his shoulder, and he's gently rocking her side to side. When his eyes meet mine, he almost looks apologetic. Or is it helpless? Maybe it's that he's drowning in a sea of sorrow, and he's not sure how to find the shore. That's a feeling I understand.

I hate that I'm the source of their pain.

Feeling dejected, my gaze falls on one of the big rig semi-trucks parked nearby. I consider hitching a ride to spare Paul and Diana any more of my company. I try to see past the reflection on the large windshield to the trucker who might be inside. There is something terrifying but also exhilarating about the idea of climbing into an 18-wheeler. I get the appeal of disappearing into the vastness of the open road with the task of moving items back and forth in an endless loop. The trailer boasts snack cakes, which seem friendly enough on the surface.

My brain instantly ridicules me. Snack cakes? As opposed to what? A trailer advertising torture equipment or vampire blood supplies?

"Tamara," Paul calls out as if he hears my thoughts. He motions his fingers to wave me over as he continues to rock Diana.

The teenage girls' chatter comes from behind me. I think about this intersection of lives, of all the people this rest area sees in a day, everyone moving from one piece of their life to another. I don't belong on any of these paths.

The sunlight feels good against my skin, and the warmth gives me a sense of safety. We're in public, and it is still light out. Nothing bad will happen right now.

I feel myself moving toward Paul like I'm outside of my body. We're about to reach our end. Just one more small ride, and then it's over.

The anticipation of that event makes the feelings inside me worse. I'm having a hard time seeing what tomorrow should be.

"I'm sorry," is all I manage to say to them.

Diana won't look at me. Paul shifts her weight onto one arm and reaches to open the passenger door for me before carrying his daughter around the vehicle.

I hold on to the door and glance around the rest stop. The teenagers are getting into the back of a minivan. The sound of slamming car doors effectively cuts off their laughter. A semi-truck's engine revs to life.

"Tamara?" Paul asks from the driver's seat.

I nod and climb inside the SUV.

"Plop!" Diana cries out.

The sound startles us, and we both turn in our seats.

Diana is hugging the stuffed animal to her chest, refusing to look at me. I can tell that its fur is muddy like it had fallen into a dirty puddle.

"You found him," Paul says. "That's great, honey."

"Where was he?" I ask. "Can I see him?"

Diana glances at me and pointedly looks away, not answering. I can't help but wonder at the psychological damage I've inflicted on her from being in her life.

"Paul?" I insist. "We looked everywhere for that thing. Where did it come from? Did you see anyone by the car?"

"The car was locked, and I was in view of it the whole time," Paul says as he starts the engine. "It was probably stuck under the seat. It's fine. I'll wash it when we get to my parents' house. I'm just relieved we found it."

I get out of the car and look in the back windows to ensure no one is hiding inside. Then, I search the surrounding grounds for anyone watching us too closely, wishing there was some neon sign pointing into the bushes, blinking the message, *"Watch out. Ghoul hides here."*

I find nothing. Someone once told me that female mosquitoes drink blood and buzz at a difficult-to-hear frequency. When you hear buzzing, that's the males, and you're safe. It's when you hear nothing that you need to worry.

Well, right now, I see nothing, and I'm definitely worried.

I slowly get back into the car.

Paul backs out of the parking spot and puts the

SUV into drive. I keep watch, trying to take note of all the cars and semi-trucks in case we see them again later. That could mean we're being followed.

"I knew you'd never leave me, Plop. I knew it." Diana hugs the toy tight and rocks it back and forth.

"Seat belt," I whisper. She pointedly ignores me.

"Seat belt, munchkin doodle," Paul orders. This time, she listens.

CHAPTER
TWENTY

Mr. and Mrs. Turnblad live in precisely the kind of quaint Midwest suburban house I'd expect from decent foster parents in a made-for-TV family movie. It's small but well taken care of with a fresh coat of paint in a warm, inviting color and a white picket barrier around the flower beds surrounding the house. Toys are scattered about the fenced play area, but I don't see the children who go with them. At first glance, it appears the Turnblads have created a happy environment for their foster children. I can see why Conrad remembers them fondly.

"This looks better than the last neighborhood," Paul says as he cranes his neck to check out the house.

"Thank you for the ride." I reach for my backpack behind me, hooking it with my arm as I clutch my phone. My eyes meet Diana's. She holds her dirty stuffed animal. "May I say goodbye to Plop?"

Diana thinks for a moment and then hands the dog to me. I work my hands over the toy, squeezing it and checking the seams for signs that someone has messed with it. It appears harmless enough, but I don't like how it showed up after we all looked for it.

"Goodbye, Mr. Plop." I reluctantly hand the animal back. To Diana, I say, "Thank you for being kind to me when I needed it. You're a very remark-able person. I'll miss you. I..."

What more can I really say? Nothing is sufficient enough to express what I'm feeling, and no amount of pouring out my desperation will make their lives better.

"Goodbye." I get out of the car and push the door shut behind me.

"Hey, wait, Tam—" Paul's voice is stamped out as the door slams.

I turn and lift my hand to say goodbye, but I can't make eye contact. It takes all my energy to focus on walking toward the house.

Don't look back.

Don't look back.

The words are like a mantra as I take each step. I feel the phone vibrate in my hand and glance down.

A text from Conrad reads, *"You there?"*

I type back, *"Just arrived. All good."*

I hear the front door open and plaster on a smile as I look up. A kindly man greets me. His fingers are splayed as he waves from the porch. He wears a pink and white apron with ruffled edges over a button-down shirt and khakis. I assume the apron embroidered with the words "Queen Chef" belongs to his wife.

"Mary?" the man calls out from the small porch. "I'm Larry. Welcome! Welcome! Come on in. We've been expecting you."

Larry is excited to see me. It's a strange feeling.

"I hope you like pot roast," he says, holding open the door as I approach. "Marge took the kids to a skating party, but they'll be back in a jiff."

I reach the concrete steps leading to the porch. I listen for Paul to drive away, but his engine idles behind me.

Before I can answer, Larry is talking again. "How was your trip? You're coming from New York, right? Con—"

"Tamara!" Diana's hoarse scream forces me to turn around. Her car door is open, and her small legs fall out of the back seat. "Don't leave me!"

"Who's this?" Larry asks.

I ignore him as I move to intercept Diana.

"Diana," Paul says sternly, getting out of the car. "You can't keep jumping out..."

I bend down to catch the girl as her small arms wrap tightly around my neck. The impact of her weight causes me to stumble slightly, but I manage to keep my balance. As I'm about to stand upright, I soothe, "It's okay—"

Boom!

A deafening explosion resonates behind us, and a wave of intense heat engulfs my back. My body flings forward. I can't stop the fall, so I instinctively turn to shield Diana from impact as we plunge onto the grass. A storm of fiery debris rains around us, and the all-too-familiar smell of smoke soon follows.

Diana screams in terror. I roll over to protect her, hoping the worst is over. Paul dives onto the grass and slides next to us. He covers us with his body.

Diana trembles violently. Paul's weight presses into my back, and his leg pins me down. I hear thuds as pieces of the house land all around us. The force of the explosion leaves my head stunned as if someone struck me on the back of my skull with a baseball bat. My hammering heartbeat is the only thing I hear as everything else becomes muffled. I'm not sure how long we stay like that, muscles braced for the worst, thoughts frozen in fear as we will the seconds to pass.

"We're okay," Paul says, but the words are more like a plea than a statement.

Gradually, noises start to invade the numbed silence. Neighborhood dogs bark erratically, adding to the chaos. Shouts erupt from people coming out to see what happened.

I try to steady my breathing, and we're slow to untangle our limbs. When I manage to turn, I see the fiery husk of the home in ruins. Flames eat at the wood, sending smoke and sparks into the air. The embers catch my eye, reminding me of the night of my birthday when I watched fiery butterflies turn to ash. I had been drunk and high then and probably hallucinating a little, but I'm sober now, and I can still see the shape of them in the dying embers.

Larry is on his stomach on the lawn.

"Larry!" A man in a bathrobe appears next to him. "Who's inside?"

Another man in workout gear is trying to get near the front door. He shields his face as he tries to brave the fire.

"Stop," Mr. Bathrobe yells. "They're not home."

I didn't hear Larry answer, but he must have.

"Diana, look at me." Paul moves behind me. "Does anything hurt?"

Dazed, I watch the pandemonium unfolding in front of the burning house.

Another fire? This can't be happening.

Three fires in my proximity can no longer be written off as a coincidence. I can't deny the truth. Someone wants me dead, and they have no problem taking out innocent bystanders to do it. I think of the foster kids who could have been home. By the grace of some universal force, they had a skating party. I would not have been able to bear it otherwise. There has been too much death around me.

"Are you all right?" A woman appears over us. The flames backlight her red hair, making it seem like she's on fire. I recoil from her.

Paul's hands move over my body as he examines me. "We're all right. We're all right."

The only person he seems to be convincing is himself.

Eyes from the gathering crowd move from us to the house and back again. We sit in a clean patch of grass. Miraculously, the debris has fallen in a perfect circle around us.

"You're lucky you weren't hit," the redhead says. "Give thanks. Someone up there is looking out for you."

Why is the woman staring at me as she says it? Did she have something to do with this? I want to ask her what she knows.

Paul grabs my face, forcing me to look at him as

he stares at my eyes for several seconds. "Your pupils look normal. I think you're okay. Just in shock."

"I have my hose," a man shouts as he tries to use a garden hose to fight the flames. He assumes a wide stance and blocks the stream with this thumb to make it spray farther. It would be comical if it weren't so dire.

"The fire department is on its way," another neighbor adds. "Wet Jack's house. Keep it from taking out the neighborhood."

The amateur firefighter redirects the stream of his garden hose to the neighbor's siding.

"Move the cars. Clear a path," yet another neighbor shouts. "Take those kids down the block, Janet!"

"Come on." Paul shoves my backpack at me before lifting Diana into his arms. "We're getting out of here."

I follow his lead as we get into his car. The man in the bathrobe waves him to drive as they try to clear the road for the emergency vehicles.

Paul weaves the SUV through the debris and then keeps driving. No one tries to stop us. I roll down the window to look. The wind whips the back of my head as I watch the scene disappear from view.

Dark smoke filters into the sky, marking where the house is located. Sirens echo, but I don't see the fire trucks. The SUV seatbelt alarm starts to ding, warning me to get into my seat and buckle up, but I ignore it.

I roll up the window. The inside of the car smells like smoke, and I realize it's emitting from our clothes.

"Diana?" Paul asks, breaking our heavy silence.

The girl sniffles in response.

The sound springs me into action, and I crawl into the back seat and slide next to her. I place my arm around her and pull her against my side. Plop is on the floor, and I grab the stuffed animal to bring it into our hug.

Diana isn't shaking like I expect her to be. Is she in shock? Two explosions in less than a week, plus a funeral, plus the motel. I can't help but think I've irreparably scarred the poor child.

I tried to do the right thing by them, and something terrible happened. Again.

"There were toys in the yard," Paul says, stunned.

"The Turnblads are foster parents," I say. "The kids and wife weren't home."

Paul nods that he hears me. "Thank goodness. That could have been so much worse."

Conrad said the Turnblads are good people. They don't deserve this. None of them deserved to meet me. I'm cursed, and it's affecting those I encounter.

What the hell is going on? Who is doing this? Why?

"It's all right, honey," Paul says. "Everything is going to be all right."

I know he's not talking to me, but I take comfort in his reassuring tone.

"I know." Diana's hand snakes up to toy with my necklace. "I'm not scared. We're protected."

My eyes meet Paul's in the mirror.

"It's pronounced protectus," I correct.

"What?" Diana frowns in confusion.

"I didn't tell her about that yet," Paul says.

"It's like a magic spell," I tell her. "Whenever someone scary frightens you, tell them you're Devine protectus."

"I'm Devine protectus," she repeats.

I give her a light squeeze. "Good. Don't forget it."

"Does this mean I get a magical necklace like you?" she asks.

"No, sweetie, this necklace isn't magical. It's just a necklace," I answer.

She looks at me like I'm lying. I think of the circle in the debris on the Turnblads' yard. Then, I remember the feeling of heat from the gas fire at the apartment. And the vampires at the motel. We should be dead. All of us. But we're not.

I touch the amulet. Surely, I would feel it if magic was at work.

I think of my birthday as proof that it's not magical. If not for the firefighter, I would be a pile of char next to Costin. That pain was unforgettable and very real. I almost died.

"Does this mean you're staying?" Diana asks.

"No, I can't." I hate the idea of having to say goodbye to them again. Each time, it gets more difficult.

Grief, regret, and guilt trap me in their relentless vortex. They weave around me, tightening their web with each passing second. I feel like I'm locked in a whirlwind of negative emotions and can't fight my way free.

"But why?" Diana insists, her voice a borderline whine. Her arms tighten.

How are all parents not just walking around in an exhausted haze all the time? I can't even be classified as a parent, and I feel the total weight of Diana's neediness on me. I want to comfort her, but I also want a break to figure out my own head so I can say the right things.

There's that guilt again. I shouldn't be such a selfish asshole. She's just a kid, and this is my fault.

She's looking at me with such need and trust.

"I have to visit someone." I don't know how much to tell her. I direct my voice toward Paul. "Just drop me off. I'll get a taxi."

"No." My arm muffles Diana's voice.

Paul grips the wheel. His lips move, but he doesn't speak the words aloud. Our car navigates the sea of traffic, smoothly keeping time with the other vehicles. I'm unsure where he's going, and I don't think he even knows. I glance into the windows of passing cars for signs of danger. Eyes briefly return my stares from blank expressions. None of them act as if they recognize me, but I can't help but feel danger is lurking everywhere around us.

I don't want to die.

I don't want to be alone.

I'm not sure either reality is up to me.

Paul takes a deep breath and keeps his death grip on the wheel. "We're close to my parents. I will drop Diana off with them, and then I'll take you where you need to go."

"I'm not sure that's a good idea," I say. What if the curse follows me to his parents?

His knuckles have turned white. I sense the worry he tries to suppress.

"I don't mind calling for a ride," I insist. "I can figure it out."

"We should talk," he answers.

"I think I might be..." I look at Diana whose head is buried against my arm. She clings to me. *"Unlucky."*

He nods and reaches for his phone. When we come to a stoplight, he dials. Seconds later, I hear an inaudible voice answer.

"Hey, Dad, we're in town. We made it," Paul says. The light turns green, and we start to move forward. "I have to drop off a friend somewhere, but is there any chance you can meet me and pick up Diana first?"

I hear what sounds like excitement, but I can't make out the words.

"Yeah, how about the parking lot outside that old barbeque place where you took Mom that one year for your anniversary?"

I hear laughter coming from the other side of the call.

"Just don't bring her back any ribs," Paul says. "I'm not sure you're out of the doghouse yet for that one."

More laughter.

"About twenty minutes? Great. See you there." Paul hangs up.

"You're not supposed to talk and drive," Diana scolds.

"I know, honey. I'm sorry. But grandpa and grandma are so excited to see you. He says your grandma is making five different kinds of cookies."

"With fairy sparkles?" Diana perks up a little.

"I don't know. I guess you'll have to find out." His voice is upbeat, but it doesn't match his expression. "He also said they have new board games in the closet. I bet if you ask him, he'll let you pick one out."

"Why can't you come, Tamara?" Diana is back to pouting and making me feel guilty. "You like eating fairies. You can have as many as you want."

"Diana, we've already explained that Tamara has to visit someone. She's an adult, and adults have responsibilities. We can't hold her hostage." Even stern, Paul's voice is kind.

If I ever dared to question my father, he'd have bristled in irritation and then waved me away, thus cutting off all communication for the rest of the day. On the other hand, if I questioned my mother, I'd find myself running an additional hour on a treadmill or with an evening of extra homework. Lady Astrid believed that if I had the energy to annoy her, I had enough energy to better myself. If my childhood was any indication, I annoyed her often.

For all their bad qualities, I still miss them.

The burn of tears threatens my eyes, but I force them back.

I wish I could keep the memories from triggering. I want my brain to stop dwelling on the past. It's not helping anyone, especially me. I've been feeling sorry for myself ever since I woke up in hospital quarantine after the first fire.

Warm tears slide down my forearm. My little duckling mimics me again, and she doesn't even know it.

"I don't want you to go," she whispers.

I don't want to leave. All I can do is hold her. There is nothing more to say.

TWENTY-ONE

Ben Cannon looks exactly as I imagine Paul will in thirty years, with salt and pepper hair and a thicker middle. They have the same kind eyes and easy smiles. I'm struck as I watch them. The happiness they feel at seeing each other radiates. They genuinely care. I notice them whispering and can only imagine it's about Nancy's death as Ben checks in on how his son's handling things.

"Papa!" Diana runs, arms wide, toward Ben. Her legs kick in anticipation of being lifted off the ground. He gives her a little twirl.

I feel a twinge. I miss my grandfather.

I have to look away. My eyes fall onto a restaurant boasting the best barbeque in Kansas City. The smell of cooking meat permeates the air from a smoker somewhere outback, overtaking the scent of the city. The bright red and white paint mimics the colors of the local football team. A beefy, hairy gentleman in flannel standing at the window looking out at us makes me think this place would make a perfect beacon for werewolves. Something about his large hands reminds me of the fist trying to hand me a sweaty handkerchief at the funeral.

"How was the trip?" Ben asks.

Paul says something polite and non-alarming in return.

Even though we're in a city, it doesn't feel like New York. No place feels like New York City. It's hard to explain. The vibe is gentler here. Strangers make more eye contact.

Or possibly they're making contact because I'm staring first.

"How's mom?" Paul asks.

"Doing better," Ben answers. "She hated not being there for you."

"I know," Paul says. "But I'm glad you didn't have her make the trip. Is she feeling better?"

"She gets tired easily." Ben forces a smile to hide his worry. I've seen Paul do that exact same thing. "But knowing a certain little girl is going to pay a visit has put a pep in her step."

"Oh, yeah, sorry. Dad, this is our friend, Tamara," Paul says, forcing me to turn my attention back to them.

I'm aware of how messy I look, and I give a nervous nod. "Nice to meet you, Mr. Cannon."

"Oh, Ben, please," he automatically corrects. "So, what brings you to Missouri?"

"I thought we were in Kansas," I answer in surprise.

"Almost," Ben laughs. "Common misconception being as it's called Kansas City. The state line is a short drive that way, which cuts the city in two. So what brings you to almost Kansas?"

"Oh, um." I glance at Paul for help. "I'm just passing through. Paul was considerate enough to give me a ride."

"Me, too," Diana says as her papa lets her slide to the ground.

"Right, Diana, too. She was nice enough to let me tag along." I absently work the tip of my finger against a jagged thumbnail, picking at it.

"So, how do you all know each other?" Ben smiles as if he is well-versed in the art of polite conversation. The question is meant to break the ice, but there is a natural undercurrent to it that is hard to ignore. His eyes have no judgment when he looks at me, and I'm grateful for that.

I wonder how much Paul has told his parents

about his situation with Nancy. Technically, Paul was still married up until a few weeks ago. Even without the added complexity of the paranormal reality, my being with them could appear unseemly.

"It's a long story. I'll tell you about it later," Paul answers.

"Her parents and brother died," Diana pipes up matter-of-factly. "Their funeral was by my mom's."

The unexpected answer catches Ben by surprise, and I see him struggling to find the right words to respond. The instant concern in his expression reflects his sincerity as he clears his throat and says, "I'm sorry for your loss."

I nod. "Thank you."

He doesn't pry for details, and I'm thankful for that.

"Are you hungry?" he asks, motioning toward the restaurant.

Paul gives a small laugh. "What would Mom say if she found out you were crashing your diet?"

Ben gives a playful frown and waves his hand. "Who wants to live forever if all you get to eat is salmon and salad? Besides, what she doesn't know..."

"I'll tell her," Diana inserts. "And you'll be in *trouuu-ble!*"

"Oh, you'll tell on me, will you?" Ben feigns disappointment as he reaches for her, but it's clear from the twinkle in his eye that he has something mischievous planned. He tickles her, and her childish laughter echoes through the empty parking lot, filling the air with her infectious joy. It warms my heart to hear her playfulness. Anything is better than crying and clinging to my arm in the car, begging me not to leave her.

I don't belong here. Wanting something and getting to have it are two completely different things. I hug my arms to my waist and wait. I want this moment to be over, like ripping duct tape off your skin. The ripping off a band-aid metaphor doesn't do my heartache justice.

Paul's eyes meet mine, and he glances toward the car as if silently telling me we're going to leave soon. I nod once.

"Speaking of diets, Grandma's kitchen is currently covered in cookies," Ben tells Diana. "I have it on good authority if I bring back a certain little girl, and if that little girl asks nicely, she'll let me have some."

"You get fish!" Diana teases.

Ben recoils. "Fine. Then you distract her, and I'll steal some anyway."

Diana lets out an impish laugh and nods in agreement at his plan. She hunches her shoulders and holds out her fingers like grabby claws to show how she'll sneak for the cookies. "Like ninjas!"

"Cookie ninjas," Ben agrees. "I bet I can eat more than you."

"Nuh-uh," Diana counters.

"Ugh-huh," Ben banters.

"Dad." Paul grimaces and shakes his head with parental concern. "Try to throw a vegetable in there, would you?"

"And ruin the sugar rush?" Ben teases. "Sorry, *Dad*, but grandparents don't have to do vegetables. Our whole job is to spoil. I retired from vegetable duty when you moved out of the house."

"Yeah," Diana mimics, "sorry, Dad!"

Ben affectionately slaps his son's back. Paul drops his head forward in mock defeat and shakes his head.

The familial scene only makes the ache inside me worse. What would it have been like to have a life like this one? They're so effortless in their affections.

"Say your goodbyes, kiddo," Ben instructs. "Your grandma is going to have my head if I don't take you to her."

Diana's cheerful demeanor suddenly shifts as she looks at me. Her smile fades, and I see sadness creeping in. Before I can say anything, she rushes toward me and tightly wraps her arms around my waist. For a moment, it's like she's holding on for dear life.

I get it. Her world has been shaken, and she doesn't want to lose more.

"Dad, let me talk to you for a moment." Paul motions his father away from us and starts talking in a low tone. Ben glances in our direction with concern.

I pet Diana's hair. "I want you to remember a couple of things for me."

She looks up at me.

"First, fairy sprinkles taste better after they float."

She nods as if it's the most logical advice in the world.

"Second, do you remember the magic spell?"

"I'm Devine protectus," she answers.

"Good job. It'll keep you safe." I cup her cheek. "If anything scary like those men from the motel bothers you, you yell that at them as loud as you can to make them go away."

I hope and pray it's true.

"Come give me a hug." Paul crouches to be at her level.

Diana leaves me to give him his hug.

"Let's go, squirt," Ben says.

"I'll be by later tonight," Paul says. "Call if you need me."

Ben offers his hand to Diana and walks with her to his pickup truck. "Nice to meet you, Tamara."

"Nice to meet you too," I call after them. I watch Diana.

"Ready?" Paul pulls out his keys.

I nod even though I don't want to leave. It's not lost on me that I wanted this moment over seconds before, but maybe the metaphorical duct tape can restrain me a little longer before I tear it off.

He comes to stand beside me as we watch them climb into the truck. Tears threaten as I think of never seeing Diana again. I want to take back all those moments of irritation I felt on this trip with her.

"Did you warn him to be careful?" I ask.

Paul nods. "I had to say something. Diana will surely mention seeing the fires."

Worry etches his features, and he tries to hide it behind a smile. Even though he doesn't look directly at me, his hand reaches for mine, squeezing it.

"He'll keep her safe," he says, almost to himself more than me.

"You should go with them." I pull my hand from his. "I'll be all right on my own."

"No. We need to have a conversation," Paul says.

The burly man in flannel watches us from the restaurant window. Logic says he's probably checking to see if we're customers, but I don't like the attention. It would make sense, though, if a werewolf opened a barbeque joint. They do have ravenous appetites.

"You're right. I owe you at least that much." I get into the SUV and glance into the empty back seat.

I've had moments alone with Paul, but Diana was always nearby like a mini chaperone. Now, we are totally alone, and I find myself nervous.

My gaze moves to watch his strong hands as he starts the car. "Where to?"

"Bus station," I answer. Yes, Conrad has an airplane ticket waiting for me and flying might be faster, but I don't want to be stuck at thirty thousand plus feet in the air with supernaturals after me. At least with a bus, there is a chance of escape.

Paul grabs his phone as the SUV idles in the parking lot.

Assuming he's looking for directions, I lean my head against the window and stare out at the restaurant. Mr. Flannel is no longer at his post, and Diana and Ben are gone.

"The bus to California doesn't leave until eleven thirty tonight." Paul places his phone on his lap and puts the SUV into gear. "We have time before I have to drop you off."

I watch him navigate into the city traffic. The car

hums softly with the gentle vibration of the engine. He seems to know the area.

Paul had mentioned earlier that he wanted to talk, but now he's silent. He seems lost in thought, staring ahead at the busy street in front of us. The view is a mix of opposites. Public spaces filled with trees are nestled between blocks of cement structures.

Watching him drive, I'm mesmerized by the movements of his hands as they guide the steering wheel. I remember what they felt like holding me when we kissed behind this very vehicle at the motel. The memory brings with it a flood of sensations. My lips tingle, and I long for his mouth, soft and warm against mine. I want the heat of his body pressing close as his hands roam with a passion that leaves me breathless.

But he might as well be a million miles away.

The ache of wanting something so bad and knowing I can't have it is worse than any punishment I've ever endured.

We pass by a hotel, and I reach for his arm.

"Stop here," I whisper.

He looks over in surprise. I don't blame him. I surprise myself.

Paul enters the small parking lot and finds a spot before turning off the car.

The red brick·hotel looks like the kind of place you don't want to be caught after dark. I see a bony figure sleeping in the shadows next to the building. She's wearing shorts and a tank top, and I detect red scabs on her skin. There's a sadness to the façade evident in a century of dirt and mold staining the once proud exterior. I can imagine all kinds of human tragedies emanating from inside its walls. Why not add my heartache to the mix?

The one thing the hotel has going for it is that it's here. I'm tired of being in the car, staring at Paul's hands, mile after mile. I'm tired of the annoyingly persistent ache inside my body. I'm tired of feeling alone, scared, and on the run. I want to be somewhere no one will think to look for me, and this forsaken place in the middle of Kansas City is it.

I don't dwell on the fact that no one should have been looking for me at the last two locations.

Nor do I let myself think about how self-centered I am by dragging Paul once more into my vortex. I'm greedy and selfish. I want at least one moment to carry with me after I say goodbye.

"Diana seems like she's going to be all right," I say, more for myself than for him. I remember Paul mentioning that his dad had been a firefighter. Somehow, that knowledge makes me feel better.

"She loves hanging out with my parents. They

spoil her rotten and hardly ever say no." Paul gives a small laugh. "It'll be good for her to be around family."

I'm going to miss that little duckling. Our parting was not the dramatic goodbye I thought it would be. In the end, she just drove off with her grandfather. No tear-stained eyes pressed against the glass as they faded into the distance, like the turning point in some movie.

But life isn't a movie. This nightmare is all real.

TWENTY-TWO

We sit in the car, not moving, both of us hesitant to leave. My nerves are on edge. I'm as eager as a bookish freshman being invited to a senior prom afterparty by the football captain. I want to be with him, but I'm suddenly anxious now that the moment is before me. My hands shake, and I hope he doesn't see it.

The hotel looms like an unspoken question neither of us will ask, even as it silently beckons us to enter. The growing sexual tension between us is palpable.

"I guess I'll start," Paul says with a deep breath.

"Let's get a room," I say at the same time. I know he thinks we need to have a deep conversation right now, but that's the farthest thing from my mind.

"Here?" He frowns and leans to look at the building. He shakes his head. "Let me take you somewhere else."

"It's here. We're here. No one will think to look for us inside." My heart is beating fast, and I feel breathless. We're adults. We both know what I'm after.

For a torturous moment, I think he might say no.

"Okay," he answers.

The word is soft and not as confident as one might hope after such an offer. I imagine he is silently fighting with himself, trying to talk himself out of this. There are so many reasons why we shouldn't.

I know what I want. It's the same thing I shouldn't have.

One taste. I make myself promise that it will only be this once. Then I will leave him alone.

My hand continues to shake as I reach for the handle. My senses are on overdrive. As the door opens, the smell of the city hits me in the face. It reminds me of the inside of a parking structure with a combination of car exhaust and old motor oil mingling with a fragrant bush in a concrete pot near the street.

My eyes turn downward to a section of wet

parking lot where a tiny stream flows from a leaky hose. It runs over chipped concrete and loose gravel. A beetle runs toward it. I step over, feeling like a giant towering above a tiny village. A butterfly starts to land. The door slams shut behind me, startling the insect and sending it fluttering away.

As I join Paul at the back of his SUV, I glance to ensure no symbols are drawn in the dust. If supernaturals wanted to track the car, they could use the license plate, but I have a feeling the symbols were more of a taunt. Some creatures like to play with their food.

A feeling of dread lingers on the edges of my thoughts, plaguing my mind with a suffocating sense of foreboding. It's a thick fog, relentlessly swirling like invisible ash from the raging fires I'm trying to escape. Even now, the memory of the scorching heat lingers on my skin. Flashes from my childhood try to surface, just random moments when I've felt alone and unsure.

"What is that look?" Paul reaches to touch my face. "Where did your mind go just now?"

I blink as I focus my gaze on him. His kind eyes are filled with concern.

"Please, tell me," he insists.

"When we were kids, my oldest brother Anthony and his friends invited Conrad and me to play with them in the woods. It's a game magical kids use to hone their skills called Hunter and Hunted. It's like Hide and Seek, but we draw cards, and then everyone searches for their particular thing. Anyway... Part of the rules is that the woods are enchanted, and you can't leave them until you find your target. We got split up. It felt like I was lost out there for days. The forest was so dense, and the branches kept scraping my skin like the trees were reaching for me. I could barely see the path, let alone know where to follow it."

It's a stupid story that has nothing to do with anything. I want to stop telling it the moment I start.

"What made you think of that?" he asks.

I give a small shrug. "Because I have never again felt that alone and helpless until now."

And terrified. The dark woods with those grasping trees gave me nightmares. The heavy weight of fear on my chest is oppressive.

He stands by the SUV, not trying to hurry me inside. His hand remains on my neck, strong fingers curled around my nape, simply holding me. I feel his rough calluses against my tender flesh.

Paul leans in, looking like he wants to kiss me. "You're not alone."

But I am alone. This is only a stolen moment.

And yet, the movement of his hand brings with it a sense of relief and connection.

"I know you're scared, but you found your way out of the forest. You'll find your way out of this." He gives me a comforting smile. His stroking fingers stir my pulse to racing.

A driver blasts their horn as two cars zip through traffic, nearly causing an accident. The sound amplifies my uneasiness.

I take Paul's hand and hold it as I pull him toward the hotel entrance. I want to get out of public sight. My heart is beating so hard that it nearly chokes me. I feel tiny vibrations joining our hands as if his life force is slipping into mine. I know that's not a real thing, but I feel like it is every time I touch him.

It's a surreal feeling walking into the hotel with Paul, like I'm not really me, and I'm not really here. But I force myself to remember each passing detail. I don't want to forget him or this moment.

The lobby is surprisingly clean, even if it is run down. The small black and white hexagon tiles on the floor look like they've been there since the 1920s. They create the kind of pattern that will make a person dizzy if they stare at it for too long. The textured walls are uneven, but the chips in the paint have been brushed clean so they don't curl from the surface.

A man with a cloth rag twitches as he rubs it in jerky circles against a small window. His green sweater has patched holes. With each stroke, he blows from tight lips to make a soft whooshing noise. For a second, I worry he's supernatural, but one look at his face tells me it's more likely he's on meth. Sometimes, it can be difficult to tell the difference.

I go to the front desk. Without looking up from his car magazine, the clerk waves his hand over a clipboard and says, "Eighty bucks. Sign in."

The varnish on the wooden counter has been worn clean in spots. On an old clipboard, I see several Mr. and Mrs. Smiths staying at the place. A pen is attached to it by a yellow string. I release Paul's hand to write the same sign-in names. There's comfort in knowing this place values secrets.

Paul places cash on the counter.

"Rob, you're done," the clerk says as he turns to grab a key out of a basket next to him without getting up.

The meth addict swipes forty dollars and drops the rag over the rest before darting out the door. The clerk tosses a key next to the rag.

"Up the stairs. Number's on the key." The clerk flips his page and sighs like he was forced to run a marathon. Almost as an afterthought, he mumbles, "Check out is at nine."

Paul takes the key and stares at it in his hand. "You deserve nicer."

It's sweet but unnecessary. We all deserve a lot of things that we're not going to get. That's life.

Scratch that thought. He's more than I deserve.

I can't help but be captivated by the exquisite details of his face. A hint of beard shadows his jawline, giving him a rugged masculinity. His hair is messy from being blown around outside, but he doesn't nervously fuss with it. His lips are slightly parted in breath. His mouth is beautifully chiseled and perfectly firm. Whoever crafted his design had the talent of a classical sculptor. I imagine godlike hands molding him with the sole purpose of tempting me.

None of that compares to his light brown eyes and how they make me feel when they penetrate me. All I want right now is to be alone with him. I put my hand over the key to hold his. The rough calluses on his palm tell me he's good with his hands.

I don't see an elevator, so I lead Paul to the stairway. His eyes stay on me as if he's also trying to memorize the moment. It's as if he sees through me, down to my very soul, and he's not turning away from what he finds there.

I hear movement on the floor below as the front door opens and feet shuffle. A strange groan greets us from above. Tortured human in the grips of addiction? Or a grumbly goblin hiding out until dark falls over the city?

I step faster, exhilarated and terrified all at once. I wish I knew the supernatural population of Kansas City so I would know the odds of running into something, but the truth is I never bothered to wonder about it until now. The thing about being a New Yorker is you tend to think New York City is the center of the universe. And not to be elitist, but it kind of is.

Is this finally happening?

I say a silent prayer that this building doesn't catch fire, at least not before I quench the flames inside of me.

Is that wrong? It feels like that comparison might be a little wrong.

Who cares. I can't feel bad about that now. Desire aches deep inside me, swimming in an empty cavern, desperate to be filled. I need this to happen.

Anticipation builds as we near the top of the stairs. The air feels electric against my skin, snapping with the unspoken desire pulling us together like two magnets. I can't help but stare back at him, barely watching where I'm going.

Someone passes us on their way down, grunting with each step, but I don't see a face. My mind has stopped clinging to the details of our surroundings and is now focused entirely on Paul. All that matters is getting him alone so that our desire can completely consume us.

Fuck, I want him.

I want him so badly that every piece of me hurts with the longing.

I'm not a virginal wallflower. Sex has never scared me. I've never seen it as scandalous. Trust me, there is plenty in this world that should frighten us. Maybe it's because supernaturals tend to be a little less puritanical compared to most humans. Old fashioned in their ideas, yes. Discreet in their affairs, sure. Puritanical about bodily functions, no. I should know. I'm a product of my parents' apparently open marriage. As long as public image is maintained and we do what is expected of us, no one cares what vices a person has in the bedroom.

But this feels like more than an animalistic connection. Paul is different than other men. I care about him.

I feel the hard keychain in our clasped hands as our shared body heat makes them sweat. We reach the second-floor landing, and I can't contain myself. I swiftly turn to face him. I use my free hand to pull his neck toward me. My body melts to his, and each inch of contact sends a shockwave through me. Our lips meet in a fury of movement.

Nothing is stopping this from happening.

All the voices in my head shut up except for one primal creature that propels me onward. The world falls away until nothing matters but this, us, him. Paul.

"Paul." His name escapes my lips only to be swallowed by our kiss.

My heart races. His back comes up against the hallway wall. Painted red doors offer privacy, but I can't be bothered to open them. His chest is hard to my soft, molding my breasts through our t-shirts. Fingers splay my lower back. I want to feel his hands where they belong, gliding warmly against my naked skin.

I feel my body turning, only to become trapped between Paul and the wall. Someone clears their throat, but we ignore them. They don't matter.

Raw hunger and need consume me.

"I call next ride," a man says as he passes.

Paul reluctantly breaks the kiss and glares after the guy. I grip him tighter to keep him from defending my honor.

Our labored breathing fills the narrow hallway, the harsh sound a testament to our passion. He releases my hand, and I feel the hard edge of the key gliding up my wrist before skating along my arm, causing me to shiver. The sensation of his kiss lingers on my lips, and I can still taste him.

Paul leans to study the door next to us. He lightly touches its room number before pulling back and glancing at the key in his hand. A sense of urgency brews between us as he grips my arm and leads me across the hall.

Paul unlocks our private sanctuary. My hands roam over his back, urging him to hurry. The wood creaks open on loud hinges, revealing a room suffused with warm, soft light.

This place isn't pretty. Melancholy clings to its walls like barnacles on a sinking ship, but I can think of nowhere else in the world I'd rather be.

Dust particles lazily swirl in the sunlight that streams through the parted curtains, casting long, slanting rays across the room to illuminate the sparse decoration. The walls are painted a yellowed white with lighter squares left over from missing paintings. The empty nail holes are still burrowed into the wall. There is a strange silence, punctured only by the sound of our breath and the swish of our feet on a worn brown carpet.

He shoves the door shut, and it reverberates with a decisive thud that amplifies my growing desire like a playful slap on the ass. I feel my insides jolt in excitement.

Paul sucks in a deep breath and lets it out slowly. It's sexier than anything he could have said.

He crosses the distance to me, and we crash together in a passionate embrace. He's everything I've ever wanted—sexy, kindhearted, mortal like me.

I cling to him like I cling to this moment, pulling at our clothes to get them out of my way. I hook the heels of my shoes with my toes to kick them off. My shirt lifts over my head, trapping my arms briefly. Warm hands on my waist steady me as I struggle to toss it aside. My mind wants to savor, but my body doesn't listen. It needs to end the ache that has been simmering below the surface since the first time I saw him at the cemetery.

As I toss my shirt onto a small table and begin work on my bra, Paul follows suit. He's more graceful than I am. Muscles move beneath his skin, beckoning my fingers to their peaks and valleys. I see the tiny scars attesting to an active life. His strong hands move to his waist, and I watch him unbutton his jeans. I can barely stand the anticipation of this moment. I love his confidence. But why shouldn't he be confident? He's beautiful.

When he comes to me, I push my pants down my legs, taking the underwear with it. Paul walks me back toward the bed, pausing only to pull the covers back to inspect the sheets. They appear clean, and I fall back onto them, pulling his arm so he comes with me. Nothing about this moment represents my normal life. That makes me love it more.

I want this. I want this more than anything. I would give up all the money, power, and knowledge I have for a life with Paul, even if that life was spent in hotel rooms like this one because he would be with me.

I want to ask him how Nancy could have cheated on such a perfect person. There's a small fear that wonders if she saw something I'm not seeing. My judgment with men hasn't always been stellar in the past. But that's the last thing that I'm going to ask about. It's the last thing I want to think about.

Knowing this is my only chance to be with him creates a strange urgency, as if I need to fit in as much as possible into the short timeframe. We're all hands and scratches as we claw at each other. Our mouths move in a frantic rhythm. I can't tell who is trying to devour whom.

I want to absorb him into my skin. I want to remember his smell. I want to lock this moment into eternity.

Why does life have to be this hard?

Why can't I have this one thing for me?

The ache is almost too much to bear as it wars with the desire inside of me. My mind keeps trying to skip to the end as if bracing itself for the pain that is sure to come. I force my thoughts back into the moment. I notice the way his hand cups my breasts and how his thumbs tweak over my peaked nipples. I feel the threads of passion weaving from those movements.

Threads of passion? Did I actually think that? Suddenly, I'm in a cheesy romance novel.

A tiny laugh escapes me, and Paul pauses to pull back and look at my expression.

"That tickled," I lie.

Paul grins and rubs his thumb over me again, sending a tiny shiver over my body.

His head nudges mine aside. His mouth finds my neck and ear. He braces his weight as his chest presses against mine so as not to crush me.

I explore his back and waist before my fingers roam lower to cup his ass. My legs are intertwined with his, and I wiggle them free to open myself to him. I pull his hips forward, begging for more. I can't take this damn empty ache.

"Shit," he whispers.

The comment takes me by surprise, and I freeze.

"Condom," he mutters.

The departing weight of his body leaves mine

cold. For a shocking moment, I worry he might not come back. I lift up on the bed to find him digging through his jeans for his wallet.

I guess I should be grateful that one of us is being practical. I'm ashamed to admit I didn't even think of it—not that a baby is a great idea right now or ever.

"Please, please, please," he says to himself as he searches the clothing for his wallet.

I start to feel self-conscious and draw my limbs close to cover my nakedness. Sexual denial stings each oversensitive nerve ending. If fate cock blocks me in this moment, I will never forgive the bitch. It would be beyond cruel.

"Yes. Got it!" Paul displays the small metallic packet in victory before rushing back toward me. In obvious relief, he says, "That was a close one."

He sits on the bed and tears the package open with his teeth. I reach for his back, rubbing it as I watch him put the condom on. With a small moan, he rolls back on top of me to resume where we left off.

He's breathing heavily, and I can see the effort it's taking for him to remain in control of himself. His hips settle between my legs. I feel the cool, intimate brush of a condom along my thigh. I can't contain the shiver of anticipation that runs over me. He draws his arousal confidently against me, and I stiffen in the seconds before he thrusts inside.

I pull his hips with my legs. He glides deep to fill me completely. I cry out at the pure pleasure.

This. This is what I needed. Him. Deep inside me. Connecting. Being. Here. Now. More.

The deep ache only gets worse as the hunger grows. My body wants to fuse itself to him so he can never leave. His kiss is tender as he thrusts his body against mine. Lids partially cover his eyes as he watches my reaction. I've never felt more connected to another person. He wants me, no games, no manipulations, no ulterior motives. He's here despite all the reasons he should run away from me.

There is something fragile and perfect about being with another human. There are no aggressive power games or magical restraints. It's more meaningful because we're both temporary.

Paul's hand wraps my wrist and holds it against the mattress.

Well, okay, now. Maybe there is a little aggressive restraining. I'm definitely here for it.

Time. It haunts us. It takes and takes and rarely gives. And right now, I will take every single second fate will let me have.

I want to go slow, but my body doesn't listen. We come together in frantic, desperate thrusts. He grips my hair. I bite his lip. Our limbs are a tangle of move-ment. I shift my weight, pushing him onto his back as I ride him onto the mattress.

Pleasure comes too fast, taking siege of my body. My fingers dig into his chest as his hands grip my hips to hold me to him. I want to cry out, but my breath catches in my throat. Warm gratification floods me, stretching over my core to my limbs as I tremble with release.

For the sweetest of seconds, we are perfection.

A loud, sharp rasp sounds as I finally manage to pull in a deep lungful of air. Heart hammering wildly, I try to catch my breath. His harsh pants match mine in a beautiful melody that only lovers can appreciate.

The tremors of my climax take time to settle, and all I can do is stare down at him. I know when they stop, reality will come crashing in, and I don't want it to.

This can't be the end of us.

This can't be our only moment.

Fuck. There it is. Reality.

Fucking reality.

I struggle to hold back my tears as I move to curl up next to him, seeking comfort in his near-ness. As I settle in, I can feel the cool sheets against my skin, the scratchy texture creating a sharp contrast to the comforting heat emanating from his body.

My fingers skate along his chest in lazy motions, and I watch where they make contact. His hand covers mine, pressing my palm down to stop the movement.

"I hate that I brought you here." Paul sighs as he stares upward. I follow his gaze to see the stained acoustic tiles of the drop ceiling. Someone had launched a pencil into a panel, which now hangs stuck overhead.

"I hate that I brought chaos into your life," I counter.

His brow furrows, and he turns onto his side to study me. "I have to ask you something I've been wondering about."

My stomach tenses. "Ask."

He cups my cheek. "What particular thing were you supposed to find in the enchanted forest game?"

A tiny laugh escapes me. "A fairy ring. I thought it was jewelry. Turns out it's a ring of mushrooms."

"How did you get out if you didn't know what you were looking for?"

"My grandfather ended the game when I didn't come home. He came to get me." I briefly touch my necklace. This isn't exactly what I want to be talking about right now. "I think he would have liked you."

"I take that as a high compliment." He lightly taps the stone of the amulet before jerking his hand back with a laugh. "It shocked me."

"That's weird." I touch the stone and don't feel anything. "We must have worked up a static charge."

He traces his finger along my cheek and jaw before gliding down my neck. "Not surprising. You're electric."

I chuckle at the compliment and swat at his hand. "You're a little cheesy."

He shrugs. "I'm okay with that. You're a lot beautiful."

I enjoy the intimacy of being next to him like this, but it can't last. I'm only making it harder for myself. He's looking at me with such an open expression.

"I think Diana might be right. This stone is magical like your grandfather said." He smiles but avoids touching the amulet again.

I bite my lip, widen my eyes, and shake my head in denial. I firmly believe I would know if that were true.

He sighs in frustration. "Gah, you are a frustrating woman sometimes. Something has been keeping us safe. Haven't you noticed how the light changes with a blue tint when danger is near?"

"It's..." I try to think of a way to explain it. I force

myself to sit on the bed and turn so my feet dangle over the floor. "Dumb luck."

I'm not magical. I don't have magical things. I can't cast spells. I'm not supernatural. It's the one fact that has been drummed into me since birth.

He touches my back. "Did I say something wrong?"

I have to be firm about this. "No, we just did what we came here to do."

Ick. I want to swallow the words back into my mouth. I sound like an insensitive ass.

"I came here to have a conversation." The bed moves behind me, and his hand continues to roam over my back and hip. "The sex is great, don't get me wrong, and I'll gladly do that anytime you want, but there are some things we need to talk about."

"Like what?"

"Us." The word comes out a little too quickly. He didn't even need to think about it.

"There is no us, Paul. We can't allow ourselves to pretend that this has a future. We're just a moment in time. This one moment. When I leave tonight, that's it."

His hand drops away, and I instantly want it back.

"What if I don't see it that way?" He sounds irritated. I can't say I blame him. I'd be irritated dealing with someone like me, too. "I'm not going to freak you out by saying that this is true love, but I mean, we could be...*something*...you know? Tell me you don't feel it, too. Tell me you didn't feel it in that first moment at the cemetery like we were being pulled toward each other. I know it's not the romantic story that every girl dreams of, but you're not every girl."

"The fires? The vampires?" I whisper before I glance back at him. "You have all the evidence you need about my life."

He lightly touches my waist, tracing the curve. "I like you."

"I like you, too, but—"

"But what? That should settle it." He gives my hip a light slap.

It seems letting him down gently is not the way to go. Or doing it rationally, for that matter.

"What more evidence do you need?" I stand, frowning. "Everywhere I go, something explodes. Hell, this hotel might catch on fire soon."

He glances around. Why is he not scared?

"To be honest, I'm more worried about germs and junkies," he says.

"Three fires," I state, hands on hips. His eyes dip over my naked body, and I realize I should probably get dressed. I start looking for my clothes as I continue, "and a vampire attack. That's not normal. I know I'm not blowing shit up. I don't have that kind of pyrokinesis power, but something is happening. I'm cursed. It's not safe for you, and it sure as hell isn't safe for your daughter."

I find my underwear and pants. Shaking them out, I pull them on at the same time.

The mention of Diana changes his expression. Good. Finally. I seem to be getting through to him.

"Let's think about this logically." He sits up on the bed. Sheets cover his lap, but barely. The sexy indent by his hip shows. My hand flexes, and I want to touch him there so badly. "Who would want your family dead?"

I shrug. "They were some of the most extraordinary magics in the world, but feared and loved are not the same thing. They probably have enemies I don't even know about."

"Who would want you dead?" He looks at me like he already suspects an answer.

I find my bra and turn my back to him as I wrap it across my back and fumble to latch it against my stomach. My hands shake. "No one. I'm nobody."

"Who had the addresses for all three fires?"

"No one," I dismiss.

"Who knew you'd be at the motel?" he persists.

I hate his tone. It's know-it-all, and it's pissing me off. "We didn't even know we would be there."

I hear a loud sigh as he moves on the bed. I keep my back to him. Why won't this stupid bra latch?

"The first fire was my birthday party. Everyone knew about it. Lady Astrid invited a who's who of the supernatural world." I finally get one latch to hook, and I twist it around so that I can loop my arms into the straps.

"And the second was where?" He sounds a tad condescending now.

If I were a puncher, I'd hit him. "Conrad's birth mother's house. No one knew about her. He kept her a secret."

"And the third?"

"Conrad's foster parents," I mutter the words, not wanting to say them.

"And who did you tell we'd be at the motel?"

Damn Paul. Damn him to hell.

"It's not my brother," I yell, twisting around to glare at him. "Get that out of your head right now. You don't know. You don't understand what our life was like. You can't just go accusing him of-of... Of things!"

"Then who else knew?" Paul stands naked by the bed, utterly unashamed that he's dangling for the world to see.

Well, for *me* to see.

I avert my gaze, refusing to be distracted. Even angry, I'm attracted to him.

He holds up his hand and begins listing off his evidence with flicks of his fingers. "Conrad's family. Conrad's remaining sister. Conrad's birth mother. Conrad's foster family."

"So you think someone wants to hurt Conrad?" Even I don't fully believe my conclusion. "Like he made someone mad, and they want to hurt him in retaliation?"

"Why would he tell someone who is mad at him where to find you all those times?"

I realize this is the reason Paul insisted on being alone with me to talk.

"It's not..." I shake my head. Part of me hates Paul for even putting this doubt in my mind. "He's my brother."

"Did you text him where we were staying before the vampires came?"

I give a half nod. A hot tear slides over my cheek before dripping onto my chest. I did tell him. He worries about me. I wanted someone to know where I was.

"Do you think your phone is compromised?"

I want to say yes, but all our phones are magically protected from hacking. I can barely get the admission out. "It's not likely."

His expression says more than he ever could. I can't meet his gaze.

"And if you're out of the way, who gets all that Devine power and money?" Paul's tone softens at my tears. "Who is there now making all the decisions regarding the estate? Who is dealing with the lawyers? I know you don't want to see it because you've lost so much, but I say this because I care. Often, the simplest answer is the right answer. Tamara, I'm sorry, but I think your brother is trying to kill you."

TWENTY-THREE

Devine Country Estate, Eighteen Years Ago...

"You're not supposed to be in here," I warn.

Conrad hunches over the spell books in the library. We're not allowed to touch them, let alone read the secrets inside, but he has never shown fear of the rules. If he's told he can't do something, it's a sure thing that he'll want to try.

"I'm just reading." Conrad dismisses. His tie is abandoned on the floor, and he'd thrown his suit jacket over a bust of some old wizard. The sleeves of his shirt are rolled up to his elbows, and I can see a stain he's trying to hide. "In case you haven't caught on yet, touching things will not make your insides explode. That's just Lady Astrid's version of Santa Claus—an acceptable lie you tell children about magic. I'm almost thirteen. You might be a baby, but I'm not a child anymore."

"I'm not a baby," I protest.

Touching the books and paintings might not poison us like she claimed it would, but trying to wield magic as a mortal would end up just as badly.

He gives a tiny scoff. "You probably think Santa is real."

"I'm not stupid." I frown at his sour mood. "If any supernatural creature were to go around giving presents to a bunch of children in the middle of the night, I have one word for them."

"Pedo?" Conrad mutters.

"Run," I say at the same time. I'm not sure what his word means, but I'll never admit it.

I watch him, waiting for him to give me his full attention. I'm bored and want to be distracted.

"What do you want? Are you going to tattle on me again?"

The accusation hits me like a slap to the face, and I bow my head. When he says nothing more, I look back to where he's sitting by a lamp. I slowly make my way over and sit on the arm of the couch.

"What are you reading?" I ask.

"You're too young to understand." He waves me away.

I slide onto the couch cushion and inch closer to

him. I try to see the words on the page. "I'm almost as old as you."

"But you're not." He dismisses me by angling his back toward me like a wall.

"Do you want to go outside?" I ask him. "Charlotte says it might rain, but I don't care."

"No." He turns a page.

"Come on. Anthony has his special lessons all weekend, and I'm bored." I inch closer and nudge him with my elbow. "Let's build a fort."

He makes a point of pulling away from my touch. "I should be the one taking lessons. I'm the oldest."

I notice he likes pointing out that he's older than both Anthony and me, not that it matters. I could say that we've been in the family longer, and in that way, Anthony is the oldest, but I know from experience that arguing only feeds his displeasure. I think Conrad enjoys quarreling with people.

"They should be teaching us what they're teaching him," Conrad continues. "This is our world, too. It's like they want us to be helpless."

I shrug.

"I'm never going to be helpless again," Conrad swears. "No one is going to hurt me. You watch. I'm going to do what I want when I want."

This conversation is boring. I don't want to have it again. "Anthony is magical. We're mortal.

There's nothing you can do about that. Just accept it."

"I can become a vampire," Conrad disagrees.

"Ugh, gross!" I wrinkle my nose and try not to gag. "They drink people and have no souls. And they always feel cold, like meat in the fridge."

He sneers. "You don't know what vampires feel like."

"I do so. Costin touched my hand once."

"His name is Constantine," Conrad corrects.

"He said I could call him Costin."

"That's stupid. Constantine sounds scarier. I'd pick a better name than Costin if I were a vampire. He sounds like he belongs in the bargain bin."

"Whatever." I want to tell him this conversation is stupid, but I don't.

"Maybe I'll be a necromancer," Conrad considers, tapping his book.

"Ew. That's worse. They play with dead people." I shake my head. Then, teasing, I say, "What about a werewolf? Then I can finally have my puppy."

"No. Werewolves are filthy beasts. No one respects them." Conrad frowns. "I can use potions and learn spells. I'm just as good as the rest of them. I'm smarter than Anthony."

"Mom and Dad—" I start to say.

"They're not my real parents." Conrad glares at

me. "They're probably not really your parents either. That's why you're nothing."

I know that's not true. My parents are my parents. They wouldn't lie about that.

He's in a cranky mood. He gets like this when Anthony goes on his special trips.

I flop back on the couch and stare at the ceiling. I don't like the paranormal, not like Conrad does. He's always trying to find ways to be in that world. I just want the supernatural to go away so I can live a normal life. I want to go to the parties when the house is full of guests. I want to go to school and not a room with a tutor. I want to play baseball in the park with other kids when we are back in Manhattan.

"Do you want to raid the kitchen?" I suggest. "You can lift me up so I can reach the cookies."

"Astrid is going to make us run an extra hour if she catches you," he warns. "Now, leave me alone so I can finish this chapter."

"Want to see if we can summon Mr. Farty's ghost?" I ask, using the supernatural as a last-ditch effort to entice him away from his task. "I know how to make a spirit board."

"Ghosts are stupid. When I summon something, it'll be a demon, and he'll burn everything in the fires of hell." He flips another page.

I hate it when he's like this.

"Go away," he says. "I have to keep to a schedule if I want to get through all these books."

I look at the shelves, and my eyes drift over the towering wall of ancient tomes that rest there. The worn and faded spines attest to their age despite being well cared for by my family for centuries. The sheer number of books is staggering, and the task of reading all their boring words seems insurmountable. Many hands have flipped over their pages—supernatural hands. Their knowledge is not meant for us. The second Conrad broke the code to make them readable, he's been obsessed.

"We're never going to be them." I try to tell Conrad, but my words are too soft, and he only glances at me in annoyance. He might be older, but there is one thing I understand better. We can't alter who we are. We're mortals, and no amount of wishing is going to change that fact.

TWENTY-FOUR

"*Ego sum avis stultus.*" I stare at my hands as I sit on the bed. Paul is close enough that I can feel his heat, but we're not touching. He put on boxers but nothing else. I know he's giving me time to process what he's concluded. I don't want to believe him. I mean, it's Conrad.

Conrad. My brother. My family. Out of everyone in my life, he knows what our childhood was like. He knows the isolation and fear we grew up in. He understands the burden of not being extraordinary.

"What does that mean?" Paul asks.

I give a small, humorless laugh. "I'm a stupid bird."

"I don't understand." Paul lifts his hand as if to touch me but holds back.

"You're not meant to. It doesn't matter. It's just a

thing we used to say as kids." I touch my arm, remembering what it felt like to be broken, as I stared up at the empty high balcony where Conrad had given me the fake fairy dust. Then, the vampire Costin appeared.

I think of Costin turning to ash under my hands. If I let myself, I can still feel the pressure releasing against my fingers as he poofed into his eternal rest. The guy could come off as a creeper, but I didn't wish him dead.

There are so many memories. My brain can hardly sort through them. I see all these moments—young Conrad putting his arm around me when I'm crying, him tormenting the staff, staring into bonfires, endlessly reading on the couch. And then I see us older, standing quietly under Lady Astrid's inspections, holding my hand while I dangle from the balcony as we sneak out of the country estate, holding the elevator outside the Manhattan penthouse as I run toward it. Arguments. Make ups. So many moments. So many tiny things build to create a relationship between two people.

Standing, I find my shirt and tug it on before retrieving my shoes and socks. I move because I don't know what else to do.

Conrad? There must be another answer.

I can't think of one that makes as much logical

sense. There are things about my brother's personality that I don't want to see. I always forgive them because I know what our lives are like. He's not perfect, but he's not a killer.

He can't be.

"You're wrong about Conrad," I say, hoping my firm tone will convince Paul I'm right. "You don't know him."

"I don't know your brother, but maybe that means I can see things you can't. You're too close to—"

"Shut up. Just shut up," I command, practically yelling. My hands are shaking, and my entire body feels tight. "I know my brother is not perfect. I know he has his issues. Who doesn't? I mean, look at his childhood before he came to live with us."

Paul stares at me but doesn't comprehend what I'm talking about. Of course, he doesn't. His parents are normal, and his family is uncomplicated compared to mine.

The truth is that Conrad never talks about his childhood before he came to live with us. I know he was adopted. I know he bounced around foster homes before my father found him. I've seen scars that look like old cigarette burns. I met his drugged-out wreck of a birth mother. He has reasons to be messed up.

Have I been blind when it comes to him?

Conrad has always craved power. He has a desperate obsession with being what we are not. He wants to be supernatural, wield magic, and have the kind of fearful respect that comes with the greatest of authority.

I never thought he'd turn that obsession against me.

Maybe he hasn't. Paul could be mistaken.

This is my world. Not Paul's. He must be wrong.

I hate this. We should be cuddling on the bed, basking in the aftermath of pleasure. I don't want to be thinking about any of this.

"We should go." I look around the room. It no longer feels like a sanctuary. "You need to be with Diana."

"You didn't text your brother that we're here," Paul says, getting dressed. I hear him moving, but I keep my gaze averted. "I didn't give you my parents' address, so he shouldn't have that."

I finally look at him. "That's why you had your dad meet us at that restaurant instead of at his house. You didn't want me to know where they lived."

"She's my daughter, Tamara." It's not an apology. I don't expect it to be one. "And to be clear, I don't want your brother to have the address or any other information about us. I might be wrong about him, but I'm not taking that chance."

I nod. "You're a good dad, Paul. That's why I know you'll let me go. You have to protect Diana."

He wants to protest. I see it in his face.

"You know I'm right about this." I try to smile, but I'm not happy. I hate this.

"And you know I'm right about your brother." He reaches for me, and I step back. If he touches me, I'll find myself back in his arms. I need to hold on to my sanity. "I don't feel right abandoning you to deal with all of this. You shouldn't be alone."

My loyalties are torn. I hate him for saying that stuff about Conrad. I don't want to believe any of it.

"You have no choice." I pull on my shoes and look for my phone before realizing I left it in his car. It doesn't take a master manipulator to figure out his weakness, but it does take a bit of an asshole to exploit it so bluntly. "If you love your daughter, you'll protect her and forget all about me. Diana just lost her mother. Do you really want to risk her losing her father too?"

The words have their desired effect. I see the shock. It's worse than if I had just slapped him. Then comes the doubt and guilt, crossing over his features in predictable waves. It's almost too easy to get him to do what I want. I guess I learned more cruelty from Lady Astrid than I thought.

Resignation radiates from him. "Promise me you'll be careful."

"Sure." I try to smile but soon give up the effort.

Something has shifted between us, and I know I caused the wedge. I finally did what was right, but the loneliness of that decision looms over me. My family is dead. Conrad can't be trusted. Everyone else in my life is supernatural, and they look at me like a pet human.

I'm not just losing Paul in this moment. I'm losing the secret wish he represents, that hope of family and normalcy.

I feel it hardening me. I've been locked under a haze of grief and depression since before the funeral, but now I feel anger peeking through at the injustice of it all. The ground beneath me had been shaken the night of my birthday party. I've been a broken version of the woman I fought so hard to become.

"We should go." I look around the room but don't see anything else that is mine.

Paul is dressed, and I catch him doing the same before he looks at me like he can see through me and all my posturing. "I feel like we could have been something."

The words are so surprisingly honest. They shake me to the core, and I can't answer.

He sighs and goes to the door. I can't be sure, but I think to hear him whisper, "I'm sorry you're determined to throw that away."

The details of the hotel no longer glimmer with the promise of anticipation. I see it for what it is—a sad place filled with miserable lives.

I can't judge those around us. I'm here, too, aren't I? This place now keeps the memory of my broken dreams forever within its walls. They're as real as the stains on the carpet.

It occurs to me that endings are always unhappy, and my life currently feels like a series of endings.

CHAPTER
TWENTY-FIVE

There is nothing more to say. That doesn't mean wishes aren't bubbling up inside me, screaming to get out as I watch Paul open the driver-side door to his car. He's asked me again to let him drive me to the bus station, and I've adamantly refused. If I get in his car, I'll never leave him.

Don't go.

Tell me again that we have something.

Refuse to leave me.

Say you love me and want to be with me. Only me. Forever.

Don't leave me alone.

Don't leave me. Don't leave me.

Don't leave me...

I project my thoughts toward him like I have some kind of psychic power to make him hear them. I don't, and he doesn't. I'm mortal. I can't make him read my thoughts. And it's wrong for me to say them out loud.

So here I find myself, standing beside his vehicle, holding my phone and backpack like some vagabond, saying nothing and feeling everything.

Paul gets into the SUV and sits with the door hanging open. His hands rest on the steering wheel like he doesn't know where else to put them. His fingers work restlessly, rubbing along the circular curve.

"I'll be back in New York next week." He reaches for the door. "I'm sure you can find me."

As he's pulling it shut, I step forward to block it. The door hits my backpack, bumping me toward him. I touch his arm. All these thoughts are in my head, pleading with the universe for the perfect solution.

I want to keep touching him. I feel the tiny familiar shiver traveling from my fingers where they make contact with his skin. The feel of his kiss is embedded on my lips.

"Thank you," I manage, "for..."

What more can I say? I give a small shrug.

"Thanks for the ride." I release his arm and step back.

"You know where to find me." Paul pulls the door shut with a firm thud.

The finality of the sound makes me jump a little. I step back. My chest is tight as I stare at him through the window. I know this is the end of our journey.

He turns on the engine.

This sucks ass.

I take another step back and then another, forcing my legs to move when they don't want to. All these words and thoughts are swirling inside my mind in a jumbled mess. Everything I want in this moment wars with the nothing I can have.

My gaze sweeps over the back of the SUV. There are no more symbols drawn in the dust. He waits with the vehicle idling for a long time, and I simply stare at his window, hoping for magic to ripple over my life and change its course into something better. I touch my necklace and will the flash of the blue he was talking about to happen. I wish it could protect me and change the past so that this moment, this ache inside my chest, never happened.

Fate hates me.

Magic doesn't come.

He puts the car in reverse. His eyes meet mine, obscured by the reflection of light on the glass. I wait for him to nod or wave, but he doesn't. His attention turns forward, and he drives out of the parking lot.

I don't know how long I stand watching the road before I feel a vibration in my hand. It shakes me out of my thoughts, and I slowly look down at my phone.

Conrad.

I don't answer. I just let it ring until it stops.

When I look at my missed calls, I see he has tried to reach me sixteen times but has left no messages.

I remember the fire. Is he worried I'm dead?

Or is Paul right, and Conrad is checking to ensure he's finished the job?

I hate myself for thinking it.

I look up directions to the bus station and hike the backpack on my shoulder. Maybe it's big-city elitist hubris, but the streets of Kansas City have nothing on New York. I would almost feel sorry for anyone who tried to fuck with me right now.

Desperation and anger make very complicated bedfellows, and right now, they are duking it out inside me like two tweakers over the last batch of meth.

Speaking of tweakers, I noticed the man Rob from the hotel lobby curled up in a covered stairwell. His eyelids fall heavy as he stares past me in a daze. I know I should feel better about my situation. Other people have worse demons to fight.

I must be selfish. That thought doesn't turn my darkening mood around. My heart beats so loud I can hear it in my ears. It causes my feet to move faster until I'm striding down the cracked sidewalk.

I don't know what to do. I don't have any answers.

Usually, I'd call Conrad to talk it out, but I don't know who I can trust. I kept thinking all three fires were connected to me, but they were more connected to him. Paul was right. I don't want to see it.

This is my new reality. There is no one to bail me out.

My phone dings, and I stop walking to read a text from Conrad. *"Call me."*

He's my brother. When I think of him, I see that lost kid being thrust at me on my sixth birthday. I remember a domino of moments, crashing into each other—studying with the tutor, sneaking candy, daring each other to make eye contact with an unshifted werewolf, moving out of the family penthouse, and subsequently having to move back in when life proved to be more challenging and more expensive than we thought.

Could he betray me? Yes, a part of him is broken, but I love him, and I know he loves me in his way. I don't want to doubt him.

I don't stop to consider while I dial the phone. As it rings, I start walking quickly along the route to the bus stop.

"Law offices of Mabon and Beck," a cheery woman answers.

"Tamara Devine for Mr. Mabon."

"One moment, Miss Devine."

"Tamara." Mr. Mabon's deep, boisterous tone reminds me of a drunk politician commanding attention at a party. I don't know why. It just does. There's an unappealing arrogance to him with just a hint of smarmy. I'm unsure if that's the lawyer part of him coming out or the hint of the siren in his ancestry. Sirens are known as master manipulators who use their voices to persuade victims.

Still, I guess confidence is something you want in your attorney.

I'm unsure why I called him or what I expect to learn. Maybe I just want him to reassure me or to be a kind voice on the other end of the phone. I don't have anyone else I can talk to about what's happening. And, I mean, that's what he is paid to do—answer my call.

"I didn't get a chance to tell you how sorry I am about your family," he says when I don't speak, but he has told me several times. "What can I do for you?"

"Is this call protected?" I ask.

"Are you on your secure cell phone?"

"Yeah, I—"

"Go ahead."

I keep my eyes forward, only glancing side to side when I have to cross the street. "I want to know how much trouble I'm—"

"Can you be more specific?" He has a habit of talking over me, starting his sentences before mine are finished. I'm used to it.

That question is ominous. How many problems do I have? "The fire—"

"Do you mean to ask if the family estate is liable for the damage?" Mabon clears his throat. "No. Nothing to worry about there. They might not want your family's patronage for a while, but there are other event venues. I'm sure they'll come around when they realize they need the supernatural more than we need them."

Does he seriously think I'm worried about future party planning?

"I mean the detectives," I insist. "The ones that came to the funeral looking for me."

"Ah, yes." Mabon clears his throat before chuckling to himself. "NYPD's finest. Don't you worry about them. Your parents' past contributions have not been in vain. They'll huff and puff as the old fairytale goes, but they're not blowing down any doors."

I feel a tiny inkling of relief at his assurances.

"If there is someone to blame for the fire, the vampires will find them for us," he continues. "Supernaturals have ways the local law enforcement does not."

And just as quickly, that relief drains away.

"I don't want you to worry. Worrying is what you pay your lawyers for. You just take care of yourself. Like I told Conrad, the estate paperwork is all set. It will be here waiting for you to sign as soon as you two return from your trip. You're one lucky little lady. Your parents made sure you're well taken care of."

You two? Why does he think Conrad is with me?

"We'll see you when you get back from California. Goodbye now." Mabon hangs up the phone.

The call was supposed to make me feel better. It hasn't. Coldness creeps over my body. Mabon doesn't know anything about the police coming after me, at least not in the way Conrad claimed. And why does he know I'm going to California? My brother clearly didn't think I'd call the firm as I trusted him to just take care of things—well, trust with a healthy dose of avoidance. I'll own it. I can avoid with the best of them. And if Paul hadn't put that doubt in my head, I wouldn't have checked in.

How many lies?

I hate this path I'm on. I hate feeling like I have no one I can turn to. I could call Uncle Mortimer, but he'd only want to discuss a suitable supernatural stud to my broodmare. I could call some of the people I used to work with, but work friends aren't the same as family. They'll just mumble apologies for my loss and then pry for answers to things I can't discuss. There's the staff at the houses, but I'm not sure they even like me.

As I walk along the sidewalk, lost in my thoughts, I suddenly become aware of a man approaching me from the opposite direction. I hear him chuckle under his breath and glance in my direction. I leave my expression neutral and keep walking, giving him no reason to pursue me beyond this brief interaction. He licks his lips suggestively, and his smile widens into a smirk as if his silent cat call will make me lose my pants as I follow him to the nearest flat surface.

I am not in the mood to be objectified by this asshat. Still, confrontation in these situations is never advised. Anger mixes with fear as I quicken my pace and try to put some distance between us.

If I disappeared, would anyone even notice?

Logic and feelings don't agree inside of me. I find myself dialing the phone, wanting to hear Conrad's voice reassuring me that everything will be fine.

It's ringing before I can think of stopping myself. "Tam?"

His voice rushes at me. He sounds the same as he always does.

"What the hell is going on, Conrad?" I demand before flinching at my disagreeable tone.

"I was about to ask you the same thing. What did you do, Tamara?" He sounds just as irritated.

I stay on the defensive. "I didn't do anything. The Turnblad house exploded the second I arrived, just like at your mom's apartment."

"Don't call her my mom. She didn't earn that title." Conrad's in a mood. I can hear it in his voice. Everything about him is so familiar, built on decades. I can easily forgive his tone. "I need you to level with me. What's going on with you?"

"What do you mean?"

"How are you escaping all these fires if you're not setting them? I've been to the banquet hall. There was no way you should have made it out alive. And the apartment building? The apartment is on the second floor." He breathes heavily into the phone.

I think of the heat coming at me during the explosions and the circular debris field around me at the Turnblad house. I don't want to tell him I'm starting to believe the amulet works. "Of course, I

406

didn't start the fires. How could you even ask me that? Are you saying that in order to prove my innocence, I should let the next one kill me?"

"Don't yell at me. I'm not the enemy," he counters. "I've been trying to get you out of this mess."

Mess? Such a tame word for my life being flushed down the toilet.

I hate that I suspect him and that I'm analyzing everything he says, but it's true. I don't fully trust him anymore.

"But you have to admit. It's almost like something is protecting you," he insists.

"Or someone is just really bad at trying to kill me," I counter. At least neither of us is trying to chalk it up to bad luck. "Can you think of anyone who might want me dead?"

He doesn't answer.

I should have planned out this call before making it. Do I accuse him outright? Do I ask him about Mabon? About California?

"How are things going with the lawyers?" I ask, testing the waters. I hope I'm wrong about him.

Conrad sighs. "The detectives are still an issue, but they're working on it. I'm afraid of what will happen if they connect this latest fire to you. There are a lot of unanswered questions. It doesn't look good."

The lie hits me like a punch in the face.

Still, I pray I'm wrong.

"Did you talk to Beck or Mabon?" I ask.

"Mabon, of course. He handles the Devine estate," he answers. "Beck is a tool. He couldn't litigate his way out of a whorehouse raid."

If he had said Beck, there was a chance I could believe Mabon and Beck had not communicated with each other about what's been happening.

"Do they seem like they want to help us?" I'm desperate for a reason to trust my brother.

"We pay them, don't we? We're in charge of the estate. They know who they need to be loyal to." The way he says it drips with elitism.

"You sound like the rest of them." I don't mean for the insult to come out.

"What?" Conrad demands. "I didn't catch that."

"How about the estate paperwork? Everything in order?"

"It's a mess," he says. "It's clear our parents never expected us to take over. Everything was going to Anthony. It's going to be a while before we can sign. Don't worry. I'm taking care of it."

More lies. Why? There has to be a reason. Is he trying to protect me from something worse? Is he trying to keep me out of the city?

"I want to come home." I keep my head down as

cars pass and avoid glancing in the windows of the buildings I pass. Part of me hopes to disappear into the concrete landscape. The other part hopes a car will jump the curb and put me out of my misery, so I don't have to deal with any of this.

As soon as the thought creeps in, I get pissed off at myself. This is not who I am. I'm not a weak flower desperate for someone else's sunlight. I'm not suicidal or hopelessly negative all the time. I remind myself that I am a Devine. Sure, a mortal descendent, but still. It might not be magical, but Devine blood courses in my veins. That must count for something.

Conrad stays quiet, and I pull the phone back to see if the call dropped. It's still ticking off the seconds. "Conrad?"

"I don't think that's a good idea," Conrad denies. His voice is so familiar. It draws me in, offering comfort in its familiarity. I don't want to believe the worst.

"I don't feel safe out here." I stop to wait for traffic at a crosswalk. "Alone."

"What happened to, uh..." He lets his voice taper off.

"Nothing. He gave me a ride, and we parted ways." Pain centers in my chest as I say the words, forcing my tone to carry a nonchalance I don't feel. A heavy weight presses down on me, and I struggle to maintain my façade.

"I'm sure if you call him, he'll keep you—"

"How's your driver from the funeral?" I interrupt.

"What? How should I know?"

"I'm sorry. I thought you wanted to talk about strangers who drive us places for money." I dismiss the course of his conversation.

"So that man means nothing to you?"

"Seriously? It's like you said, what am I going to do? Play housewife to some working-class stiff?" That's exactly what I want, not that I'd ever admit it. It's vital that everyone forgets about Paul and Diana. "Give me a break, Conrad. You told me to leave the funeral, and I found some dude to give me a ride. End of story. Can we drop it already?"

"What about California? Your birth mother?" he asks. "Why don't you go there?"

"I'm twenty-eight years old. If the woman wanted to have a relationship with me, she would have found me before now. It's not like she didn't know where I was. We have enough to deal with. I should be there in New York to help you with the estate issues. Maybe I should call Mabon and see if I can add some insight to—"

"No. I got it under control with the lawyers.

There is no reason for you to contact them. You have enough to deal with."

"I don't mind. If I can help..."

"No. Just concentrate on you. Besides, you know, too many cooks in the kitchen, too many lawyers at the table, and all that. I'll handle everything." He pauses, and I can hear his breathing. "You do trust me, don't you?"

My legs stop moving. "Of course."

Lies. I don't, but I desperately want to.

"You know I only want what is best for you."

Lies. I don't know that.

I nod as if the movement will force the words out of my throat. "Sure, I know."

"We're family. We're all we got." He sounds so sincere, and it breaks my heart. "No one else matters."

Lies. Lies. Lies.

I wish he'd talk to me and tell me what is really going on. What is he keeping from me?

"I feel like I'm tiptoeing around you lately when all I want to do is make things better. You know what? Go to California, Tamara. Get it over with. Confront her. Meet her. Talk to her. Whatever you need to do to get your head on straight. Even before the fires, you weren't yourself. You haven't been since Astrid told you about Lorelai. Then, come back to

New York. I think you'll regret it if you don't. Maybe it'll be..." He struggles for words.

"Yeah, maybe."

"I want my sister back," he says.

The words feel like a slap on the face. They also feel like a manipulation.

I hate all this uncertainty. When I hear his voice, I want to trust it. I mean, it's *Conrad*. But there is a wall there now. Paul's words have planted doubt inside of me. I don't know what to do or think.

"I'll call you when I get to California." I hang up and gasp back a sob.

I don't know how, but I find myself on the ground. My knees and palms press against the hard sidewalk. My backpack is by my hip. My phone is face down between my hands, and a tear drops onto the case.

I thought I felt low before the funeral, but that's nothing compared to now.

There is absolutely no one left. I feel alone.

I see feet move past. They come too close for comfort, and I turn my head to look. Seconds later, I feel someone trying to grab my backpack on my other side. I swing around to grab hold of a strap as it's being lifted off the ground, and I jerk hard. Momentum topples me onto my ass, and I kick at the closest pair of legs.

"Fucking bitch!" a man swears as I make contact with his knee. He releases the bag.

Rage erupts inside me, shutting me off to reason. I'm so tired of things being taken from me. I charge up from the ground, screaming and swinging my backpack at him. The sounds leaving my mouth aren't even words. They're the nonsensical banshee rantings of a madwoman. Each time the bag makes a satisfying thud and the man yelps, I feel a rush of relief coursing through me.

"Get her off! Get her off," he yells between thuds. "Get her the fuck off me!"

I keep swinging, not seeing him through the blur of movements. Someone tries to grab me from behind, and I screech as I swing my backpack at a new target. I miss. The bag arches through the air. I let it carry me around to re-aim at the would-be thief. He's limping away as quickly as he can run with the support of his accomplice.

But my energy isn't expended. The rage still boils, and it feels fantastic compared to the depression and grief. I scream after them, my jaw pulled open wide as I shake with the force of it. The sound becomes hoarse, tearing at my throat, but I barely stop for quick breaths.

I see people jaywalking over the street to avoid me—the crazy lady having a meltdown in the middle of the sidewalk. I don't care. Let them think I'm insane. What does it matter? What else can they take away?

I have no idea how long I stand glaring around without really seeing anything. My feet don't feel as if they touch the ground. I'm not connected to any of it.

Rage slowly dissipates, leaving me empty and numb.

I find my phone on the ground. When I pick it up, I discover the screen protector is cracked along one of the corners, but it's still functional. My first instinct is to call Paul just to hear his voice. I resist the temptation. It took everything in me to walk away from him, and I can't do it again.

The textured warmth of his mouth, the way it molded perfectly with mine, is imprinted on my lips. I can feel a shiver of movement over my skin as I remember the glide of his strong hands. He makes me feel safe. His scent, a mixture of musk and cologne, lingers on my skin. That crappy hotel room will forever be the number one thing I long to return to, and my mind will always go back to the intimate moments we shared there.

Life is cruel.

The walking map to the bus station is still active on my phone. I obey its route because I don't have any other plan. California or New York? Buses will go both ways. Or I could just live there at the bus station, disappearing from everything. Out of all the options, I like avoidance the best. Sadly, the world won't stop turning, so I can curl into a ball and never get up. I can't help feeling that there is nowhere for me to go.

CHAPTER
TWENTY-SIX

Darkness surrounds the tinted windows, obscuring the passing landscape and forcing my attention to remain inside the vehicle. I barely remember getting on the bus, but here I am, trapped between the window and an elderly gentleman who keeps clearing his throat as he tries to sleep. At least the seats are cushioned, and my travel buddy isn't one for awkward small talk.

The hours spent sitting in the bus station before that were a blur. The later the time, the stranger the clientele inside the station became. I spent most of it on a bench constructed of thick, plastic-coated wires with a tile wall back, clutching my backpack in my lap and watching for signs of the supernatural.

I'm pretty sure there were plenty hanging out. Travel depots make for a great place to find victims.

People are traveling, isolated, and often alone. They don't know the area and are distracted. I guess that's why human muggers like to hunt in the same locations. I suppose getting dragged into an alley to be robbed and murdered is just as bad as being dragged into that same alley to be a late-night snack to a vampire. The end turns out the same.

The boy who spent too much time by the vending machines loading up on sugar had a certain goblin twitch. I stared for so long that I saw his human glamour malfunctioning to reveal the gnarled creature hiding beneath the cloaking magic. He was harmless enough, as he basically begged for change to feed his sugar addiction.

A soul eater lingered outside the restrooms, "accidentally" (feel the air quotes) bumping into people as they went in and out. I caught her eyes lighting up as she fed on tiny slurps of her victim's energies.

The man behind the counter moved like a zombie, but to be fair, I think he probably just resented his job.

The digital ticket on my phone says San Francisco, California. I keep checking to make sure. I've turned the volume down to ignore any messages. I don't want to talk to anyone. I have nothing to say.

I bought the ticket online and used my fake name. Still, it was paid for with my actual credit card, so I feel trackable. What else could I do? The damned thing was nearly five hundred bucks.

I should have flown. An airplane wouldn't take two days.

I'd also be trapped in the sky if something threatening followed me onboard.

I watched the other passengers load, and none of them stuck out as dangerous. But I'm paranoid and can't help but think that every time a murderer is arrested, a neighbor is talking about how shocked they are that they have been living next to a killer. What if this entire bus was filled with supernaturals in disguise, and I don't see it? If I were a supernatural wanting to hurt people, I'd take the night bus.

I'm torn. Logic can't make up its mind. On the one hand, I want to be hidden and safe. On the other, I want the vampires to chase me and leave Paul and Diana alone.

"Should I just give up and let them have me? Then it will all be over."

My travel companion glances at me, and I realize I've started talking to myself out loud. I give a slight shake of my head to indicate the words weren't for him and purposefully turn my attention to the dark landscape. I can't see much, even when streetlights illuminate the interstate.

"It will be light out when we get to Denver," the

man tells me. "Won't the mountains be pretty? Hard to be sad when you see God's creation."

"Sure," I mutter.

He closes his eyes, presumably to go back to sleep.

Tension has found a permanent home in my stomach, and I haven't been able to eat. Yes, the bus will make stops, but I'm not sure I want to leave my seat at night. When the sugar goblin was trolling for loose change, I managed to stuff a few candy bars and a bottle of water into my backpack, just in case. I'm running low on cash, and soon, I won't be able to afford much else.

Unless I use my cards, which seems dangerous. Isn't that how they track criminals?

Does it matter since I used my card for the bus?

Maybe I should drain one of my accounts at an ATM. Then I'd have cash. I could disappear, and Mary Bennett could get a job. I could start over in witness protection for one.

That won't work. Conrad and several of Anthony's friends know the name on my fake ID, and it's possible the vampires already know about it, too.

Well, crap. I can't use that name for too long. Not for the first time since this hellish adventure started, I think about how I would make a lousy criminal.

I see something blur past the dark window. My

heart jumps a little in my chest, and I press my forehead against the glass. Knots tighten in my stomach. All I see is the side of the road passing by at sixty miles an hour.

"Calm down," I whisper to the glimpses of my reflection I catch in the glass.

I'm exhausted, but I feel Paul when I close my eyes. The rumble of the vehicle and the constant sound of tires on the road remind me of him, and it's almost disappointing to open my eyes and see he's not next to me driving. I even miss the thump of Diana's feet hitting the back of my chair in boredom as she whines about waffles.

Instead, someone behind me is snoring.

I reach for my phone to check if he's texted, desperate to feel the tiniest connection. Instinctively, I know that Paul would be concerned. It would be in his nature to check on me. The fact that he hasn't means he is making a rational decision not to.

My thumbs hover over the keypad, and I compose a message in my head.

Dear Paul, I wanted to again thank you—

What the hell? This isn't a letter to grandma.

Hey, what's up? I just wanted to—

What? Act like a psycho and pretend things aren't fucked as I text in the middle of the night?

Apologize for nearly getting you and your daughter killed by bloodsucking monsters?

I move my thumbs. Pretending to type, I hover them over the keypad while I mouth those words he said, leaving the hotel room. "I feel like we could have been something."

I can almost hear his voice in my head.

I exit the messages. Tears burn my eyes but don't fall. It's for the best.

I detect what sounds like something pinging across the roof and look up, ears trained for more. After several minutes, I tell myself it was probably a pebble kicked up by a passing semi-truck's back tire.

I travel in this self-made purgatory, afraid to sleep. The bus stops a few hours in. I don't get out. The bus moves and then stops again soon after that. I can't help but think for five hundred dollars, we should get fewer interruptions. It's not lost on me that Lady Astrid would have tipped five hundred dollars not to be inconvenienced by traffic driving two blocks.

Topeka, Junction City, these places mean nothing to me beyond the anxiety caused by the motionless bus. By the time we roll into Salina, Kansas, at three in the morning, my back is aching, and I need to stretch my legs.

My calf muscles are stiff as I hobble off the bus

into the parking lot between a hotel and a gas station. I hope the cool breeze will help me clear the cobwebs forming in my brain. I need to stay awake, at least through the night. Only a few of the passengers get off with me.

I carry my backpack, not trusting my co-travelers. The parking lot is bright, and there aren't many cars. I see the hotel and wish I could walk inside to find Paul and Diana waiting for me. They're probably sleeping like a nice, normal family.

I start to picture myself in some ranch-style home, sitting at a polished wood table with his family, playing those new games he told Diana about. The fantasy lasts all of two seconds before I stop myself. That's not how you get over someone.

Survival mode. That's the only mindset I can allow myself right now.

Even though we're technically in a town, gas stations in the middle of the night feel isolated by design. My senses are heightened, and I can't shake the feeling of dread that has become my constant companion. Beyond the darkness, I imagine prairies stretching out for miles. I hate to admit that my image of the Midwest automatically reverts to the olden days when people crossed the countryside by covered wagon. Seeing the clerk behind the counter wearing a prairie dress, made famous during the pandemic, does not help this impression. I know it's not a realistic description, but that feeling of emptiness and aloneness adds to my anxiety.

I don't belong out here.

I don't know what I'm doing.

Each step feels like a chore as I make a beeline for the front door. Every nerve in my body tingles in warning, and every tense muscle yells at me to run, but I have nowhere to go. Thankfully, the lights are on in the parking lot and shining through the convenience store window.

I focus on reaching the door handle and pulling my way inside. The bored cashier forces a smile and mumbles a mandatory greeting, but she's not paying attention to me as she scrolls on her phone. That's good. I like it when people ignore me.

I think of my limited amount of cash and pause to look at the chips on an end cap. I'm tempted to shove some into my bag since the cashier isn't paying attention to us. But in the end, I can't do it. I feel too guilty and clearly still suck at being a criminal. I skip the shelves. Breakfast will have to be the vending machine candy.

Seeing the restroom sign, I head toward the back of the store and push my way inside. There are several stalls, and I automatically head to one at the back of the line. It feels safer, somehow.

As I reach for the door, the color reminds me of the banquet hall, and I get a flash of feeling dizzy as I had the night of the party before passing out. I start to breathe heavily, unable to control it. My stomach churns as it did then, only this time, it's not booze and pot; it's stress and fear.

Every part of me wants to hide on the toilet. The only thing stopping me is the idea that the bus will leave without me. The brusque driver had announced as much at each stop.

I hear flushing and then footsteps leaving as someone exits a stall. Only the quiet buzzing of fluorescent lights remains. I take a deep breath, then another. I need to calm myself before walking back to the bus.

It's three in the morning. That means what? Three hours left until dawn.

"I can make it," I whisper. "Just three hours. That's nothing."

The pep talk does little to ease my apprehension. I know I'm lying. It takes one second for a vampire or some other supernatural creature to mesmerize someone. They could do a lot in three hours.

"It's okay," I tell myself as I hike the bag on my shoulders to carry it on my back. "Get a grip, Tamara. No one knows where you are."

I keep telling myself I'm fine.

I turn the stall lock and hear it release.

I'm fine. I got this.

As I swing open the door, the lights flicker overhead.

I freeze, not seeing anyone in the room with me. I lean over to look for feet. No one else is here. The only noise is my loud breathing. I inch toward the sinks. The lights flicker and then pop, leaving me in darkness.

Oh, fuck.

The restroom is pitch black, and the only sound is now the buzzing in my ears accompanying the drumbeat of my frantic heart. I feel a tear slip down my cheek, and I start to shake. I hold my breath, waiting for the lights to come back on, praying that they will, begging the universe for help. I think about digging for my phone, but it's shoved in my bag, and it feels like it would make too much noise to try to find it.

A cold chill runs along my spine. It takes all my willpower to lift my hand into the black, and I sweep it back and forth as I inch toward where the door should be. I try to be as quiet as a mouse. My knuckles hit the wall, and I jump in fright, even as I rub my hand along the wall to find the door.

As I pull it open, I see all the lights are out except for what looks like a small red dot near the ceiling running on battery backup. Someone holds up a phone, the soft glow acting like a flashlight.

"Take it easy, everyone. It's just a blackout. Looks like it's the whole block." I recognize the cashier's voice. She sounds more annoyed than concerned. "I'm calling my boss. Sorry, your purchases are going to have to wait."

Through the window, I see that the streetlights are also out, but the moonlight and running lights from the parked bus help.

I hear someone fumbling in the aisle.

"Please don't steal. The cameras have night vision," the cashier says before muttering, "They don't pay me enough for this."

I can tell that the woman doesn't even believe what she's saying. I hear more rummaging, and I'm not sure her halfhearted warning worked.

I need to get back on the bus. I should never have gotten off.

I stride for the door, intent on running across the now-dark parking lot. Before I can reach it, the doors blow open on their own. The cashier yelps in fright, and I see the light of her phone dropping to the floor. Large flying creatures burst through the opening, screeching high-pitched sounds that hurt my ears. A woman screams, and I hear crashing as someone knocks over a metal shelf.

Vampires.

They've found me.

The sound of their flapping bat wings is unmistakable.

I don't think. I run toward the door in a panic, pushing past the heavy glass before it swings closed. It knocks me on the back, but the contact only makes my legs move faster. The bus feels too far away, so I head toward an ice machine and duck beside it, away from the door. I hear crashing and screaming inside as I get my bearings.

I want to help those within, but there is nothing I can do.

I huddle in the corner, willing the bus driver to see we need help and move closer. Fuck, why couldn't I have been born with psychic powers?

I hear a light tap behind me and slowly turn around to see a vampire standing in the window, smiling like a predator who just found his prey. He has a handsome face and short blond hair, but then again, all vampires have a sexiness about them. I'm told it's to help them lure their victims. I don't recognize him, but that's not surprising. What I do recognize is the glow of hungry intent in his eyes. He taps his long fingernail against the glass. The steady rhythm is meant to terrify me. It works. To be frankly honest, if I had not already gone to the restroom, I'd be pissing myself.

I push up to run toward the bus. Maybe I can convince the driver to step on the gas and get us out of here. I surge to my feet and stumble a couple of steps but make it no further. A vampire bat flies in front of me seconds before the vampire who attacked me at the motel lands on the parking lot between me and the bus. I don't know how it's possible, but he looks even more enraged than before.

I hear the echoing thought from my old self-defense instructor advising me to run.

What else can I do? I dart towards the edge of the building. I don't know where I'm going as I turn the corner. I hear the flapping of movement behind me and the thump of feet running as they give chase.

Any fleeting moment of hope is soon lost. There is no outrunning a brood of vampires on the hunt. I round the back of the building only to skid to a stop. I'm confronted with three impressively large male vampires and a much shorter female. I slide on the loose gravel, falling on my hands and knees. I feel it cutting my palms.

For all their scary sizes, it's the woman who instantly demands my attention. She's vaguely familiar. Though she wears tight leather, and her straight black hair is severely angled at her chin, I picture her with longer curls and a blue gown. I've seen her in a painting somewhere, possibly in a book.

Recognizing her is not a good thing. That means she's probably old and very powerful.

I lift my hands in a useless attempt to stop her from coming forward. At the gesture, I hear a collective inhale as the vampires get a whiff of my blood. I feel a drip running down my palm to my wrist, and I wipe it against my shirt as if it will somehow erase the temptation from their nostrils. The small wound stings, but it's nothing compared to what's coming.

"Please," I beg. "You're making a mistake. I didn't hurt Costin. The fire was not my fault. This is all a misunderstanding, and I promise I will do everything I can to figure out who is responsible. I lost people too in that fire."

The woman taps her fingers against her thigh as she stares at me. She seems unimpressed with my pleading. I suppose for a vampire, having humans beg for their lives is nothing spectacular. I doubt any of their food wishes to die.

"Humans." That single word comes out of her mouth in a rasp.

Usually, vampires have an air of boredom to them. Like the centuries have just added up into a long eternity of nothingness that they're trying to fill. But right now, the way they're looking at me, they're not bored. They have a purpose, which is more terrifying than anything I can envisage. I can only imagine that what they have planned for me is not an easy ending.

"I had no reason to hurt Costin," I state, trying to sound confident and firm. I hear movement behind me and glance back to see we're not alone. I turn my back toward the gas station wall as I try to keep them all in my eyeline. Getting trapped against a wall isn't great, as it cuts off any exit, but it's better than being exposed. "We were..."

I stopped short of claiming we were friends. We weren't friends. Costin was friendly with my parents.

"We were on friendly terms," I manage.

"You're braver than most blood sacks. I can see why my brother liked you," the vampire answers, flicking the back of her nails against her short hair. "Although Costin always did have questionable taste in pets."

"Costin was your brother," I state the realization out loud.

Well, crap. This is not good news.

And he *liked* me? I'm not sure I buy that.

The woman arches her brow at the comment as if she's surprised I didn't know. How the hell was I supposed to know Costin had a sister? It's not like we chatted at parties. Usually, our interactions were limited to him calling me "little castoff" and looking at me like I was an amuse-bouche he wanted to devour.

"You can call me Elizabeth," Costin's sister says.

In the few seconds I turned my attention fully on Elizabeth, another half dozen vampires congregated behind the gas station. I didn't even hear them land.

"I'm a Devine," I say.

The smirks I get in response are about what I expect from the hollow warning.

"But are you? Really?" Elizabeth laughs.

"I didn't kill Costin," I insist, yet again.

Elizabeth bobbles her head a little and rolls her eyes as she says, "There is no way *you* could have taken out my brother. So much for old men and their prophecies."

I don't know what she's talking about.

"We talked to Conrad," Elizabeth continues. "He made an intriguing proposition."

I sigh in relief. Oh, thank goodness. Conrad talked to them. This performance art is just to scare me. I take a deep breath and try to relax my tensed muscles.

"So, we're good? This is over?" I can't keep the hopefulness out of my voice.

"Sure, it's over," Elizabeth nods, "as soon as we kill you."

"But..." I lift my hands in front of me like a shield. The tension comes rolling back as I prepare for a fight. I no longer care that they're smeared with blood. "You said Conrad made a deal."

"Oh, you don't..." Elizabeth laughs, prompting the others to do the same. The evil sound surrounds me like a chorus.

I wish somebody was coming to save me, but there's no one. I'm all alone in the world. Who would even care that this is happening?

Uncle Mortimer might. Someone has to carry a supernatural baby, and that won't be Conrad.

I start to think of Paul but quickly push him out of my mind. Rumor has it that vampires can read thoughts, at least some of them. And I don't want them digging out that one.

"Sweetie." Suddenly, Elizabeth is in front of me, cupping my face. Her fingers feel like ice cubes against my skin, and the scent of ash lingers like perfume. When I stare into her eyes, I see a cold emptiness. She doesn't bother to try to mesmerize me into submission. "Conrad did make a deal with us. We kill you. We turn him. And we gain access to the great Devine empire."

Tears spill from my eyes, and I know they're hitting her fingers because she pulls one hand to her mouth to lick them before lightly slapping her wet hand against my cheek.

"Brothers! Am I right?" Elizabeth laughs harder.

"I don't believe you." I don't want it to be true. I don't care what all the evidence says. I don't care how logical Paul was in his reasoning. It's Conrad. It's my brother. Family.

Family has to mean something.

"You do know he tried to sell you to my brother in exchange for turning him." Elizabeth is enjoying herself. "Costin refused, of course. This offer, though? Yeah, I'm going to take it."

Please, anyone, say it isn't so. More tears fall, and I'm shaking. I lift my hand to swat her away from my face, but when the backs of my fingers hit her wrist, it's like slamming against a brick wall. The blow has absolutely no impact on her.

"Gah, you're so..." Elizabeth shakes her head, almost disgusted. "Mortal."

"Let's eat her," one of the vampires suggests. "I'm hungry."

"Yeah, such a tasty little treat," someone else adds.

I can't see who's talking. Elizabeth is still in my face, stroking my cheek with her corpse-like fingers. I again try to knock her away, swinging my arm as hard as possible. The vampire is unaffected as her fingers bounce away from my face.

Her lips part, and I hear a soft hiss coming from deep within her throat. Sharp fangs appear like razor blades to capture my full attention. I've never seen a vampire's mouth this close before, and it's more terrifying than I have ever imagined. I feel a ripple of tension filter through the others. Their eyes become fixated on me, and their bodies tense, ready to pounce.

I have no choice but to try. I go into full attack mode as I punch and kick. She stumbles back, and I land several solid blows before Elizabeth backhands me to make me stop.

"No, no, no..." I beg, unable to make any other coherent thought pass my lips. I taste blood in my mouth where my teeth cut my cheek.

Knowing I'm going to die, I feel only one regret. Paul. I regret that I did not have more time with him. I should have told him how much I care. Dare I even think it? We could have been in love. Maybe? I guess now I'll never know.

It all happens within an instant. Elizabeth's fingers slip into my hair and wrench my head to the side. The forcefulness of the movement sends pain down my spine. Her mouth opens as she surges forward to bite. The motion is like a cue to the others, and they all converge on me at once, swarming me like hungry insects. They push me to the ground. I land on the backpack, wobbling like a turtle on its shell, as I feel their hands clawing into me, gripping my body and puncturing my flesh.

An unholy sound unleashes from my throat as I cry out in terror. The scrape of Elizabeth's teeth hit my neck, almost like a tease lingering in the horrific moment. Time becomes suspended. I see quick flashes like a carousel of photographs scrolling past my vision. So many moments are going by so fast that I can't focus on a single one. Only these are not my moments. They're ship battles and fire and bullets shattering stained glass. They're falling and swords and convulsing underwater. The impressions they leave make them feel like they belong to me, but I don't recognize them.

Is this death? Are these Elizabeth's memories invading me?

Death is supposed to be my life flashing before my eyes, not scenes from horrors I know nothing about.

I hear the bus horn as if the world is calling me back.

Why doesn't she bite?

I struggle to push them off, barely wiggling an inch under their tight hold.

A blue light flashes so fast I'd miss it if it didn't bounce off Elizabeth's ear blocking my view. I feel a release of pressure like a pulse is sent out into the universe. The vampires fling away from me in a flurry of pitching limbs and surprised screeches. Some transform into bats and fly away. Others fall to the earth like boulders from the sky, thudding and cracking on the ground.

I don't have time to question it. I scramble to my feet, pushing off the ground while using the gas station's brick wall for support.

Elizabeth is crouched like a predator, ready to pounce. Bloody tears come from her red eyes. At my attention, she hisses and instantly crawls backward with supernatural speed, blurring into the shadows as she leaves her companions behind. The blond vampire lies unmoving as another pulls him by the arm, dragging him away.

And just like that, they're gone, leaving no evidence they were even there.

I can't explain what happened. All I know is I'm free, and I have to run. I dart around the side of the building. I'm wobbly, but that can't matter. I weave a path toward the front of the gas station and then dart across the dark parking lot. The bus's running lights call me like a beacon.

Even as he sees me through the open door, the driver honks a quick warning. I climb inside.

"You almost missed it," the driver says, shutting the door behind me. "Next time, I leave without you."

I try to mumble something, but my heart is beating too hard, and I walk back to my seat. A few cell phone lights shine as people look at their phones. Others are sleeping or at least trying.

They are all blissfully unaware of how close they were to death.

"The girl inside thinks it's vandalism," someone whispers in conversation. "Like when all those groups attacked the power stations up north."

"Did you see those birds flying around inside? I think they were vultures," another passenger says.

I walk by a kid with a suspicious amount of candy bars stuffed into his jacket as he shoves one into his mouth. Guess he didn't get the memo about not stealing. His mother is next to him on her phone and is either apathetic about what her son is up to or doesn't care that she's raising a thief.

The elderly gentleman in the seat next to mine looks up in surprise. "What happened to you? Are you all right?"

I let my backpack slide off my shoulders as he angles his legs to the side to let me pass. My body aches, and my bloody hands sting. I feel far from all right, but I nod. "Yeah. I had an accident when the lights went out. Wrong place, wrong time."

I collapse into the seat with the backpack dropping by my legs. The gas station's outside lights flicker back on. I reach to touch my amulet. Every inch of me hurts from the scuffle, but I'm alive.

How am I alive? There should have been no escaping that.

I grip the amulet tighter, not caring that it digs into my scraped hands. My grandfather was right. It's enchanted. That's the only explanation that fits.

For a tiny moment, I can feel him there with me, protecting me, and I cling to the memory of him and his kindness. But with those memories come thoughts of Conrad and how he pushed me from the balcony, thinking we could fly.

How had it come to this? I wouldn't rank vampires at the top of the honesty pyramid, but why would Elizabeth lie at that moment? Just to taunt me? She definitely enjoyed doing that. I can still picture the look on her face as she told me of Conrad's deceit.

My mind automatically tries to find reasons not to believe her. But there comes a point when the facts are piling up so high they can't be denied. I know my brother's faults. I've known them for years. I've seen firsthand his obsession with becoming supernatural. I know that he's always wanted to be more than the mundane mortals we were born as. He's never been able to accept otherwise. I know he wants power, immortality, and respect. I just never thought he'd sacrifice me to get it.

The betrayal is almost too much for me to feel. I don't know how to describe it. It burns like hot lava in my chest, ready to explode out of my mouth like a volcano. Or that alien monster that rips open people's chests to be born. No words that I can think of do it justice.

Conrad betrayed me.

My brother wants me dead. And for what? Power over the family estate? Like I would have ever fought him for that. It belongs to both of us. I don't want to be in charge of the great Devine legacy. I don't want that responsibility. I never have. He can have it.

What am I supposed to do with this knowledge? I'm utterly alone. I have no one. I have nothing left.

I rub my scraped hands as if I can erase everything they represent. I want to go back to those moments before my party. I want to erase everything that has happened. Please, universe, don't make me stay here.

"Take this," the gentleman hands me a tissue and

a single wet wipe packet from his fanny pack. "You should clean those cuts." He resumes searching his pack. "I should have some antibacterial gel in here, too. My wife always said I was an accident waiting to happen."

"Thank you." I tear open the wet wipe and clean the blood off my trembling hands, mainly because the man expects me to. I keep an eye on the sky as we pull out of the parking lot, but I don't see the vampire bats flying around us. Whatever the amulet did scared them away.

Does that mean I'm safe?

The thought is fleeting. I already know the answer.

Are Paul and Diana safe? That's the more important question right now.

Conrad doesn't know what Paul means to me, and I have never been so glad that I lied about my feelings. As long as I don't make contact with them again, Conrad will have no reason to pursue them.

That only leaves my birth mother. Conrad knows I'm on the way to see Lorelai.

The gentleman beside me tries to hand me a tube of antibacterial gel. I don't take the ointment as I dig into my backpack and pull out my phone. The man continues to insistently hold the ointment for me to take.

I take the tube and hold it in my fist, but I don't use it. Instead, I pull up Lorelai's phone number and begin typing. The woman is a stranger to me, but thankfully, she knows about the supernatural world.

"This is Tamara, your daughter," I write. *"We talked the other day on the phone. I am on a bus traveling to San Francisco to see you. I think my brother, Conrad, is killing people by starting fires and sending vampires after them. I think he wants me dead. I don't want to believe it, but I think that's what might be happening. I hope I'm wrong. But just in case, you need to be careful. He knows about you and where you live. I think he might be coming after you next because you're my birth mom. And he already killed his birth mom and possibly the rest of our family? I don't know. I don't have all the answers right now. But you know what this world I live in is like, right? So, be careful. Don't trust anyone. Maybe don't go home? I don't know how protected you are. Just be careful."*

I look at the rambling text message. It makes me sound like a psycho. Let's try this again.

"This is Tamara," I amend. *"I'm sorry for the suddenness of this message and wish I did not have to send it. If anyone contacts you, please be careful. I believe someone wishes to harm people in my life. It's a long story, but I'm currently on a bus to San Fran-*

cisco, and I will explain everything when I get there. It arrives at 8:30 tomorrow night. I hope it's nothing, but please be safe."

Send.

This is not exactly how I imagined the first text to my birth mother would go. But there we have it.

My seat buddy watches me, and I realize I still hold the ointment tube. I open it and squirt the gel onto my finger before handing it back to him. He nods in approval.

As I'm rubbing it over my palms, I watch the phone. Lorelai doesn't answer, and I again turn to the window. We're back on the quiet interstate. I see a shadowed reflection staring back at me. I barely recognize myself anymore.

TWENTY-SEVEN

Exhaustion overtakes me, and I fall asleep. There's comfort in knowing I have my grandfather's protection. Well, to be honest, I'd rather the amulet didn't let me get beat up before it decided to intervene because I feel like I've been thrown through a woodchipper. Every part of me aches, and the constant bumps in the road don't help.

Mortal beggars can't be choosers.

When I open my eyes, light peeks over the horizon, and I'm greeted by the sight of the candy bar thief puking his guts out in front of a fast food restaurant. The bus is empty as everyone goes inside to order food. The engine isn't running, and it feels almost peaceful.

I check my phone, unable to stop myself from

hoping Paul's name appears in my missed messages. Instead, I find no one has contacted me.

No one. Not my birth mother, not Conrad, not Paul.

Did my birth mother get my message? It's early yet, not even five in the morning in California. She could be sleeping.

Does Conrad know what happened yet with the vampires he sent?

Does Paul... I sigh. Does he miss me? Does he regret me?

I grab my bag and walk the aisle, stretching my legs. Blood stains my shirt from where I wiped my hands, reminding me of all that has happened.

Something has to be done about my appearance. I quickly leave the bus and jog my way to a side door of the restaurant near the restrooms. The stalls are full, but I set myself up at the sink. I wash my hands and arms, splash water on my face, and use wet paper towels to clean under my shirt. I watch the people entering and exiting, making sure no one pays too much attention to me.

Turning my shirt backward, I put on the jacket to hide the blood on my back. It's no fashion show, but it'll do. At least I no longer look like I lost at fight club.

I see the amulet bump beneath the material. I

expected an enchanted object to feel differently—like a tingling eruption or the surge of the magic ball Anthony let me hold that burned my hand as a kid. This just feels like a necklace.

But I suppose that doesn't matter when it did its job. I'm alive. For what, I'm not sure at this point.

I wish my grandfather were here to give me advice. The isolation and loneliness are overwhelming. It leaves a hollow pit inside of me, and there is a prickling sensation in my chest. I imagine tiny supernatural creatures living in there, carving out a bigger home with their minuscule knives, and they won't stop until there is nothing left but a bag of skin. The pit will slowly grow like a cancer until I become one of those wild people living in the woods—so secluded that I forget how to speak or interact with other humans.

What am I fighting for? Why am I even here on this journey? I don't recognize my life.

In a silent toast, I lift an invisible glass toward my reflection in the mirror and whisper, "To the fall of the Devine legacy."

I take the pretend drink, wishing it were real. Why couldn't this all be some magic drug-induced hallucination? Maybe if I lay on the restroom floor and close my eyes, Anthony will come and find me— laughing at the fact I can't hold my liquor and pot.

All that magic. All those great big lives. And it boils down to this hot mortal mess staring back at me.

The door opens, and I recognize a woman from my bus. She touches the diamond ring on her finger like she wants the world to know she's not alone. The gesture reminds me of the comfort I get from knowing the amulet is there. Or maybe she's scared I'll steal it.

"Oh, excuse me," she mumbles, even though she's not nearly close enough to bump into me. Her eyes sweep over me, and I see her lips tightening. I'm really not in the mood to be judged by a stranger, so I leave the restroom.

I'm tempted by the smell of food but feel the need to conserve my cash reserves. If anyone is tracking me, I don't want to be found. I have no clue if they are, but it feels safer this way.

Before leaving, I refill my water bottle by the drink dispenser. I don't linger in the parking lot. I see people watching me, but I don't keep eye contact for too long. I might be protected, but anyone who comes into my life will be a moving target.

I'm the first person back on the bus, and I settle into my little corner next to the window. It's brighter outside now, and I feel resigned to my path.

Mabon said Conrad is in California. Paul and Diana should be safe. My brother thinks I've used them and ditched them. They should be fine as long as I continue to resist the urge to hear their voices. I like to think Conrad can't hack my phone because it's protected, but I don't want to take any chances. And what's to say he won't hack the people I contact? Nothing I believed in makes sense anymore.

I look at my bare hand and touch my ring finger. I'm jealous of that judgy woman in the restroom. How could Nancy throw Paul away? I'd give anything to have that perfectly normal life with him.

Instead, if I somehow make it through this, my world will never look the same. I'll be alone.

No, scratch that. I'll be married to a supernatural of Uncle Mortimer's choosing.

The idea is so repulsive that I clench my hand into a fist and squeeze hard as if I can erase the image of being married to anybody but Paul. This is my fantasy, dammit.

"Oh, god, please don't let it be Chester Freemont."

If my parents had written a will stating that I am to inherit everything, I'm sure they would have included a clause forcing me to align with the Freemont family and bear a flock of little Chesters. I suppose that's one good thing about no one expecting I'd outlive the rest of them. They didn't bother to put their wishes in writing.

"Death or Chester?" I mutter to myself, still clenching my fist. "Well, this is the worst choose-your-fate game ever."

I flatten my hand and rub it against my thigh before reaching for my phone.

"Death," I belatedly answer my own crappy game.

I need to get out of my head or at least focus on solutions instead of self-pity. A quick check tells me no one has messaged me. Still, I look at Paul's name in my contacts like it's some mystical link to let me feel him with me. I don't call it. I need to delete it, but I can't make my fingers press the button.

Instead, I text Lorelai, *"Sorry to be a bother. Please let me know if you got the message and are safe."*

I hover my finger over the device before finally forcing myself to send it. Two messages aren't too much, right? I mean, if I send another, then I'm heading into needy stalker territory. It's too early to call California. I know nothing about this woman. Does she sleep with her phone off? Does she sleep until noon? Did she block my number after I called because she didn't want contact with me?

I hear someone getting on the bus, and I burrow down into my seat. People are filtering inside. The break is over, and we're about to get back on the road.

I'm glad for it. I'm ready for this journey to be over. Knowing there is a day and a half left on this bus isn't helping.

My stomach growls, and I dig into my bag to look for that candy bar from the bus station. Sweets are not what I want, but it makes me think of sparkle pancakes.

Everything reminds me of Paul and Diana.

What if I just get off at the next stop and walk away? Toss my phone in a trashcan, drain my bank account for all the cash I can get to tide me over until I find a job, and just disappear into the ether? Forget about Conrad's bounty on my head. Forget about the vampires. Forget about the birth mother, who probably never wanted to hear from me.

I'll never find another Paul, but there must be someone out there who'd marry a sad woman with a fake name who doesn't want to bring kids into this world. Or I could just live in the forest and adopt a bunch of cats.

A strange sensation comes over me at the thought, making me physically incapable of following through with the idea. I'm not sure what this feeling is, but it's intense.

Guilt? Sense of duty? Familial responsibility?

Cowardness?

My phone rings, and I nearly jump out of my

skin at the sound. I fumble to check who it is, hoping it's Paul while knowing he shouldn't be calling me.

Lorelai's name pops up.

My birth mother is calling.

I take a deep breath and answer, "Hello?"

"It's," she makes a confused noise, "um, Lorelai. I got your message. Are you all right?"

"Yeah, I'm," I look at people filing onto the bus, "good."

"You're safe?"

"Yes," I answer.

"Good." She sighs into the phone.

"I'm sorry if my message was cryptic. I wasn't sure how to say—"

"Don't talk about it on the phone. You need to get here." I notice her voice is soft, almost like she's trying to whisper. "Listen, I checked flights. You'll be in Denver in a few hours. Once you get to the bus station, get on the train that goes to the airport. There is one leaving every fifteen minutes. The ride is just under forty minutes. When you get to the airport, hop on the one o'clock flight to San Francisco. I'll be waiting to pick you up."

"But—"

"Do you understand?" she insists.

"Um, yeah, but—"

"Okay. Good. I'll see you then. Be safe." Lorelai hangs up the phone.

I pull it back, confused by what had just happened.

"I got you something." The older gentleman sits next to me and hands me a food bag. It takes me a moment to react to him. "It's not healthy, but it's better than candy for breakfast."

His words have a parental tone, the gentle yet firm scolding that comes from raising kids. Paul uses that same tone when he corrects Diana's behavior.

I nod my thanks, and I take the bag. Why is he buying me food? Do I look that desperate?

Never mind. I know the answer to that. I'm scraped up and wearing my shirt backward.

"My name is Walter, by the way, but you can call me Walt."

"Mary," I answer.

"Good to meet you, Mary."

"Thank you, Walt." I open the bag and pull out a breakfast sandwich. I refrain from telling him how much this gesture means to me. How this one little simple act of kindness fills me with just a bit of hope that this dark period will go away.

"My wife used to pick young families dining at restaurants and would pay their bills. She would tell me, Walt, no matter how little we have, someone always has less. We have to keep putting good out into the world. It's the only way to live."

I notice that he uses the past tense but still wears a wedding ring. This is the second time he's referred to his wife. It's safe to assume he feels as lonely as I do. I feel like he wants me to ask about her. I don't want to. I don't want to take in more loss. Walter is a kindhearted, possibly lonely guy who just bought me breakfast. I want to savor the positive moment.

Even with all that in my mind, I find myself saying, "She seems like a wonderful person. When did you lose her?"

"Last year," he says with a small tremble in his voice. "Aneurysm. It happened suddenly. One moment, she's laughing, and the next..."

I can see that a year has not taken away his pain or lessened his love. He doesn't need to say much more. I can picture what he had.

The polite thing to do would be to share a bit about myself. To tell them that he's not alone in his grief. I don't mention my family.

"I'm sorry," I say. "That must be rough."

I think of all those phrases people said to me at my family's funeral. None of them helped. Not really. Words didn't change facts.

He nods. "I take her with me on trips. I've been

spreading her ashes everywhere I go. She's in my bag now."

"Oh?" I nod.

"I suppose some people think that's weird," he says. "But I like having her with me. How about you? Do you have someone?"

"Nope. Completely single."

I envy Walter. I'll bet he never had to worry about vampires chasing him or magical legacies. I want what he had, even if, at the end of it, I end up sitting alone on a bus with Paul's ashes.

Fuck, my brain is morbid. Even my fantasies end badly.

I realize the bus had started to move while we were talking.

All these people have no clue about what is happening around them, and they have no clue how lucky they are. I wish I didn't know the things I do.

Walter produces a worn paperback and settles into his own quiet thoughts. I eat the breakfast sandwich and return to my post, staring out the window at the flat countryside. I don't know if this is Colorado or Kansas, and I guess it doesn't matter. The sun is lifting over the prairie, hitting the ground in such a way that, in the breeze, the rolling grass looks like water rippling over the fields. I imagine they've looked like that since the beginning of time, watching centuries of humans come and go.

I'm the last remaining Devine. If I turn my back on that, centuries of a proud legacy die.

"It can die."

"Not today, Astrid." I push her voice out of my head.

Walter glances at me, and I wad up the wrapper to my finished sandwich. I shove it back into the bag. "Thank you. This was amazing."

He smiles and nods before turning back to his book.

Lorelai called me. She's safe for now. It barely feels real, but she wants me to come. Sadly, I'm too jaded to believe it's for a happy reunion. I suppose I'll find out the reason soon enough.

Stress must be taking its toll on me. My body feels heavy, and exhaustion is creeping in. I close my eyes, wondering if there is any reason to stay awake.

TWENTY-EIGHT

My tongue is thick, and my mouth tastes funny. I don't know where I am. I feel the vibration of a vehicle rumbling through me, and I instantly smile and turn my head. As I open my eyes, I mumble, "Paul."

I start to reach for him. He's not there.

I stare at the empty seat next to me in confusion. It takes a long time for me to piece together that I'm on a bus. Too long.

What the hell is going on?

I open my mouth and move my tongue around. Feeling drool on my chin, I swipe it with the back of my hand. Yawning, I look out the window to see we're parked at a large bus concourse. The word Denver catches my attention.

There is something I'm supposed to do in Denver.

Why am I hungover in Denver?

The thoughts in my head tick slowly. I grab the seat in front of me and pull myself to my feet. My leg bumps into something. I glance down and see my backpack.

Pulling the bag onto my shoulder, I see my phone on the seat. I take that, too, as I look around for anything else that might belong to me.

The bus idles, and only a few people remain on it. I bump into the seats as I make my way along the aisle. As I exit, I look around for familiar faces but don't see any. Sounds run together, and words are hard to pick apart. It's all a jumbled mess of tones, like everyone is talking at once.

Nothing about this feels right.

What am I supposed to do in Denver?

A sign directing people to the airport shuttle catches my attention. I'm supposed to go to the airport and fly to San Francisco. That's right. I'm meeting my birth mother.

Reality slowly comes into focus through the haze. Before I realize what I'm doing, I find myself walking to get on a train. Someone stops me. They want my ticket. I forgot you had to pay for things.

I dig through my bag, looking for cash. It's missing. My wallet is open like someone rummaged through it. Both of my driver's licenses are askew, and my credit cards are still there.

"Hurry, hurry, hurry," a mother shouts, dragging her son behind her as they rush to board the train.

The words aren't meant for me, but they prompt me into action. I use my card to buy a ticket at the vending machine and hurry to find a seat on the train.

A loud thud rouses me, and I jerk awake.

"Sorry," someone mutters an apology. I'm not sure if they're talking to me.

I don't remember passing out, but my head is a little clearer. I'm on a train to the airport to visit my birth mother because my brother is trying to kill me. My body still doesn't feel right, but at least I can focus my thoughts.

A heaviness has invaded my muscles and dulled my nerves. It reminds me of smoking pot in the closet at my birthday party.

Am I drugged?

I rise from my seat and look around for supernatural creatures. There are a few candidates I should keep an eye on.

I automatically reach for my necklace and am relieved to feel its bump beneath my shirt. Apparently, it only protects me from death, not suffering.

Or being roofied.

How...?

"Fucking Walter," I grumble in realization. He gave me the breakfast sandwich and waited for me to pass out before robbing me.

Oh, come on, now.

I was so focused on protecting myself from the supernatural that I forgot to guard myself from another basic predator: humans.

That's like, 'How to be a Girl 101'. Don't ingest anything from strangers.

Damn. And he seemed so nice, too, talking about missing his dead wife and carrying her ashes with him. So harmless.

Yeah. *Harmless.*

For fuck's sake. Now, I feel drugged and violated.

I look at my clothing. At least we were near people on the bus. I doubt he would have molested me while I slept. Still, the not knowing for sure leaves me feeling gross.

Fate really has it out for me. What did I ever do to that bitch?

I get on my phone to check flights. I would have bought my ticket earlier, but I was too busy taking food from strangers. I'm surprised that I actually find a flight, even though the cost of the three-hour trip is more than the bus ticket.

When the train comes to a stop, I duck my head and draw my arms close. I keep to myself as I navigate through security to my departure gate. I can't be certain, but I think I catch a security officer's inner eyelid membranes blink in the wrong direction like a lizard. I pretend not to notice.

The plane is already loading when I get there, so I just walk on. My seat is in the very back against a wall. It doesn't recline and isn't the most comfortable, but whatever.

Waiting for takeoff, I pull out my phone to charge it and text my arrival times to Lorelai. She instantly answers that she'll be at the airport waiting in Terminal Level Four, past the baggage claim. I want to keep the conversation going so as not to feel so alone, but I don't know what to say. Instead, I end up giving her a thumbs-up emoji.

I click on Paul's name and stare at his number. I would give anything to have him and Diana next to me instead of being squished between a woman with too much perfume and what I can only assume is an angsty teenager. Not that I can judge. I was an angsty teen not so long ago.

Regardless, I won't make the mistake of becoming friendly with my travel companions again. Lesson learned.

The plane begins to move, and the flight attendant is doing her presentation. I ignore her. If the plane goes down, it won't kill me. The amulet won't let it.

On the surface, that might sound like a blessing, but I'm beginning to understand that it might be a curse. Nothing against my grandfather. He meant well. He did his best to protect me.

I'm anxious about flying. What if the lizard security guy recognized me and told someone? Conrad had indicated people were looking for me. The supernatural can be a tight-knit network of busybodies. If there is a bounty on my head, any number of them will be happy to claim it.

Can I even trust anything Conrad said? Has my whole life been a lie?

I feel so betrayed. And heartbroken.

I should be excited and nervous about meeting my birth mother, but all I want is to curl into a ball and never get out of bed. Four months ago, I had a family and a life that made sense. And, if not sense, it was at least familiar. I knew my place in the universe. My adoptive brother loved me. My mother was my mother, for better or worse.

I should have been a better daughter. Then Astrid wouldn't have told me about Lorelai. If I had to pinpoint a moment my life started to take a nose-dive, it's that one. Everything has been an upheaval since.

Astrid's voice echoes in my brain, telling me that self-pity helps no one. That it's a tool of the weak. Growing up, I always thought of my mother as a cold woman. Now, sitting here on a plane all by myself, I realized the gift she gave me. She was teaching me how to survive in a cruel and ugly world without protection. She tried to make me resilient. She tried to provide me with all the tools she thought my human self would need to survive. Somehow, she knew that I would not be able to depend on other people and that, in the end, I would need to rely on myself. I miss her greatly. And I wish I could lift her out of that mausoleum and tell her I understand. That I don't hate her. And I'm sorry.

And, yes, it can die.

I think now that I understand those words. You don't have to take someone's life to kill them. There are much crueler deaths.

The plane gains speed, and I feel the moment the tires leave the tarmac. Gravity pulls me back in my seat as we head into the sky.

I don't know what the world will look like with Lorelai in it. I feel a little too beaten down for hope at this moment. All I can do is trudge forward.

I think the last of my hopes left me when I

watched Paul drive away. He took my mortal dreams with him.

"Whoa, hey, are you okay?" The teenager gives me a strange look.

I realize that my eyes are wet. I swipe them with the back of my hand. "I hate flying."

"You, uh...?" He timidly offers me his hand.

I'm not making friends. Life has been pretty clear about that lesson. People I'm friendly with either hurt me or get hurt. There is no in-between. I might survive a crash landing, but these people won't.

I shake my head in denial. "No, thanks, I got this. *Ego sum avis stultus.*"

CHAPTER
TWENTY-NINE

Despite my resolve to harden myself and be strong, I can't help the nervousness causing my hands to shake as we disembark the plane. I think a big part of me never believed this moment would happen. And if I'm honest, I have to admit that a big part of my personality likes to put its head in the sand and avoid difficult situations. My entire life, I've had somebody else there to take care of things for me. My parents protected me. Anthony gave me emotional support. Conrad had always been ready to beat up the bullies. I can't say it's my most flattering quality or that I'm proud of the cowardice.

I should have emotionally prepared myself better. Questions I can't answer whirl around my thoughts. I've never even seen a picture of my birth mother. Does she look like me? Will she know me?

What is she like? Will I feel like I belong with her? Will there be an instant connection?

What if she rejects me?

What if I don't like her?

What if she is like Conrad's mom, a druggy prostitute looking for a cash cow to pay her rent in a sketchy vampire-controlled neighborhood?

What if this is a trap?

I wish I had someone to talk to about this. I want to call Paul. I want to hear his calm voice as he tries to fix the world around him. I want him to fix me.

I just want him.

But I'm alone. I don't think I can do this.

The blend of hope and fear creates a deep anxiety that makes it hard to breathe. My heart thumps so heavily that I feel like it's trying to choke me. I don't know what I should feel at this moment. Should I be grateful that she came to the airport to get me or angry that she abandoned me, to begin with? I'm curious and terrified.

This is one emotional rollercoaster I don't want to be on—not now, not with everything else exploding around me.

I touch the amulet. Why didn't my grandfather tell me about her? He must have had a reason.

I should run. My self-defense instructor told me the best course of action for a human who feels danger is to run away and hide. There are plenty of places for me to hole up. I pass seating for people waiting for a flight, and there is a restroom. No one will think anything of me hanging around. There was that movie about that guy who lived in an airport. How hard could that be?

Somehow, I manage to walk with the flow of pedestrian traffic toward the airport's exit. People are talking and laughing, happy to be on a journey. A few annoyed businessmen drag their roller bags behind them as they weave the crowds like they're on a mission. One nearly knocks into me with his suitcase and doesn't stop to apologize. Overhead announcements blare, but I don't hear the words.

The sense of safety I feel at being inside the secured area evaporates as I pass the checkpoint to leave. My movements are stiff, and I can't lift my arms. All I can do is concentrate on putting one foot in front of the other while my head screams at me to run in the opposite direction.

I take the escalator down to where she said we'd meet. I see people holding signs, but none of them say Tamara. As I travel downward, I search the crowd for a woman who looks like she might be waiting. No one sticks out in the crowd. I then look for danger in case this is a trap.

I stand in the terminal, slowly turning in circles

to look around. Of all the scenarios that played out in my head, I never considered that she would flake and not come. I'm unable to describe the disappointment I feel at the idea that she has abandoned me for the second time in my life.

Making my way around a new city isn't exactly difficult. I have her address, and I can get a taxi. It might be better if I arrived at her place to check things out before meeting her.

I walk outside and look at my phone. It must have dinged, but I'd been too anxious on my walk from the plane to hear it. Lorelai wants to know if I'm here yet. In all my nervousness, I forgot to tell her I landed.

The California air feels warm against my skin, even in the shade. I look at the line of cars waiting to pick people up. My jacket looks a little out of place, but I can't remove it. The blood stains on my back might be problematic.

Texting back, I write, *"Outside the terminal now."*

"Driving to get in line. Blue car," comes the answer.

She didn't forget me. I hate the surge of excitement I feel at the knowledge. It's like I'm setting myself up for heartache, but I can't help it.

I walk along the line of cars, eagerly peering into

every blue vehicle's window. Anticipation mounts, fueled by uncertainty. I feel the adrenaline surging through my veins. Each step feels like it takes an eternity.

Then I see light reflecting off a crystal hanging from a rearview mirror. I stop walking. My attention goes to the driver. It's her. I know it as sure as I know the shape of my own shadow.

She has my hair.

What an odd thought. I have no clue why that's my first impression.

Seconds later, Lorelai leans forward, and her eyes lock with mine. She lifts her hand from the wheel in a small wave. I manage to lift my fingers in return. It's a small gesture, but I'm nervous. I draw my arms around my waist as I move to meet her vehicle.

Lorelai parks the car and gets out. The world feels like it's in slow motion. The breeze isn't hard, and still, she looks windblown. I don't know what I expect, but this woman is not it.

If Astrid reflected refined wealth and perfection, Lorelai is her polar opposite. Her hair is a tangle of wild curls, held back by the sunglasses pushed on top of her bright scarf headband. She doesn't wear makeup, and her layered Bohemian dress appears homemade. Eclectic costume jewelry boldly adorns her ears and wrists, but on her neck is a thin chain with a medallion.

One thing both women have in common is that they neglected to teach me about motherhood. I think of Diana and how she is better off without me. I lack the skills to give a child what she needs, not for any meaningful amount of time. People talk about an unbreakable bond between mother and child. I don't feel it when I look at Lorelai. She's a stranger. And I never felt it with Astrid.

When she starts to come around the car, one of the airport security guards appears next to me. "Hey! No parking. Stay in your vehicle. Pick up lane only."

"Okay, okay, I got it." Lorelai holds up her hands like she's being robbed. She nods at the car and tells me, "Get in. I live about a half hour from here."

I glance back at the security guard. He's already moved on from the encounter to continue patrolling the line of cars.

She leans over the passenger seat to push open my door from inside. The smell of patchouli oil wafts from within. Plastic bins and art canvases fill the back seat. As I slide into the car, I feel like an intruder.

"Let me look at you, Tamara."

When I look over, her hands are already outstretched to cup my face. She presses her palms to my cheeks. They're clammy, as if she'd been holding them in fists. Her gaze keeps steady on mine as if she's trying to read my thoughts. I break eye contact first. A faded butterfly tattoo is on the center of her chest.

"I've thought about this moment for so—"

A knock on the window interrupts her, and she lets go of me as I spin around in fright. The security guard is motioning for us to drive.

Lorelai lifts her hands again and nods.

"Just trying to have a moment with my daughter. The machine cogs are moving, officer." She grabs the wheel and puts the car into drive. "Reptilians are such sticklers for the rules. You must be unflinching with them. They respond well to authoritative attitudes."

Daughter. The word strikes me in the chest. She said it easily without stumbling or awkwardness, as if it were the simple truth.

I watch the guard as we pass. He looks human. "How do you know he's reptilian?"

"He's got the aura," she answers.

"Are you...?"

"Supernatural?" Lorelai chuckles. "No. I'm super enlightened. I've had lots of practice and a little help. I'm one hundred percent human. You get that from me."

She says it with such ease. I'm not sure what to make of this. I can't stop staring at her, studying her, and, *yes*, judging her. This moment is hard for me, and she's so...*breezy*.

"You're thinking I'm a bit much," she concludes.

"I'm trying to picture you with my father." It's an honest answer. I can't see it. She's no Astrid.

"Ah," she sighs, and her lips tighten. "That Davis was a charmer."

I wait for her to expand. She doesn't.

That's it? A charmer? That's my origin story? I'm in existence because my dad was charming?

Is it bad etiquette to demand more? Astrid would. I'm not Astrid. I want Lorelai to like me. I also want her to show remorse for giving me up and staying out of my life. I promise myself not to start a fight. She has the answers I desperately need about where I come from.

"Can you see all kinds of supernatural?" I ask.

"Oh, sure." She nods. The car picks up speed as she navigates traffic a little too fast. Glancing at the cars as we pass, she says, "Human. Human. Shifter. Human. Human. Councilman with not his wife. Human."

Lorelai pulls her sunglasses down as bright light pours into the front seat. It's impossible to tell if she's being truthful or trying to impress me.

I know I have all these questions, but I can't think of what to say as we drive in silence. Finally, I manage, "Thank you for coming to get me."

She smiles. "Thank you for texting to warn me."

We should discuss that, but it feels like a lot to dive into Conrad's betrayal and my family's deaths.

One of her hands drops to her lap. "This must be strange for you. I'll admit, you took my breath away when you finally called. I knew someday you would find your way back to me."

"You could have called me." Crap. My tone is harsh. I promised myself I wouldn't start an argument with her. What if she drops me off and leaves for another twenty-eight years?

"No. I couldn't have." She pulls in a long breath and lets it out slowly. I wonder if her breezy attitude is a shield protecting her from the ugliness life throws at us. "I didn't want to talk about this while we were driving. I was going to offer you tea, and... Well, I suppose there is no good way to delve into things. No number of practiced speeches is going to make this easier. Shall we rip the bandage?"

I nod. "Please."

"I promise you complete honesty. I refuse to live anything but an authentic life. I'm not surprised your father never told you about me. He was never good with hard emotions. I mean, I don't have to tell you that he avoided the messiness of life. Oh, but he knew how to have fun, and we did."

"He was married," I remind her.

"Sure, but I guess marriages are different when you're that rich and supernatural and have been together for hundreds of years. You know, I met Astrid. She knew about me and the others. I don't think she minded." Lorelai glances at me. "You're an adult. I can't be telling you anything you don't know. You're old enough to have figured out all this by now."

Knowing and hearing it said out loud, so matter of fact, are two different things.

"How did you meet?"

"The same way most cliched people meet in New York, at a bar. I was drunk. He was sexy and funny. That was that. He smiled at me through the crowd, and I was totally his. For a while, I wondered if he had cast some kind of spell over me, but I don't think that was it. I was young and partying, and he was Davis. He introduced me to the world of magic. I introduced him to body shots and the artist's lifestyle. It was a beautiful few months we shared."

"And then you got pregnant," I prompt.

"And then I got pregnant," she confirms.

"And you gave me to Astrid." So much for not being confrontational. I can't help it.

Our speed increases as she blows past the speed limit. I worry about being pulled over as she weaves through traffic.

"Not at first. I tried to keep you. Davis gave me child support, but he couldn't give me time. He had a family and responsibilities. Romances like ours are never meant to last. We drifted apart when I was pregnant. What we had wasn't love. It was a good time." She reaches over to stroke my arm. "But he loved you. He was there right after you were born."

"Was it too hard being a single mom? Is that why you gave me to him?" I feel myself trying to understand and making excuses. I think of Diana. She's a sweet girl, but I see how much responsibility Paul has on his shoulders. I wonder if I'd ever have enough patience to be a parent. Davis and Astrid handed their children off to staff and nannies. And it sounds like Lorelai might have been too overwhelmed.

"I promised you honesty. If you don't hear anything else, hear this. I have loved you since the moment you were born. I looked at that face, my perfect, beautiful little baby's face, and I knew I would never care for anything as much as I cared for you. Time has not changed that." She again touches me, letting her hand linger on my forearm to squeeze it and not let go.

I hesitate before resting my hand on top of hers. I

don't move as I stare at the contact. So many emotions are flooding me that, in a way, I feel numb. How different my life would have been with her—to have a mother who loved me and thought me perfect the way I came into this world.

"Then why?" If she loved me so much, why did she disappear?

"Part of love is sacrifice. I couldn't protect you. I could give you love and a home, but I couldn't shield you from the supernatural bloodline you came from. As a human and a baby, you couldn't protect yourself. Word about your birth got out. That's when the monsters came. Whoever had you had a link to manipulating your father and the Devine empire. We were chased by werewolves in the park. Vampires outright offered me a million dollars for you. When I didn't take it, they threatened me. Your father sent bodyguards, but there was only so much they could protect us from. Necromancers would send ghosts at all hours of the night to inspect you and try to influence you."

I think of Leviathan and his eyeball ring. Those creepy bastards are still magically trying to inspect me.

"I tried to stop it," Lorelai insists. "I did everything I could imagine. I put mystical objects around your crib. I poured salt and circles around wherever you were. And then the goblins came. I used to sleep in a rocking chair by your bed because I didn't want you to ever be alone. One night, I awoke to the sound of you gasping for breath. Goblins had tied me to a chair and magically gagged my mouth while I slept, and with the bodyguards right outside in the living room, none the wiser."

Her hand trembles beneath mine, and I give it a small pat. I need her to keep talking.

"And they were stealing your breath. Davis said the necromancer sent them because..." Lorelai pulls away. She swipes her fingers beneath her glasses and sniffs back tears.

"Because necromancers don't control the living. They control the dead," I say for her.

She nods. "Yes."

"How am I not dead?"

"You had this butterfly mobile I made you over your crib. You loved it." She touches the butterfly on her chest. "That's what I used to call you. My little butterfly. I got this tattoo to keep you close to my heart after you were gone."

"That doesn't say how I'm not dead. What stopped the goblins?"

"One of the goblins must have bumped the switch. The butterflies began to fly in circles, and it frightened them away. When the goblin magic slipped, I was able to scream. I yelled for the guards. They untied me and reported back to your father. He arrived with Astrid, and we agreed that it was best— *safest*—for you to go live with them as Astrid's daughter."

She rushes over that part of the story like she's trying to force it out. I watch her continue to swipe at her eyes under the glasses. There it is. The remorse I hoped for. And now I feel like an asshole for wishing to see it.

The car goes faster and weaves. I grip the door for support. "Should we slow down?"

"They don't pull people over here. Too much traffic," she dismisses. Then, nodding as we pass a sports car, she says, "Wood sprite in the passenger seat. Those are rare sightings."

I glance at the pretty woman but quickly dismiss the sprite. She looks human to me.

"As I was saying, they told everyone I was a surrogate. I never thought anybody would believe that because of how much I felt connected to you. It was inconceivable to me that everyone couldn't feel our bond. The second you were born, I told everyone you were mine. I underestimated the supernatural." She scrunches up her face in thought. "It's such a particular hierarchy system, the super-naturals. No one questioned that a woman like

Astrid would not want to ruin her figure or be slowed down by pregnancy or breastfeeding. They all accepted it. I think I was even blamed for your mortality. Like they somehow picked the wrong carrier for their baby. Your father gave me enough money to move as far away as I could get, which was California, and I opened a small gallery. I knew if I were in the same city as you, I wouldn't be able to stay away."

I know the Devine dynamic well enough to understand that they would have seen my connection to Lorelai as a problem. If she were my mother, then her ties to the family would pose a threat. It's not like they could have moved Davis's mistress into their house for protection. And Astrid wouldn't want his mistress hiding in plain sight in her home. Regardless of what Lorelai thinks, a big part of me believes Astrid was affected by my father's affairs. How could she not be?

"Life is complicated." That's all I can think to say.

Lorelai nods in agreement. She puts her hand back on my arm. "What about you? Is there anyone special in your life?"

Yes.

Paul. Paul and Diana.

"No." I shake my head. I will protect them and

keep them out of my mess until the day I die. "I'm all alone."

"You're never alone. You have me, for what that's worth to you. You're here now, and you finally know the truth."

"Did you have other kids?" I ask. "Are you married?"

"No. No kids. Marriage isn't really for me. I'm a serial dater. I guess you can say I have commitment issues after everything that happened."

I touch my necklace, pulling it from inside my shirt.

"Your grandpa, George." She lifts her hand toward my necklace but doesn't touch it. "I liked him. He was a good man."

"Yeah, he was. I miss him."

"We spent a long time trying to track that amulet down."

"You helped find this for me?"

"Arts and antiques tend to go together. I knew people, and since I'm not a Devine, I wasn't on the supernatural's radar." She smiles. "How much did he tell you?"

"You're not like the rest of the family, Tamara," he told me in the hospital. *"You have our blood, but the magic didn't take root for some reason. But our blood, our lives, who our family is, all of that puts you in*

danger. Wear this. Always. And know that every time you look at it, you are loved."

Then, he materialized butterflies for me.

I've had a piece of her with me this whole time. He couldn't tell me the full truth, but he told me what he could the only way he knew how. I just didn't understand.

Lorelai takes the wheel in both hands and zooms toward an exit. She slams on the brakes, and I lurch toward the dashboard. I brace myself. My birth mother is a crazy ass driver.

She's waiting for me to answer.

"He said that once I put it on, it's mine. And then made up a story about a Pagan goddess and trolls."

"Those Norwegian trolls are hard negotiators." Lorelai dramatically shivers. "And their caves smell funky. I had to burn all my clothes."

I wrap my fingers around the stone.

"But it was worth every minute of those three months dining on cave bugs to know you are safe." The car comes to a stop sign, and she uses the moment to reach for my face. She brushes my hair back. "My sweet butterfly."

A horn honks, prompting her to drive. We go through an artistic community filled with colorful murals and small galleries. Even the people seem more vibrant. When I think of San Francisco, this is exactly what I imagine.

I touch my face where her hands lingered. I can't describe the depth of my feelings. I suppose some emotions don't have actual words.

My life is a mixed-up batch of puzzle pieces. The edges are put together, and I know what the picture should look like, but it will never be complete because I haven't been given all the pieces.

I wish my grandfather would have spoken plainly so I could have thanked him for all those things he did without my knowledge.

"The amulet works? It keeps you safe?"

"It keeps me alive." I remember the blood staining my back. Safe might be too strong of a word, but I don't want to complain. "I didn't think it worked at first, but then I survived the fire that broke out on my birthday when I shouldn't have."

I'm unsure why I keep talking, but the words tumble out. Maybe it's because she listens, and I've felt so alone. I tell her about the fires and the vampire attacks. I talk about the blue light reflecting off Elizabeth's face when she tried to bite me. I even mention Walter stealing my cash. The amulet didn't protect me from being drugged, but then it only seems to work when death is on the line. I'm not sure if that means I'm immortal. Honestly, I can't think about that now.

The only thing I don't mention is Paul and Diana. That memory is too precious to share, and I must keep them safe. Those moments are mine. They belong only to me.

I finish with the realization that my adoptive brother wants me dead and sent vampires to kill me when the fires failed. The betrayal chokes my voice.

"That is why I left that cryptic message," I say. "He knew I was planning on coming here to see you. I don't know what he'll do or who he'll send. I'm sorry for bringing you into this Devine family mess. I wanted to meet you. When I hired Mr. Wick to find you, I didn't know where life would lead me."

"It's right you came." She gives a firm nod to punctuate her point.

We go up a hill past restored Victorian homes, only to pull into the driveway of a brightly painted three-story house. The deep blue exterior is accented with gold trim. Large bay windows extend along the first two stories. Intricate woodwork adorns everything from the roofline to the porch. With the angle of the hill that we're on, the stairs leading to the porch are steep. At the top, I see a stained-glass butterfly in the front door.

"Welcome to my painted lady." Lorelai parks the car near a detached garage.

"Do you think it would be better to stay somewhere else? Off the grid?" I ask.

"No, everything we need is here. I've worked hard to protect this house."

"Aren't you worried that it might explode when we go inside?" After all I told her, she should be.

"This house has been blessed by more protection spells than you could imagine," Lorelai answers. "Besides, you have the amulet. I'll just stand close to you in the circle of your protection when we go in."

It occurred to me that is exactly what happened when I was holding Diana. She also emerged unscathed from the deadly incidents.

I start to reach for the handle, but Lorelai doesn't readily get out of the car.

"Are we...?" I glance toward the home.

"George liked to say that the world is filled with butterflies and dragons," Lorelai whispers. "When we go in there, I'm going to need you to be a dragon."

CHAPTER
THIRTY

Lorelai doesn't elaborate on her enigmatic words as she unlocks her front door to let me inside the entryway, and I'm a little scared to ask her. I hope it means she is telling me to be brave. I find solace in the fact that Lorelai has been kind to me so far. The historic neighborhood hardly looks dangerous. On the surface, I'd say the most dangerous thing would be ghosts since the houses are so old. That's ignorance, though. I know that we must look beyond the surface.

I don't have time to gather my nerve to enter. There is no choice as I walk closely behind her. Tension fills me as we pause for a few seconds in the entryway. I brace myself for something that doesn't happen. Conrad has no clue when I will be showing up at this house. That thought gives me some comfort. He knew everyone would be there at my birthday party. At the apartment he gave me an exact time. Then, with the Turnblads, he texted me on my way in the door. In hindsight, everything should have been so obvious. I just didn't want to see it. I still don't. There remains a tiny voice inside of me praying that I'm wrong, that it's all a conspiracy.

A second interior door leads to a foyer adorned with high ceilings and polished hardwood floors. I slip the backpack off my arm and drop it on the floor. The interior is dimly lit, and the drawn shades cast long shadows across the spacious home. I hesitate to venture further, allowing my eyes to adjust to the low light. The expansive layout opens to a cozy living room boasting floor-to-ceiling bookcases and a charming reading nook. Art easels displaying vibrant canvases compensate for the absence of a table in the dining room. The open staircase beckons, vanishing into the upper levels of the house.

"Water? Coffee? Tea?" she asks.

"Um, water."

The house is quiet. Lorelai moves through the dining room. I follow her and listen to her in the kitchen. My hand strays to the phone in my back pocket. I want to call Paul to tell him I met my birth mother and that she's nothing like I feared. He's the only one I can think of who'd care to hear about it. Of course, I don't. He and Diana are probably having fun with his parents right now. I need him to be in Kansas, safe and out of my insanity.

I miss them.

Dust particles dance in peeks of sunlight coming through the sides of the curtains. Protective charms hang in each window. I see them casting shadows on the blinds. The small sculptures gracing various surfaces would look like arty decorations to the layperson. To me, they appear to be totems. These are all things Conrad had dismissed as useless human magic when we were younger. Charms in the window and oil-anointed candles rarely stopped the really dangerous creatures.

A sideboard with photographs catches my attention. I couldn't see it from the foyer. Moving closer, I realize all the photos are of me throughout my life. The largest, in the center, is Lorelai holding me as a baby. We're in front of a crib with a butterfly mobile, and she's smiling. I see a rocking chair in the room where she described the goblin attack. Around that are other snapshots of us together. There is even one with the back of my father's head. From there, I grow up slowly, my age progressing as my gaze moves outward from the center vortex of baby pictures. An ancient bowl holds salt next to them as if this is an altar, and she's trying to keep me safe.

I draw in a shaky breath. My mother looks so happy

holding her baby. Her smile is bright and full of life. She's been doing everything she could to protect me—the salt, the amulet, living in banishment from my side of the country. It dawns on me that all this time, there has been someone out in the world filled with concern and love for me. The revelation strikes me hard, and I press my hand to my chest. I never suspected.

There is not one picture of Astrid holding me like that, with that love emoting from her face. This house could have been my house. This life could have been my childhood.

"A shrine is no replacement for the real thing." Lorelai comes up behind me. I didn't hear her footsteps. She hands me a glass of ice water. "But it's all I had."

I hold the glass, not really wanting it.

"May I...?" Lorelai lifts her arms slowly like she's trying to corner a feral cat about to dart past her. I don't move. She leans into me, arms moving around my shoulders as she pulls me into her hug. Her breath catches in her throat, and she trembles. "It's been so long. I can't believe you're here with me."

I lean my head into the embrace, still holding the glass. When she pulls back, her eyes are wet with unshed tears.

She again takes my face in her hands. In this

light, it strikes me that we have the same shade of hazel eyes. I couldn't tell earlier in the car. We're also the same height.

"Know, whatever happens, I love you," she says.

"I..." The words are difficult to get out. Emotion overwhelms me, and I can't speak.

She pats my face. "I know. I know. A mother knows. You should drink your water. It's easy to get dehydrated here."

I try again. "I—"

A loud *thump* sounds overhead.

I instantly set the glass on the sideboard and put myself between the stairs and Lorelai to shield her. I stare at the ceiling. "Is someone here?"

Another loud *thump-thump* answers my question.

"Hide," I order as I move toward the foyer to go upstairs. I touch my amulet for support.

Lorelai grabs my arms to stop me. "This is what I have been working my way to tell you."

The thumps come angry and fast.

"Now, don't freak out," she soothes. "After I got your message, this man showed up asking if I was your mother. It was too coincidental. Nobody here knows your name. All my friends think those pictures are of my second cousin living in Europe. It allows me to disappear on your birthday and holidays to be alone. They think I'm over there."

Thump. Thump-thump-thump.

"This guy seems way too interested in getting information. He's human, but there is something off about him. He kept evading my questions, so I drugged his tea." She glances upward. "It sounds like it's wearing off."

Conrad's here? Mabon believed my brother was in California. Or did he send someone?

"Did he bring anything with him? Was he alone in the house at any time?" I ask.

"He didn't have time to plant a bomb if that's what you're worried about," she answers.

Of course, that's what I am thinking. My brother apparently likes to blow shit up while trying to pin it on me. The cops probably think I'm a serial arsonist.

"He didn't even carry a wallet, just some cash in his pocket," she continues. "Who doesn't keep an ID or phone on them? Contract killers and kidnappers, right?"

If I hadn't survived what I did over the last few weeks, I would have thought she sounded unwell. "So you kidnapped a kidnapper? What are we supposed to do with him? Torture him for information?"

Lorelai's expression says she's not opposed to the idea.

None of this is good. I don't torture people, at least not on purpose. Conrad once told me that my singing makes siren's ears bleed. I guess I could...sing at them?

"He comes after you then he deserves what he gets." Lorelai uses her hold on my arm to force her way past me. As she takes the stairs, she says, "I'm sorry I made you an accessory to kidnapping. If this goes wrong, I'll take the blame."

I don't ask what she means by goes wrong. I feel like everything in my life has been going wrong.

I know it's best if it's Conrad. Then I'll know where he is and be able to ask him whatever I want. Let the lawyers get me out of detaining an arsonist. That sounds a lot better than *being* the arsonist.

Yet, a part of me hopes it's not Conrad. I'm terrified of confronting my brother. I'm not ready for it. My emotions have been on a rollercoaster ride through a dark tunnel called denial, and I haven't had time for self-care to get my head screwed on straight.

Can any amount of self-care make me accept what Conrad is doing?

"I didn't know what we were dealing with," Lorelai continues in a whisper as we tiptoe to the second floor. "I didn't know what questions to ask, and I didn't think texting you that I just drugged a stranger was a great course of action. Digital trails and all that CSI stuff."

That is why she wanted me to take the flight and get here sooner.

Hopefully, it wasn't the only reason.

The stairs creak and give away our ascent. I'm not sure why we're trying to sneak up on a guy who's supposedly detained. I'm beginning to believe I inherited my criminal abilities from my birth mother. Masterminds, we are not.

"This is where you come in." Lorelai pauses as we reach the top and turns to rub my arm in reassurance. I hear the thumping coming from one of the closed doors off the landing. "You'll know what questions we need to ask. Then, we can figure out what needs to happen."

What needs to happen?

What the fuck have I gotten into?

In my mind, I hear a hypothetical stranger asking, *How was it meeting your birth mother for the first time?*

To which my sarcastic brain responds, *Oh, we had a lovely visit. We discussed family trauma, managed to avoid a speeding ticket, worried about dying in an explosion, and then kidnapped and tortured my murderous brother together. You know, normal bonding, nothing special.*

Fuck me.

"Hey." Lorelai gives my shoulder a firm tap. "You here with me? If you can't do this..."

"I'm here. I can do it." I have to confront my brother at some point, and sooner is better than later. I can't keep going on like this. "Let's get it over with."

My heart thunders in my chest, and I feel it threatening to explode. Fear sends shivers down my spine. I clutch my enchanted amulet, feeling the comforting weight in my hand as I stare ominously at the closed door. I know whatever lurks behind it cannot bring about my physical demise, but life has recently taught me all too well that there are things worse than death.

I hear the echoes of the past swirling in my thoughts. Desperately, I try to banish the memories of my childhood haunting me, the ones that bind me to Conrad and fill me with an overwhelming sense of betrayal.

Please don't make me do this.

I'm breathing heavily and don't want to face the truth. Each step closer tightens the invisible grip on my chest.

Please let me go back to the way things were, to ignorance and innocence. Let me rewind time and fix this—fix that broken piece in my brother that would have caused him to become so dark and twisted.

Lorelai reaches for the door handle. I want to stop her, but I don't.

The door groans open on its hinges, and the sound of struggling instantly stops.

A small end table, cluttered with totems and sculptures, stands between the door and a headboard. The shades are drawn in the guest room, keeping it shadowed. Yellow wallpaper, frilly bedspreads, and antique furniture hardly set the scene for a kidnapping scenario. There is an abstract painting of an evil eye as if to summon protection from harmful spirits.

A sturdy wooden chair with a tall back is securely fastened to the bedpost at the foot of the bed. The man sitting on the chair has his back to me, and the bed obstructs my view. A floral pillowcase drapes over his head to conceal his identity. Our prisoner jerks against his restraints. The rocking causes the loud thumping noises that had reverberated through the downstairs. His hands appear firmly bound at his sides, rendering him immobile.

"Don't worry, he can't escape." Lorelai moves to stand in front of him. She puts her hands on her hips. I see the determined set of her mouth. She's trying hard to look in control. "He can't hurt you."

The man issues an angry, muffled response.

I step along the side of the bed to get a better look at him. On the floor near his feet, Ogham Stones inscribed with traditional Celtic runes are placed in a circle around him. They're meant to trap people within their boundaries. Lorelai doesn't take any chances when seeking to protect her home, and she's clearly influenced by several cultures.

The man grumbles again. I can't understand his words.

I find it hard to catch my breath. As I round the foot of the bed, I realize immediately by the breadth of his shoulder that this isn't my brother. Pink unicorn duct tape wraps his chest and waist to keep him seated. My eyes are drawn to the wrist restrained to the arm of the chair with matching duct tape. He jerks violently, trying to free them.

I gasp in shock. I know those hands. I love those hands.

"Paul?" I rush toward him and jerk the pillow-case off his head.

He blinks heavily and shakes his head, butting it forward like he's going to fight. I cup his face to make him look at me. The pink unicorn duct tape is over his mouth.

"You recognize him?" Lorelai asks.

"Paul, what are you doing here?" I start to peel

the tape. It's sticky, and my attempt looks painful, so I stop. "Is Diana with you?"

He shakes his head in denial.

"Is she with your parents? She's safe?"

He nods.

"You're sure?"

He nods again.

I sigh in relief.

"I'll take that as a yes," Lorelai answers her own question.

"Yes," I tell her belatedly. "Paul is a friend. Get some scissors. Help me cut him free."

Lorelai hesitates.

"He knows this is a misunderstanding. He won't hurt us." This is one thing, maybe the only thing I know for a fact anymore.

"I'll be right back." Lorelai leaves.

I stroke the hair back from his face and whisper to him, "I'm sorry."

Paul looks upset, rightfully so. I feel bad. Lorelai did drug him and duct tape him to a chair. He'd probably been sitting here for hours.

"I hate that you're here, but I'm so happy to see you. That's my birth mother. We just met about an hour ago. I never told her about you. She thought Conrad sent you to hurt us." I want to make him understand why this is happening. "You were right about my brother. I didn't want to see it, but... Some things have happened since I left you in Kansas City. It's a long story, but I have confirmation that you are right. And not just about Conrad. You were right about my necklace protecting me. I don't know if this makes me immortal forever or what, but it keeps things from killing me."

He tries to tell me something, but the words are muffled.

"Why are you here? How did you even beat me? The last time I saw you, you were on your way to..." I furrow my brow. He can't answer that.

I touch his face. He feels like Paul. Lorelai said he was human. Surely, it's really him and not some magical glamour to trick me.

"Paul?" I search his eyes. They're the same eyes that drew me in from the beginning. I want to trust him.

He mumbles a response. His fingers lift in my direction but can't reach me. His eyes dart to where Lorelai left as if he's trying to warn me.

I follow his gaze only to turn back to him. "I'm sorry. I don't understand what you're saying."

He mumbles again and jerks his head toward the door.

"You think she's dangerous?" I ask, trying to peel the tape again. He winces in pain, and I stop.

He nods frantically.

I hesitate. He was right about Conrad.

"Is this because she drugged your tea?" I can see why he'd be upset about that. I think of the glass of ice water. Had she tried to drug me, too?

No. This is a simple misunderstanding. She thought she was protecting me.

I wanted to trust Conrad, too. Perhaps I'm not the best judge of character.

Lorelai did say she habitually disappears on my birthday and holidays. Was she confessing to being in New York when the fire started? Had I just not caught the slip?

"Are you sure about this?" Lorelai appears with scissors, startling me. "He's a big guy. We're not getting this chance again."

I try to push away the self-doubts, but I don't know who to trust. I try to keep Lorelai in my peripheral as I reach for the pink unicorns over Paul's mouth. "I'm sorry. I'm going to take this off you. It'll hurt. Moan if you want me to stop."

He looks intensely at me. I slowly pull, instantly seeing the strip of irritated flesh it leaves behind. I get to his mouth and try to go slower. Paul jerks his head back and to the side to rip it faster. The end of the tape hangs from his cheek as he takes a deep breath.

"Get me out of this," Paul demands with a small struggle.

"What are you doing here?" I ask. "How did you even find this place?

"You're not exactly Fort Knox when it comes to shielding your phone screen. I saw you staring at it several times," he says. "I've got a good memory."

"But what are you doing here?" I ask again. I see the redness around his lips. I'm tempted to kiss him. I never thought I'd be this close to him again.

He sighs and looks at Lorelai. "Can you untie me? I don't want to talk about this in front of an audience."

I glance back to where Lorelai has moved to stand behind me. Her arms are crossed, and her stance is wide while she stares at us. She grips the scissors in her fist like a weapon. It doesn't look like she intends to move anytime soon. I rearrange my position so I can see both of them.

"Answer her questions first," Lorelai orders.

"Fine," Paul grumbles at our hesitance to cut him free. "I thought if I could just make myself drive away from you, the hardest part would be over. I knew I'd made a mistake the second you were out of sight. I booked a flight almost immediately to come and see you. I showed up here thinking Lorelai might know when you were expected to arrive in California. The last I knew, you were going by bus, but I couldn't be sure."

"Likely story," Lorelai interrupts. "What kind of man walks around without a phone or wallet? That's pretty shady if you ask me."

He answers but directs his words at me. "Tamara, I'm not stupid. There is no way I was showing up here with my address printed out in my pocket and a phone containing the contact information of everyone I care about. I hid them before coming inside. Judging from my current position, I'd say I was right to be cautious."

"Why not text her?" Lorelai asks. "If you're friends."

"Some things need to be said face to face," Paul answers, still holding my gaze. "I knew you were angry about what I said about your brother and needed some time. And with what I..."

His eyes turn toward Lorelai. It looks like he wants to say more, but not with witnesses.

I reach my hand toward her. "Hand me the scissors, please."

She puts them in my palm. I sigh in relief. She's not going to try to detain us.

Staring at Lorelai, he says to me, "I also wanted to make sure your mother was a decent person and that you'd be safe here. What kind of man would I be if I let you do this by yourself? I couldn't let you face her alone. That's a difficult thing under the best of circumstances, but with what Conrad has been up to? You could not have expected I would go off and be fine abandoning you. I knew if I tried to call or text to say something, you'd probably bite my head off again."

"Actually, I probably wouldn't have answered," I admit.

I start cutting the pink duct tape along his side, trying not to poke holes in his shirt material. I whisper, "I think I know someone who would think these pink unicorns are a good look for you."

"She misses you," Paul whispers back.

"I won't apologize for protecting my daughter," Lorelai interrupts loudly. "I'm not sorry about any of this."

Finishing at his waist, I move to a wrist.

Paul's expression tightens. "Then I guess there is nothing for me to forgive."

The second his wrist is free he lifts his hand to my face briefly before reaching to pull the piece of tape hanging off his cheek. He tosses it on the floor.

"As long as we understand each other," Lorelai quips. "Next time you come to someone's house, introduce yourself properly, young man. Seriously, if you had just told me you were infatuated with my daughter, I probably wouldn't have made the duct tape so tight."

Lorelai wasn't kidding. She's not apologizing.

I cut the second wrist free. Paul instantly starts to pull the tape off his chest. It comes off in one big strip. I cut the tape holding his ankles down.

"And you, Tamara, could have told me earlier that you had a boyfriend who might come looking. This isn't 1955, and you're not a teenager. I expect you to have a man. Or woman. Honestly, I'm good either way." Lorelai shakes her head. "I can see by the nervous looks you're giving me that you two have much to discuss. You can stay in this room. Guest supplies are in the nightstand. Towels in the linen closet. I'm ordering Chinese food. Come down in about forty-five minutes for dinner."

Lorelai leaves us.

"She's a nut job," Paul says.

I can't blame the outburst. "I don't think she's out to harm us. If she was, she wouldn't have let me free you, and I don't think she would have left you alive. I think we can trust her."

"Yeah, probably, but she's still out there," he mutters.

Paul surges to his feet the second he's completely free. He stretches by arching his back for a few seconds before he wraps his arms around me in a giant hug and squeezes. A small eruption of surprise leaves my throat, and he releases me. "Your mother is…"

"I know." I shrug helplessly. "My family is different than most. I'll understand if you want to fly back to Kansas. I promise you won't be abandoning me. You can leave with a clear conscience."

I say the words, and I believe them to be true. They don't *feel* true. I don't want him to go—I never want him to go—but nothing has changed. I'm still me, and danger still lurks. Even if I get past this current turmoil with Conrad, that doesn't mean there won't be more trouble standing in line right behind him.

I think of Uncle Mortimer. What would he say if I brought home Paul to rule the Devine magical empire with me? How long would that empire last without supernatural protection? I would never bring him and his daughter into that life.

Out of all my current traumas, this one hurts the worst.

"Tamara, what your mother said about me being infatuated with you," he begins.

I shake my head to stop him. "You don't need to say anything. She's a little bit of a free spirit. I don't expect her to speak for you."

"That's not it. I was going to say that I'm not

509

infatuated with you. The reason I came here to California is because I wanted to tell you that I'm all in. I don't know any other way to love someone. What I feel is not infatuation. It might be sudden, but it's not some fleeting whim. I lived in a bad relationship for years. I know what I want and what I don't. I'm here to say I love you. I don't know what you do with that. I don't know where we go from here. I wish I knew the answers to everything. But I know how I feel at this moment."

Warmth floods me at his words. My heart beats fast, and I don't want him to stop talking. I don't move, scared of breaking the spell.

"Leaving you in front of that crappy hotel was one of the worst feelings I've ever experienced. I know how bad that sounds, considering where we met." He takes a deep breath and releases my face. "Now, if you excuse me..."

Before I can answer, Paul runs out of the room. My mouth hangs open in shock at the sudden departure. "Paul?"

I hurry after him in time to see the bathroom door closing. I cover my mouth to muffle the laugh that tries to escape. To be fair, he'd been tied in that chair for a while.

He loves me.

Love.

The word fills me with such aching joy. It's everything I could ever want—to belong with Paul, to be with him.

My damned mind instantly sabotages the moment. I remember the danger. I think about giving up my inheritance. To whom? Conrad? That would never work, not after all this. After I deal with my brother, maybe Uncle Mortimer will take over. I know he's never shown a lot of interest in taking on more responsibility when it comes to my father's businesses. My uncle has a lot of rules about how the supernatural should conduct itself, and I am the remaining blood heir. But wouldn't he be forced to do it if there is no one else?

Uncle Mortimer's solution is to make me conceive a supernatural baby so the bloodline lives on. If he took over, he'd probably find a way to make that happen. I'd never abandon my baby in that world. I'm not my mother. I can forgive Lorelai for her decisions because she left me with my father, but knowing what I know, I'd never leave a baby to be raised without me.

No matter how hard I try, the math doesn't work. Paul plus me doesn't equal happily ever after.

THIRTY-ONE

"I love you too," I whispered to the bathroom door. I know he can't hear me. This might be my only chance to say it. "I want nothing more than to spend the rest of my life with you and Diana. I want to belong in your world. To be safe. To feel wanted. If I could have any wish, that would be it. But the baggage I carry is not just a suitcase. It's a giant angry monster, and it's hungry and selfish and demanding. There is no hiding from it. It will devour us whole. There is no witness protection program from the rich and supernatural. What I want doesn't matter. What I want will destroy everything."

I hear the water faucet running. Moments later, Paul opens the door, almost knocking into me. He stops to gather me into his arms. Warm lips meet mine as he kisses me. His skin is moist, and his hair damp as if he splashed water on his face.

Paul holds my face and keeps kissing me as he walks us toward the guest room. When we go inside, he kicks the door shut with his foot. The reverberating sound of it slamming shut causes me to pull back in surprise.

He flashes a smile, and I can see the glint of mischief in his eyes. His intentions are clear, and I'm not going to stop him. The universe is taking pity on me and giving me another moment with him. I'm going to embrace it. I'll savor every second I can get.

There are so many reasons not to do this, now and here, but for once, my brain takes a back seat and lets my body have control. Pure instinct and emotion flood my senses. I want him. He wants me. This is everything.

He gazes into my eyes with such concentration it penetrates me. He cups my cheek before running his hand back into my hair. A thumb caresses the rim of my ear, sending a shiver of anticipation over my body. I feel his thick arousal along my stomach.

I don't need a slow seduction. I'm ready for him now. The feel of him has haunted my every breath— the texture of his firm lips, the way his eyes pierce me as if he really sees me. I place my hand over his heart, feeling the rapid beat against my fingers. Formed muscles mold against my hand. I love that he's not all soft and pampered like most of the refined gentlemen in my family's circle. He's animalistic and hard, primal like a werewolf, without the unfortunate side effect of sprouting hair and fangs. And he's much more kindhearted in temperament.

Every concern I have melts away until all I can see is Paul. He licks his lips as he stares at my neck. I wonder if he can see how fast my pulse is racing. He leans forward, drawing his lips along my neck to my ear. I feel the light scrape of his teeth against my skin. He takes a lobe between his lips.

My knees weaken at the sensation, and I grab hold of his shoulders for support. He moans at the reaction and intensifies his efforts. I fall against him, pushing into his chest. I hate that our clothes separate us.

I think about savoring the moment by drawing out the pleasure. My body disregards the suggestion. I push him away. I try to take my jacket and shirt off at the same time but end up trapping my arms above my head. The clothing surrounds my head in darkness as I wiggle to get free.

Paul chuckles as he comes to rescue me. He yanks my shirt and jacket off and drops them on the floor. "There she is."

I thread my arms through my bra straps and push it to my waist. His shirt is off as he pulls me against him. I've missed his smell. It makes me tingle with awareness. My need for him is so deep it burns.

Paul jerks back the covers on the bed. We slide the remaining clothes off our hips, cherishing the moment. This place is significantly improved compared to our first time together.

I fall into his embrace. He instantly lifts me off my feet and spins me around to lay me on the bed. The cool, clean sheets caress my back as his warm body comes over me. I feel the weight of the amulet slide along the side of my neck into my hair.

The rough texture of his hands feels better than I remember. I'm obsessed with them—so strong and confident and protective. I feel safe when he touches me.

Paul caresses the length of my body, teasing and giving pleasure at the same time. I grope at his neck, trying to make him kiss me, but he resists. My eyes close when his hand slides from my hip to my inner thigh. I want to make him go faster, but he takes his time.

"I take back what I said earlier," he whispers.

I open my eyes to look at him, not understanding.

"I am infatuated with your body." He leans over to kiss my nipple. "I can't stop fantasizing about you."

I smile.

His mouth moves between my breasts as he works his way down. Hands grip my thighs, parting my legs. I watch him move lower, intimately kissing my sex. The firm press of his tongue sends a jolt of electricity through me, causing goosebumps to erupt over my flesh and my toes to curl.

I writhe beneath him, squeezing his shoulders with my legs. I try to pull him back up, but he's too strong for me to move. I can't force him to do anything.

"Please," I beg.

Paul chuckles against my body, the seductive sound vibrating against me.

My thoughts are focused on him. Every nerve reaches out in the hope of his touch. A hand runs down my leg before trailing along my hip. He follows the hand with his mouth, kissing his way to my belly button before licking a path back to my neck.

Suddenly, he stops and groans. He breathes heavily against my shoulder. "I don't have protection."

I hate to admit that I once again forgot about condoms. That's not like me. My mind is not focused on responsible lovemaking when I'm with him. Of course, he does, though. He's the most responsible person I know.

"Guest drawer," I say.

"What?"

He lets me up so I can roll to look inside the nightstand. The drawer is filled with travel-size toiletry bottles, toothbrushes, and a box of condoms. I give a small laugh as I produce a condom for him to put on. As if by mutual agreement, we don't comment on it.

I return to his arms, maneuvering my legs around him. He thrusts deep, and I can't help the moan of approval that escapes my lips. We're a perfect fit in every physical way. Being with him is all I want. That desperation fuels my need. I want to absorb him into my skin and make him such a part of me that they can never tear us apart.

We rock our bodies in unison. I bite his lip. He licks mine.

Paul grabs my hand in his, pinning it close to my head. His eyes hold mine. We thrust faster. The tension mounts. So close, so close, so...*here*.

I once heard someone describe climax as a little death. I think they're wrong. The building pleasure is all that matters, a representation of striving for what we want, needing that finish at the cost of all else. That's life, the striving for fleeting perfection. Death is what comes after, when the trembling is finished, and we're left with a cold reality we cannot change.

Death is a locked mausoleum. Being with Paul will never compare to that.

The shattering release washes over me in waves, making my stomach tense in response. Paul's hips jerk against me. My heart thunders in my ears. I feel the pants of his breath hitting my cheek.

He gently kisses me, moaning softly before rolling to rest next to me on the bed. My attention falls on the yellow wallpaper, instantly reminding me of where we are.

"Hey," he cups my cheek. "Stay with me."

My gaze darts back to his.

"Your life is not a giant angry monster," he says.

My throat catches a little. "You heard that?"

He nods. "What you want does matter. You matter, Tamara. If we love each other, we'll figure the rest out."

He touches my amulet thoughtfully.

"I'm not saying we won't have to be cautious," he continues. "But that's life. We protect our families, our kids, ourselves. When danger came, when it mattered, Diana was safe with you. I'm not saying we expose her to vampires or more fires, but once we figure out how to deal with your brother—"

I kiss him. How can I not? This is the sweetest thing anyone has ever said to me. He chooses me. Paul knows the mess I am. For the first time in my life, things feel right. I feel like this is where I belong, with humans who love me.

"I love you." The words just come out. I've never meant them like I do right now.

"I know," he says. "And that's why we'll get through this—together."

THIRTY-TWO

If ever there was a close-to-perfect day in my life, this one might be it.

I mean, not counting the psychotic brother who wants me dead so he can become a vampire and take over a supernatural empire.

Apparently, an entire box of condoms was an invitation neither Paul nor I could ignore. We made love again in the shower. After he saw my bloody shirt on the floor, I had no choice but to tell him everything that had happened since we parted. Not that I mind. I want to tell him everything.

For lack of anything clean of my own to wear, I raided Lorelai's closet. The peasant skirt and tank top are not my usual style, but today, I am not my usual self. Lorelai took one look at the stolen clothes and nodded in approval. I even saw her tear up, but she tried to hide it from me.

When we came down for Chinese food, Paul disappeared outside only to return with his wallet and phone, which he'd hidden in a planter. When he checked in with his parents, they were at the aquarium with Diana. They sent a picture of her dressed in a princess gown with fairy wings, pressed against a giant tank surrounded by fish.

I miss that kid, but I'm glad she's safe.

Lorelai ordered enough food options to keep us fed for days. The containers spread across her coffee table in the living room. The shades are still drawn, but two table lamps are turned on, giving plenty of light. Paul smiles as he offers me an egg roll. For a moment, I let myself fall into the fantasy of normal.

"You two are adorable." Lorelai eats noodles out of a container with wooden chopsticks. "I'm happy to see you worked things out."

Paul's grin widens, and I know the meaning of that twinkle in his eyes.

"However, I'm afraid I need to interrupt this Rockwellian moment to address the explosive elephant in the room." Lorelai sets her noodles down. "As relieved as I am not to have to bury your body in the backyard, Paul, the fact that you're a friend means we have no way of finding out what Conrad's plans are."

"I'm happy not to be buried in your backyard," Paul answers wryly.

I glance at my phone. Conrad has not tried to contact me again after Elizabeth and her crew tried to kill me. It only affirms the truth I'm trying to accept. He betrayed me. The vampires would have reported back to him by now. If they hadn't, he would have called. If he was innocent and something had happened to Conrad, Uncle Mortimer would have been right on top of it, trying to make me claim the throne.

Yeah, yeah, so it's not technically a throne, but it might as well be. I mean, Lady Astrid did occasionally wear a tiara.

A sudden wave of grief over my family's deaths takes me by surprise. Paul touches my shoulder and squeezes gently. I give a small smile at his questioning look. I don't want to talk about it in front of Lorelai.

"I could call Conrad. Ask him for a meeting," I suggest. "If I see him, I should be able to talk some sense into him. Or at least get to the truth."

"And what does sense look like?" Lorelai asks.

"Prison," Paul answers without hesitation.

"Mental health facility." I still have a hard time

reconciling my feelings for Conrad with the facts in front of me. "I need to believe he can be saved."

Paul and Lorelai share a doubtful look, and I can't help but feel they are ganging up on me. They don't know Conrad like I do. They weren't there.

He's my *brother*.

The grief tries to resurface, and I shove it down. I feel as if I've lost my entire life—my parents, Anthony, Conrad, and the security and familiarity they represented. We might as well add my sanity to that list. The thoughts feel like a betrayal of the new family I'm making with Lorelai and Paul.

But they're new. Conrad and I have a history.

How could Conrad choose vampires over me?

I touch the amulet. "This protected us before when we were in the fires. I can protect us again."

"It will only work if you're in direct danger," Lorelai counters. "Like protecting those in your immediate circle to keep you from exploding. It might not work for an individual attack. The amulet's protection magic is only meant to save you."

"Then you should hide. Let me deal with my bother," I say.

"And if he brings more friends," Paul shakes his head. "No. I'm not hiding while you go to battle. Not happening. Pick a different plan."

I have a feeling that even if I locked him in a cellar, he'd find a way to break free to be by my side.

"The house should be vampire-proofed," Lorelai says, pulling a decorative box off a high bookshelf and setting it on the floor, "but it never hurts to be over-prepared."

Paul goes to open the lid. He pulls out a wooden stake with symbols carved on the end.

"Ash wood." Lorelai moves toward the kitchen. "It repels evil."

Paul drops the stake back into the box. "There has to be a better option. I don't want to kill anyone."

"If it's us or them..." I stare at the box. There are enough stakes to take out Elizabeth's army.

"Of course I choose us." Paul frowns. "It doesn't mean I have to like the thought of stabbing someone in the chest."

The room suddenly gets darker, as if clouds have blotted out the sun. What little sunlight snuck through the edges of the closed blinds is disappearing.

"Looks like we're expecting a storm." Lorelai reappears, holding several jars of what looks like garlic. She drops them on the floor by the box before crossing to the window to peek outside.

Good. Let the weather match my darkening mood.

Gentle, uneven taps begin on the window panes as rain strikes the glass.

Paul lightly strokes my back in a comforting gesture.

"I don't feel right," Lorelai mumbles. "Do you hear that?"

"I hear rain." Paul looks at me for verification.

"Laughter?" Lorelai frowns and stumbles on her way back from the window. "Who's there?"

Paul surges to his feet to catch her before she falls over. He lifts her onto the couch. I rush to their side and check her wrist for a pulse. I feel the reassuring beat of her heart.

"Lorelai?" I tap her cheek. She's out cold. "Can you hear me?"

"What was she talking about?" Paul goes to the window to look out.

My hands begin to tingle, and I stretch my fingers. "I don't—"

"Tamara." Paul pulls the curtain aside so I can see. "Is that...?"

Pink glitter rains from the sky, glistening as it hits the window. I've seen this before.

"Why is it raining a glitter bomb?" Paul asks.

"Fucking fairies," I mutter, my stomach tightening in dread. "Paul, get away from the window. It's a fairy portal."

Lorelai doesn't move.

"A what?" Paul drops the curtain and slaps his cheek.

"Fairies," I repeat. What do they want?

I stand, turning in circles as I search the room for changes. The temperature begins to rise. "I know you're here. I don't think you know who you are messing with. I'm a Devine. Show yourselves, and let's talk about this."

"Are they with your brother?" Paul asks.

I don't have time to answer him.

Suddenly, Paul starts swatting at the air like a swarm of flies is attacking him. I detect the sickly sweet scent of magic. Paul begins to weave on his feet. I rush to support him before he falls, slipping my arm around his back and walking him toward a chair. He's too big for me to carry, and when he starts to fall, I spin him around so that he lands in the seat. He doesn't move.

I put my body in front of him like a shield. As the last person standing, I wait, tense and at the ready. The second one of these flying pests shows itself, I'm smacking it out of the air into the nearest wall.

I feel a prickling sensation buzz past my neck. I don't react as I wait and listen. It happens a few more times before a sparkly image materializes before me.

Sadly, all those cliché images people have in their

529

heads about the fairy court are real. The vain creatures never met a puffy-skirted ballgown they didn't like. I think it's to make up for the fact they have to magically glamour their makeup. Without it, most of them resemble a gnarled piece of reclaimed barn wood.

The creature before me spins in a circle, spreading her fairy dust all around. When she finally stops her little production, she poses in a recitation handclasp as if prepared to perform poetry. She looks vaguely familiar.

"Have we met?" I try to place her. There were so many family parties. "Did my brother send you?"

I could see Conrad seducing a fairy. My eyes dart to the vampire kill box. Stabbing a fairy might not kill it, but it would make her leave.

"Mistress Devine," the fairy states firmly. "I have come to serve you with a summons to appear before the high fairy court."

"Uh, no." I rub my temple as my eye twitches in annoyance. I do not have time for this. "Go away."

I'm not sure where that response came from. It's like I'm suddenly channeling Lady Astrid. No one ordered her around.

The fairy stutters a little but persists. "Y-you are being charged with—"

"Send it to my lawyer," I interrupt. "Or make an appointment with the Devine personal secretary."

She drops her hands in irritation and shouts, "You are being charged with a most heinous offense!"

I flinch. "What is it you think I did?"

What lies has my brother told them to piss them off at me? Fairy magic hardly seems like it would be his preferred method of attack, seeing as they are such flighty, emotional things, but what the hell do I know anymore?

"Threaten..." Her voice is still shrill, and she clears her throat, resuming her hand-clasped pose and moderate tone. "Pretending to consume fairies in some sick game and teaching a human child that it is all right to attack us—"

"You're that grumpy waitress!" I finally realize where I've seen her. "At the chicken tuxedo diner place. Viney, Biney...?"

"Ivy," she corrects, moving her hands to her hips.

"Let me stop you right here, Ivy." I wave my hand in annoyance. "We didn't mean anything by it. I'm not facing a fairy court over a donut with sprinkles. I'm sorry you felt disrespected, but people eat human-shaped cakes all the time. It doesn't mean we're contemplating becoming cannibals."

Okay, sure, it's usually erotic cakes that are made in the naked human form, but my point stands.

She hems and haws a little before managing, "Well—"

"And, for the record, that little girl idolizes fairies." That should make her vanity happy. "Is there anything else?"

"Yes. You didn't tip well," Ivy accuses.

Why is she wasting my time?

"Seriously? You disappeared and never refilled drinks, you made a kid almost cry, argued when we tried to order because you didn't like our choice, and practically threw the plates at us when you dropped off our—"

"Well, you ate an offensive donut!"

For fuck's sake.

Ivy makes a strange grunting noise before hocking up a loogie and spitting it at me. I jump back in repulsion. Before I can counter, she does a fast spin and poofs into a sparkly huff.

I hold very still, arms at the side, as I hesitate to touch the gross spot staining my skirt. I stand, listening and waiting. When the sound of the fairy portal against the window stops, I grab one of the napkins that came with the food to clean my skirt.

Is this my life now? Are supernatural creatures going to grow bolder now that I don't have protection? Are they all going to take a run at the dwindled Devine family?

"Everyone enjoys watching a giant fall," I mutter. It's like those people who see a famous person in a bar and try to fight them to up their street cred.

Lorelai and Paul both moan as they wake up. Lorelai stretches on the couch, rubbing her eyes. Paul leaps up from his chair, ready for battle even as he's wobbling on his feet. He grabs the side of his head and groans.

"What happened?" he demands, confused as he watches me with the tissue.

I wad it and throw it inside an empty food container. With a sigh, I tell him, "Ivy, that crappy waitress, is evidently a fairy. She came to spit on me for not tipping better."

Well, it's almost the whole truth. Ivy wouldn't dare attack Diana for this, and Paul has enough to worry about with Conrad.

"How long was I asleep?" Lorelai sits and stares out the window.

Paul and I turn in unison. He reaches for the curtain, pulling it back slowly. A magenta sky indicates the sun is setting.

"Like a minute," I answer. "Fairy portals can mess with the time. It helps keep what they're doing hidden from detection."

"Fairies were here?" Lorelai stands and begins searching her house. "What did they take?"

"A single fairy was here," I correct. "She's gone. It's handled."

"The waitress from that place with the chicken statue?" Paul asks as if his thoughts are starting to focus. "We did tip her. I felt bad because she was so terrible at her job."

I'm not sure how much more stress I can take.

"I'm going to check all the windows and doors," Lorelai says. The sounds of her footsteps disappear into the kitchen.

I stare toward the yard, watching the light change on the Victorian house across the street. Paul puts his arm around my waist, keeping me close to him. I love the feel of him next to me, the sound of his soft breath, the scent of his skin. Each second seems like a time bomb ticking away inside of me. Damn that fairy. She robbed me of precious hours. I am supposed to have the entire day with Paul before the threats of night come for us. I wanted to make love to him again, to savor more stolen moments.

I hate not knowing where Conrad is.

I hate not knowing the future.

Why does fate keep taking things from me?

I want so badly. I feel better when I'm by Paul, but the deep ache of longing never really goes away because I fear this is temporary.

"I love you," Paul whispers. "Whatever is coming, we'll get through it together."

I feel better for a fleeting moment.

"I love you, too." The words feel strange and new.

His grip on my waist tightens.

Streetlights come on. I see a flutter of movement cross over the yard.

"They found us." Lorelai comes up behind us. "Here. Take these."

I feel a vampire stake slip into my hand. Paul lifts his stake, adjusting it in his palm. So much for a normal family.

"Come here," Lorelai orders. The smell of garlic wafts from behind.

I turn to find her holding a jar. She dips her fingers in and rubs garlic on her neck before doing the same to me. My nose curls at the strong odor. I want to point out that no one is biting me with the amulet, but it's already done.

"They won't drink through this," Lorelai tells Paul as she slathers his neck, "but don't forget you have other arteries."

"Whatever happens," Paul says.

I nod. "Whatever happens."

"Whatever happens," Lorelai repeats as she joins our battle mantra. She puts her hand on my shoulder.

Their nearness gives me strength. Even so, it's not lost on me that they're in danger because of me. Two people who just recently came into my life are more willing to protect me than my supernatural family.

We remain by the window, the curtain drawn aside, peering out at the multiplying shadows. They move like vampires.

"I count thirteen of them," Lorelai whispers as more join the others to increase the number. "We need more stakes."

Elizabeth clearly called for backup after my amulet stopped them last time. I try to pick out which shadow might be her. For all the times Costin has mocked and scared me, he'd always shown restraint. I don't see that same quality in his sister.

Dread seems to be a permanent rock in my stomach. We stare at the gathering vampires. I'm unsure what to do. My trainer would say run. But we can't run, and I know from experience at the gas station that I don't have the skills to take down an entire brood. All the defense moves I know would have the effectiveness of trying to beat on a brick wall when it comes to vampires. Sure, I might chip it, but I'm the one who ends up bloody and raw.

I touch the amulet. Lorelai and my grandfather meant well, but I wish it did more than protect me.

What good is immortality if everyone around me isn't also protected?

As suddenly as they arrive, the vampires disappear. They move at once, spreading toward the house like a plague, dispersing to each side while a few dart upward. Loud thuds land on the roof. We look up in unison. They're not trying to hide.

A tap sounds on the window, startling us. We step back. Paul lifts his stake and tries to put himself in front of me.

Elizabeth stands on the other side, chin dipped down toward her chest as she stares in. Her wide grin at that angle looks creepy as fuck. I think she knows it.

The vampire looks at me and motions that she wants me to come outside. My heart is beating fast. What were we thinking? Did we believe we had a chance tonight?

"What if we don't invite them in?" Paul asks.

"Forget what the Victorians taught us about vampire lore," Lorelai answers. "They don't have to wait for an invitation to enter your property. They aren't obsessive counters. They don't have to sleep in the dirt of their ancestral homelands. Stakes, sunlight, garlic, that's what matters. This house's protection spells should make it more difficult for them to come inside."

"What is she doing?" Paul stares at Elizabeth.

She wants me to come out. My heart is hammering in my chest, and it's all I can do to keep my breathing quiet. I hear them on the roof walking around. They want me to hear the noisy threat. They want us to know they're everywhere. I hear more tapping on the windows in the dining room. This is not a battle we can win, but maybe if they get what they want, Paul and Lorelai might have a chance.

Lorelai is pulling stakes out of the box and unscrewing lids on the garlic. I inch toward the door while their attention is distracted. I don't dare say goodbye. If they see me, they'll try to stop me.

I unlock the deadbolt. The click is loud and instantly causes them to look at me.

"Tam—" Paul begins.

"Don't follow me!" I open the door, darting through and slamming it shut before they can stop me.

I run toward the empty street to where the street-lights illuminate the road. I ignore the steep stairs as I fall and slide down the grass next to them. My skirt rises and exposes my thigh to the ground. Only when I reach the bottom do I realize I still clutch the stake.

"I'm here!" I yell. My leg stings, but I don't care.

I turn in eager circles, expecting them to land. I

watch Lorelai's neighbor's curtains shift as they look out at me. None of them come out to investigate.

"You want me? Come and get me!" I scream, trembling with a combination of fear and fury.

Tears stream down my cheeks, and I can't stop shaking. It's all I can do to hold on to the stake. I stare up at Lorelai's house. I don't see the vampires—not Elizabeth in the window, not lurking along the roofline, not in the bushes.

Then I realize that Paul doesn't come after me, and he's not looking out the window.

"Paul!" I rush to get back inside. "Lorelai!"

I stumble over the uneven curb and find myself crawling up the steep cement steps leading to the porch. Gasping for breath, I push to my feet and rush back to the door. In my haste, I slam into the wood frame as I twist the doorknob to get inside. A sudden, painful impact knocks me in the stomach. The wind rushes out of my lungs, and I fall face-first onto the wooden floor in surprise. The stake flies out of my hand, leaving me defenseless.

The house is quiet. Too quiet.

"Please, no, no, no..." I mouth the words, willing all the bad to go away.

I cradle my stomach, too scared to lift my head. I don't want to see what the vampires have done. As long as I don't look, it hasn't happened, and there is hope.

So much for my perfect day.

I force myself to my hands and knees. A sharp pain radiates from where I was hit. Each breath is like a knife stabbing me in the ribs. The skirt is tangled around my limbs, making it difficult to maneuver. A tear drops to the floor beneath me, splatting into a tiny pool on the wood surface.

I can't keep going on like this.

I manage a raspy breath.

"Hey, sis," Conrad's voice penetrates my frantic thoughts. There is a dispassionate edge to his tone. The sound makes my blood run cold.

THIRTY-THREE

It feels like an eternity since my birthday party. I have to believe that I've somehow veered off path, that my life diverged into the wrong timeline. I'm inhabiting another Tamara's existence instead of my own. If only I could find my way home from this horrible parallel universe.

"Yoo-hoo, Tam-tam," Conrad mocks. He gives a slight whistle. "This way."

I finally make myself look. First, my gaze skates across the floor, looking for blood and bodies. Instead, I find Conrad's boots.

I hold my side as I amble to my feet. It takes everything in me to lift my head. I follow the black slacks up Conrad's legs. He's dressed like the young vampires in a silk shirt. Our eyes meet briefly before I follow the line of his outstretched arm. He holds a gun pointed at the couch.

They're alive.

I exhale in relief to see Paul and Lorelai staring at me. Though they are not bound, they're not moving. Their lips are pressed tightly together. Paul looks like he wants to yell, but he keeps the words inside. The gun holds them in place.

"Don't mind them. I told them if they moved or made a sound, I'd shoot everyone." Conrad grins. His glassy eyes shine like he's high on something. Any lingering doubts I had as to his culpability are forced away. I see the evidence before me. "So good to see you, Tamara. Are you going to introduce me to your new friends?"

I glance between the couch and Conrad before looking up the stairs and behind me. I don't see any vampires. "No need to introduce me to your friends. We already met."

The gun bounces between Paul and Lorelai as if he's trying to decide which one to threaten.

"Hey," I try to get Conrad to listen to me. "What are we doing here? Come on, Conrad. Look at me. It's me. Talk to me. We're family."

His brow furrows, and he lowers the gun a few inches. I don't know if it's drugs or mental illness, but

I can get through to him. I know I can. I just need to remind him of what we are to each other.

"Remember when we were little? Those nights on the balcony? Those days breaking the rules in the library? It was you and me against the supernatural world. We always took care of each other." I lift my hand and slowly move toward him. If I can just reach that gun and disarm him, I can end this. "That never changed. You and me. Family."

"Family?" He gives a short, humorless laugh. "Stop being so naïve. We're not family. We've never been family. Do you know what I remember? Davis shows up at the Turnblads' house, asks to inspect the kid who had a run-in with goblins at the group home before coming to stay with them, drops off a wad of cash, and takes me like a puppy he picked up at the pound. Lady Astrid made it very clear that my only purpose was to take care of *you*, entertain *you*. Be Tamara's brother. Go to school with Tamara. Take care of lonely Tamara. Watch out for Tamara. She's gullible and easily manipulated by others. Never tell Tamara. If anything happens to Tamara, you'll find yourself back at the pound. So, because you needed a friend, I got to spend the next decade as your babysitter."

His words hurt. I'm too stunned to speak.

Conrad grits his teeth. "Every time you messed up or got hurt, I was punished, even as an adult."

"You know that is not how it was," I argue.

"Grow up!" he yells, swinging the gun toward me. "Open your eyes, sister."

"Watch it," Paul orders. "Point that over here."

Conrad ignores him. "And do you know what the final straw was? I find out that I'm not even in their will. Anthony was. You are. Uncle Mortimer even gets a piece. The only way I get anything is if all of you are dead, and that's because, legally, I'm next in line. They acted like I was a servant, not their son."

"Please tell me you didn't do this because of money." I recognize his face. I remember the love, but I don't know this man. "I would never have let anything happen to you. I would have given you half the estate. I don't even want it all."

Conrad's eyes turn downward, and his words lose a little of their heat. "They didn't love me. But they did teach me that in this life, it's everyone for themselves."

"I believe you," Lorelai attempts to soothe. "I know firsthand how Davis and Astrid could be. But they're gone now. You don't have to do this. Tamara is not them."

"Shut. Up," he enunciates with points of his gun. "No one is talking to you, birth mother."

I touch my amulet, feeling its comfort. "I'm not saying our parents were perfect. They weren't. No one is. They might not have known how to show it, but they loved us."

Paul tenses and lifts a little in his seat as if waiting for an opening to pounce on Conrad.

"Sit down!" Conrad warns. He points the gun at me before swinging his arm back to threaten Paul. "Or I'll shoot her."

"You can't hurt her," Lorelai says. "She's protected. You never get what you're after. If you leave now, we'll forget you were here. Tamara has already promised you'll be taken care of."

Conrad takes a deep breath, seeming to center himself as he continues to steady the gun on Paul and Lorelai. He talks toward me. "Right. Protected. You know, I kept wondering how on earth you managed to survive all those times. I waited until you and Anthony were high in the closet with his boy toy. There is no way you should have escaped that hallway. Even Costin couldn't escape that hallway."

"And your mother?" I prompt. "Why her? She was already living in her own hell."

He's enjoying this evil villain monologue. I let him talk as it buys time. All I need is for him to make a mistake. The next time he points it at me, I'll charge him. He can't kill me. I hold my rib, trying to ignore the pain. I only hope I'm fast enough.

"Dear old whoring mom. I enjoyed watching her like a little rat in her dirty cage. She played god with my life when I was a baby, so I played god with her. I knew I'd eventually end her when I got bored. I figured two problems, one explosion."

"And the Turnblads sold you," I conclude.

He taps the gun against his temple before re-aiming it at Paul. "You're catching on."

"Oh, Conrad. You hurt so many innocent people," I whisper, shaking my head.

"Supernaturals believe they are so superior. I'll show them humans are the ones to be feared. They underestimate us. They'll never underestimate me again." He smiles. "When you survived all of that and the vampire attack at the motel, I knew no one was that lucky. Elizabeth agreed to handle your death personally. When she told me what happened, I realized that necklace isn't just a story."

"Conrad, I—"

Conrad swings his arm toward me and aims at my head.

"Tamara!" Paul cries out, leaping in my direction.

Conrad fires the gun.

Bang!

Lorelai screams.

I duck, covering my head. At this range, there is no way it will miss me. I hear the bullet shatter glass behind me.

Paul sweeps me into his protective embrace. His hands move over my body to check for injury. I flinch in pain when he touches my sore rib. "Tamara?"

Conrad laughs and does an excited jump. "Holy shit, it's true!"

I hold my side. Ducking has jarred my ribs and has made the throbbing worse. There is little comfort in knowing the severe pain is not going to kill me.

"Stand up," Conrad orders Lorelai. He motions for her to walk toward me. "Get over there."

Lorelai holds her hand up and moves toward us. I hear her feet shuffling.

Conrad lifts his free hand toward me. "Give me the amulet."

"No," Paul answers for me, putting his hand in front of me to stop any transfer.

"It won't work for you," Lorelai says.

"She's telling the truth. Remember, I told you what our grandfather said," I remind him. "Once I put it on, it bonded to me. It doesn't work for anyone else."

Conrad frowns and gives a big sigh of irritation.

He aims the gun at Paul and fires. The loud *bang* causes me to jump in surprise.

I turn toward Paul in shock. His wide eyes stare at me, and his lips part as if he's trying to speak. Blood pools over his heart, coming from his chest.

"Paul?" I can barely get the word out as I wrap my arms around him. He tries to hug me back, but his arms drop to his sides. His weight pulls me down as I hold on. I feel the wet warmth of his blood against my chest. "Paul!"

We fall to the floor. My rib shoots with pain, but it doesn't matter. I can't let go.

I cradle Paul in my arms, holding him close. I press my hand over his heart, but how can I stop a wound like that?

"Paul, baby, look at me," I urge. "Stay with me. Don't leave me."

His lips move, but whatever he's trying to tell me is lost in an ugly gurgle. Lorelai is by my side, trying to help. I push her hands away as I pull Paul closer. His eyes lock on mine. I feel the moment he stops breathing. The tension drains from his body. His dead eyes continue to stare at me.

For the longest moment, I hold still in shock. I refuse to breathe, willing time to reverse and take this back. But I can't control time any more than I can control fate.

There is no describing the feeling that rolls through me. It's unlike any pain I've ever felt. Every cell in my body feels like it's suffocating. My stomach turns in on itself, and my heart implodes, taking all my faith with it.

I think of Diana all alone now and know it's my fault. Conrad might have fired the weapon, but I brought Paul into my world when I asked for a ride.

"Tamara," Lorelai whispers, stroking my back in what little comfort she can give.

I gather Paul as close as I can, holding tight. Blood smears my hand, transferring to his cheek when I touch his handsome face. His skin is still warm, and I kiss his mouth even as I cry against him.

I shake my head to deny death its meal. I remember it swallowing my family into the inky depths of the mausoleum. And now that great monster is taking Paul.

I scream as loud as I can. The incoherent sound has no word or definition, but everyone knows its meaning.

When I look at my brother, he's watching my grief like he'd watch a play.

"All those times," I manage through my hoarse throat. "I made excuses for you. I told people you had a hard life but were good deep down."

He smirks.

He thinks this is funny? I want to swipe that look from his face.

"But they were right. You're broken. You're..." I sob as I try to breathe. My attention goes back to Paul.

"Let's try this again," Conrad says. "Hand me the amulet, or I shoot Mommy."

"Don't. He'll kill us both anyway," Lorelai says.

Conrad steps forward and pushes the gun to Lorelai's head. Tears stain her cheeks, but she shakes her head in denial, telling me not to listen. Her trembling hand reaches to hold mine.

I don't want to live, not in this parallel world. Immortality is not worth this sacrifice.

"Tick-tock," Conrad prompts. "Necklace or Mommy?"

I reach for my neck, yanking the chain over my head. It tangles in my hair, pulling out the strands. I throw it at him. "Here. Take it. I hope you choke on it!"

"No," Lorelai dives after the amulet and tries to catch it. She misses.

It lands at Conrad's feet. He swoops it up, holding it by the chain so he can examine it. "You should have listened to her. I am going to shoot you both anyway. Thank you for making it so easy."

I don't care if I die. There is nothing left for me.

"To think, all this time..." he says to himself, spreading the chain with his fingers to loop it over his neck.

The amulet gives a little shimmer as it settles around his neck. Conrad breathes heavily in excitement.

Lorelai wraps her arms around me as I continue to hold Paul. She's crying and trembling. I wish I could comfort her. But what can I say? I should have never looked for her. She was safer not knowing me.

Everyone I love turns to ash. I pray that this is the end of Conrad's wrath, that he doesn't know about Diana and leaves the girl alone.

Conrad points the weapon at us. I close my eyes tight. I hear an echo of gunfire. I wait for death.

I take a breath. Then another. I wait for Lorelai's arms to release their hold.

A strange noise comes from Conrad.

I look up from the floor. Blood runs from a bullet wound in his neck.

"How...?" I look around to see who could have shot him.

The amulet gives off an eerie green glow. The new color overtakes the red jewel. The pulsing light surrounds him, emitting a buzz that grows louder and softer with the magic. He drops the gun and grabs his throat. A new wound opens on his neck, and he begins to bleed like he's been bitten by a vampire. Fire erupts around his feet. His mouth opens, and he gurgles as he tries to cry out.

I hold Lorelai's hand as I watch my brother suffer and burn. As the ash of his body begins to fall, the amulet's weight pulls the chain through his neck. His head tumbles to the side and crumbles on the floor.

"Tamara," Lorelai's voice sounds far away. The buzzing grows louder as the green glow dissipates, and the room goes completely dark.

CHAPTER
THIRTY-FOUR

"Tamara."

My head is fuzzy. I can still smell Conrad burning.

"Tamara."

I'm standing on a sidewalk, choked by the acrid smell of smoke and ash. I stare at the hand that had been stained with Paul's blood, my vision blurry, forcing me to blink. Instead of red, it's now smeared with black soot.

"Tamara!"

I blink and turn to the sound of Lady Astrid's voice. She's reaching for my face, patting it. "You're all right. Don't move from this spot. I'm having them bring the car around."

"Paul?" I try to answer, but my throat feels like I swallowed fire. I don't understand what's happening.

Time feels like it's sped up for everyone but me. People move around me, appearing frantic and busy as I stand completely still. I hear the staticky voices on a radio calling out commands.

Lights from emergency vehicles flash over the scene, but they are nothing compared to the orange glow in the windows of the old stone building. Smoke pours out of the broken windows of the banquet hall, drawing my eyes toward the sky. Familiar embers flutter against the night like dying butterflies. Their ash drifts down, a fine snow landing on top of everything.

Spotlights move over the clock tower gargoyles. I experience a sense of déjà vu as the stone creatures appear to be moving their heads with the shifting light. Something lands next to them and then flies away. I've been here before. It's my birthday party.

But this is not what happened.

Confused, I look over the crowd. I see Louis jogging backward down the sidewalk as he watches the building burn. Anthony stands near the paramedics where Conrad had been the first time, watching Louis. Lady Astrid is ordering people about. My father is talking to a group of powerful supernatural men.

Relieved, I realize my family made it out of the fire.

Was it all a nightmare? My head is fuzzy. Am I still high? What the hell did Anthony lace that pot with?

Where's Conrad?

I reach for my necklace, seeking the comfort of the amulet. It's not there, but it's always there. I rub at my neck and chest, looking for it, but I don't find it loose in my clothing.

I search on the ground by my feet. The necklace is on the sidewalk. The red stone is now green and shattered into pieces.

Conrad put the amulet on, and it turned green.

I kneel on the concrete and lift a shard to peer through it. The sharp edge slices my finger, and I let go.

A shadow appears before me, and someone grabs me before I can react. Cool fingers hold my wrist.

"Hello, castoff."

I inhale sharply and try to jerk my hand away. Costin holds firm.

His eyes are focused on my cut. I see him breathing in my scent as he leans over to pull the bloody digit into his mouth. His lips are warmer than I expected, and he makes a tiny sound of pleasure. My eyes round in surprise at his boldness. I don't know what to do. There are too many people around. Surely, they see what he's doing.

His eyes change, swirling with an inner light. He releases my finger from his mouth, but I see he wants more. The bloodlust is taking over.

He's not going to try to eat me right here, is he?

"You can't..." I try to deny him, but the words don't come out.

"You saved me," he whispers. Costin licks his lips. "Now I can always find you."

Before I can respond, he's gone. My hand remains suspended in the air where he held it, my wet finger pointing upward.

What the fuck was that about?

"Rooms on this end are clear," a voice says over a radio, "we have survivors coming out the north doors."

"Stacy," a man yells.

The paramedic runs past me, pushing a gurney to where firefighters are pulling a body out of the building. The person is badly burned.

"Easy now. I'm Stacy. We're friendlies. We're taking you to the private clinic."

The memory surfaces as I watch the woman and her partner over a body. Whoever it is, the injured person is not moving.

Stacy lifts a limp hand to her lips and bites. She makes a face and recoils, tossing the arm down. I see her lips move, appearing to say, "Human... dead."

Dead?

Paul.

I stare at my hands in panic, expecting to see blood. Nausea unfurls in my stomach. I hate that everything is under this drugged fog.

Astrid appears next to me. "You broke your necklace."

I start gathering the pieces, careful not to cut myself again as I cup them in my palm.

"It's Conrad." Anthony appears next to us, his face stricken. "That body they found. It's Conrad."

I remain on the ground, staring at them as they stare at me. Tears flow down my cheeks as I touch Anthony's leg. The image of them being carried into the mausoleum is so vivid. I know that it happened. I'm not crazy. I saw the wizard sealing him inside the tomb. But here he is—alive!

"Anthony," our mother orders, "get her off the ground. We need to get her to the car. People are staring. This is a private family matter."

Anthony loops his forearm under my armpit and pulls me to my feet. I lean against him.

"You're alive," I whisper.

"What the hell happened in there?" Anthony asks. I can see his eyes are as glazed as I feel.

My feet stumble as I walk away from the chaos to a limo. Nothing makes sense.

Someone holds open the door as I'm ushered inside. I fall onto the seat. My feet are on the floor as I lay to the side, unable to push myself up as I clutch the broken amulet against my chest. The door slams shut.

"Hand me the yellow vial," my mother orders, "then go find your father. Tell him we're going to leave without him if he doesn't hurry."

I hear the door open, and Anthony gets out of the car.

Astrid appears next to my head. She strokes my hair. "Sit up. Drink this."

I want to ask what is in the vial as I force myself to sit upright. It doesn't matter. She's holding the potion to my lips. I dutifully swallow what's inside, hoping it will clear my thoughts. Instead, my eyes blur as everything goes out of focus.

"That's it. It will calm you down," Astrid soothes. "Just rest. Let the potion take all your pain away."

THIRTY-FIVE

Two weeks later…

I can die.

I touch my neck, feeling the bare skin where the necklace should be. With the broken amulet tucked away in my jewelry box like some old memento, I am no longer protected. Any immortality the stone gave me is now gone.

Astrid kept me in a potion-induced haze for over a week. I know she thought she was helping, and perhaps she was in her own twisted way. The woman never really understood what it means to be a mother, but she tries. I see that now.

When my mind finally returned to reality, the pieces began falling together. Whatever enchanted magic the amulet had was destroyed when Conrad put it on. It was never meant for him. All the times I should have died were transferred onto him, and the magic transported me back to the first time—my birthday fire. I guess I'm lucky I didn't die as a teenager. I'd hate to be reliving those years.

It's like the rest never happened.

The road trip with Paul and Diana never occurred. There were no sparkle pancakes or grumpy fairy waitresses. I even miss that dancing turtle shirt and endless whining about waffles.

The death of Paul's wife has been in the news and all over social media. Memes making fun of the woman who died in a car accident while giving head have gone viral. Without the story of my family dominating the news cycle circus, the vultures and internet trolls have found something else to entertain themselves.

Conrad's death barely got a mention. There was a respectable article about the tragic death of the adopted son of Davis and Astrid Devine in a downtown fire. That's it.

Now, as I stand outside the family mausoleum with Anthony and our parents, I mourn the loss of my brother. No one knows what he did, and I see no reason to tell them. If they even believed me, there is no point in sullying his name. I tell myself I choose to remember him as I believed him to be before he tried to kill everyone.

Conrad's mother remains in her apartment, turning tricks and chain-smoking cigarettes. I slipped the article about her son under her door. I wasn't sure what else to do, but I feel a mother should know— even a mother like her.

The Turnblads are none the wiser in their Kansas City home. No massacre happened at a road-side motel. No police are investigating me—if that was even true. It's all been erased. Time has reset and righted itself. The fire was ruled an accident, prob-ably because no one cared enough to dig further.

What? Am I supposed to tell them Conrad set it?

Then there is Lorelai. I haven't contacted her again, but it helps to know she's out there in the world. I picture her in her home, painting with her artistic Bohemian friends. Even if she doesn't remember my visit, I can still feel her love inside me, and it helps me get through the days.

We don't have a big funeral service for Conrad. There is no standing room only guests come to pay respects, no overhead drones or police detectives. Instead, it's just immediate family.

The weather is warm, just as I remembered it to be. Conrad was so severely burned it was decided to put his cremains in an urn. My father holds him against his chest. When he leads the way inside the mausoleum, I can see the ghost of a memory overlaying the new reality. Before, three coffins had been carried inside. Now, those same three walk upright.

I follow my family into the gothic depths of Conrad's new home. My father places him in an inlet.

"You will be missed," he says, tapping the lid.

"Sleep well," Astrid adds.

"I'm going to miss you, brother." Anthony sighs and drapes his arms over my shoulders.

They all look at me. What can I say? There are no words.

"Goodbye, Conrad," is all I manage.

Guilt fills me when I don't cry. I feel the grief settling into my bones. It will always be there like an internal scar.

We file out of the mausoleum. My mother places her hand on my father's arm as he walks her across the grass toward where the town car waits.

I don't follow them. "I think I need to be alone for a bit."

They all turned to look at me.

"Are you sure?" Anthony asks. "I thought we'd raid the wine cellar and drink until we forget there is a tomorrow."

"Maybe later." I take a step backward and touch my purse. "I have cash. I'll take a taxi home."

"Very well," my father says, continuing toward the car.

I don't watch them leave as I pull off my heels and cut through the graveyard. I dodge the old tombstones with only one goal in mind: to get to the stone bench by the fountain. Conrad is not the only person being laid to rest today.

The route is longer than I remember, and I find myself running. Finally, the sound of water on concrete calls to me like a siren song. I must get there.

I pass the giant sundial and the reader with her leashed dog. I focus on the bench—our bench. Diana has already come out to look at the fountain. My heart beats violently. I start to approach, trying not to look too eager. I can't remember exactly what I said last time to get Paul to give me a ride, but I'll think of something. I've been barely able to think of anything else. This is my chance to start over.

With my parents alive, I have Devine family protection again. No one will care who I date. Paul and I can be together. I just need to remind him that he loves me.

"Hello," I say, my voice soft as I approach Diana. It's chilly in the shade, but I don't care.

The girl turns to look at me with her swollen red eyes. I see the heartbreak in her gaze, and I want to make it all better.

"Diana!" Paul appears. The sound of his voice is like a balm to my soul. He looks rougher than I remember, and I can only guess that the public attention has made a difficult time worse.

I start to smile and lift my hand. Before I can speak, the temperature drops. I see a dark figure materializing on our stone bench. The transparent image comes into soft focus.

Conrad, dressed all in black, lounges as if he's been waiting for me. His arm stretches along the back of the seat as he stares at me with that same evil grin he had at Lorelai's house before he shot Paul.

I drop my hand and don't call out. Conrad's gaze shifts to Paul, and his smile disappears. He lifts his thumb and slowly draws it across his neck in warning before pointing a finger gun at their heads. He pulls his fake trigger twice. The threat against Diana and Paul is clear. If I go near them, Conrad will kill them.

I remember all too well what it felt like to have Paul die in my arms. The pain was unbearable. I could not survive it a second time.

"Hey, I told you not to wander off," Paul says to his daughter before he glances at me. Our eyes hold for a second, and I watch to see if there is a glimmer of recognition.

Conrad walks up to them, still holding his finger

gun as he lifts it to Paul's head. They don't see Conrad's ghost.

Paul ushers Diana quickly away from where I stand. "I told you not to talk to strangers. It's like we discussed. They just want a story about your mom. We can't give them one."

"I didn't," Diana protests.

Paul lifts Diana in his arms and holds her close. He glances at me warily. "It's gotten cold out here, huh? How about we go home and find some hot chocolate?"

I'm forced to watch them leave.

Conrad's eyes appear to turn black, and suddenly, he's standing before me. He tilts his head. I watch his lips move but can't make out the words.

I glance to where Paul and Diana disappeared.

"Conrad. Don't do this," I beg. My heart is breaking into a million little pieces. This moment was the one thing keeping me going for the last two weeks and he is taking my happiness from me. Again.

Conrad smiles as he steps through me. The smell of ash lingers in the air as it clings to his spirit. The feel of him invades me, chilling me to the bone. Before he disappears, I hear his voice whisper, "They can die."

To be continued...

Okay, I know what you're thinking, my wonderful, amazing, patient, loyal readers: *"What the hell, a cliffhanger? Tamara should be with Paul in a happily ever after. It's destiny. That's... Heck no. Go back into your writing cave, Michelle, and fix it. No more brownies for you!"*

Yes, I know cliffhangers can be a love-hate experience, but trust me, it's all part of the plan to make Tamara's journey as captivating and thrilling as possible. Let me reassure you: I have plans—so many plans for Tamara. I can't help it if her situation is a little messed up. I mean, you've seen her family, and that Conrad is no walk in the park. I promise that her adventures have not nearly begun. You can watch for the next leg of her journey in book two, Mostly Shattered. I want to thank you for being on this wild ride with me. You have my love and gratitude, as always.

Also, please don't take my brownies.

Love, Michelle

MERELY MORTAL SERIES

Merely Mortal
Mostly Shattered
Barely Breathing
Nearly Dead
More Planned!

Visit MichellePillow.com for details!

ABOUT MICHELLE M. PILLOW

New York Times & *USA TODAY* Bestselling Author

Michelle loves to travel and try new things, whether it's a paranormal investigation of an old Vaudeville Theatre or climbing Mayan temples in Belize. She believes life is an adventure fueled by copious amounts of coffee.

Newly relocated to the American South, Michelle is involved in various film and documentary projects with her talented director husband. She is mom to a fantastic artist. And she's managed by a dog and cat who make sure she's meeting her deadlines.

For the most part she can be found wearing pajama pants and working in her office. There may or may not be dancing. It's all part of the creative process.

Come say hello! Michelle loves talking with readers on social media!

www.MichellePillow.com

facebook.com/AuthorMichellePillow

x.com/michellepillow

instagram.com/michellempillow

bookbub.com/authors/michelle-m-pillow

goodreads.com/Michelle_Pillow

amazon.com/author/michellepillow

youtube.com/michellepillow

pinterest.com/michellepillow

tiktok.com/@michellempillow

threads.net/@michellempillow

PLEASE REVIEW

THANK YOU FOR READING!

Please take a moment to share your thoughts by reviewing this book.

Thank you to all the wonderful readers who take the time to share your thoughts about the books you love. I can't begin to tell you how important you are when it comes to helping other readers discover the series!

Be sure to check out Michelle's other titles at www.MichellePillow.com

Made in the USA
Las Vegas, NV
25 July 2024

92905115R00324